DYING TO SIN

STEPHEN BOOTH

Dying to Sin

HarperCollins*Publishers*

This novel is entirely a work of fiction. The names, characters and incidents portrayed in it are the work of the author's imagination. Any resemblance to actual persons, living or dead, events or localities is entirely coincidental.

HarperCollins*Publishers*
77–85 Fulham Palace Road, London W6 8JB

harpercollins.co.uk

Published by HarperCollins*Publishers* 2007

1

Copyright © Stephen Booth 2007

Stephen Booth asserts the moral right to
be identified as the author of this work

A catalogue record for this book
is available from the British Library

ISBN 978-0-00-724342-6

Set in Sabon by Palimpsest Book Production Limited,
Grangemouth, Stirlingshire

Printed in Great Britain by
Clays Ltd, St Ives plc

Mixed Sources
Product group from well-managed
forests and other controlled sources
www.fsc.org Cert no. SW-COC-1806
© 1996 Forest Stewardship Council
FSC

Dedicated to the officers and staff of Derbyshire
Constabulary B Division, with particular thanks to
Divisional Commander, Chief Superintendent Roger Flint
(the man with all the best anecdotes), and PC 2204
Rachel Baggaley

For he that is dead is freed from sin.

Romans 6:7

1

Thursday

The mud was everywhere at Pity Wood Farm. It lay in deep troughs under the walls of the house, it surged in wet tides where the cattle had poached the ground into a soup. And it was all over Jamie Ward's boots, sticky and red, like blobs of damson jam. His steel toe-caps were coated with the stuff, and smears of it had splashed halfway up his denims – long, fat splatters, as if he'd been wading in blood.

Crouching in a corner of the yard, Jamie stared down at the mess and wondered when he'd get a chance to wipe it off. He couldn't remember if he had a clean pair of jeans back at his parents' house in Edendale, whether his mother had done his washing this week, or if he'd thrown his dirty clothes behind the bed again, where she wouldn't find them. She'd been complaining for the past month about the amount of dirt he brought into the house, the number of times she had to clean the filter on the washing machine. He wondered what she'd say about this latest disaster when he got in.

And, as he heard the first police sirens wailing up the valley, it occurred to Jamie to wonder whether he'd actually be going home tonight at all.

'Damn it, boy. Why didn't you just cover it up again? It would have been for the best all round.'

Jamie shook his head. You couldn't just do that, could you? No matter what anyone else said, it wasn't right, and that was that. He'd done the only thing he possibly could, in the circumstances. He'd done the right thing, so there was nothing to regret.

'Throw some dirt on it and forget it. There's no need for all this.'

He felt bad about it, all the same. It was bad for Nikolai and the other blokes. This was a nightmare they didn't want, and some of them couldn't afford. Just before Christmas, too, when they needed the money more than ever, he supposed. He was going to be popular, all right.

Jamie felt his muscles beginning to stiffen. The longer he stayed in one spot, the more he felt as though his boots were sinking into the ground. If he stayed here long enough, perhaps the blood-tinted earth would slowly close in and swallow him. His own weight would bury him.

Of course, he knew the mud only looked red because the soil here was clay when you got a few inches down. It was so unusual for this part of Derbyshire that he'd noticed it as soon as he started digging. Clay and mud, tons of crushed brick and corroded iron. It had been a nightmare of a job, almost impossible for his spade to deal with. Jamie's rational mind told him that the colour was only because of the clay. And if the stuff on his boots looked *too* red, too dark, too wet . . . well, that was just his imagination, wasn't it?

Jamie Ward thought he had plenty of common sense. He was educated, after all – not like most of the other lads on the crew. He would never be a victim of superstition and ignorance. He wasn't even particularly religious – he didn't cross himself when they passed a church, or hang a statue of the Virgin Mary over the dashboard of the van, the way Nikolai did.

But this mud was *so* sticky, and *so* smelly. It stank as though it had been rotting for centuries. Now, when Jamie finally straightened up, he saw a thick gob slide from his boot on to the ground. It formed a sort of oozing coil, like the dropping of some slimy creature that had been living on the old farm, left to itself when the owners moved out and the cattle disappeared. He pictured something that only came out at night to feed on carrion, scavenging among the ruins of pigsties before slinking back into a dark, damp corner between those abandoned silage bags.

'*Damned fool. Kretyn.*'

He remembered the way Nikolai's fist had gripped his jacket, the feel of the older man's face pushed against his, rain glistening in his thick eyebrows and on his moustache. Jamie couldn't believe how angry Nikolai had been, not over something like this. The foreman had tolerated his bungling and his ignorance of the building trade with raucous good humour – until now. Yet suddenly this morning he'd been a different man, a wild thing, dangerously on the verge of violence. And all over a muddy hole.

Jamie swallowed a spurt of bile that hit the back of his throat. He'd been trailing backwards and forwards over this same patch of earth for days now. Shifting stacks of breeze block for the brickies, unloading bags of sand from the lorry, stopping for a quick fag behind the wall. Damn it, his boot prints were all over the place. Anyone who cared to look would see the pattern of his rubber soles, pressed deep in the mud. His eyes followed the criss-crossing trails he'd left, curving in long arcs that stretched twenty yards or more. His tracks were so numerous and extensive that they were probably visible from space like the Great Wall of China, placemarked on Google Earth. They were so distinct that they might as well be the swirls of his fingerprints. Jamie Ward's signature on the job, perfectly clear and complete.

Soon, people would be talking about him and pointing at

him. Before much longer, he'd be answering questions, endless questions, re-living over and over the moment he was trying to forget. He'd seen the TV cop shows, and he knew they never let you alone once they had you in one of their little interview rooms.

He could hear two sirens now, their yelp and wail teasing playfully against each other, fading and getting louder as the cars took one of the bends in Rakedale, dipping behind stone walls and clumps of trees until they reached the top of the hill and turned into the farm.

Jamie thought back to the morning he'd got out of the van, stretched his legs and stepped on to Pity Wood Farm for the first time. It was strange to think there had been grass growing here when the crew arrived on site. Now the whole gateway was churned up, and the soil either side was bare and exposed. In one corner, a wheel rut from a reversing truck had sliced through his boot prints.

He didn't remember noticing anything unusual that first time. Well, maybe there had been a slight difference in the level of the ground just here, a low bump that was only notice-able if you happened to be pushing a wheelbarrow load of sand over it. And perhaps the grass had been a bit greener, too – only a tiny bit, if you looked closely. Perhaps the blades had gleamed with faintly unnatural health in the winter sunlight. He wouldn't have looked twice at the time, and he'd never made anything of it. No one would have done.

But then Nikolai had asked him to start digging a trench for the footings of a new wall. Jamie had dug barely more than a few inches into the ground before the soil changed colour. It had taken him a while to get even that far down, though. There were so many stones to be prised free with the spade and lifted out, not to mention lumps of concrete and long splinters of rusted metal. Without his gloves, his fingers would have been raw by now.

After half an hour, he'd been starting to think that Nik had

4

given him the job as a punishment for something, or just because he was the youngest on the crew and a student at that, the one they called 'The Professor'. Or maybe it was on account of the fact that he didn't understand what they were going on about when the blokes started joking around on site, and they were taking advantage of him. Probably there wasn't going to be a wall here at all. Nobody had ever shown him the plans for the new development, so he couldn't be sure. But during the last few days Jamie had made his own plans. He reckoned that if he'd bought the farm himself, he'd have kept the old dry-stone wall and turned this bit of ground into a nice patio. All it needed was a few yards of paving, not a fancy brick boundary wall that needed some idiot to dig a trench for twelve-inch footings.

Damn that trench. Just the thought of its moist, slippery sides made Jamie feel like throwing up. If it weren't for all the other blokes standing around gabbling to each other in Polish, he'd have lost his breakfast ages ago.

Even in his distracted state, Jamie noticed that one or two of the labourers were looking a bit nervous as the police sirens got nearer. No papers, he supposed. Illegal workers. Well, it wasn't his business, and he bet the cops wouldn't care either, not today.

Nevertheless, Jamie automatically counted up the men. Nine, all present, but standing behind Nikolai for safety.

And all of the crew were looking in the same direction now – at the cluster of objects Jamie had accidentally uncovered with his spade. There wasn't much to look at, not really. A strip of plastic sheeting and a scrap of rotted leather. A bulge of cloth, torn and faded, a surprising eggshell blue where patches showed through the dirt. And there had been a faint glint of metal, slick with the dampness of clay, reflecting a glimmer of light and the movement of his spade.

But most of all, he knew they were staring at the only thing worth seeing – that unmistakable object laid out in the mud, like a bird trapped in cement, or an ancient fossil preserved in the clay. It was like a five-limbed sea creature, bony and white.

It was the shape of a human hand.

Detective Sergeant Diane Fry stepped out of her car on to the muddy ground, drew her coat tighter round her shoulders and wiped the rain from her face. All the activity seemed to be taking place on the other side of the track. Uniformed officers setting up cordons, SOCOs climbing into scene suits, a bunch of bystanders gaping like idiots. She looked around with a weary sigh. A week before Christmas, and wouldn't you know it? A major enquiry in prospect, if she wasn't mistaken.

Fry slammed the door of her Peugeot, her hands already wet and slipping on the handle. There was only one ray of hope. From the initial reports that had come in to Control, this air of activity might be misleading. Something quite different was going on here.

In fact, everyone was waiting with barely restrained anxiety for a verdict on the age of the body that had been unearthed. If it was recent, the entire division was in for a ruined holiday. If they were lucky, it could prove to be a historic burial, the remains of a medieval graveyard disturbed by the construction work. And then they could hand it over to the archaeologists and drive off home with a cheery wave and shouts of 'Have a good Christmas.'

All right, that was probably too much to hope for. But even a decade or two on the bones would be good news. At least they could take their time making enquiries. Victims who'd been missing for ten or twenty years would wait a little while longer for their identity to be established.

Besides, what family wanted a knock on the door over Christmas and a police officer standing on the step to inform them that their missing loved one had been found in a shallow grave in some godforsaken spot at the back of beyond? That sort of thing could ruin Christmas for ever.

She called to a uniformed officer in a yellow high-vis jacket. 'Is DC Murfin here somewhere, do you know?'

'Yes, Sergeant. Shall I fetch him?'

'Please.'

Yes, Christmas. In Fry's experience, there were already far too many families who were unable to regard it as a time for gladness and joy. This time of year had a nasty tendency to bring back memories for people. Recollections of happier times, of opportunities lost, of friends and relatives who had passed on to celebrate Christmas in a better place.

No, the festive season wasn't all about peace and goodwill, not these days. Anyone in the emergency services could tell you that. Christmas didn't make much difference to the lives of all those poor, pathetic and dysfunctional people who cluttered up the police stations and courts from one month to the next.

A few days ago, two men wearing Santa Claus outfits had raided a building society in Chesterfield. They'd been carrying baseball bats inside their fur-fringed sleeves, and a customer had ended up in hospital with a fractured skull when he got in their way. The suicide and domestic violence rates jumped at this time of year, the number of road accident victims multiplied, and the streets of Edendale were full of brawling drunks. The cells at West Street were never fuller, the hospitals were over-stretched, and hosing out the divisional vans was a full-time job. Lots of ho, ho, ho.

But perhaps she was just a bit jaundiced in her view. Personally, she hadn't celebrated Christmas for over a decade. Not in a paper hat and cracker, turkey and mistletoe sort of way. There had never been a decorated spruce tree standing in the corner of her damp little flat in Grosvenor Avenue, no tinsel over the mantelpiece, no *Nine Lessons and Carols* on the radio on Christmas morning. She was lucky if she had a present to unwrap – at least, one that she hadn't sent to herself for appearance sake. What was there to celebrate?

DC Gavin Murfin appeared at her side, teetering dangerously on the edge of the mud. The bottom four inches of his trouser legs were rolled up to reveal a pair of green paisley socks and a strip of deathly white flesh. Fry looked away, feeling suddenly queasy. On balance, the sight of a partially decomposed corpse might be preferable.

'Do you think there'll be any overtime on this one, boss?' asked Murfin as they approached a PVC body tent erected over the makeshift grave.

'You're already rostered for duty over Christmas anyway, aren't you, Gavin?'

Murfin looked crestfallen.

'Damn, you're right. I'd forgotten.'

Fry heard the dismay in his voice, but felt no pity. 'If it's a historic burial, you could be the officer in charge for a while.'

'Great. That's just . . . great.'

'Most DCs would appreciate that kind of opportunity,' said Fry.

'It makes a change from processing nominals, I suppose.'

Reluctantly, Fry smiled. Ah, nominals. The official name for the area's most prolific criminals – the repeat offenders, all those individuals the law makers called 'recidivists'. They came into custody at regular intervals, might even get a short prison sentence if they were unlucky. But, before long, they were back out there on the litter-ridden streets of the Cavendish Estate – or 'the community', as it was known in the criminal justice system. Edendale's nominals would be celebrating Christmas, all right. No one wanted them cluttering up the custody suite.

Murfin was silent for a moment as they watched the medical examiner directing a SOCO where to uncover vital parts of the body. The exposed edge of a bone here, a bit of decomposed flesh there.

'Diane, do you mean there are people who'd prefer to attend a postmortem than be at home carving the turkey?' asked Murfin.

'There isn't much difference, is there?'

'Now that you mention it. Not the way I do it, anyway. And the company might be better in the mortuary – especially since we have to visit the in-laws at Alfreton on Boxing Day.'

Fry peered over the tape into the grave. The hole was gradually getting bigger, even as she watched. The hand that had been exposed by the workman looked fairly fresh. But the torso that was now being painstakingly revealed seemed to be badly decayed.

A cold case, or a warm one? Fry was unashamedly ambitious – she wanted the next move up the promotion ladder, and for that she needed cases to her credit. Successful cases, airtight prosecutions that led to convictions. Clear-ups, not cock-ups. It would be PDR time in April, the annual round of dreaded staff appraisals. She had to file something away that she could point to as a recent triumph, evidence of her outstanding skill and expertise, proof of her ability to manage an enquiry to a successful outcome, blah, blah, blah. Senior management believed it if it was down on paper, typed on an official form. Would Pity Wood Farm give her that case?

'OK, let's move these people back behind the cordon. What are they all doing here anyway?'

'They're witnesses, Sergeant.'

'All of them?'

'So it seems.'

'Well, get their names and addresses and put them somewhere out of the way, for God's sake.'

'They don't seem to speak English.'

'Oh, Jesus.'

Rain had begun to fall again – big, fat drops splattering

on to the roof of her car and pitting the already treacherously soft ground. Around her, uniformed and paper-suited figures speeded up their actions, as if suddenly instilled with a new-found sense of urgency. Within a few minutes, they were all sheltering against the walls of the farmhouse or sitting in their vehicles.

And it was only then that Fry really noticed Pity Wood Farm for the first time. Until this moment, she'd been concentrating on the ground, trying to keep her footing in the slippery mud that was coating her shoes and trickling in between her toes. But she looked up, and she saw it in all its glory.

She was confronted by a collection of ancient outbuildings leaning at various angles, their roofs sagging, doors hanging loosely on their hinges. By some curious law of physics, the doors all seemed to tilt at the opposite angle to the walls, as if they were leaning to compensate for a bend. Some door-ways had been blocked up, windows were filled in, steps had been left going nowhere. Mud ran right up to the walls of the outbuildings, and right up to the door of the farmhouse itself. From the evidence, Fry thought it probably continued inside the house, too. The exterior was grimy and flecked with dirt, a bird's nest trailed from a broken gutter. Piles of rubbish were strewn across the dead grass of what might once have been garden. Was this really a farm?

'Who else is here, Gavin?' she asked, in despair.

'The DI's on his way,' said Murfin. 'But in the meantime, it's you and me, boss.'

'DC Cooper?'

'Ben? He's on a rest day. We don't know where he is.'

'Strange,' said Fry. 'This is *exactly* his sort of place.'

Crouching uncomfortably, Detective Constable Ben Cooper studied the withered object carefully. In all his years with Derbyshire Constabulary, including seven in CID, he'd never seen anything quite like this. There had been plenty of dead bodies – some of them long dead, others nice and fresh. And some of them perhaps not quite dead, after all. But this?

The flesh had shrivelled away from the fingers, leaving them thin but not quite skeletal. The fact that there was still a layer of leathery skin shrunk tight to the fingers somehow made it worse than if he was just looking at bones. The result was that the hand appeared to have been shrink-wrapped in a film of wrinkled, yellow plastic. The thumb was bent strangely out of shape, too, as though it had been broken and never re-set. The severed wrist was ragged, and the tattered skin looked as though it had been sealed with some kind of sticky substance.

He straightened up, easing the painful muscles in his back. He'd been playing squash this morning, and his opponent had smashed the ball into his kidneys when he was out of position recovering a drop-shot. You could never trust police officers not to get you in the back.

'The hand of glory,' he said. 'They're very rare these days.'

'Mmm.'

'Very rare. Not rare like steak, but rare as in *very* unusual. There aren't many of them about.'

Cooper had the suspicion that he was babbling, spouting nonsense. He did it just because there was a silence that had to be filled. It wasn't the first time it had happened. Not even the first time today.

He looked at his companion, unsure of her reaction because of the silence. 'What do you think of it, then?'

'It's gross.'

'Gross?'

'Like, totally yucky.'

Cooper nodded. 'Yes, I suppose it is.'

It wasn't exactly a technical assessment – but accurate, all the same. There were many occasions when a police officer in E Division might want to use it. A Saturday night on drunk patrol, for example. Another body lying in the gutter on the

High Street? *I'm not touching that, Control – it's yucky.* Yes, that would work.

But today was his rest day, and he'd volunteered to take his eldest niece out for the day, since the Christmas holidays had started. So he had an obligation to be interesting and informative. Volunteered? Was that really the right word? His recollection was that he'd happened to be hanging around at Bridge End Farm chatting to his brother Matt, when Amy had kidnapped him. But he'd never prove that in court. He had no evidence.

'The "hand of glory" supposedly comes from an executed criminal and was cut off the body while the corpse was still hanging from the gibbet,' said Cooper, reading from the guide book.

'There's a recipe here,' said Amy, interrupting him. She was eleven now, and strangely adult in some ways. Cooper was starting to feel sorry for the teachers at Amy's new school. She could be merciless if you were boring her.

'A what, Amy?'

'A recipe.'

'Like Delia Smith? That sort of recipe?'

'I suppose. *"The recipe for the preparation of a hand of glory is simple,"* it says.'

Cooper looked down at his niece, surprised by the sudden change in her tone. Now she was interested. It was yucky just to stand and look at a preserved hand, but learning how to preserve one yourself – now *that* was cool. He supposed he shouldn't be surprised.

'*"Squeeze the blood out of the hand. Embalm it in a shroud and steep it in a solution of saltpetre, salt and pepper for two weeks. Then dry in the sun."* What's saltpetre, Uncle Ben?'

'Erm . . . I'm not sure.'

Amy snorted gently. '*"The other essential item is a candle made from hanged man's fat, wax and Lapland sesame."* What's Lapland sesame?'

12

'Erm . . .'

'Sesame seeds from Lapland, obviously.' She frowned. 'Do sesame plants grow in Lapland?'

'I, er . . .'

'Never mind.'

'I know how the hand of glory was used,' said Cooper desperately. 'You fixed candles between the fingers of the hand, and then you lit them when you broke into a house.'

'When you did what?'

'Well, it was used by burglars. According to the legends, it made them invisible. It was also supposed to prevent the owners of the house from waking up.'

There was a final bit on the little interpretative panel that he didn't bother reading out. Wicks for the candles were made from locks of hair dipped in grease from the murderer's body and the fat of an old tom cat, then consecrated by saying the Lord's Prayer backwards. Ah, the old Lord's Prayer backwards – that always worked, didn't it?

They moved on through the museum. Cooper glanced out of the window, and saw that it was still raining. He didn't mind Edendale in the rain, but Amy objected to getting wet. And since it was the start of her Christmas holidays, and only his rest day, she got to say what they did and where they went. And that didn't involve going out in the rain, thanks.

In the centre of town, Victoria Park had been taken over for a Victorian Christmas Market. These things seemed to be very popular, judging by the crowds coming into town. There was a smell of roasting chestnuts in the air, and the sound of a fairground organ. And there was an innovation for Edendale this year – a Continental market, where stalls sold French bread and German sausages. Some of the stallholders spoke with foreign accents and might even be French or German. You never knew these days.

In the evenings, mime artists, stilt walkers and clowns would mingle with the crowds, and Santa would turn up on his sleigh at exactly the same time every night. A couple of weeks earlier, a local TV presenter had been brought in to switch on the lights, but the headline act on the main stage tomorrow would be an Abba tribute band.

They stopped by a costume display. The rough trousers and leather knee-pads of a lead miner, the gowns and bonnets of an elegant lady.

'So how are you liking school, Amy?' he said, aware of an unfamiliar silence developing.

'It's so cliquey. They're all goths or emos. Or chavs.'

'Chavs, eh?'

'They're so stupid. There aren't any *real* people, Uncle Ben.'

'Would you rather be at home, or at school?'

'Well, home is all right. I like being around the farm and the animals. But Mum and Dad are so immature sometimes.'

'Oh, are they?'

'They only think about money and possessions – they're very materialistic. I can't believe they never stop and think about serious subjects now and then.'

Cooper found himself trailing after his niece, as if he was the child demanding attention. It was supposed to be the other way round, but it never seemed to work like that in reality.

'Well, they're very busy looking after you and Josie,' he said. 'And they have to try to make sure the farm makes enough money to support the whole family. It's very hard work, you know.'

Amy didn't seem to hear. He could see that she was thinking about something again. It was very unnerving the way she did that, switched to auto pilot while her brain concentrated on some totally different subject. Perhaps she was already learning to multi-task, practising that skill all women claimed to have.

'It's just like Draco Malfoy, in that shop in Knockturn Alley,' she said.

14

Cooper frowned, stumped again by the turn of the conversation. 'Is it?'

His brain turned over, trying to pin down the reference. It was humiliating to find that his brain worked so much more slowly than Amy's but he was finding it more and more difficult to keep up with his nieces' interests these days. Their lives seemed to change so quickly, the pop stars they liked being different from one week to the next. Even the language they used evolved so rapidly that it left him behind.

'Wait a minute – Draco Malfoy, did you say? That's *Harry Potter*.'

'Of course it's *Harry Potter*.' Amy could barely conceal the contempt in her voice. 'It's in *The Chamber of Secrets*. Draco Malfoy finds a hand of glory when he's in the shop with his father. *"Best friend of thieves and plunderers,"* that's what the shopkeeper says.'

'*"Best friend of thieves and plunderers."* OK, that would make sense.'

'So it's magic,' said Amy.

'Yes, of course. What did you think it was?'

'I thought it was for real. Well, it's in the museum, isn't it? All this other stuff is for real – the costumes and the tools, and the old furniture.'

'Yes.'

'But the hand of glory isn't real – it's magic.'

'It's a genuine hand,' said Cooper defensively. 'A hand that belonged to a real person once.'

'But it's still magic. Magic is make-believe. *Harry Potter* is made up. It's fiction, Uncle Ben.'

'The fact is,' said Cooper, treading cautiously, 'people in the past believed those things were for real. They didn't know that magic was just something out of stories like *Harry Potter*. They actually thought it worked, in real life. The hand of glory, all kinds of stuff.'

They got to the door of the museum and looked out on to

the street. There were fewer umbrellas being carried by the pedestrians now, so the rain must be easing.

'People can be really weird, can't they?' said Amy. 'They believe in such stupid things.'

The old man's dreams were worse during the day. He drifted in and out of consciousness, hardly aware of his surroundings, pressed down into the darkness of sleep by a great weight. At times, he wasn't even sure he was still alive, it felt so impossible to wake up. It was so difficult, so far beyond his strength.

Our dawns and dusks are numbered. They'll steal our land next, and our hills. I always thought the place would last for ever, but now I don't care. I wouldn't pass on the curse. It'll die with me, and none too soon. It will an' all.

Dark filth, cruel brutes. Coming to my home for their evil purposes, stealing away my life. Our life. They turned up in their white vans, and they went away again. Dark, some of them. Speaking in tongues. They might as well have had the number stamped on their foreheads. Them and their minions, traipsing all over the shop. A load of rammel in the sheds, I don't know what . . .

Words and phrases repeated in his head, meaningless yet desperately important, the only thing that mattered.

For he that is dead. For he that is dead.

Aye, it were silin' down again. That morning, he was fast on, so I didn't waken him. He'd only be lorping around the house, the old dosser. Yammering about his mad ideas. Sacrilege and superstition, damnation and desecration.

The night before, they'd all been popped-up again. I thought I'd go scranny if they didn't stop. Look, he's a wick 'un, I said. I told you he was a wick 'un.

The old man opened his eyes for a moment, aware of movement and light, but sank back into sleep before his brain could focus.

But he was sickly, and always was. Weak in the head, and

sick in the body. Sound, me. I'm sound, I always said. But him, he was badly. I never cottoned on how badly. But it makes no odds now, does it? It's all for the best, in the end.

For he that is dead.

For he that is dead.

For he that is dead is freed from sin.

2

A single hair follicle was enough to make a DNA match. Polymerase chain reaction and short tandem repeats could get a result from one head hair, or even an eyelash. Invisible stains would work, too. Stains of saliva. Tears and blood.

Watching the activity at Pity Wood Farm, Diane Fry despaired of being able to rely on modern scientific techniques. Even the fingerprints Jamie Ward had left on his spade a few hours ago would have bloomed in the damp atmosphere and become useless.

Yet more vehicles had arrived at the scene, jockeying for parking places on the drier patches of ground. They were wasting their time, because there wouldn't be a dry inch left by the end of the day. Even now, the sound of spinning wheels whined in the air as a driver churned another rut into the mud.

'Well, I see the builders have trampled all over the job long before we got here.'

Fry turned to see Detective Inspector Paul Hitchens approaching the inner cordon, casually clad in jeans and green wellington boots, as if he'd only popped out to walk the dog on a Sunday afternoon.

'Morning, sir.'

'Morning, Diane.' He looked down at the sea of mud. 'That's just great. What a start. But I suppose it makes a change from our own plods doing the trampling.'

'Does it? I can't see any difference from where I'm standing. All size-twelve boots look the same to me. I'm not bothered what type of helmets they were wearing when they were doing the trampling. It's not as if they were bouncing around on their heads, is it?'

'True.'

'If we found an imprint of a Derbyshire Constabulary cap badge in the mud, that would be a different matter,' said Fry. 'Then we'd be looking for some uniformed idiot who'd tripped over his own feet. And we'd have a list of potential suspects right under our noses.'

Hitchens laughed. 'Shall we have a look at the centre of all this attention?'

With DC Murfin trailing reluctantly behind, they followed a line of wooden planks borrowed from the builders to create a temporary bridge. Their feet thumped on the planks as if they were walking out on to a pier at the seaside. Blackpool, with mud.

And here was the end-of-the-pier show – a sort of gipsy fortune teller lurking in her shadowy tent, consulting the bones.

The Home Office pathologist, Mrs van Doon, straightened up as they approached. She brushed a stray lock of hair from her forehead, leaving a smear of dirt from her glove across her temple.

'I shouldn't worry too much about contamination of your crime scene,' she said. 'This body has been here long enough for half the population of Derbyshire to have passed through the area on their way to the pub and back again.'

Murfin looked suddenly interested. 'There's a pub?'

'In the village,' said the pathologist, gesturing with a trowel. 'About a mile in that direction.'

Hitchens grunted impatiently. 'How long has it been here exactly?'

'*Exactly?* Is that a joke, Inspector?'

'Make an estimate, then. We won't hold you to it.'

'On that understanding . . .' Mrs van Doon gave an apologetic shrug. 'A year or so? I assume you'll be getting the forensic anthropologist in to examine the remains. Dr Jamieson might be able to give you a better estimate.'

'At first glance, the body looks pretty well preserved to me,' said Hitchens.

'Oh, you're looking at the hand. Well, the hand isn't too badly decomposed, that's true. But it had been well covered up and protected from the air – at least, before some individual stuck the edge of a spade through the plastic sheeting. There are some old rips in the covering at the head end, though. So the condition of that area of the body is a bit different.'

'At the head end? That sounds like bad news. What are our chances of an ID going to be?'

Mrs van Doon shrugged in her scene suit, rustling faintly. 'It's too early to say. But I can tell you the victim has lost quite a bit of flesh on the left side. Down to the bone in places. I'll know more when I can get her back to the mortuary. That might take a bit of time, though.'

'Why?'

'We need to be careful digging her out. Some of the skin is sloughing off, and the less of her we lose at this stage, the better. Wouldn't you agree?'

'It is a "her", though,' said Fry. 'You did say "her".'

'Yes, I'm pretty sure of that, Sergeant,' said the pathologist, her boots squelching as she squatted to peer into the hole. 'Unless you've got a cross-dresser with a penchant for tights and blue skirts on your missing persons list.'

'Not that I know of.'

'I'll pass the remains into Dr Jamieson's care when

20

he arrives. We can consult later, when she's safely in the lab.'

'Thank you, Doctor.'

As they re-crossed the plank bridge, Hitchens cast an eye over the farm buildings.

'What do we know about the occupants?'

'Apparently, the farm was owned by two elderly brothers,' said Murfin, producing a notebook and demonstrating that he'd actually been doing some work while everyone else was standing around gassing. 'One of them died quite recently, and the other is in a care home in Edendale.'

'*Was* owned?'

'Well, the place has been bought for development – hence the presence of all these builders in their hard hats. Development, or conversion. I'm not quite clear what they're telling me.'

'So who's the present owner?'

'A Mr Goodwin. He's a lawyer, lives in Manchester. Mr Goodwin is the man employing the builders. I've got his contact details from the site foreman. But that seems to be all the bloke knows.'

'Get on the phone, Gavin, and find out everything you can about the previous owners,' said Fry. 'We need names, dates, relationships. We need to know who else was in the household. Dig out anything that's on record about them. Get some help, if you need it.'

'If?' said Murfin. 'If?'

'The body has been here for a year at least, according to the pathologist.'

'That puts the victim *in situ* before Mr Goodwin took ownership, then. The sale went through only three months ago, I gather. The farm has been empty for about nine months, after the surviving owner went into care.'

Fry looked at their surroundings in more detail, the farm buildings beyond the stretch of mud and the track and the parked vehicles.

21

'Does that explain the state of the place? How could it get like this in nine months?'

Ben Cooper would probably tell her that all this was evidence of the evolution of the farm over the centuries, as its owners adapted to new ways of working, changed the use of their buildings from cattle to sheep, from hay storage to machinery shed. Or whatever. To Fry, it looked like dereliction and chaos, pure and simple. Not an ounce of design or planning had gone into the farm, not even in the newer buildings.

Of course, farmers were a law unto themselves in so many ways. They were even allowed to create these shanty towns, reminiscent of the slums of some Third World country where there was no running water or drainage, and rubbish was dumped in the streets. In Rio de Janeiro, you might expect it. But not in Middle England.

'What a place,' she said, unable to avoid voicing her feelings for once.

'The builders have hardly started on the house or outbuildings yet,' said Murfin. 'The foreman tells me they've been doing some work on the foundations and building an approach road. Then they have to tackle some of the exterior walls where they're unsound. And of course there's the roof. Not much point in trying to do any work on the interior until you've sorted out the roof, is there?'

'What is it going to be when they've finished?' asked Fry.

'The foreman says a gentleman's residence. Office suite, swimming pool, guest annexe.'

'They've got a hell of a job on.'

Unrepaired splits in the iron guttering had allowed rainwater to run down the walls, dragging long grey stains across the stone. Wires sagged from the telegraph pole. Two black crows swayed on the wire in the wind, flicking their wings to keep their balance.

Fry noticed a large shed behind the house. A very large

shed indeed, with a convex roof. Wheel tracks led from one end of the shed towards the stretch of ground where the body had been found. Old tracks that had been made when the ground was soft, but whose ruts had hardened and survived until the recent rain. That was the sort of building where anything could go on, out of sight of the public. Out of earshot, out of mind.

The rain was getting heavier. That could be a problem.

But then Fry corrected herself. There were never any problems, only challenges. No obstacles that couldn't be overcome.

At least the FOAs had been right on the ball, getting that body tent over the makeshift grave as soon as they saw the conditions. By now, this rain could have washed away the evidence if they hadn't acted quickly. Lucky they'd had one in the boot of their car. In these circumstances, there was an evens chance that they would have had to sit and wait for one to arrive.

According to their advertising, these tents were supposed to go up in ten seconds, but she bet it had taken a good bit longer than that. The peg-down eyelets looked none too secure in the soft ground, and the guy ropes were slippery with mud.

'Duckboards,' someone was saying into a radio. 'We need duckboards here. Lots of duckboards.'

Fry turned back to Murfin again. 'So where's this builder who found the body?'

'Waiting in the van over there. Ward is his name – Jamie Ward, aged twenty. I'd hardly call him your typical builder, actually.'

Fry looked at him. 'So what *would* you call him, Gavin?'

Murfin closed his notebook. 'Terrified,' he said. 'That's what I'd call him – a terrified kid.'

Matt Cooper had loaded some sheep into a trailer and was doing the paperwork in the Land Rover when his brother arrived. Ben could see a sheaf of forms resting on a clipboard.

Pink copy for the destination, blue for the haulier, yellow for the holding of departure.

Matt opened the door, the usual frown caused by paperwork clearing from his face.

'Hello, little brother. How was Amy? Did she have a good time?'

'Oh, yes. She was fascinated by the recipe for preserving a severed hand.'

'That sounds about right. She's been in a funny mood recently.'

Matt was still putting on weight. That was a new set of overalls he was wearing, and they were a size larger than the last ones. He was only in his mid-thirties, so he still had middle-aged spread to look forward to.

'Amy talks in quite a grown-up way sometimes, doesn't she?' said Ben.

'Oh, you noticed that. Yes, it's a bit of a new thing. I think it's some influence at school – she must have some new friends, or something.'

'Or a new teacher she's got a crush on?'

'Do girls have crushes on teachers?'

'Yes, I believe so, Matt.'

'I mean . . . well, I think they're mostly female teachers that she has at that school.'

'Even so.'

Matt was silent for a moment. 'I'll ask Kate to have a quiet word,' he said.

Ben turned to look at the farmhouse, conscious of its presence behind him, the old family home. Now that he no longer lived here, he noticed that Bridge End Farm was starting to look middle-aged, too. The house hadn't been painted for a while, and he could see that some work needed doing on the roof of the barn. He supposed there wasn't much money in the bank to spare for repairs these days.

'It'll just be a phase Amy is going through, won't it?' he said.

'Are you sure?'

'It could be a lot worse, Matt. She's a sensible girl.'

Matt put his paperwork aside. 'Ben, how come you know so much more about pubescent girls than I do? I'm the dad around here.'

'You see all sorts of things in the job.'

'I suppose you do. And of course, you don't always talk about it, do you, Ben? Especially these days. Whenever you come to the farm now, you seem to have changed a little bit more.'

Ben watched Amy coming across the field, walking with exaggerated care, instead of running in an uninhibited way, as she once would have done.

'Perhaps some of us are maturing faster than others,' he said.

Ben couldn't deny that he was losing his sense of connection to Bridge End Farm. The ties were no longer quite so binding since he'd moved out and rented his own flat in Edendale. Memories of his childhood at the farm were objects in the far distance, unless he stopped to think about them. And then the details could spring at him with unexpected ferocity, like wild animals that hated to be stared at.

'Nothing much happening, then?' asked Matt. 'No urgent crime on the streets of Edendale to take you away from us? If you're at a loose end, you could help me batten down for the weather. It's not looking too good.'

Ben turned and looked at the hills in the east, where the bad weather came from. A bank of cloud was building up, dark and ominous. Those easterly winds had been a feature of his early years. At Bridge End, when the wind blew from the east it made all the shutters bang and the doors of the loose boxes rattle against their latches. The trees on the eastern ridge would be bent over at unnatural angles, their bare branches flailing helplessly against the power of the gale. At night, animals would stir uneasily in the barns as the young

Ben lay listening to the banging and the moaning of the wind, jumping at the crash of a bucket hurled across the yard or a tile dislodged from the roof.

Just when Cooper was thinking that nothing would ever make him jump with alarm like that any more, the phone in his pocket began to ring.

Jamie Ward was shivering miserably in the front seat of the crew bus that had brought the builders to Pity Wood Farm. It was a converted Transit, smelling powerfully of cigarettes and muddy clothes. The seats were worn thin, the floor scuffed by dozens of work boots. Fry moved a hard hat aside, slid in next to him, and wound the window down to prevent the interior steaming up. Rain covered the windscreen, blocking out the view of the farm.

'Are you all right?' she asked.

'I'll be OK.'

He didn't sound very sure, but Fry let it pass. The sooner she finished with him, the better it would be. If he went into shock, he'd be useless.

Murfin had been right about Jamie Ward. He was younger than any of the other men she'd seen standing around the site, and he had an entirely different look about him. His hair was streaked blond, and was gelled up at the front – hardly the typical builder's style. But he was a well-built lad, six feet tall at least, a good build for a rugby player. His hands were powerful and broad, just as suitable for hard physical work as for playing rugby.

'I'm studying Microbiology at Sheffield University,' said Jamie when she asked him. 'But I need to find work whenever I can, you know – to get some dosh.'

'You work as a builder's labourer? That's a bit of an unusual vacation job for a student,' suggested Fry.

Jamie shrugged. 'It suits me. It beats working in McDonald's, anyway. I like to be outside in the open air, doing a bit of physical work. I'd go mad otherwise. I don't have any skills or training, but I can use a spade and push a wheelbarrow about.'

'And carry a hod full of bricks?'

'We're not allowed to use hods any more,' said Jamie. 'Health and Safety – you could do your back in, or drop bricks on someone's head.'

'Really?'

He nodded. 'Besides, we're not using bricks on this site. It's going to be entirely stone on the outside, to match the original walls. Breeze block on the inside, of course.' Jamie wiped off a few inches of condensation and looked at the figures moving about in the rain. 'Funny, really, when there's all this clay lying about. But stone is much more fashionable. That's what the owner wants.'

Fry saw him relaxing a little, now that he had managed to get off the painful subject of the body he'd found.

'So you like to be outside in the open air?' she asked, thinking that Jamie Ward reminded her a little of Ben Cooper. 'Are you from a farming family, by any chance?'

'Well, I used to help my grandfather around his place when I was a teenager. Just at weekends and during the school holidays. He doesn't have the farm any more, though – Granddad sold up when it stopped making money.'

'Sensible man.'

'Right. Well, I wouldn't have wanted to spend my life doing the job that Granddad did. He was at it twenty-four seven. There was no let-up from looking after the animals. Livestock farming is for losers, don't you think? Anyone with any sense is getting out as fast as they can.'

They both sat for a moment peering through the patch of cleared glass at the buildings of Pity Wood Farm, like divers examining a deep sea wreck.

'I mean,' said Jamie, 'look at this place, for example.'

'You're right there.'

Ward glanced sideways at her. 'But you want me to tell you what happened, don't you? How I came to find the . . . well . . .'

'I know you'll have gone through it before, but it would help me if you could describe the incident in your own words, Jamie.'

'The incident, yes. I suppose that's what it was.'

'Take your time. I'm not going anywhere for a while.'

'Nik had me digging this trench, see. To put in some footings for a new wall, he said.'

'And Nik is . . .?'

'Nikolai. He's the gaffer, the foreman. Polish, of course, but he's OK. He leaves me pretty much to myself most of the time. I don't get the best jobs, obviously – I'm just a labourer. In fact, they sometimes send me up to the village for cigarettes, if they run out. Anyway . . . I'd been digging this trench for a couple of days. It was hard work – that soil is so heavy, especially when it's wet. You can see how wet it is.'

'Yes, I've seen how wet it is,' said Fry, becoming aware of the dampness soaking into her feet where the mud had overflowed her shoes.

'And there's all kinds of stuff in the ground here. You wouldn't believe the rubbish I've turned up. Nothing that'd interest an archaeologist, but I've thought once or twice of asking the Time Team to come and give me a hand.'

There was silence for a moment as the full deadliness of his joke drifted through the van like a bad smell. Fry saw him go pale, and thought she was going to lose him.

'Are you all right, Jamie?'

He gulped. 'Yeah. Thanks. It was mentioning the hand. Not that I meant that hand, but . . . Shit, I'm not making any sense. I'm sorry.'

'You're doing just fine. You were telling me about the rubbish you had to dig out for the trench. What kind of thing do you mean?'

28

'A lot of it was rusty lumps of metal, half-bricks, nails, broken buckets. It looked as though the farmers had used that area for a tip. I cursed Nik a few times, I can tell you. There were even some of those glass jars that people use for making pickles, with lids that have an airtight seal. Do you know what I mean?'

Jamie was making gestures with his hands to indicate the size of the containers he'd found.

'Mason jars?' said Fry.

'That's it. Oh, and an old, broken cross on a chain, some Coke bottles, and a packet of coffee filters. The things people chuck out. Why don't they use their wheelie bins – some of that stuff ought to be recycled.'

'Where did you put all these items you dug out of the trench?'

'In a barrow, then they went into the big skip round the back of the house.' Jamie paused. 'Why are you asking questions about the rubbish?'

'Because some of the items you dug out might have belonged to the victim,' said Fry as gently as she could.

'Oh, God. I never thought of that.'

'An old, broken cross, you said.'

'It was nothing. Just a cheap crucifix on a chain, with part of the base chipped away. A bit of worthless tat.'

'You didn't notice any personal items, did you?'

'Such as?'

'A purse, jewellery, coins,' said Fry. 'Items of clothing.'

An entire handbag would be nice, she was thinking. A driving licence, credit cards, a letter from an embittered ex-lover?

'No, nothing like that,' said Jamie.

'I don't know if anyone has mentioned that the body is that of a female, fairly young?'

Jamie swallowed again. 'Well, some of the blokes have been listening in, you know. Word got around.'

'I mention it because there might have been items you were unfamiliar with.'

Jamie shook his head. 'Only the – what do you call them? Mason jars.'

So she might have been making pickles when she was buried, thought Fry. That helps. But she knew she was being unfair on the young labourer. Why should he have taken any notice of what he was tossing away in his wheelbarrow? It would be up to the SOCOs to go through the contents of the skip. Who was going to tell them about that job? Mrs Popularity, she supposed.

'All right. Let's move on. How far down had you dug before you noticed anything wrong?'

'Nearly three feet. I was shifting a big lump of stone out of the clay. It was heavy, and I was thinking of calling one of the other blokes over to give me . . . I mean, to help me lift it. But they laugh at me if I ask for help, so I tried to manage on my own. I'd climbed down into the trench, and I managed to get both hands round the stone and hoist it up. I remember it came out with a sort of sucking sound, and it left a big, round impression in the clay where it had been lying. I must have stood there like an idiot for I don't know how long, watching the water slowly fill in the hole where the stone had been. And there it was – the hand.'

Fry kept quiet. She could see that he was in the moment now, living the experience. This was the time he might remember the little details best.

'I shouted then, I think,' said Jamie. 'And I dropped the stone, too – I've just remembered that, I dropped the stone. Somebody came running over straight away, one of the other blokes working nearby. They thought I'd hurt myself, of course. I could already hear Nik swearing in Polish and calling me an English cretin.'

Jamie finished with a laugh. 'And he's right – that's what I am. What an idiot for making all this fuss.'

'Not at all,' said Fry. 'You did exactly the right thing.'

Jamie didn't look convinced. He rubbed his own hands together, as if trying to remove the mud he'd seen on the thing he'd uncovered.

'So you could hear Nik cursing. Was it him who came running over when you shouted?'

'No, someone else. Nik turned up a bit later. I can't remember who it was who came first. I didn't take any notice at the time.'

'But it must have been somebody working nearby.'

'Yes. Well, it must have been.' Jamie shrugged apologetically. 'But I don't know who. It was a bit of a blank by then.'

'Don't worry. You've done really well, Jamie.'

'You know what I'm thinking now?' he said. 'Thank God that woman's hand was under that stone. If I'd been digging and hit it with my spade, I'd have sliced right through it. Well, I would, wouldn't I?'

'Possibly.'

He looked pleadingly at Fry. 'I need to go outside now,' he said. 'Right now. I'm sorry. Tell everyone I'm sorry.'

Strips of plastic sheeting that had been ripped from passing lorries were snagged on barbed-wire fences and hawthorn branches. They streamed and fluttered in the wind like tattered pennants. No need for windsocks here. It was always obvious which direction the wind was blowing from.

Cooper had Peak FM on in the car and was listening to a series of tracks from seventies bands. UB40 and Dire Straits. A bit of Duran Duran even. Well, it was that or BBC local radio, where the playlists seemed to be regressing to the sixties, with more and more artists that he'd never heard of. The Beatles maybe, but most of it was stuff his parents must have listened to when they were children.

Pity Wood Farm, according to Control. He'd never heard of it, but he knew where Rakedale was – the southern edge

31

of the limestone plateau, maybe even beyond the limestone, somewhere down past Monyash and Hartington. Much further south, and this body would have been D Division's problem.

The peat moors were the brownish yellow of winter. An oddly shaped cloud was rearing over the hill, as if there had been a nuclear explosion somewhere near Buxton. Bare, twisted branches stood outlined against the skyline, gesturing hopelessly, as if they thought the spring would never come.

Cooper found Fry inside the outer cordon, shaking the rain from her jacket.

'Diane – what do you want doing?'

'We're going to have to start on the house and outbuildings some time, but I don't know where's best to begin. Take a look around, will you? Give me your impressions. Perhaps you could start with that shed over there.'

'Shed?'

'That shed over there. The big one.'

'No problem.'

Cooper watched her go. Impressions, was it? That wasn't normally what she asked him for. Fry was usually hot on firm evidence. Maybe there was something about this place that bothered her. If so, she wasn't likely to say it. She was putting that responsibility on to him – let DC Cooper come up with the impressions, the vague feelings, the gut instincts. Then she could always dismiss them, if necessary. Cooper's contribution could be trampled underfoot, without any shadow on her own reputation.

Oh, well. Fair enough. It seemed to be his role in life since Diane Fry had become his DS. He either had to accept it, or find somewhere else.

When the police had finished with him, Jamie Ward looked around for a few minutes. There were a lot of cops here now, and some other people he took to be forensics. He could imagine the blokes in his crew blabbing to the police. *Yes, that's him over there. We call him the Professor.* But not all of them would be eager to talk to the authorities, he bet. A few of them would make out they didn't speak any English at all.

Nikolai was standing over by the house, talking to a bunch of the men. He was speaking quietly in Polish, almost whispering, though it was unlikely anyone would understand him, except his own lads. Jamie frowned, and counted them again. Seven. He looked around, wondering if he could be mistaken. But no. There were seven, plus Nikolai. Two men short.

He sighed, foreseeing more complications, and more trouble. Jamie recalled that faint glint of metal, slick with the dampness of clay, reflecting a glimmer of light and the movement of his spade. He remembered the impression he'd had, the thing that had made him stop digging, his spade frozen in his hands as he stared down into the hole. For a second, that flicker of light had looked like an eye – an eye that had turned to watch him from its muddy grave. He thought he would probably still be able to see that eye in his dreams tonight.

3

It was more than just a shed. When you got right up to it, the building that Fry had pointed out was more like a vast, corrugated-iron tunnel. When Cooper walked into it, he felt as though he was entering a cathedral, with airy space all around him and light filtering down from the roof, shafts of it striking through cracks in the iron sheeting. Water dripped somewhere ahead of him, and the sides gleamed with patches of damp as he moved.

Many of the older farms in this area still used wartime Nissen huts for storage, relying on the fact that they were built to last a long time and took many years before they finally collapsed from age and neglect. But this thing was bigger than any Nissen hut Cooper had ever seen. A hundred feet long at least, with central posts holding up the ridge of the arc high above him. The structure was open to the elements at both ends, but the middle was dry and sheltered.

Inside, he found two tractors parked on a concrete base alongside a pick-up truck. More vehicles stood outside – a lorry fitted with a winch, an old Escort with a pig trailer attached to the tow bar. The equipment stored in here included an interesting yard scraper made from twenty-four-inch tractor tyre sections. Matt would love that. Cheap, but effective.

Heaps of old tyres lay around the yard, and the vehicles were overshadowed by a huge fortress of silage bags. At first glance, the bags looked like plastic boulders painted black, with strips of loose wrapping stirring in the breeze. Cooper pictured them in summer, with bumble bees buzzing around the stack, attracted by the sweet smell of the silage. But a shiver of cold air reminded him that it was December, and the silage shouldn't still be standing here, untouched.

Outside, the sides and roof of the shed were starting to turn from their original yellow to rust red. The branches of a hawthorn tree scratched restlessly against the sides – the only sign of life in the abandoned farmyard.

Behind the farmhouse stood a typical skeleton of an open Dutch-style barn, its timbers supporting only a few tatters of roof. He could see that the ridge of the house sagged in a couple of places, and the windows at the back were hung with dusty curtains. A grimy caravan stood in what might once have been the garden. Ancient bales of hay were visible through a ragged hole in the wall of a stone byre.

Another range of old stone buildings was practically in ruins. Cooper found himself inhaling whiffs of a powerful smell here and there as he moved around. A hint of ammonia suggested the presence of a number of cats. Farm cats, that lived outside and prowled the barns and sheds for rodents, doing a job of work.

Beyond the Dutch barn, a few yards down the slope, he found a series of dilapidated poultry sheds. They weren't all that old, but had never been maintained properly. He peered through a dusty window, expecting rows and rows of battery cages. But there were none to be seen. So the sheds must have been deep-littered with straw for the birds, unless the cages had been removed.

Cooper was already starting to find this place depressing. Parts of Bridge End Farm might be deteriorating because there was no money for maintenance and repairs. But Bridge End was a model of modernity, compared to Pity Wood.

He turned his attention to the house itself. Limestone, with those distinctive gritstone corners called quoins. Some of the walls had been rendered with cement to combat the effects of the weather. But, judging from the scabrous patches where the render had flaked off, the weather was winning. In fact, it had been winning for some time. This farmhouse had thrown in the towel.

If there were any answers to how the body had ended up in that shallow grave a few yards away, they would most likely be found inside the house. Cooper enquired who'd taken possession of the keys, and he eased open the back door.

In the hallway, the first thing he saw was a huge, black family Bible, laid out on a table like a warning.

Fry knew she had to get control of the scene and protect any forensic evidence – though what kind of evidence might have survived the slow decay and partial demolition of Pity Wood Farm she couldn't imagine.

These were the critical hours. If any evidence did turn up, she had to be able to demonstrate chain of custody. It was so important to look ahead to the possibility of a trial some time in the future. If the prosecution didn't have chain of custody, it presented a gift to the defence. No matter what happened between now and that hypothetical date, her present actions could cast doubt on an entire investigation or provide it with a solid foundation.

The SOCOs had a rule of thumb. If an item of potential evidence was vulnerable, if everyone was going to walk over it on the way in and out of the scene, it should be removed or protected. If it was out of the way, it could be left in place.

There could be evidence that had already been walked over several times on the way in and out.

So those builders had to be kept clear, to minimize any contamination to that they'd already caused. The digging operations had to be done in a controlled manner – someone would have to keep an eye on the diggers and stop them wandering around the farm.

And those vehicles parked up on the muddy track and in the entrance to the yard . . . well, it was already too late, probably. No matter what action she took now, there was no way she could turn back time.

'Sutton,' said Murfin breathlessly, breaking into her thoughts. 'Sutton.'

'What?'

'The previous owners of the farm. Name of Sutton. Raymond is the brother now residing in a care home back in town – we don't know which yet, but we'll find out. He's quite elderly, in his late seventies, we think. There was a younger brother, Derek, who died about a year ago.'

'Not bad, Gavin.'

'Thanks. Unfortunately, we can't find any sign of anyone else in the household at that time, other than the two brothers. We've checked the electoral register, and they were the only two adults listed.'

'So no women?'

'No women,' said Murfin. 'Just peace and quiet.'

Inside the farmhouse, Cooper found the rooms to be a strange mixture of conversion and preservation. Passing from one room to another for the first time was an unpredictable experience. Some spaces were littered with building materials and tools left behind by Jamie Ward's workmates. Sacks of sand and cement, piles of breeze block, buckets, a ladder, a couple of steel toolboxes. These rooms had been stripped of their original contents – all dumped in the yellow skip he'd seen outside the back door, presumably – and they'd been transformed into building sites instead.

Other rooms, though, had yet to be touched by anyone. Those still contained evidence of the farm's occupants and their day-to-day existence – two pairs of wellington boots by the back door, a smelly overcoat still hanging in a cupboard under the stairs.

Upstairs, there were three bedrooms. It was difficult to tell which of them had been occupied most recently, since they were all equally full of junk and old clothes. The middle bedroom overlooked the yard, and it seemed darker and colder than the other two. If Cooper had been choosing a bedroom, it would have been any one but this.

The kitchen seemed to be the part of the house that was most intact. A black, cast-iron cooking range dominated one end of the room, and near it a tap still dripped in a Belfast sink, as if someone had only just failed to turn it off properly. All the furniture was still here, too – a large pine table with scarred and blackened legs, two ancient armchairs, a dresser filled with plates and cutlery.

In the corner and along the back wall, Cooper unearthed a number of less identifiable objects. He counted a dozen cardboard boxes, some standing on top of each other, the bottom one crumpling slightly under the weight. There was a heap of clothes on a chair near the cooking range and more coats and overalls hung behind the outer door. It was a *Marie Celeste* of a kitchen, frozen in time, preserved in the moment that the owners had finally walked out one day.

Even the fridge was still here, an old Electrolux with a split rubber seal. But that wasn't still working, surely? Cooper opened the door, and was surprised to see the interior light come on, and feel a draught of cold air on his face. But then he saw why it was switched on. The builders had been keeping their milk in it, ready for their tea breaks. Their carton of semi-skimmed sat among some less reassuring items – jars without labels, tins that had been opened and left to grow mould, as if someone had been trying to culture penicillin. The contents of the nearest jar had crystallized and lay on the bottom, defying him to figure out what they'd originally been.

The smell was disturbing, and Cooper shut the door again quickly. The fridge responded by breaking into an unsteady hum, rattling slightly on the tiled floor.

As he moved around the house, Cooper felt the skin on the back of his neck begin to crawl. The surroundings were innocuous enough, if depressing. But the atmosphere was really bad. His instincts were telling him that something awful had happened here at Pity Wood Farm. Painful memories had imprinted themselves into the walls, the aftershock of some traumatic event still shuddered in the air.

Cooper shivered, and tried to put the sensation aside. It was the sort of feeling that he couldn't mention, particularly to Diane Fry. He'd been accused of being over-imaginative too often to risk the put-down. Evidence was all that anyone was interested in, and he had none of that.

He might describe his feeling to Liz when he saw her – she would understand what he meant. Cooper glanced at his watch. Hopefully that might be tonight, if he was lucky. The sense of urgency that pervaded most major crime scenes was missing from Pity Wood – presumably because the body was judged to be too old. The twenty-four-hour rule didn't apply here. Vital evidence that could disappear in the first day or so after a murder was long gone in this case. Anything that was left would be preserved down there, in the mud with the body – or here, inside the house. Better to take it slow and carefully, so that nothing remaining was missed.

That's what he'd be thinking if he was SIO, anyway. Not that he was ever likely to reach that position – you needed to be promoted at regular intervals to achieve it. He'd probably slipped too far behind already when he failed to get his promotion to DS. He was thirty, after all, and there would be eager young officers overtaking him before he knew it. Just the way it had happened to Gavin Murfin, and many others.

Cooper looked through the kitchen window and saw DI Hitchens standing in the yard with the crime scene manager, Wayne Abbott. Right now, Abbott was doing the talking, and the DI was nodding wisely. He did that pretty well, the nodding bit. From a distance, he looked intelligent and in control, a man who knew exactly what the plan was. Cooper knew he could never look that way himself, whether from a distance or close up. He'd always just look like a confused DC who was having uneasy feelings that he couldn't explain. Fry had told him that often enough. *Keep your mouth firmly shut, Ben – that's the best way. Don't give them an excuse to laugh at you.*

He heard a noise behind him, a faint crunch of cement dust underfoot. He turned to find Diane Fry standing in the doorway, her usual silent approach thwarted by a layer of builders' debris. Her gaze roamed around the room, taking in the furniture and the yellowed walls. Cooper tried to think of something intelligent he could say to her, a few words that would make it look as though he'd been gathering useful evidence, rather than dwelling on eerie atmospheres.

'Jesus,' said Fry, before he could speak. 'Don't you feel as though something horrible happened in here?'

In the more distant outbuildings, there had been that powerful smell of cat urine. Yet Cooper had seen no sign of any cats as he walked round the property. He wondered what had happened to them when the Suttons left. Dispersed, like everything else, he supposed.

But everything hadn't been dispersed, had it? Far from it, in fact. There was all that machinery and equipment in the big shed, the silage bags, the hay, and the vehicles parked in the yard.

'You know, it would be normal practice to have a farm sale in these circumstances,' said Cooper as they went back outside.

'A what?' asked Fry.

'A farm sale. I don't mean the sale of the buildings themselves. Before it got to that stage, they would usually sell off all the equipment – the tractors and trailers, tools, field gates, spare fencing posts. There are buyers for most things. They could probably sell the silage and the tyres, too, maybe even this shed itself. But they should have done that before the house and land were put on the market, so there was a tidy site for buyers to look at. I can't understand why all this stuff is still standing here. It doesn't make sense.'

Fry shrugged. 'Perhaps they're planning to do it later. There's no law against it.'

'I'll enquire at the local auctioneers, Pilkington's – they'd almost certainly be the people called in for a job like that.' Cooper shook his head. 'But it's really bad planning to do it this way round. They should have cleared everything out first.'

Murfin stuck his head round a corner. 'Oh, there you are. Mr Hitchens wants everyone out front for a confab.'

'We're coming.'

DI Hitchens was Fry's immediate boss, the man whose job she might have to get if she planned to stay in Derbyshire E Division. But the thought of staying here wasn't part of her future plans, and places like Pity Wood Farm only confirmed her view. There were times when she longed for the city, or even for the peculiar urban fusion that was the Black Country where she'd grown up.

Hitchens looked calm and unruffled, allowing the rain to fall on his head without flinching. As he waited for the officers to gather round him at the RV point, he wiped some moisture from his face, flashing the white scar that crawled across the middle knuckles of his fingers.

'Well, as some of you already know,' he said, 'this body has been in the ground for a year or more.'

'So there's no point in us rushing around if the case is so old, sir?' asked someone.

'Well . . . that's not something I want to hear anyone saying publicly. But it does mean we can let the anthropologist and forensics team do their thing for a while yet, and the mince pies might not have to go cold.'

There were a scattering of half-hearted cheers, but the relief was palpable.

Hitchens acknowledged the reaction with a slight smile. 'Meanwhile, a few basic procedures are in order, to make sure we've covered the ground. If we do have to open a murder enquiry later on, I don't want to hear that we missed vital evidence in the early stages because someone was in too much of a hurry to do their Christmas shopping. Understood?'

'Yes, sir.'

'For a start, we need information on all these workmen – anyone who's been on site. Names and addresses, dates of birth – you know the drill. Then we can run them through the PNC if necessary.'

'What about their status?' asked Fry.

'Status?'

'I was thinking that some of them might have residency or immigration issues. You know how difficult it is to get information when they're worried about being arrested or deported.'

'I thought someone told me they were all Polish?' said Hitchens. 'Poles don't have residency or immigration issues – they're members of the EU, so they can come and go when they like, and they don't need work permits either.'

Murfin raised a hand, enjoying being the man with the answers for once. 'Apparently, most of these blokes work for an agency, which sends them wherever the work is. It means they don't have a settled address, sir. They live in digs, bed and breakfasts, caravans, whatever is available. They say it's worth their while – they get about twice the minimum wage, enough to send money home, if their families aren't in this country.'

Fry glanced across at the little huddle of builders in their safety boots and yellow hard hats. 'We're only assuming they're all Polish. The foreman is, but we haven't checked the rest out yet, so we might get some surprises.'

'Don't tell me we're going to have to find translators,' said Hitchens. 'At Christmas? Their statements alone could take weeks to process.'

'Well, maybe we don't need them.'

'No. You're right, DS Fry. Let's prioritize, shall we? We're dealing with the foreman and the lad who actually found the body. What's his name?'

'Jamie Ward.'

'Jamie Ward, right. The rest can wait, as long as we know where to find them. Meanwhile, we need everything we can get on the family who lived here. Two brothers, Raymond and Derek Sutton, and anyone associated with them. I'll be speaking to the surviving brother myself this afternoon, when we establish which care home he's in. There's a village over that way somewhere, called Rakedale. We'll be starting house-to-house there tomorrow morning. Everyone OK with that?'

There were murmurs of agreement and a general shuffling. Everyone was now anxious to get finished and go home.

Cooper fell into step with Fry as the impromptu meeting broke up. Their feet squelched as they walked back towards their vehicles from the outer cordon.

'What do you think, Diane? Are we going to have to interview all the builders?'

'I hope not.'

The crew working on the conversion of Pity Wood Farm had created their own access, widening an old field entrance and laying down a gravel roadway to reach the back of the farm. The area they'd been working in was getting very muddy, and Scenes of Crime had managed to lay a series of duckboards to reach the site of the grave, which would protect evidence better than their temporary bridge. Anyone who stepped off those duckboards was getting splattered with mud. One or two of the more carelessly parked vehicles might have to be towed out at the end of the day.

Cooper could see Liz Petty talking to two of her SOCO colleagues. They were probably awaiting the arrival of the Northern Area Scientific Support Officer, who was based at C Division headquarters in Chesterfield.

He badly wanted to acknowledge Liz, but they'd agreed to keep their relationship low profile when they were at work. Not secret, exactly – it would never be a secret in E Division. But they both felt it was important to be professional, and not to give anyone cause for complaint.

When he saw the front of the farm, Cooper realized why the builders had gone in the back way. The main access must already have been an ocean of mud when they arrived. It looked as though the previous owners had allowed their cattle free rein. The ground was seriously poached, right up to the walls of the farmhouse. The lane from the gate past the barn would be almost impassable on foot, unless you were wearing waders.

Cooper shook his head. No one would have allowed that to happen unless they no longer cared about the farm, or had no stake in its future.

He pulled his Toyota over towards the wall and leaned on the topping stones for a while. He could see that someone had been into Pity Wood this way, and quite recently. Tyre tracks ran through the mud, where a vehicle had churned deep, wet ruts. The tracks didn't run all the way up to the house, but stopped near the barn. If he looked a bit more closely at the ruts, then asked around to find out when cattle were last in here, he could probably have a good stab at how long it was since the vehicle had come and gone.

But it didn't matter, did it? This crime wasn't recent enough.

Cooper felt sure they'd be looking into the past to find the information they needed, studying that little time capsule of a kitchen, not the cement-covered building site. The answers would lie in the lives of the people who'd abandoned Pity Wood Farm to its fate.

4

At The Oaks residential care home in Edendale, Raymond Sutton was sitting in the big lounge – the one with a view of the fields at the back, where he got an occasional glimpse of cattle grazing in the distance. Holsteins, but it was better than nothing. The TV was on, of course. Some of the old girls watched it all the time, though they didn't always know what they were seeing. Most of the stuff that was on during the day was rubbish – brainless quiz shows, old films, kiddies' cartoons. He'd never been one for sitting indoors watching the telly. Raymond liked the news, though. Just because you were old and getting a bit stiff in the joints, it didn't mean you should let your brain cells die.

He saw a car enter the gateway from the road and head up the drive. Thanks to his new hearing aid, he could hear the tyres crunch on the gravel. There were many sounds that he'd missed when his hearing started to fail, but the noise of cars wasn't one of them. His home at Pity Wood had been far enough off the road to save him from traffic.

He didn't recognize this particular car. Red, which was unusual these days. Everyone seemed to go for grey or silver, which made it difficult to distinguish between them. He could see it was a four-wheel drive, too. Japanese – Mitsubishi,

Toyota? One of those makes. He might have known the difference once, but it didn't matter that much any more.

Four-wheel drive, though, and very muddy around the wheel arches and the bottom of the doors. Somebody who knew the countryside, then. He wondered which of the residents they were visiting.

One of the carers came into the room. The one called Elaine. Young, dark-haired, one of the nicer ones. She was always gentle with him when she had to get him out of bed or into the bath. A little bit of kindness could make his last days more tolerable.

'Raymond,' she said. 'Are you feeling up to visitors? There are some people here asking to see you. They're from the police.'

Cooper felt he could probably have done a better job interviewing Raymond Sutton on his own. But DI Hitchens was in charge of the investigation for now, so he was within his rights to do whatever he wanted. Some might say that the Senior Investigating Officer should be back at the office co-ordinating the enquiry and allocating resources, but what did he know? He was just a DC.

They were shown into a lounge by the care assistant, whose name badge said she was called Elaine. Mr Sutton had either been put in there on his own, or the other residents had been moved out somewhere else when they arrived. Whichever it was, they found the old man in splendid isolation, perched in one of those big chairs that only old people ever sat in. There were other, similar chairs ranged round the walls of the room, and a big television set stood in the corner, mercifully switched off a moment before. Many interviews conducted in people's own homes resulted in conversations shouted over the noise of the telly. It was often a temptation to take someone down to the station just for the sake of being able to hear what they were saying.

'Mr Sutton? I'm Detective Inspector Hitchens, and this is Detective Constable Cooper. From Edendale CID.'

Hitchens offered a view of his warrant card, as procedure recommended. But Sutton held out his hand instead to greet his visitors, and Hitchens was obliged to shake it. Cooper did the same, grasping a hand with paper-thin skin that trembled slightly in his palm. The old man smelled of soap, and his clothes were clean and neat, though the cardigan he was wearing no longer fit him so well as it once might have.

They sat on chairs either side of him, and Hitchens opened the conversation.

'Mr Sutton, you are the former owner of Pity Wood Farm at Rakedale. Is that right?'

'Aye. That's where I live. Pity Wood.'

Hitchens shook his head. 'That's where you *used* to live. You sold the farm, didn't you?'

'I did. You're right. I don't remember who bought it.'

'We know who bought it, Mr Sutton.'

'Who was it? I can't remember their name.'

'Mr Goodwin, from Manchester.'

'I don't know him. It was all done through the estate agents and solicitors. You'll have to ask them where he is.'

'No, we want to ask you about Pity Wood Farm.'

'Pity Wood, that's where I live.'

'You don't live there any more. Don't you remember?'

Sutton laughed – a dry, crackly laugh, with little humour in it, as if the DI was tormenting him with a feather in a sensitive spot.

'I remember some things quite well. But I don't recall this feller that bought the farm. What did you say his name was?'

'Goodwin.'

'I don't know him.'

'No sir –'

The old man turned away from Hitchens and studied Cooper

instead, his eyes glinting. 'You'll come to see me again, won't you? I don't get many visitors.'

Hitchens became impatient then, and made the mistake of putting his hand on Sutton's sleeve to get his attention. The old man drew his arm away abruptly and stared at Hitchens in indignation.

'Just a minute, young man. Take your hands off me, or I'll get them to send for the police.'

'Mr Sutton. We have to ask you some questions, I'm afraid, sir. There have been human remains found at Pity Wood this morning. The dead body of a woman. We need to know how this person ended up buried on your farm.'

'Questions? Well, you can only try. Open the barn door, and you might find a cow.'

Hitchens opened his mouth, but shut it again quickly, as if he'd just found the cow and didn't want it to escape.

They left Mr Sutton sitting in the lounge on his own, and found the care assistant who'd let them in to The Oaks.

'I'm sorry if you didn't have much luck, Inspector,' she said. 'Raymond has good days and bad days. You'd be surprised how much he can remember sometimes. His brain is still quite active. But other times, he gets a bit, well . . . confused, even distressed. It's perfectly normal for his condition, but you can never quite tell what's going to upset him. Memories, I suppose.'

'If he has a good day, would it be possible to bring him out for a couple of hours?' asked Hitchens. 'We'd like him to come and see the farm.'

'His old home? Oh, I'm sure Raymond would love that.'

'I take it he's physically fit enough?'

'Oh, yes. He has no major health problems, considering his age. In fact, the doctor says Raymond is quite a tough old bird. He'll probably still be around in ten years' time, when all our other residents have gone. It must come from being a farmer, I suppose.'

'And the wonderful care he gets here, I'm sure.'

'Why, thank you, Inspector.'

Hitchens nodded, turning on his most charming smile. Cooper couldn't help raising an eyebrow. Personally, he didn't think Raymond Sutton would love a day out at Pity Wood Farm at all, but perhaps he was wrong about that, too.

'Yes, if the weather is decent, we'll put a wheelchair into the minibus and Colin will drive Raymond up to Rakedale to visit the farm. But you won't tire him out, will you?'

'Not at all. We'll send him back as soon as he wants to come.'

'Fine, Inspector. Can we give you a call when we think he's ready?'

The DI produced his card and handed it over with a gesture almost like a small bow. Cooper felt like gagging. But then, he wasn't the person the Hitchens charm was being aimed at.

'Sir,' said Cooper as they were leaving, 'do you think Raymond Sutton knows who buried the body at the farm?'

'Almost certainly.'

'Could he be in danger? Might someone want to make sure that Mr Sutton doesn't talk?'

'They might. But how would they get to him in The Oaks? Their security is pretty good, and the staff know where every resident is twenty-four hours a day.'

'I hope you're right,' said Cooper.

With a weary curse, Nikolai Dudzik tipped his yellow hard hat back from his eyes. 'Look at these outbuildings. All the roof structures are rotten. Completely rotten. The whole lot will have to be stripped off, you know. We're talking about a massive amount of new timber for the joists alone.'

Fry could see that Dudzik's workmen had dug a network of trenches behind the barn for the new drainage and water supply. No pipes had gone in yet – they still lay in heaps at the edge of the field. But the trenches were half full of water, thanks to the rain that continued to fall intermittently on Pity Wood Farm. She could see that the clay must be non-porous. Further north, the limestone would let rain water through like a sieve. It was one of the few geological facts she'd learned since leaving Birmingham for the Peak District.

'There must be some old drains over that way somewhere,' said Dudzik, gesturing towards the tumble-down ruins of a cowshed. 'We haven't found them, and we're not looking for them any more. God knows what state they'll be in. They must be very, very old.'

Inside the outbuildings, someone had started chipping the old plaster off the walls. Layers of dust covered the floor, and the exposed stonework looked inexplicably damp.

'If it was up to me, the whole thing would come down,' said Dudzik. 'Then we could start from scratch and do a proper job. But we have to retain the original features. Original features! Bits of old stone and rotten timbers. What's the point? I ask you.'

Fry let him talk for a while longer. Then she thought of a question. 'Why haven't you dug up the old drains, did you say?'

Dudzik shrugged. 'There's no way of knowing where they are exactly. There are no records for these old places, no proper site maps, yes? And the drainage often goes off at odd angles, when it's so old. It will be sections of clay pipe, you see – useless by now. Useless. Besides, there's nothing in the new plans for that area. It'll just be a bit of garden or a paddock, so what's the point of us digging it up?'

'And this area where Jamie Ward found the body – there wasn't supposed to be a wall here at all?'

'No, no. There was no wall here. It was a job I gave to Jamie, you know – to keep him out of the way.'

'Can I have a look at the plans, please?'

'Sure.'

Dudzik pulled a rolled-up plan out of his back pocket and handed it to her.

'It looks as though this area was going to be left pretty well untouched,' she said. 'It's shown as grass on the drawings.'

Dudzik shrugged. 'I know. But what a waste. This is the perfect place for a nice patio. Some good paving, you know. A water feature maybe. We could have made it nice.'

'That's pretty much what Jamie said too.'

'That boy. He's not stupid – just not practical, you know.'

'He would have noticed soon enough that no wall was being built, wouldn't he?'

'I guess so, Detective.'

Fry had been listening to his accent. She knew he was Polish, but it was only the sound of his vowels that gave him away. His command of idiom was very good, and he hadn't faltered on the use of tenses, which was often a problem for non-native speakers.

'Your English is excellent, Mr Dudzik. How long have you been in this country?'

The builder looked wary. 'Eight years, Sergeant. I learned English back home, when I was a kid at school in Poland. When I came here, I talked English all the time with the people I met. Some of my fellow countrymen, when they come now, they don't think they have to bother to learn English. It's too much trouble for them. They think things will be translated into Polish for them, because they are so many. But I was one of the first to come, before my country was a member of the European Union, even. I always wanted to live in England, so I learned English. It's the only way to fit in, yes?'

'Yes, of course.'

He looked at her, still uncertain. 'My papers are in order.'

'I'm not doubting it,' said Fry. 'But you could do one important thing for me. Would you give my colleague, Detective Constable Murfin, a list of the men who have been working on your team here at the farm?'

*　　*　　*

52

Raymond Sutton stood to one side of the window and watched the police officers get into their car at the end of the drive. Quietly, he muttered a sentence to himself.

'And they answered and said unto him, Where, Lord?'

As the car passed out of sight, he let the curtain drop. He turned back to face the room, looked around him for a moment, and finished the quotation.

'And he said unto them,
Wheresoever the body is, there will the eagles be gathered.'

'I'm sorry, Raymond? Did you say something?'

Sutton stared at Elaine, confused by her presence. He hadn't noticed her come into the room. He'd been thinking that he was somewhere else, far away, in another life almost.

'The Gospel of St Luke,' he said. 'Chapter seventeen, verse thirty-seven.'

'I see, Raymond. Are you ready for your tea yet?'

'King James version. Obviously.'

'I'll fetch it in, shall I?'

'You can do what you like. It makes no difference now.'

5

A team from Sheffield University had been unloading equipment – shovels and trowels, wire-mesh screens for sifting bone
fragments from the soil, evidence bags, tape measures and
orange markers. One of the students was already using a video
camera to record the position of the remains from every angle
before the team approached it.

Fry knew that digging a dead body out of a grave was never
as easy as burying a fresh one. When an unprotected corpse
was placed in the ground, it formed an intimate union with
the earth. Flesh rotted, fabric disintegrated, the skull, spine
and pelvis became embedded in the soil. A casual digger would
soon despair of freeing the entire body, even after it had spent
a year or so in the ground. If anyone removed a body to bury
it elsewhere, they were bound to leave a few bits behind.

'We're being allowed to approach for a few minutes' consul-
tation with the anthropologist,' said DI Hitchens. 'But then
we have to keep clear. Dr Jamieson says he wants to protect
himself from assumptions.'

'Whose assumptions?'

'Ours, I think.'

The forensic anthropologist's task was the recovery of
human remains, and the determination of age, sex, stature,

ancestry, time since death, and any physical trauma that might indicate manner of death. Beyond that, he was not part of the investigation.

Fry laughed. 'Are we allowed to speak to him at all?'

'You could probably wish him a Merry Christmas.'

When he heard the laughter, the anthropologist looked up from the excavation with a suspicious scowl. He had a pale, bald head, almost the same colour as the paper scene suit he was wearing. Water gleamed on his scalp. From rain or sweat, it was impossible to tell.

'How is it going, Doctor?' called Hitchens.

'Mixed fortunes, I'm afraid. A dry soil would have preserved the body better. But this is, well . . .' He scooped a handful of mud that seeped through his fingers.

'Too wet?'

'Correct. *Much* too wet.'

'But there's some good news, I take it?'

'Well, you know, there are plenty of opportunities on an isolated farm for disposing of a body. If your aim is to reduce the remains to something unidentifiable, then burial is actually one of the slowest and least successful ways to achieve that.'

'It's much quicker just to leave it exposed somewhere, if you can get away with it,' suggested Cooper.

'Yes. How do you know that?'

'Every livestock farmer knows that a dead sheep left out in the open during the summer will be reduced to a skeleton within a month.'

'Exactly. Burying a corpse just slows the process of decomposition. A deeply buried body can take eight times as long to decompose as one exposed on the surface. In this case, burial and the use of plastic sheeting are the two factors which might enable the victim to be identified.'

Protective clothing was being distributed to the forensics team – coveralls, hair caps, gloves and shoe protectors. Trace evidence was transferred so easily that it could be carried away from a crime scene just as easily as it was carried there.

Next to the grave an area had been provided for the scientists to work in, preventing any more disturbance of the grave itself than was necessary. Soil would be removed by lifting it in layers of about ten inches at a time, then it would be passed through sieves of various mesh sizes to extract evidence. They would be trying to locate fragments of bone, personal items, anything that had been dropped or didn't belong in the area. Some of the anthropology students had begun cursing when they saw the condition of the soil they were supposed to sieve.

'Yes, buried bodies can be said to be protected from the elements to a large extent. If the soil is acidic, the body will tend to decompose more rapidly. In temperate zones, or areas with severe winters, the processes of decomposition are slowed. Did you know that fat people skeletalize much faster? It's because their flesh feeds huge armies of maggots. It's not a weight-loss programme I'd recommend, but maggots can strip forty pounds of surplus flesh off an obese body in twenty-four hours.'

The remains would have to be exposed completely before they could be lifted from the grave. There was too much risk of losing body parts to the sucking grasp of the wet clay. The excavation team had come equipped with an array of small tools – dental picks, bamboo sticks, paint brushes and hand trowels. Fry could see that this was going to be a long, slow, painstaking job. And even after the remains had been removed, the excavation would continue. The anthropologist had called for a further ten inches of soil to be taken from below the body, in case small bones or other evidence had been left behind.

The whole process was being recorded by video and digital photography, as well as handwritten records at every stage. Items that were discovered with the body which might indicate an identity couldn't be assumed to belong to the victim.

Intentional placing of false documents had been known. Anything to confuse investigators.

Fry leaned forward to get a view of the remains, her shoes slipping on the edge of the duckboard.

'Some parts of the body look very grey, Doctor.'

'Saponification. It's a factor that can affect a body after burial, especially if it's buried in a moist area or directly exposed to water and kept free of air. The fatty tissues of the body turn into adipocere. That's the greyish, waxlike substance you can see.'

It was that unnatural greyness that Fry would remember most about the victim at Pity Wood Farm. There was a big difference between a violent death and a natural death, between the killing of another human being and death as part of life. The latter she'd come to accept. The former she never would.

Cooper found himself drawn back into the farmhouse by some irresistible urge. It was if the house was calling to him, coaxing him into its rooms so it could tell him its story.

This time, he noticed that the whole kitchen had a curious yellow tinge. The wallpaper above the table might have been lemon once, and the cupboards were made of that golden pine which never seemed to darken completely. But there was also a sort of patina over the ceiling and the walls, particularly near the armchairs. Cooper guessed the Sutton brothers must have been heavy smokers. He could picture them sitting in those two armchairs in the evening, one either side of the fireplace. They would be puffing away, not talking to each other much, if at all. Thinking their own thoughts, but keeping those thoughts to themselves.

Turning away from the kitchen to look back into the sitting room, Cooper found himself disorientated. With the black range and the dripping tap behind him, and the smell of paint and fresh cement in front of him, he felt as though he was standing on the threshold between two worlds. For a moment, he wasn't sure whether he was standing in the present, looking back into the vanished past, or somehow occupying a brief second of history, sharing the forgotten warmth of the Suttons' kitchen while getting a glimpse of the future.

He wished he could pin down his sense of life and the lack of it, why some of the rooms were different from others. He was sure there were no scientific data that would back up his impressions. It was more a question of a feeling in the walls, a faint gleam that reflected the generations who'd survived an uncomplicated existence here, accepting life and death as it came. So why was that feeling lacking in some parts of Pity Wood Farm? Why was the gleam missing from the kitchen, why did the shadows seem blacker and more permanent in that middle bedroom on the first floor?

Outside, it was getting dark quickly. No surprise, since it was almost the shortest day of the year. At this time of year, darkness snuck up on you almost without you noticing, so that suddenly it was pitch black. Cooper could just make out the corrugated-iron roof of the shed and the faint gleam of the cars parked in the yard. The mountain of silage bags seemed to be spreading dark shadows across the farm.

But someone had pulled their fingers out and got the flood-lights up. Now, part of Pity Wood Farm was bathed in a yellow glare that turned the muddy ground into a corner of the Somme. Mud and trenches and decomposing bodies.

The anthropology team were still working, but Scenes of Crime had gone home for the night, and only a couple of uniformed officers were left on scene protection duty. Soon, the farm would be settling back into its ancient silence.

When darkness descended totally, all he could see beyond the floodlights were the distant, isolated lights of scattered farmhouses. There were no streetlights out here, not even on the B road down in the valley. There was no upward glow from the lights of a town to reflect off the sky. There were no towns near enough. Soon, the shadows would have taken over the world. Or the whole of Rakedale, at least.

To the south of the farm, Cooper could just see Pity Wood itself, or what was left of it. Dark clumps of trees, their bare branches dripping with rain. And from the direction of the big shed, the only sound he could hear was the incessant *scratch, scratch, scratch* against the corrugated-iron sides.

As if Fry didn't have enough on her plate, Ben Cooper was behaving oddly. Well, even more oddly than usual. She could see him stopping periodically, and sniffing. Sometimes he even crouched and sniffed close to the ground. Quietly, she came up behind him, realizing that he was totally absorbed in whatever he was concentrating on. When he stopped to squat on the ground again, she tapped him on the shoulder.

'Hey, what are you supposed to be? General Custer's Red Indian guide?'

Cooper almost overbalanced, and had to push a hand palm down in the mud to stop himself falling.

'Oh, for – Diane, don't do that.'

She found him a clean tissue in her pocket, noting that he'd been so taken by surprise that he didn't even bother to correct her inappropriate use of the term 'Red Indian'.

'What's with all the sniffing?'

'There's a strange smell in this area,' said Cooper. 'I thought at first it was just cat urine, but there's more to it than that.'

'It's a farm,' said Fry. 'Farms have smells like dogs have fleas. Haven't you noticed that before?'

'Not a livestock kind of smell. It's a chemical odour. Ammonia, but something else too.'

'This must have been the machinery shed. There'd be diesel, lubricating oil. Damn it, there must have been fertilizer and herbicides, too. Disinfectant – all kinds of chemicals. What's one whiff among friends?'

'Can you actually smell it?' asked Cooper.

'No. But, then, I think I'm getting a cold.' Fry turned her face up to the drizzle that had started while they were speaking. 'And if I stand out here much longer, it'll be pneumonia.'

Fry sent Cooper to see if the DI needed anything doing before he went off duty. She shook her head as she watched him go, despairing at her inability to understand him, even now.

There were so many things about Cooper that bothered her. She was aggravated by his tendency to look hot and flustered, as if he'd only just got out of bed. These days, he'd probably been in bed with that SOCO, Liz Petty. Or maybe it was just the stress of running from one obsession to another. At least he didn't look quite so dishevelled as he used to, so maybe he'd learned to wash and iron for himself since he moved out of the family farm into his little flat at Welbeck Street.

When she first met him, Fry had mostly been struck by that disarray and by his air of innocence, which was lacking in those around him. He looked as though he'd hardly left the sixth form at High Peak College. Now, she wasn't so sure whether what she saw was innocence any more. For a start, his hair wasn't quite so untidy. It no longer fell over his forehead, but had been styled. His tie still needed straightening, though, and that scuff mark had been on his leather jacket for months.

She looked up as Cooper's car passed, catching his profile as he drove by. In retrospect, it was amazing that he'd ever seemed innocent at all.

Fry recalled the day he'd told her about his father, Sergeant Joe Cooper, and his death on the streets of Edendale at the hands of a gang of thugs. *'Three of them got two years for manslaughter, the others were put on probation for affray. First-time offenders, you see. Of course, they were all drunk too.'* And then there had been his mother, the psychiatric illness and the complications that had taken her life only a few months ago, with Ben at her bedside in the nursing home.

Fry wanted to be fair to him, she really did. In the circumstances, she supposed it was surprising that Cooper still retained a positive outlook on life at all, let alone the concern he so often showed for the problems of other people. He ought to be cynical. He ought to have grown as cynical as she was herself. She wondered how he managed to avoid it.

Before she left Pity Wood, Fry took another look inside the inner cordon to see how work on the remains was progressing. Under the floodlights, the shadows of the diggers against the sides of the PVC tent. The body was emerging bit by bit, but it was a painstaking job.

Something dark and fibrous in the soil caught Fry's attention. She couldn't make out what it was at first. Then she realized it was a hank of black hair that had become detached from the head.

In a way, she found it more bearable when a corpse had started to decompose. At least it definitely looked dead. Fresh bodies were more disturbing, because they still had the look of life about them, as if they might spring up at any moment and carry on as normal. At those times, it was hard to be unaffected by the most distinctive things about a dead body – the coldness, the utter stillness, and the knowledge that a human life had just been snuffed out an hour, or even a few minutes, before you arrived.

In other ways, a body left in a shallow grave for years, undiscovered and unidentified, was the saddest sort of case. Somewhere, there must be family and friends, wondering even now what had happened to this woman.

Fry knew that hand would live in her memory for a while. It was bent into a gesture, welcoming, almost inviting. It was as if the dead woman was greeting her visitors, enticing them down into her grave.

She'd waited a long time to have company. And it must have been lonely down there.

6

Oh, I'm a man from a distant land,
A place where camels roam
It's hot and flat, and dry as bone
And if they don't like your face, they'll cut off your hand
It's the place that I call home!

The Pedlar turned to the chorus, who joined in with the song. They were all dressed as Chinese peasants – colourful tunics and coolie hats. Within minutes, the scene had shifted to the street outside Widow Twankey's house, which meant the Emperor Ping Pong would soon arrive with his beautiful daughter.

Edendale's Royal Theatre was full for the highlight event of the year, the annual Christmas pantomime. Ben Cooper was sitting several rows back from the stage, behind dozens of excited children waiting for the chance to boo and hiss and shout 'Oh no, you *didn't*' at any opportunity.

There were many variations on the script for *Aladdin*, but Eden Valley Operatic Society seemed to have opted for one of the more politically incorrect versions. Not that there was such a thing as a politically correct *Aladdin*, with the characters of Wishy Washy and Inspector Chu of the Chinese Police Force. But he was particularly doubtful about Abdulla

O'Reilly, listed in the programme as 'an Irish half-wit'. And then there was Ugga-Wugga, chief of the cannibal tribe.

Cooper squirmed in his seat. Criminal investigations had been launched for less blatant examples of racist humour. But this was panto, and it was traditional. Surely no one came into the theatre without having a good idea what to expect? Cheap jokes, comic names, a cheerful confusion of racial stereotypes.

In the next seat, Liz nudged him and whispered. 'Ben, have you had a think about coming to my parents' on Christmas Day?'

'No,' hissed Cooper back.

'No, you haven't had a think? Or no, you're not going to come?'

'We'll talk about it later.'

'Oh, yes. You're always so busy, though.'

A chorus of boos heralded the first arrival on stage of the wicked wizard, Abanazar. Within seconds, it was clear that he was being played pretty much as an evil Arab who'd accidentally wandered into a Chinese city. It certainly gave an extra edge to the lines of the opening song: '*And if they don't like your face, they'll cut off your hand.*'

Cooper settled a bit lower on his seat, hoping not to be recognized. Some hopes. He'd already been greeted by a dozen acquaintances as he came through the lobby.

Liz nudged him again. 'What's the matter?'

'Nothing.'

'You look shifty.'

'Thanks.'

'Aren't you enjoying it?'

'Yes, it's great.'

'Only, we can't leave. Not until after my friends have been on for their bit. They're Chinese policemen, and they don't appear until halfway through Act Two.'

Oh, God. The Chinese policemen. There were bound to be

a few bobby jokes, and people would be looking at him when they laughed.

'No, I'm fine, I don't want to leave. Stop talking, or people will get annoyed with us.'

Every panto had its stock characters. There was always a very obvious villain – in this case, Abanazar, who had a large and challenging role, especially if he was going to carry off that turban and scimitar convincingly. And, of course, there was the pantomime dame. This Widow Twankey ran a Chinese laundry in the time-honoured way, allowing for the usual hoary old jokes about being closed for sock-taking, and so on.

Cooper turned to his programme, squinting to read the print in the subdued light of the theatre. Many of the names of the cast were familiar to him. If he didn't know the performers themselves, he'd often come across their parents. Or, in the case of the children's chorus, their grandparents. But most of them were individuals he'd made contact with in a positive way. Pantomime seemed to attract the respectable classes.

'What are you thinking about, Ben?'

'Nothing,' he whispered. 'I'm just looking at the programme.'

'You're not thinking about work?'

'No, of course not.'

'No "of course" about it. I know you.'

Reading down the list, Cooper found the names of the Chinese police officers. Apart from Inspector Chu, the performers were women. Their names were all local, too – Beeley, Holmes, Wragg, Marsden, Brindley. The latter was probably related to the actor playing Abanazar, since they had the same surname. He wasn't sure which of them he was supposed to be watching out for.

'Liz, what are your friends called again?'

'Cheryl Hague and Harriet Marsden.'

'Hague? Do I know her?'

'Probably.'

'Is she the attractive blonde we met in the pub last week?'

'Hey. I thought you said not to talk.'

A storm of booing and jeering greeted Abanazar as he grasped the magic lamp triumphantly and rolled an artificial rock across the cave entrance to entomb Aladdin. That meant there would be a genie making his appearance soon.

Cooper glanced at Liz, but she was completely absorbed. And she was right, she *was* starting to know him. They'd been going out for a few months now, a lot longer than any previous girlfriend had lasted. One of the things he liked was that he discovered new aspects of her character all the time, and glimpsed unsuspected parts of her life. She surprised him constantly. This year, she'd even bought a Christmas present for his cat.

And he hadn't realized Liz was interested in pantomimes until a few days ago. He supposed he was lucky she wasn't actually up there on stage in a costume. God forbid, she might even try to persuade him to join the cast.

Cooper shuddered, then pulled his jacket closer, trying to give the impression he was cold rather than filled with revulsion.

'Are you sure you're OK, Ben?'

'Absolutely fine. Loving every minute.'

And here they came, at last – the comedy policemen. A little troop of them, six or seven women of various sizes wearing tunics and tights, and carrying little comic truncheons. Their drooping Fu Manchu moustaches made them unrecognizable, but Liz seemed happy to cheer them indiscriminately.

Well, perhaps they'd actually arrest the villain and Cooper could cheer, too. But in the meantime, they had to get through a few more awful jokes.

When *Aladdin* was over, they squeezed out of the theatre with the crowds, hoping to find somewhere to eat before all the restaurants filled up. It wasn't the first *Aladdin* Cooper had been to. He remembered seeing the same show at the same theatre when he was a teenager. In fact, he thought he'd probably watched slightly different versions of it three or four times.

There were only a handful of traditional pantomimes, and they seemed to come round regularly, as if on a strict rota. *Cinderella* one year, *Mother Goose* the next. But he'd sometimes heard of different stories being used. *Peter Pan, Sinbad the Sailor, Robinson Crusoe. Robinson Crusoe?* A story with only two characters? Maybe he'd have to be a bit adventurous one year and seek out somewhere that was doing the show, to see how they bent the plot to introduce a pantomime dame on to a desert island.

In Victoria Park, the fair was in full swing. Among the fairground rides, a big wheel spun green lights across the park as it turned, and a carousel made the faces of the crowd glow with pink luminescence. Free mince pies and glasses of mulled wine were being handed out to visitors.

This was by far the busiest time of year in Edendale's social calendar. There was an E Division pub crawl planned for later in the week. Another annual tradition. This year, the officers organizing it had settled on a theme – seasonal ales, which they intended to track down all over town. There were plenty to be found. Every year, the breweries produced beers like Rocking Rudolph, Hark and Black Christmas.

But Cooper wouldn't get a chance to try them. He wouldn't be with his colleagues on the pub crawl this week, as he might have been in previous years. His priorities had changed in the last twelve months. He wasn't quite so single as he used to be.

'Well, if you won't come for Christmas with me, at least you won't forget the baptism service on Sunday, will you?' said Liz.

'I'm looking forward to it. Yes, honestly.'

Liz's best friend had married a gym instructor two years

ago, and their first baby was being baptized in Edendale on Sunday. He always thought 'first baby' when the subject came up, because he'd met the friend and he sensed she was the sort of woman who intended to have lots of children.

'It's church, so everybody will be dressed up, Ben.'

'Yes?'

'You *do* have a suit and tie, don't you?'

'Oh, er . . . absolutely.'

Cooper thought of his brother squeezing into a suit for the first time this year. Now that he was too old to attend the Young Farmers' Club Christmas Ball, Matt's only social occasion had been the end-of-term nativity play at Josie's primary school. Unlike the pantomime, this production had varied the usual plot. There had been no appearances by Mary or Joseph. In fact, there wasn't even a role for the baby Jesus. Instead, the nativity story had been told from the point of view of the Bethlehem inn keeper and his family, exploring the impact on their lives. Having to deal with a sudden influx of shepherds and wise men, for a start. Well, lots of Peak District landlords would sympathize with the difficulty of mixing tourists with the locals.

Matt hadn't been impressed by the production, though. He was turning into a real diehard traditionalist as he aged. New ideas upset him.

Later this week, Ben would be singing with the police male voice choir in the Methodist church, a concert for senior citizens, followed by a children's party. The old folk loved it, though, especially around Christmas time. It was good PR, too.

Cooper recalled when he'd first met Diane Fry on her transfer to Derbyshire from West Midlands Police. She'd been scornful of everything in those days, so prickly that he soon developed the habit of letting her comments go by unnoticed. When he'd told her about singing in the choir, she had been predictably derisive. *'Do you sing soprano?'* she'd asked. *'No. Tenor.'* And he hadn't even seen the barb until much later.

Oh, well. Fry had mellowed a bit since then, hadn't she? Surely she had. Cooper frowned slightly. There was always the possibility that he'd just become very good at letting everything pass him by.

When he lifted his hand off the gear stick, Liz took his fingers for a moment and held them gently.

'Thanks for coming to the panto with me, Ben.'

On the road out of town that night, taking Liz home to Bakewell, Cooper felt content. Below him, the sprawling outline of Edendale was marked by a network of lights, but most of the Peak District lay in darkness. After all that had happened in his life, things seemed to be coming right at last. He'd found someone he cared about. And, above all, he was in the only place he'd ever wanted to live in the world.

With a surge of blind rage, Diane Fry grabbed her sister's arm and dragged her back, pulling her off balance and throwing her on to the bed.

'Hey!' gasped Angie, shocked by the sudden violence.

'Angie, what the hell are you up to?'

Diane could hear her voice coming out in a spiteful hiss. It sounded awful, but she couldn't have changed it. Her throat was too tightly constricted by the flood of emotions overwhelming her. Anger, bitterness, a sense of betrayal. And other emotions she'd never experienced before, too fleeting to be pinned down and named.

'Me?' Angie tried to laugh it off, sitting up on the bed and straightening her sleeve as if it were just a family game, a bit of rough and tumble between siblings. 'Sis, you know I'm always up to something. The original problem kid, that's me.'

'I'm not joking here. I want to know what you think you're doing.'

'Come on, Di. Lighten up.'

Diane felt herself flushing angrily. She'd told herself she wouldn't get angry with her sister. But here it was, all that rage, bubbling just below the surface. Anything could release it, a wrong word or an unguarded expression.

'Don't try to get round me, Angie,' she said. 'Just don't try it. It might have worked once, but it doesn't work on me now. Things have changed between us. I'm not your kid sister any more.'

'Oh, really?'

'Yes, really. You've got to start understanding that, or there's no future between us.'

'But that was always true, wasn't it?' snapped Angie. 'We never had any future between us.'

'What do you mean?'

'We have a past, that's all. That's the only thing we share, the one factor we have in common. And that's all it is – the past. We'd never have stayed together, Di. I know you couldn't see it at the time, but I was always going to go my own way, and it wasn't the same as yours. We'd have split up pretty soon, and you'd have gone off to your college and your police training feeling ashamed of your big sister. You ought to thank me for what I did. It was much the best way.'

Diane felt the anger draining from her. It was replaced by a strange chill that crept over her skin, like the first indications of approaching flu.

'But we're back together again now. We have to think about what sort of future there's going to be,' she said. 'We have to sort some things out to make that future work.'

Angie got up from the bed, and Diane backed away to put some distance between them.

'You haven't been listening, have you?' said Angie. 'You just hear whatever you want to. I just said we have no future. Not just back then, but now, too. We have nothing in common, Di. And we never will have. If you imagine any different, you're fooling yourself.'

'No, you're wrong.'

'Oh dear. It doesn't fit the image, does it? Had you built

up some nice, rosy picture of Angie and Di settling down together, sharing girly chats about boyfriends and babies? Holding each other's hands when we need a good cry, giggling in bed together over a couple of good books? It ain't going to happen, Sis. So it's about time you faced up to the real world.'

'Look, I know you've changed. God knows, I've made allowances for that. All those years we were apart, we were bound to go our different ways –'

'Changed? You're damn right. Yes, I'm the one who's grown up. I grew up a long time ago.'

'Oh, yes? Using heroin isn't a sign of being grown up, you know.'

'Fuck off.'

Diane took a step forward. She saw Angie begin to edge towards the door, and realized that her sister was actually scared of her. The physical outburst a few minutes ago had taken Angie by surprise and frightened her a little. She, too, had things to discover about her kid sister that she might not like very much.

'Come on, we can make this work, Angie. We just have to be honest with each other.'

'Oh, and you want me to go first, right? Confession time, is it? "Come on, dear, tell the nice police officer everything you know. How about the names and addresses of all your friends for a start?" Di, you're just not getting it, are you?'

Diane didn't answer. Second by second, she was watching their relationship turn round, seeing her big sister become more and more uneasy in her presence, like a guilty child. For the first time in her life, Diane felt as though she was the one with the power. In some way, she had the ability to affect Angie's life, instead of the other way about. She knew this, but she didn't understand why. And the knowledge didn't make her feel any better.

Angie looked at her uncertainly, pulling on her jacket. 'I'm off to work, then.'

'You can't escape for ever. We'll have to sort things out between us some time soon.'

'Yeah, yeah. Whatever you say.'

As she watched Angie sneak towards the door, Diane found herself torn by conflicting impulses – a desire to bring her sister closer, but the urge to hurt her at the same time.

'There's one thing you're just not getting either, Angie,' she said.

'Tell me about it some other time.'

Then her sister had slipped out of the room, and her feet were clattering on the stairs as she ran towards the front door.

Diane stood at the top of the stairs, unable to control something inside her that refused to let go of the argument.

'And why did you go to Ben Cooper?' she shouted. 'Right at the beginning, why did you go to *him*?'

Angie stopped, but only to shout back. 'Because *he* cares about people.'

'Oh, yes? Well, I care about people, too. I just don't care about *you*.'

As soon as the front door slammed, Diane had begun to regret her last words. But it was too late by then.

She glared at one of the students from the next flat, who'd stuck her head round the corner to see what was going on. As the student disappeared, Diane wondered whether she might ever get another chance to tell Angie what it was that she just wasn't getting.

Diane went back into the flat and began to pick up the cushions that had been knocked on the floor. She was surprised by how much mess there was, almost as if the place had been broken into and ransacked. If it had been a crime scene she was visiting, she would have said there was evidence of a violent altercation.

Was the heroin still the problem with Angie? She didn't think so, but addicts did need large amounts of money on a regular basis. Many women were out there on the streets to feed their habit, and for no other reason. Heroin or crack cocaine, or both. OK, drugs might not have put them on the street in the first place, but it was heroin that kept them there.

Diane knew that drug dealers from the big cities had moved into smaller towns like Edendale years ago. You could find drugs everywhere, pretty much anything you wanted. They were cheap, too. Perhaps it was some kind of marketing ploy to expand the customer base, but intelligence showed that Edendale was one of the least expensive towns in the country for buying drugs. Last she heard, heroin was going for about twenty pounds a bag.

It had just gradually crept in, that link between heroin and prostitution. Now it was unbreakable. The vicious circle was in play.

Diane was surprised by a sudden taste in her mouth. Dark, bitter, comforting. It was a very familiar taste, so full of memories that it seemed to sum up the whole of her life, all the low points and loneliest moments encapsulated in one brief tingle of the taste buds.

It was the return of her old craving for chocolate, and the familiarity was so intense it was almost shocking. She hadn't thought about the craving for months, not really. But some residual instinct had leaked into the nerve endings of her mouth, triggered by a moment of stress.

It wasn't so easy to get rid of an addiction. It could still creep up and surprise you long after you thought you'd beaten it. It lurked in your body and waited for a moment of weakness. But Diane Fry knew she wasn't weak, not any more.

Addictions were for everyone else, but not for her.

7

Friday

Jamie Ward woke up late next day. For a while, he lay in bed listening for noises in the house, or in the street outside, not sure what he was expecting to hear. His parents' semi-detached was in a comfortable suburb of Edendale, close to the best secondary school and the nicest church. There was rarely anything interesting to hear. The sirens were always across town, on the housing estates.

At first, Jamie's mind shied away from remembering the day before, but gradually the memories crept back. All the details were still there, fresh and vivid. The mud, the police, the argument. The hand.

And then he had a sudden conviction that this couldn't just be a normal day, not after what had happened at Pity Wood Farm. It was inconceivable that life would go on in its ordinary, routine way. Getting up, having breakfast, going for a jog, phoning his mates for a chat. It just wouldn't feel right.

Jamie went into the bathroom and found his muddy jeans on top of the laundry basket. The first day he'd turned up for work at the building site, he'd been wearing his trainers. His second best pair, not the cool ones he went out with his friends in. And Nikolai had laughed at him. So had all the other blokes, though not quite so obviously.

'Little Jamie, do you want to lose your toes?' Nikolai had said, lighting up a Benson and Hedges and blowing the smoke towards his feet. 'Boy, you won't last a day on my site. We'll find you some proper boots, OK?'

'OK, Nikolai.'

'Call me Nik.'

Most of what had gone on at the site was a mystery to Jamie. The brickies and carpenters and plasterers were skilled men who worked quickly and often silently, wielding specialist tools he didn't even know the names for.

Some of it was obvious – the trenches dug for the new drains, the gravel laid for site access. But a few things had been odd. If he'd felt more comfortable with the other men, he would have asked them the reasons for things they did. Jamie knew that you should ask if you didn't understand something, and not worry about looking stupid. If you didn't ask questions, you'd never know the answers, and that was more stupid, wasn't it?

The only good thing about the way he'd been treated on the site was that Nikolai and the men hadn't always worried about whether he was hanging around with them, or how hard he was working.

Jamie showered and hunted out some clean clothes. Then he went to find his mother, to see if he could borrow her car to drive over to Rakedale.

Cooper arrived at work that morning to find forty-three new emails in his inbox. No spam, no jokes, no personal emails – in accordance with force policy, the IT department had blocked all those. No, these forty-three were all work-related. Not necessarily related to his *own* work, of course. Unfortunately, he had to open every one of them and read it all the way through before he could be sure it wasn't relevant to him.

74

Today, he'd received a fairly typical batch. There were the usual requests from the Criminal Justice Unit for completed statements and copies of notebook entries. There was a series of directives and advisory notices from the senior management team, many of them related to key performance indicators. He had a couple of emails from the Police Federation, and there were notifications of five entirely new policies and procedures, all with start dates in the next month.

Each new policy had accompanying documents, which he was supposed to study and learn, then apply. He didn't know where to begin. But some desk jockey would be appointed as a compliance officer to monitor the new policies, so he'd have to get up to speed.

Now and then, Cooper kept some congratulatory emails about the force's Investors in People and Work Life Balance Awards. Just in case he needed cheering up some time.

'Happiness is an empty inbox,' said Murfin.

'Emails?'

'Yes. But I never read them.'

'How do you get away with that, Gavin?'

'Dunno. I tend to look at them the way I do all the junk mail I get at home, wanting to give me a bigger penis. I reckon they're meant for someone else, since I obviously don't need them.'

'There might be something about a new course for you to go on,' suggested Cooper.

'I don't need one of those, either. Not since I did my sewage training.'

Cooper laughed. Gavin had never recovered from the shock of being sent on a public order training exercise last year. Along with a couple of hundred other officers, he'd been kitted out in riot gear and deployed to the sewage works in Derby. For a couple of hours, he'd faced an angry mob of Severn Trent Water staff and special constables hurling bricks and petrol bombs at him, just to make the exercise as realistic as possible. His PDR said he'd gained valuable experience in policing a major disturbance. Gavin said all he'd learned was that shit stinks.

Still laughing, Cooper glanced at the first email attachment he'd opened. He read it a second time, trying to make sense of what he was seeing. It made a reference to something called the Community Security Policy Compliance Matrix.

The briefing that morning was relatively low-key. Detective Chief Inspector Oliver Kessen was present as crime manager for the division, though he was currently Senior Investigating Officer for a major enquiry in the Matlock area. It wasn't uncommon for the same senior detective to be SIO for more than one case at a time, but right now Pity Wood hadn't even been officially classed as a murder enquiry.

'It's too early to start combing through the missing persons reports,' said DI Hitchens when the team had assembled. 'Not until we have an idea of the age of the victim and the time of death. The list is too long otherwise – we need something to narrow it down. There are no records of incidents at Pity Wood Farm, or any missing persons reports anywhere in Rakedale. We have to cast the net wider. Any suggestions?'

'We could still start with the owners of the farm. How long has the place been empty?' asked someone.

'Nine months. But there were no women recorded in the household. Pity Wood Farm was run by two elderly brothers, Derek and Raymond Sutton. Derek died twelve months ago, and Raymond is in residential care in Edendale, diagnosed as suffering from the early stages of Alzheimer's. Perhaps the farm was sold to pay for his care. He wouldn't have been able to run it now, anyway.'

'They must have had some help with the farm work,' said Fry. 'The place is pretty run down, but two old men couldn't have managed on their own, could they?'

'Have you seen some of these hill farmers?' said Cooper.

'They're a tough bunch. Some of them just keep on going until they wear out.'

'Even so . . .'

'Well, there was clearly some labour employed at Pity Wood from time to time, but there's no indication so far that any of the help was female. The brothers must have cooked and cleaned for themselves, by the looks of it.'

Cooper remembered the state of the farmhouse, and didn't answer for a moment. There might have been some cooking going on in that kitchen, but he was pretty sure cleaning wasn't high on the brothers' agenda. Maybe squalor would be called a lifestyle choice these days.

'The trouble with that is, the more workers we trace, the more potential suspects it gives us.'

'Is there actually evidence of a crime?'

'Well, illegal disposal of a body, anyway. Someone dug the grave, then filled it in, didn't they? But as for the cause of death . . . I can't tell you. Also, I can't say whether it was murder, suicide, accident or natural causes. Sorry.'

'But what facts have we got, Paul?' asked Kessen. 'Apart from the presence of a body with an unknown cause of death, do we have any evidence of unlawful killing?'

This was a tough question, but the answer was crucial. If the SIO misinterpreted the scene and set up a murder investigation when it turned out to be a suicide or death from natural causes, he could find himself criticized for wasting resources. On the other hand, if he attributed death to natural causes and a subsequent postmortem contradicted him, then his decision could have serious consequences for the success of any future investigation. The SIO's assessment had to be made under pressure, so it took judgement to get it right, to make an accurate decision based on limited information.

'We're reserving judgement at the moment,' said Hitchens. 'There's no murder enquiry yet.'

Kessen grunted noncommittally. 'So who's going to look into the farming background?'

'DC Cooper. He's the man with his roots in the soil. All right, Ben?'

Cooper nodded automatically, not having been given any chance to think about it.

'Meanwhile, I'm hoping the forensics teams can find me some fresh evidence. Fresher than the body, at least.'

'Fresher than the body – that shouldn't be difficult,' said Murfin quietly to Cooper.

'We've got house-to-house in the village today, and that means all hands to the pumps,' said Hitchens. 'Rakedale is a small village, so we'll be hitting every household. And don't miss the isolated farms. You all know what these places are like – local knowledge could be the key. Some old biddy will provide us with that vital bit of information. So let's get to it.'

'Before you go,' said Kessen, raising his voice above the developing hubbub, 'the Chief has an announcement to make. He wants to see the CID team in his office, as soon as we're finished here.'

'Uh-oh,' said Murfin. 'This sounds like bad news.'

In her official photograph, she looked stiff and humourless. She gave the impression of a woman who wouldn't normally have worn make-up, but had felt obliged to make the effort when she posed for the photographer. Cooper thought someone ought to have given her a bit of cosmetics advice. But perhaps they'd all been too frightened of her to say anything. Instead, she'd applied lipstick and mascara with an unpractised hand, and the result was unnatural. He was beginning to feel nervous of her already.

'And this is . . .?' asked Fry.

Hitchens smiled a grim smile. 'Our new boss.'

'What?'

Their divisional commander, Chief Superintendent Jepson,

was chairing the meeting of the CID team in his office. He gestured at Hitchens to hush him.

'Ripley have finally made an appointment to the SMT,' said Jepson. 'E Division has a new detective superintendent.'

There was a moment of silence as everyone looked at the photo. The latest addition to the senior management team, another source of motivational emails.

'DS Hazel Branagh,' said Hitchens to break the tension. The tone of his voice was difficult to pin down, as if he'd made a particular effort to sound neutral.

'She's a ferociously efficient administrator,' said Jepson. 'And highly respected by her present team. All the people who work for her say the same thing. With Superintendent Branagh, they know exactly where they stand.'

'Not within striking range, I imagine,' whispered Murfin to Cooper.

Jepson frowned at the interruption, though he hadn't heard what had been said. 'You know, some managers aren't able to keep their distance from the troops. They try to be too friendly with their junior officers. I know what a temptation it is to do that – you want to be all mates together, that sort of thing. Bonding, they call it these days. But it doesn't work, you know – you just lose their respect, in the end.'

He was looking at Hitchens, and kept his gaze fixed in that direction until the DI felt obliged to respond.

'Yes, sir. Absolutely.'

'No matter how much you crave popularity, you've got to stand apart from the crowd to be a real leader. Now Hazel Branagh, on the other hand – she has *tremendous* respect from the officers in her team.'

Cooper looked at the photo again. Branagh's badly applied make-up gave her the appearance of a recently deceased auntie who'd been prepared by the funeral director. In this case, the family had been so impressed that they'd propped Aunt Flo in a chair for one last photo before they buried her.

'The word is that she won't be with us very long anyway, sir,' said Hitchens.

'In tune with the canteen gossip, are we?' asked Jepson.

'Something like that.' The DI didn't bother to point out that they weren't allowed to have a canteen any more, to discourage the formation of a canteen culture. 'I've heard the possibility discussed, that's all.'

'Well, you're right, Paul. Superintendent Branagh has already earned a reputation for herself all around the country. The next force that has an ACC's job up for grabs, it's certain somebody will come sniffing around here. You can bet on it.'

Diane Fry laid back her head and closed her eyes. Gradually, the stiffness began to ease, and the tension drained from her shoulders. For hours, she'd been staring at her computer screen, wading through figures and reports, checking online forms, reading endless emails from the SMT. It would take a while longer for the weariness to clear from her brain.

On this side of the building, they had to keep the lights on all day in December, much to the frustration of the admin officer, who'd found it impossible deal with the lack of daylight by writing a memo.

For Fry, the quality of the light was further hampered by the strings of glittery tinsel and concertinas of red-and-green decorations spelling out 'Merry Christmas' above the desks, as if no one would know what time of year it was otherwise. She was surprised that Christmas decorations were allowed under Health and Safety regulations. This was one occasion when she would have welcomed a memo. She was tempted to write one herself, but knew she'd be nicknamed 'Scrooge' for the rest of her career.

There was a desultory display of Christmas cards on top of the filing cabinets. Most of the cards were from other agencies, one from their local MP. Cooper had received a few personal messages from members of the public – 'Thank you for everything you've done for us', that sort of thing. Tasteless cards with teddy bears and glittery nativities, signed with little hearts. He'd put them among the general collection, but that only made it worse.

Fry sneezed suddenly.

'Bless you,' said Cooper. She wondered why he, like everyone else, couldn't keep the note of surprise from his voice when he said it.

'Damn it,' said Fry. 'I'd better not be getting a cold.'

'Do you get colds much at this time of year?'

'I never used to, when I lived somewhere civilized.'

'Oh, really? So they lace the water with Lemsip in Birmingham, do they?'

Fry gazed out of the window. Well, not *out* of it exactly. She couldn't see the outside world at all, only the blur of water running down the glass. Not that it mattered much, since all she could see on a good day was the back of the East Stand at Edendale Football Club.

She always tried to get into the office earlier than anyone else in CID, which in the winter meant when it was still dark. It gave her time to do the jobs she needed solitude for. First thing this morning, she'd been on her computer practising assessment techniques, ready for her first set of PDRs – personal development reviews for her DCs – next spring. PDRs were dealt with by the Human Resources manager, who had been known to return them with advice on improving their quality.

'It's this bloody weather,' she said. 'There's no way of avoiding it. I've been soaked three times this week. Is it any wonder I'm getting a cold? I'll probably be off with flu by Monday.'

'It's a weakness in the immune system, if you ask me,' said Cooper. 'It comes with urban life. You don't get exposed to nature enough when you're growing up.'

Fry found a tissue and blew her nose, which was starting to run. Hay fever in summer, and a permanent cold in winter. Welcome to the rural idyll.

There was no clear evidence yet of murder, but it could turn up at any moment. With no obvious offender, it would be a grade B enquiry, an initial maximum of sixteen officers, the DI probably doing the day-to-day co-ordination, with Kessen as nominal SIO. Fry knew she was second-guessing, but she liked to see if her assessments were accurate, whether she had learned the same grasp of priorities that her senior officers operated on.

Of course, there were other factors to be taken into account. Resources, obviously. A major enquiry would generate a ton of paperwork – statements, messages, telexes, personal descriptive forms, questionnaires, officers' reports, house-to-house forms, transcripts of interviews.

She sneezed again. 'Damn.'

'The trouble is, the winters are too mild,' said Cooper. 'Bugs don't get killed off the way they used to. It's the same with pests on the crops. At one time, no one had to spray insecticide until the spring. Now, it's a problem all year round.'

'What are you on about?'

'Global warming. I'm saying there are no frosts to kill anything off. We get a warm, wet summer and a mild, wet winter. It's no good in the long term.'

'I don't believe in global warming.'

'What?'

'I think it's all just a big scare, to distract us from more important things.'

'What's more important than the destruction of the planet?' said Cooper.

'You see? You're exaggerating. People exaggerate about it all the time.'

'Are we ready for the off, or what?' said Murfin. 'The flesh-pots of Rakedale await, boys and girls.'

Fry stood up and brushed some silver glitter off the shoulders of her jacket.

'Damn tinsel. I'm probably allergic to it.'

8

The mobile incident room was on site at Pity Wood. A thirty-foot trailer equipped with computers, drop-down screens and video and DVD equipment, and a 'front office' open to the public. It had on-board generators and floodlight masts. And, most importantly, it had heating, a fully equipped kitchen and toilet facilities. The cold rain falling steadily on the farm was enough to drive officers into the trailer on any pretext.

The initial body tent had been replaced by a larger crime scene tent to allow more space for working in. The digging team could be heard chatting among themselves sometimes, but they were more often silent and absorbed in their task, oblivious to the presence of the police waiting for them to finish their work.

As Fry and Cooper arrived, there was a burst of laughter from the excavation area, slightly brittle laughter, a release of tension.

'Anybody want a Pyrex baking dish?' said someone. 'It's still in one piece, just needs a bit of mud cleaning off. I'm giving it away. If you don't want it, I'll sell it on eBay.'

'It might be evidence,' said a police exhibits officer standing nearby with his clipboard.

The diggers groaned and went back to their task.

'Hello, what is *he* doing here?' said Fry as they reported in at the mobile incident unit.

Cooper looked around, but there were too many people to make out which of them Fry had picked out. 'Who?'

'Jamie Ward. The builder's labourer.'

'The one who found the body?'

'That's him. He's over there, at the outer cordon.'

'That's odd.'

'Normally, I'd say it was downright suspicious,' said Fry. 'Members of the public who find dead bodies shouldn't still be hanging around the crime scene next day – especially when they live miles away, as Jamie does. It makes you look guilty.'

'But Jamie can't be a suspect. Maybe he's come back with some more information.'

'We'll see.'

Fry strode over to the cordon. Jamie looked more relieved than startled when he saw her.

'I didn't recognize anyone else. I've been waiting to speak to you,' he said.

'Go ahead, then, Jamie. I'm here now.'

'I want to show you something.'

Jamie led her to the back of the farmhouse, skirting the police tape that had been strung from gatepost to gatepost and unrolled across the top of a wall. Fry could only see the large yellow skip, a lot of digging, and a cement mixer and wheelbarrows left by the builders. She made a mental note to chase up that search of the skip. God alone knew what evidence could have been dumped in there.

'See this area here?' said Jamie. 'Some of the crew have been getting ready to connect the new drains up.'

'Yes, I see.'

'But next to it there's a disturbed patch of ground. It's obvious when ground has been disturbed. The subsoil ends up on top, and it looks different. It's one thing I've learned.'

'So what do you think happened here?' asked Fry.

Jamie frowned uncertainly. 'I don't really know. I think there must have been a change in the plans some time – there was a trench here, but it's been filled in.'

'When would this trench have been dug?'

'One day last week, I suppose. I didn't see it being filled in again. I reckon Nikolai must have got somebody else to do it while I was busy round the front.'

'Well, thanks, Jamie. I'll make sure it's noted. Our diggers are a bit busy right now, but we'll be at the scene for a good while yet.'

With Cooper at the wheel, they drove towards Rakedale on a dark, jungle-green road bordered by stone walls, muddy cattle and a rushing stream. When they reached the hill into the village, Cooper found water running towards him down the road, streaming into two rivulets under his wheels.

'Oh, great,' said Fry when she saw the water. 'It's like the village is pissing on us already.'

The road was very narrow, barely wide enough for one vehicle, and the stone walls left no room for error. It wasn't used much, though – grass was growing down the road in the middle of the tarmac. There was better visibility on these roads in the winter than the summer, because the trees were so bare. But the surfaces were always slippery, especially if you had to pull over on to the verge to let another vehicle pass.

Cooper was taking care to look for any possible passing places as he went. Most of the wider verges and gateways that might have been usable in the summer were too muddy for the average car, which would be certain to get bogged down or slide off into the ditch. It was lucky he had four-wheel drive. Even luckier that Diane Fry had agreed to take his car. Her Peugeot would hardly have made it up the hill.

'Why are you driving so fast on a road like this?' asked Fry.

'There are no passing places. We don't want to meet anyone coming the other way on these straight stretches, or someone would have to reverse a long way.'

Fry sighed. 'I suppose that makes sense, of a kind.'

The place everyone referred to as a village was no more than a T-junction where the side road from Pity Wood met the B5012. There were farms either side of the road, the entrance to an old quarry, fenced off and blocked with lime-stone boulders. On the southwest corner of the junction, a stile provided access to a footpath that snaked off across the fields between the dry-stone walls, probably heading towards High Peak Trail, the old railway line to Buxton. The grass verge had been flattened and worn away here – the signs of an unofficial lay-by made by hikers leaving their cars. They'd be less willing to do that in December, the rutted mud making verges treacherous for parking on.

The main part of the village clung to the hillside just below its brow. But there were many far-flung farms, where a hard living had been scraped from sheep farming for centuries. Three or four farms clustering around a double bend formed the centre of Rakedale. There were more cattle sheds than houses, more trailer ramps and livestock gates than front doors. The only observer as they passed was a black-and-white calf peering from a pen in the corner of a yard. The calf watched them miserably, kicking at its straw.

There were no road markings here – no white lines or yellow lines, no chevrons or rumble strips. Even the edges of the road itself were unclear. At the top of the village, where they had to make a sharp right turn, the junction was pretty much indis-tinguishable. Every direction looked like a farm track.

Cooper parked in front of the village Methodist chapel and they all got out, pulling on their coats, sorting their interview forms into plastic wallets to keep them dry, and dividing the village up into three sectors. Fry looked at a giant puddle between the car and the road.

'And now I suppose you'll tell me that Derbyshire is disappearing under water because sea levels are rising.'

'No, but parts of Lincolnshire are going to disappear,' said Cooper. 'Perhaps not in our lifetime, but –'

'Oh, give it a rest.'

'You brought it up.'

Fry walked off, and Murfin nudged Cooper as they watched her go. 'I think you won that one, Ben.'

'It's not a competition, Gavin. People should be thinking about these things.'

Murfin pulled a couple of chocolate bars out of his pocket and handed one to Cooper.

'Blimey. As long we can still grow food, what does it matter?'

House-to-house. It wasn't always the most popular job on a major enquiry. Especially when it was raining.

And today, in Rakedale, it was definitely raining. From the state of the roads and the farm entrances, it looked as though it had been raining all year. The village might as well exist under some permanent black cloud that trickled constantly, like a leaky hosepipe.

Cooper crossed the road to a row of four cottages. He knocked on the door of the first house, drew up his collar and readied his clipboard. When you did house-to-house, bad weather was a useful barometer for what sort of people you were dealing with. In parts of Edendale, they'd leave you standing in the rain without a qualm, would rather see you drown in front of their eyes than let you over their threshold. If you were visiting an address on the Devonshire Estate in a downpour, you'd better be carrying a warrant, or an umbrella.

Out here, though, you'd expect members of the public to have a bit of sympathy, and not to watch you dripping on their step without a flicker of concern.

But that was exactly what the first householder did, admitting that she'd heard of the Suttons of Pity Wood Farm, but she knew nothing about them, or anyone who'd ever worked there. At the second house, he got the same response. And at the third.

Cooper paused before calling at the end house, and studied the village. There wasn't much in the way of Christmas decorations visible in Rakedale, but that was true of many Peak District villages. In Edendale, the streets were strung with lights, and almost every shop had a tree fixed to its upper storey, decorated and ready to be lit when darkness came. The same sort of thing could be found in other places – Castleton or Bakewell, for example.

But there was a difference. Some villages relied on income from tourism for their survival, and went out of their way to bring in visitors. Others had no interest in being tourist spots. Quite the opposite. Those were the places where residents didn't want members of the public clogging their streets and peering into their gardens. In those villages, there were no visitor centres, no helpful signposts, no tea rooms or picnic sites. You could drive through some of them as often as you liked and find nowhere to park. 'Keep moving' was their message.

The last cottage in the row was empty, with green paint peeling off the door. On a side lane, where the woods started, Cooper found a 1950s bungalow strung with Christmas lights, and a chained Alsatian barking in a yard. He thought it looked more promising. But, frustratingly, it was the first property on his list where no one was at home. He made a note on the sheet and turned back towards the Methodist chapel, where he'd left the car.

The chapel was a square, unpretentious building standing between two farms. Primitive Methodist, according to the noticeboard. The name was a bit unsettling, but remarkably apt.

The fact that there was no parish church in Rakedale told Cooper something about the village. He was reminded of the old social division in rural communities – chapel for the workers, church for the squire. These non-conformist chapels were where the working classes had first learned to speak for themselves, to educate themselves, and to organize. They'd been a natural breeding ground for trade unions. Once working people had tasted religious freedom, they wanted political and social freedom, too. In some of these ancient villages, the parish church was still associated with the power wielded by the lord of the manor, a symbol of servitude. The priest took the squire's money, and he preached what the squire wanted to hear.

But not in Rakedale. The nearest parish church must be in Biggin or Hartington. Villagers here were out of the gaze of any squire or landowner. And if the priest tried to visit, he would have been seen coming for miles.

Fry had made a deduction. Mud must be a perfectly normal occurrence in Rakedale. She had found brushes and scrapers by every front door for visitors with muddy boots. Not that she was allowed across the mat very often, but the possibility was at least hinted at in the provision of a scraper.

In other ways, too, everyone she spoke to seemed unsurprised to see her, as if they'd been warned in advance.

So it was a relief to come across the Dog Inn, a small pub set so far back from the road that it was almost hiding. For once, Fry didn't have to expect some sour-faced woman in a baggy sweater blocking her way. It was a public house, and she was a member of the public. So she must be welcome, right?

The Dog Inn was entered through a tiny porch, its door at right angles to the main entrance to face away from the prevailing wind. The porch door was red, matching the Russian vine covering the walls and a row of three brick chimneys on the roof, and a horseshoe was nailed to the centre panel.

Inside, Fry found a small L-shaped bar with a settle against one wall, and an open fireplace with real logs burning in it and a stone chimney breast. A tiny side room held a pool table and a battered dartboard. A man with a long, grey beard was rolling cigarettes from a battered tobacco tin and brushing the remains of his tobacco off the racing page of the *Daily Mirror*. A few other men sat at tables further down the bar, all in complete silence. She felt sure it hadn't been quite so silent before she walked in.

Fry was faced by a 'Merry Christmas' sign hanging from the beer pumps, and a row of Christmas figures over the bar counter – a few motley Santas and a snowman. She'd followed a trail of muddy paw prints into the bar that she guessed must belong to the collie dog lying on the floor.

On the jukebox she could see *Now That's What I Call Music – 1964*, a bit of Elvis Presley, and the Eagles' *Greatest Hits*. The selections were numbered one to twelve down one side, and fourteen to twenty-five on the other. Twenty-eight choices of naff sixties and seventies pop hits. According to a sign, bed and breakfast at the Dog Inn was only twenty-five pounds a night. She didn't feel tempted.

For a few minutes, Fry thought it was strange that no one seemed to be looking at her, as if they'd accepted her without curiosity. But then she realized that they *were* watching her, after all. They were making an elaborate pretence of not noticing her, but they were observing out of the corners of their eyes, letting their gaze sweep casually across her as if she wasn't there, but registering more and more details about her each time they turned their heads. Bystanders were notoriously poor at remembering descriptions, but these people would be able to draw her accurately from memory, each and every one of them. They were *all* watching her.

As she waited, a desultory conversation started up about the weather. Wasn't it wet and cold and windy, they said. Wetter and colder and windier than usual for this time of year. It would probably be even wetter and colder over

Christmas, just their luck. Somebody must have stood on an ant.

Fry finally got some attention when a middle-aged man emerged from a door behind the bar. He was wearing an old cardigan and carrying a mug of tea with 'Number One Dad' printed on it. He introduced himself as Ned Dain, the licensee.

'The Suttons?' he said. 'I remember the two old men. They're not still at the farm, surely?'

'No.'

'I thought not. We haven't seen them in here for ages. Died, did they?'

'Only one of them did.'

'Damn.'

'What do you mean by that?'

'Well, I bet that would be really hard on the other brother,' said Dain. 'They were so close they were almost like twins. Spoke the same, had a similar manner. Yet someone told me once they didn't see eye to eye on a lot of things. They kept it hidden well, if that was the case.' He took a sip of tea. 'There were a few years between them in age, I think.'

'We've been told Derek was the youngest by four years.'

'Is he the one that died?'

'That's right.'

'Damn.'

The men in the bar had moved on to discussing the Middle East problem, and whether anyone had seen the darts on the telly last night.

'Can you tell me anything else about them?'

'They always kept themselves pretty much to themselves,' said Dain. 'But there's usually somebody who knows some-thing around here. What did you want to know?'

'Was either of them married, for example?'

'Hold on. Hey, Jack!'

The man with the long, grey beard looked up. 'Aye?'

'The Sutton brothers at Pity Wood – was one of them married?'

Jack glanced slyly at Fry before answering. 'I don't rightly recall. Might have been. It was a long time ago, if so.'

'You're right,' said Dain. 'I don't recollect they were married. A set of old bachelors, I'd reckon. We mostly saw the brothers together, if we saw them at all. If there was ever a wife, she must have died, too, or walked out – who knows?'

'Well, who does?'

Dain seemed not to be able to answer a direct question.

'Derek,' he said thoughtfully. 'And then there was, let's see . . . Billy? No, of course not. That's me getting mixed up. I'm getting a terrible memory for names.'

'Billy?' The man called Jack coughed and laughed into his beard. 'There was never any Billy. You've got that wrong, Ned.'

'Raymond,' said Fry.

'Raymond. That's right. Derek, Raymond . . .?'

'Yes, Derek and Raymond. Those are their names.'

Dain gave her a quizzical look. 'All right, if you say so. Well, Raymond, now – he played the organ at the chapel. You could ask the minister about him. He's circuit, of course, based in Monyash. Or there's Ellis Bland – he's the caretaker.'

Jack spoke up again. 'Ned, they had a funeral at the chapel, didn't they? The Suttons.'

'That would have been Derek, then,' said Fry.

'Aye, Derek. Funny bugger – superstitious as all get out. Magpies, black cats, I don't know what. He thought everything he saw was going to bring bad luck.'

'He's dead now, so he must have been right,' said Dain.

'Well, we hope he was dead, since they buried him.'

Jack cackled and went back to his tobacco. Fry tried to regain the attention.

'Apart from the Suttons themselves, were there any farmworkers that used to come in the pub?' she asked.

'No, but perhaps my Dad would remember them, if they came in here.'

'Was your father the licensee before you?'

'Not him,' said Dain with a laugh. 'Well, his name was over the door, but running a pub would be too much like hard work for that drunken old bastard. No, you'd have found him sitting on that side of the bar most nights. He knew everyone around here, though. If strangers came in, he'd be giving them the once-over as they walked to the bar, and he'd know everything about them by the time they left the pub again. You could do with blokes like my old dad on the police force, if you want information.'

'I suppose he's not still around,' said Fry.

'Well, not around here, thank God,' said Dain. 'We put him in a home when he got too bad. Cracked as a tin bucket he was, by the end. Too much drink wrecked his brain. But it was his liver that did for him in the end.'

'Oh.'

'Me, I won't go that way. I'm as fit as a fiddle, and twice as tuneful.'

Dain rubbed a hand on the bar counter, as if finding a blemish on the polished wood.

'Come to think of it,' he said, 'I think the police *did* use my dad as a source of information from time to time. The local bobby would come in here himself in those days, in uniform and all. *And* he'd expect free drinks. Those were different times, I suppose. He even brought his sergeant in sometimes.'

Picturing the scene, Fry suddenly had a bad feeling about the answer to her next question. 'Can you remember the name of that sergeant?'

Dain shook his head. 'No, I don't think so. It's too long ago.'

'Shame.'

Dain ran a cloth across the bar counter. 'Wait, though . . . it was a fairly common name. Oh, that's annoying. It's right on the tip of my tongue.'

Fry waited as patiently as she could while he fumbled through his memories, but nothing seemed to be emerging.

'Cooper?' she suggested. 'Sergeant Joe Cooper, perhaps?'

'Who?' said Dain. 'Nah, that's not it. Cooper? Where did you get that from?' Then his face broke into a broken-toothed smile. 'Nothing like it. Williams, that was his name. Big Welsh bloke. We called him Taffy.'

'And the local bobby himself?'

'Oh, Dave Palfreyman? He's still around, all right. You won't be able to miss *him*.'

Outside the Dog Inn, Fry stood for a moment in the rain. Something about the conversation in the pub was worrying her. Not the barely concealed hostility, or Ned Dain's infuriatingly poor memory – if that's what it was. No, it was a faint ambiguity that she couldn't quite put her finger on. Not anything that had been said, but something that had been missing.

Fry stepped over a pothole in the car park that was slowly filling with water, and found herself thinking about the patch of disturbed ground that Jamie Ward had pointed out at Pity Wood Farm. It had been nagging at the back of her mind the way things did when she'd overlooked them, or not acted when she should have done.

She took out her phone and called DI Hitchens, who was still at the farm.

'Yes, I feel we should try to make it a priority,' she said. 'As soon as possible. Yes, I understand, sir. Resources . . . Well, Jamie Ward believed it was important enough, and I think I agree with him.'

9

Apart from the pub, the village's facilities seemed to consist solely of a small post-box lashed to a fence post. When he'd finished his calls, Cooper sat in the car and watched the rain soaking the walls of the chapel.

'There's no post office,' he said, when the others returned. 'That would be the place to go.'

'So?'

'The next village has one.'

'We could give it a try.'

He saw there was a Town Head Farm at one end of the village, and Town End Farm at the other. He supposed it helped visitors to Rakedale to know whether they were coming or going.

Most of the farms along this road were well kept. Of course, they were fully functioning enterprises, with neat signs displayed at the roadside – the name of the farm, the family who owned it, the type of cattle they bred. Friesians and Holsteins mostly, with the appropriate illustration of a proud beast under the family name. There had been no such sign at Pity Wood.

The post office in the next village was open for business only from eleven a.m. to one p.m. on Tuesdays, Wednesdays and Thursdays. Like so many rural post offices, it was operating what were officially called 'satellite hours'. Villagers here were lucky – many areas had lost their facilities altogether. But, since this was Friday, it was no less closed.

Most of the buildings seemed to be either holiday cottages or offering B&B. They were deserted in mid-winter, dormant and empty, awaiting an influx of tourists in the spring, their owners praying there wouldn't be a repeat of 2001, when the foot and mouth outbreak had destroyed their business.

The only other notable feature in the village was a farming heritage centre, which looked quite a new development. An interesting avenue of diversification, preserving the heritage instead of farming.

'Any other suggestions?' asked Murfin.

Cooper unfolded a map of the Rakedale area. 'There's another farm up the road, away from the village. We oughtn't to miss that.'

'I've been given the name of a retired bobby who lives near here,' said Fry. 'Palfreyman, he's called. Now, if he's an old-style copper, he could be a very good bet to know all about the Suttons. Well, as much as anyone here does.'

'Where does he live?'

'Hollowbrook Cottage, the landlord of the pub said. It should be up this same road.'

'I see it,' said Cooper, with his finger on the map. 'We can do both together quite easily.'

'You know what? I think you can take the ex-bobby, Ben,' said Fry.

'Oh, thanks. Is that because you think I'm the best person for the job, then?'

'Yes. Well . . . that, and the length of the drive up to his house. Someone is going to get wet.'

Some retired coppers chose to run pubs. They wanted to stay busy, they said, so they kept themselves close to the public – and sometimes a bit too close to the alcohol, as well. But ex-Police Constable David Palfreyman had hit his thirty and retired to his garden. He had a decent-sized patch behind Hollowbrook Cottage. It was a well-kept property that had been carefully modernized, and lots of money had been pumped into its appearance. Palfreyman's cottage would be worth a packet by the time he had to sell it to pay for his medical and social care in old age.

Right now, though, Palfreyman looked robustly healthy. He was a big man, a couple of inches over six feet and keeping his muscles from sagging too much by regular physical activity. Like other balding men who spent a lot of time outdoors, he had to wear a hat to avoid the damage the weather could do to his head, summer or winter. The former constable had chosen a dilapidated fedora that flopped low at the brim, shielding his eyes from the rain.

He met Cooper at the gate, having seen him coming up the length of his drive. He seemed genuinely pleased to see Cooper's warrant card, which was a rare event. And, for the first time that day, Cooper was invited in.

On the doorstep, Palfreyman paused and pointed out a passing car. 'That's Mary Greenhalgh, on her way to pick up the kids from school. If you watch, there'll be a blue Vauxhall go by in a couple of minutes. That will be her boyfriend.'

'Boyfriend?'

'Lover, if you like. He visits Mary in the afternoons, then they leave the house separately – she goes off to fetch the kids, and he drives off in the other direction, turns round and comes back. I think he lives near Buxton.'

Just as Palfreyman had predicted, a blue Vauxhall went by, driven by a man with fair hair who was straightening his tie with one hand.

'Do you know everything that goes on around here?'

'It's second nature to notice things, after thirty years in the job. Besides, I don't have much else to do with my time. There's precious little gardening in the winter.'

When Palfreyman gestured, Cooper saw that blue veins snaked across the back of his hands. But they were large hands, with the sort of palms that might have delivered a smart slap to a recalcitrant youth in the old days.

Palfreyman put the kettle on, and immediately began to talk. He revealed that he'd spent his entire career in what would now be known as 'core policing'. Beat bobbying, he called it. Never a specialist of any kind, and never a candidate for promotion. He'd made it to his thirty without a black mark on his record, and without any commendations either. A man with no ambitions beyond doing his job and staying out of trouble.

Cooper thought he knew the type. No doubt Palfreyman had spent the last few years of his service counting down the weeks and days as his retirement got closer, as so many officers did. In police stations all over the country, officers had the date they would qualify for their full pension circled in red on a calendar.

'Have a seat,' said Palfreyman. 'I won't be long.'

Cooper settled himself in the lounge, admiring a jade-green rug and an IKEA coffee table while he watched the retired bobby fussing about in the kitchen.

From what Palfreyman said, he'd been committed to the job in his own way. Lots of younger officers would have considered a posting to a rural backwater as a punishment. Not too much crime to deal with out here, was there? It was more of a PR job than proper policing, really – the visible face of the old-fashioned British bobby, providing reassurance for the public.

Palfreyman was grey-haired, but still a big man. A lot of the weight he carried must have been put on since he finished active service. He thumped around the kitchen on feet that seemed to be wearing a permanent pair of heavy boots, even after he'd taken them off in the porch.

Actually, he wouldn't have lasted much longer in the force, if he hadn't been due for retirement. Cooper couldn't see him as a modern response officer, turning up on blues and twos for a punch-up outside a pub or to chase a burglary suspect over a few garden walls. His supervisors would have put him behind a desk, where he could fill in forms. And he'd have hated it. Cooper could picture him in the corner of an office, oozing resentment and cynicism.

'So you've still got your finger on the pulse of Rakedale, Mr Palfreyman?'

'Not exactly. Not like I used to. But I know when its blood pressure is up, if you follow me.'

'But you're familiar with the history of Pity Wood Farm?'

'You ought to talk to Tom Farnham,' said Palfreyman. 'He worked at Pity Wood. He was the only one who worked there any length of time, I think. But then, he's local. All the rest of them stayed for a few months, then moved on.'

'The rest?'

'Casuals. Short-term labour.'

'Are you referring to itinerant workers?'

'Oh, aye. Lots of them have turned up at Pity Wood over the years. Coming and going all the time, they were. It made it difficult to keep track, from my point of view. I never quite knew who was living in the area at any one time. Well, I tried to persuade Raymond to keep better records, but it was a waste of breath. It's amazing to me that they didn't get into trouble. They wouldn't get away with it now, the regulations are too tight. So much bureaucracy. But then, you must know that, in the job.'

'Did you find the Sutton brothers difficult to deal with, Mr Palfreyman?'

'Difficult?' He sniffed thoughtfully. 'Well, they were a funny bunch, the Suttons. I was round there once, in the days before Tom Farnham appeared on the scene. Derek and Raymond were just sitting in that room there, one either side of the table, not speaking a word to each other. Weird, it was. Like they were afraid of breaking the silence, as if they thought something terrible would happen if they were the first to speak.'

'Was there bad blood between them? Did the brothers have an argument of some kind?'

'Not that I know of. Not in living memory, anyway. I think that's just the way they were. Awkward, pig-headed buggers. You know the type.'

'Yes, I think I do.'

Another car passed on the road outside, and Palfreyman turned his attention away.

'I see you have a cat,' said Cooper on the way out, noticing an elegant ball of fur curled on a rug in the kitchen.

'Yes. He's a Burmese.'

'Did the Suttons have a lot of cats?'

'God knows,' said Palfreyman. 'Well, probably. All farms have cats, don't they?'

Fry and Murfin were invited in, too. But the property they'd arrived at wasn't a farm, not any more. Someone had bought the farmhouse and converted it into a nice family home, but had let the land go to neighbouring farmers. If there had been outbuildings on the property, there was no sign of them now. This was pretty much what Pity Wood was intended to be, Fry thought.

A nice new Range Rover stood on the drive, the only car she'd seen for a while that wasn't plastered with mud. Inside, the home was immaculate – probably kept in that condition by the small, Asian-looking woman that Fry had glimpsed passing like a ghost from the kitchen into the passage when she arrived.

'We don't see much of the village people,' said Mrs Brindley, setting out a tray with a welcome cup of tea for her visitors. 'Not that we aren't village people ourselves, but you know what I mean.'

100

'Not really,' said Fry.

'Well, Rakedale . . . there's no reason to go there, not as far as we're concerned. Yes, even though it's only half a mile away. It's not as if it has any shops, or a post office. Or a church.'

'Just the Primitive Methodist chapel.'

'Exactly.'

Mrs Brindley was a slender, mannered woman with a carefully casual style that suited her. Both she and her husband were in their forties, pleasant and friendly. Fry wouldn't normally have put much store in those qualities, but this was Rakedale, and they were a relief.

'Our lifestyles send us further afield, I'm afraid, Sergeant,' she said. 'We need shops, restaurants, theatres. And sports facilities for the children. You won't find any of those in Rakedale. So unless we're feeling really lazy and decide to call at the village pub, we never go there. We head off to Hartington for the church, Buxton or Ashbourne for shopping and that sort of thing.'

In addition to the couple themselves, there was a teenage boy in the room, who Fry hadn't been introduced to when she arrived. About eighteen, possibly a bit younger. She was finding it more difficult to tell these days. He said nothing, but his unblinking stare was a bit disconcerting. Presumably he was one of the reasons for the Brindleys' lifestyle.

'So you wouldn't know the Suttons at Pity Wood Farm?' asked Fry.

'That's across the other side of the village, isn't it?' said Mrs Brindley. 'We've probably heard talk of them.'

'Probably? Who from?'

'I beg your pardon?'

'Who would you have heard talk from, if you don't go into the village?'

Mrs Brindley looked at her husband, confused. 'Alex?'

'There's a kind of communication by osmosis in a place

101

like this,' he said. 'People know things without you having to tell them. If you've already been to the village, I bet they knew you were coming long before you arrived.'

'Yes, that was the impression I got.'

Brindley smiled. He was a good-looking man, tall and dark, but relaxed and co-operative in a way that she'd come to regard as uncharacteristic of people in this area. It must come from meeting too many criminals.

'Well, it seems to work for us, too,' he said. 'We're aware of the Suttons, yes. Two brothers, wasn't it? But one of them died, not long ago. It was in the local paper, and they had his funeral at the Methodist chapel.'

'Yes, that was Derek Sutton.'

'But they were farmers, you see . . . We weren't on visiting terms. We wouldn't have much in common, I imagine.'

That was the truest sentence Fry had heard spoken for several days.

She finished her tea and looked out of the window. Sure enough, it was still raining. She couldn't yet see any sign of Ben Cooper standing outside getting wet.

'One last question. Have you heard of anyone going missing locally, while you've lived here? Word of that would get round, wouldn't it? By osmosis or otherwise.'

'No, and it's rather worrying, Sergeant,' said Mrs Brindley. 'We heard on the news about something being found. There was a picture of the old farm. It's terrible, what's happened.'

She couldn't even bring herself to mention an object so tasteless as a dead body.

'Yes, terrible,' said Fry.

'We're very anxious to help, if we can. But we're so busy at the moment, all of us. You were quite lucky to catch us at home. We certainly haven't had time to keep up with the local gossip.'

'How many children do you have, Mrs Brindley?'

'Just the two, Sergeant. Evan here, and Chrissie, our daughter. Chrissie is fourteen.'

Fry addressed the teenage boy who'd sat silently on the edge of the sofa, watching her throughout their visit.

'I don't suppose you know anyone in Rakedale either, Evan?'

'No, hardly anyone. There are no young people, only old – I mean, old people.'

'It's difficult enough trying to keep Chrissie and Evan away from unsuitable company at school,' said Mrs Brindley. 'We wouldn't want them going down into the village.'

'No, I see.'

'Should we be concerned about the safety of our children, Sergeant?' she asked.

'I doubt it,' said Fry. 'If a crime was committed – and we're not even a hundred per cent certain of that yet – then it happened a while ago.'

The teacups were empty, and Murfin had consumed the last crumb of the last biscuit. It was time to leave the normal world and get back to Pity Wood Farm.

'Oh, I suppose you must know David Palfreyman?' she said.

'Palfreyman? Yes, we do know him,' said Brindley carefully. 'He lives quite close, and we've said "hello" a few times.'

'He used to be the local village bobby.'

'Ah, the rural policeman. Yes, we've definitely seen him. You could hardly help but recognize what he is. I'm sorry.'

Throughout their visit, the son had sat watching Fry and Murfin as though they were putting on a show especially for his benefit. His own home version of *Law and Order* or *CSI*, maybe. Oh well, the climax would be a bit disappointing – no guns drawn, no armed officers summoned to slap on the cuffs. Just boring old police work. Just Detective Sergeant Diane Fry struggling through the mud, as usual.

10

Cooper dropped Fry and Murfin off at Pity Wood Farm and consulted the Ordnance Survey map again for his next call. To the south of Rakedale were the remains of Pity Wood itself, and a mound shown on the map as Soldier's Knoll. Some of the fields and hillsides had evocative names, too – Godfrey's Rough, Limbersitch, Biggin Hey, Callow Gore. They included a lot of leas, royds and haggs, all names for clearings in the woods. There must have been many more trees here at one time.

Tom Farnham lived near to the village of Newhaven, on the other side of the wood. There was no direct route, so Cooper turned the Toyota towards the A515.

He passed a farm called Organ Ground, where there was an even larger mountain of silage bags than at Pity Wood, though these were mostly white. Was there some significance to the different colours? Cooper searched his memory of farming practices, as he'd picked them up piecemeal during the last thirty years, but found he hadn't the faintest idea. If he'd ever known, it was gone now. He'd have to ask Matt some time.

A little red Bowers bus turned the corner ahead of him. On the way towards Newhaven, he remembered that there was no mobile phone signal in this area. The display on his phone read 'SOS calls only'. What a joke.

The transition between limestone and clay was obvious in the houses that you passed on this road. In the south of the county, the main building material was red brick, with clay tile roofs instead of stone. Many of the farms had converted their old buildings into holiday cottages. No farmworkers lived on the premises any more, and at some times of the year, temporary visitors would far outnumber the resident population.

Near the Newhaven brickworks, a small herd of black-and-white cattle bunched together round their water trough, standing in a sea of mud. Where a tractor had entered the field, the ground was completely liquefied. When one of the cows moved, its hooves splashed with a noise like a fish leaping in a river, and the legs and bellies of the animals were thick with semi-dried mud. The ubiquitous mire made Cooper long for the clean swell of the scree-scattered hills further north.

Here, the air was full of the hot smell of kilns. The clay and sand for the brickworks had all been quarried locally at one time. Even the ganister for making silica bricks had come from a quarry fifteen miles across the county at Wessington. But now all the materials used at Newhaven were imported.

Farnham's house was sheltered from the road by a belt of trees, and Cooper might have driven past without seeing it, but for a curl of smoke from the chimney and a glint of rain on a steel cattle grid protecting Mr Farnham's gateway from marauding livestock.

He found the owner of the house in a garage workshop, where he had a petrol-driven lawnmower in pieces on the concrete floor. Other lawnmowers stood against the breeze-block wall awaiting attention, along with a strimmer and a chain saw. The smell of petrol and oil was almost over-powering, but Farnham had left the garage door open to disperse the fumes. The first few feet inside the door were wet with the rain that blew in, but it was better than suffocating in petrol fumes.

'Yes, I worked with the Sutton brothers for a few years,' said Farnham, wiping a small component with grease. 'Until the business started going to pieces, that is. No one with any sense stays in a failing enterprise unless they're really tied to it, like the Suttons were. I knew when it was time to get out.'

'It sounds a bit like a rat leaving a sinking ship, if you don't mind me saying so, sir.'

Farnham was unruffled. 'Well, I wasn't the captain, so I wasn't about to go down with my vessel, if you know what I mean. I looked around for the nearest lifeboat. Tom Farnham is no fool.'

'You say you worked "with" the Suttons,' said Cooper. 'What was your role at Pity Wood, exactly?'

'I was a sort of farm manager, you might say. But one of my main tasks was to introduce new ventures, diversify, anything to keep the business going. It never worked, though. Nothing I tried worked, in the end.'

Racks of tools lined the wall of the garage, and the work bench was scarred and stained with oil from previous jobs. It looked as though Mr Farnham was the practical type, handy to have around a farm when machinery needed running repairs.

'So you were employed by the Suttons, sir?'

'Mmm. Not quite. The thing is, I actually put some of my own money into Pity Wood, so I was more in the nature of a partner than an employee.'

'You must have had confidence in your ability to turn the fortunes of the business round, if you invested your own money.'

'Oh, I did. And it could have worked. It *ought* to have worked.'

'What sort of diversification schemes did you try?'

Farnham pulled a sour expression. 'All kinds of things.

Some of them were my projects, but others . . . well, Raymond and Derek had their own ideas. To be honest with you, one or two of them were plain mad.'

Cooper's ears had pricked up when he heard the phrase 'to be honest'. It was almost invariably an indication that a person was about to lie. He wondered whether the really mad ideas had actually been Farnham's own. No harm in passing the blame to the brothers now, was there? One of them was dead, and the other in a home.

It was the second signal he'd picked up from Tom Farnham. Referring to yourself in the third person was a sure sign of evasion. *Tom Farnham is no fool.*

'The body we've found was buried on a bit of spare ground in the eastern corner of the property,' said Cooper. 'Not far from the house.'

'Spare ground?' Farnham frowned. 'Can you show me where you mean?'

Cooper took the piece of paper offered to him and drew a rough map. He was no Leonardo, but it would do for the job.

'We used to park trailers and other pieces of equipment on that bit of land,' said Farnham. 'I can't imagine how anybody would dig a grave there, even if they wanted to. The soil must have been pretty solidly compacted.'

'It wasn't easy to dig out again either, by all accounts.'

'Well, the grave must have been there a long time, then. Since before I went in with Raymond and Derek. The old boys must have used that patch of land for something else, back in the past.'

Cooper didn't respond to Farnham's invitation to put the body well outside his own time at Pity Wood. Instead, he looked at his map, noticing how the swirls he'd made looked more like a lake than a farmyard. And very appropriate it was, too, in the present weather.

'Wasn't this one of the areas considered for a reservoir some years ago?' he asked.

'Oh, that would be way back in the sixties or early seventies,' said Farnham.

'If there was a possibility this valley would be flooded, the value of properties must have crashed.'

'Yes, for a while. Blighted by the spectre of compulsory purchase, eh? The fate of the little man steamrollered by governments and local authorities.'

'So there would have been no chance of selling Pity Wood Farm during that time. If the Suttons had wanted to move on, they couldn't have done. They must have thought they were cursed.'

'But it didn't last for ever. Carsington was chosen for the reservoir instead.' Farnham laughed. 'The curse moved on to someone else, then.'

'There were protests, I think?' asked Cooper.

'Small-scale stuff. A bunch of farmers from the Carsington area got together. They never stood much chance, in my opinion.'

Cooper had sympathy for protesters, provided they stayed within the law. If it hadn't been for vigorous campaigning, there'd have been housing and industrial developments in Winnats Pass and a motor-racing circuit in the dales around Hartington. The Peak District would have been cut in half by a motorway.

He imagined the feelings of the Sutton family, watching the fate of farmers across the hill as they fought in vain to save their land. *Schadenfreude*. That would have been the only word for it. There but for the grace of God.

Cooper watched Farnham working on the lawnmower for a moment. Strong, capable hands slotted a rotor blade back into place.

'Can you think who the victim might be, Mr Farnham?'

'Victim?'

'The body we found at Pity Wood. The body of a woman.'

'No, I can't.'

'Please think carefully. Anything you can remember might help us with an identification. A woman who disappeared around twelve months ago?'

Farnham didn't even look up from his task. 'No, sorry.'

'I understand there were a number of itinerant workers employed at Pity Wood Farm. Would *that* be during your time, sir?'

This was a fact that could be checked, so a lie would soon be caught. Cooper saw Farnham working that out for himself before answering. He took a little too long fitting parts of the motor back together.

'Yes, it would. Like I said, we tried out quite a few diversification schemes. Horticulture, poultry . . . Some of them needed labour at certain times of the year. Often casual labour. So, yes – we had itinerant workers, if you want to call them that.'

'Well, we'll need records. Details of the workers employed at Pity Wood during the last couple of years. You were a sort of farm manager, so . . .?'

'Ah, well. Records.' Farnham straightened up, wiping his hands on a rag. 'Those will be at the farm, such as they are. I left the farm accounts with Raymond. They weren't the best at record keeping, you know. They didn't believe all the bureaucracy and paperwork was necessary. But anything there is, you'll find it at Pity Wood.'

'Thank you, sir.'

'Oh, if the builders haven't thrown them out already,' said Farnham, as if the possibility had just occurred to him. But his air of innocence wasn't convincing Cooper.

It was cold in the workshop. And where it wasn't wet, it was oily. Farnham had a battered white Subaru pick-up with mud-caked hub caps, but it stood outside on the drive to provide more room in the garage.

'Do you spend much time out here?' asked Cooper.

'As much time as I like,' said Farnham. 'I'm a widower, you see.'

As he drove away from Farnham's house, Cooper looked afresh at the landscape. An ideal reservoir site should have a ring of hills to reduce the amount of dam building required. Rakedale had that. It also had the necessary clay soil, which stopped the water seeping through and provided material for dam construction. That was why the limestone areas had avoided reservoir building. Much too porous, limestone. If they'd built the reservoirs a few miles further north, Manchester would be suffering a permanent drought.

Inside the mobile incident unit, a cluster of bodies was building up a warm fug. Every time someone opened the door, they were met with a barrage of complaints about letting the draught in. The inner step was a mass of muddy footprints, and more mud had been tracked through the compartments.

'Any progress towards an ID yet?' called Hitchens from the office.

'We're hoping for some results from the forensics search team, sir.'

'Oh, the forensics search team. That would be the blokes scavenging through the skip.'

'Yes, sir.'

Hitchens saw Fry, and shook his head. 'As you can see, Diane, it's organized chaos here, as usual. I've just had word on the pathologist's preliminary examination of the body. No signs of major trauma.'

'Is that it?'

'Yes, until Mrs van Doon gets a closer look. She's doing the full PM this afternoon. You can chase her up on that, if you like.'

'Oh, thanks.'

'We've managed to pull in some more diggers, though,' said Hitchens. 'They're on site now.'

'That's good news. Can they . . .?'

110

'Yes, I've told them to make a start on the disturbed ground your young builder was bothered about.'

'Excellent.'

Official-issue packed lunches had been delivered for the team at the scene, one of the few perks of an otherwise tedious and unrewarding job. But even that was causing grumbles inside the trailer.

'Somebody's had all the chocolate bars out of our packed lunches,' said someone.

'OK, where's Gavin Murfin?'

'I don't know,' said Fry as she opened the door. 'But he's probably got several alibis lined up.'

Outside the trailer, Fry looked at the mud. Her shoes hadn't recovered from the day before. The clay had caked dry by the time she got round to cleaning them. It was an unforgiving sort of dirt, and practically unmoveable, too.

'Diane.'

'Yes?'

One of the SOCOs, Liz Petty, was standing at her elbow, holding a pair of rubber boots.

'I brought these from the van. Thought you might be able to use them.'

'Oh, thanks.'

She took them automatically, and Petty walked away. Fry was left holding the boots uncertainly, looking at the mud and wondering how silly she looked.

As soon as Cooper arrived back at the farm, he searched out Fry to report the outcome of his interview.

'So what was your assessment of Mr Farnham?' she asked.

'I think he'd sell his own grandmother, organ by organ.'

Fry laughed. 'You didn't believe what he was telling you?'

'It sounded much too pat, too moulded to show himself in the best light. He'd done his best, put his own money into the farm, but it had gone wrong through no fault of his own,

111

and regretfully he'd had to pull out. If you were inclined to believe him, he's practically a saint. But he came across more like a used car salesman to me.'

'An awkward customer?'

'I'd say so.'

'Stay on him,' said Fry. 'And let me know if you want to try a different approach.'

There were accepted strategies for dealing with awkward customers. They didn't have to speak to the police, but different officers and different approaches could be tried. In some circumstances, they might decide to take an interest in another issue, such as whether his car was legally taxed and licensed. No undue pressure, obviously.

As a last resort, there was always the option of arresting someone so they could be questioned and searched. Without justification, they were open to the subject deciding to sue, and might have to pay a couple of grand out of court. But financially it was preferable to deploying expensive resources on long, fruitless enquiries when a line of investigation was blocked.

'We should try to find these farm records,' said Cooper. 'I think Farnham was right about that, at least. If the records are anywhere, they'll be inside the house.'

'Well, I'll help you later. At least it's dry inside the house, if none too clean.'

But Cooper wasn't paying attention now. He was looking at his feet.

'You know, I don't remember ever seeing mud this red before – not in this area. The real clay soils are further south.'

Murfin came trudging through the mud to hand Fry a list of the items that the forensics team had recovered from the skip. It was a very long list, but most of the material she could discount. She was only interested in what had come out of the hole, and the SOCOs had helpfully grouped some items together. These had been tipped on top of the skip in one corner, where a couple of planks had been laid as a runway to get a wheelbarrow up to the right height. There were stones here, some unidentifiable bits of rusty metal, a broken bucket, a packet of coffee filters, and some brown mason jars.

She read through the list again, more carefully, then turned to the rest of the material that had been felt less significant. The SOCOs had been right – they'd picked out the relevant items. They couldn't list what wasn't there.

Fry stared across the site at the body tent, where a forensic botanist was using a teaspoon to tease out plant fragments. She had a clear picture of Jamie Ward, squatting in the wet mud, staring in shock at the object he'd found in the trench. When he shouted, someone had run up to him, thinking he'd hurt himself, while Nikolai, the foreman, had been cursing in the background. All perfectly clear, but for one thing.

'Gavin, have you got the list of builders' names and addresses?'

'I hope you don't want them in English.'

Fry flicked through the list she was given. She could see what Gavin meant – most of the names sounded East European. She wasn't familiar enough with the different nationalities in that part of the world to tell where exactly they might be from, but the officers taking details had helpfully filled in the nationalities, too. Polish, Czech, Slovakian. Apart from two, who were Irish nationals, none of the construction crew would have English as a first language.

Then Fry corrected herself. Gaelic was being restored to Ireland these days. The two Irishmen might not consider English their first language, either. It was advisable to tread carefully on these issues. She didn't want to be sent on diversity training.

'Several of these men give the same address in Macclesfield,' she said.

'Yes, it's some kind of workmen's hostel or B&B,' said

Murfin. 'According to the foreman, most of them are employed by an agency and they move around the country, wherever the work happens to be. Just at the moment, they're living in Macclesfield. Tomorrow, the moon.'

'Gavin, round up a couple of uniforms and speak to all these men again. I want to know which of them was working near Jamie Ward when he uncovered that body. Jamie says that one of them ran up to him when he shouted, but he can't remember who. I'd like to find out.'

'OK, I can do that.'

Murfin trudged away again, looking miserable. Fry seemed not to notice.

'This woman is worrying me,' she said to Cooper. 'Not knowing anything about her is very frustrating. It means we can't piece together any relationships she had, or formulate any theories about how she died. It's possible she committed suicide, or died accidentally. And then somebody buried her.'

'Deliberately?' asked Cooper.

Fry laughed. 'Is it possible to bury a person accidentally?'

'On a farm? Well, yes. Somebody might be standing in the wrong spot and get in the way of a trailer load of silage, or the slurry hose. People get killed on farms all the time. But you'd generally know you'd done it. Even if you were looking the wrong way, or you didn't hear them scream over the noise of your tractor engine, you'd soon notice they were missing. Well, wouldn't you?'

Fry stared at the ground. 'It might depend on who it was that got buried. Nobody seems to have noticed *this* woman missing, did they?'

Cooper nodded. 'You know, despite what they say, I think everyone in Rakedale knows everyone else.'

'Yes, I agree. At least it means there's no need to spend our time looking for connections with the Suttons. An individual who *didn't* have a connection would be the one to stand out.'

'Which means they all have a potential connection to the

114

victim, too. All of the people we've talked to could have visited Pity Wood Farm at some time.'

'But we have a whole different set of people, too,' said Fry. 'These itinerant workers have been in and out of Pity Wood Farm for years, apparently. No one seems to know who *they* were.'

'How do we go about tracing itinerant farmworkers?'

'It depends on the quality of the records, Ben.'

'Poor to non-existent, I would guess.'

'They could have been illegals, then,' said Fry. 'Derbyshire has had its share of refugees over the last few years. Mostly from Bosnia, Croatia, Afghanistan, Iraq, Somalia . . . There was a reception centre for Kosovans at Alfreton, wasn't there?'

'Yes, but the numbers are quite small. At least this isn't East Anglia. We don't have seventy thousand casual workers coming through every year to work in the horticultural industries. There's nothing in this area that's labour intensive enough to create a demand for large amounts of cheap labour at short notice.'

'It sounds bad enough to me.'

Cooper shook his head. 'Go to somewhere like King's Lynn, and you'll see the difference. According to a contact I have on the force there, their illegal immigrants run into thousands, sleeping in sheds and garages. They have to keep working to pay off the money they owe for a false passport and a trip to Britain. Organized crime is entrenched in the casual labour market. I don't mean foreign students taking part in some seasonal agricultural workers scheme – those are pretty well regulated. I mean the poor bloody Chinese peasants trying to work to send money home to pay off their debts. It takes them years to work their way out of slavery.'

'Slavery? That's a bit strong.'

'It's exactly what it is, Diane. Gang masters are sometimes unscrupulous operators, but criminals have been moving in. Triad or Snakehead gangs. You see Chinese people standing outside a station with bundles of possessions. They're very suspicious of police, too scared to report anything. Very few speak English, either – and while police are arranging an interpreter, they disappear.'

'Can you talk to your friend and get some more information? It would be interesting to hear whether Norfolk have any intelligence about gangs operating in this area.'

'Of course. I should have thought of that.'

'It still gives us a lot of suspects,' said Fry. 'Too many.'

A weary voice broke in. Suddenly, DI Hitchens was standing behind them, mud ruining the casual look of his jeans.

'Did I hear someone worrying about the potential number of suspects?' he said.

'Yes, sir. Why?'

Hitchens sighed. 'Well, I don't know if this makes it any better, or worse. But the digging teams have just found a second body.'

11

Another body tent was going up, right where Jamie Ward had pointed out the disturbed earth. Fry watched three PCs in high-vis jackets struggling with the fibreglass frame, giving each other conflicting instructions. A few yards away stood a yellow-and-white crime scene tent. It was twice the size, but it seemed to have gone up more easily – perhaps, she thought, because one woman had done it on her own.

'This one is an older burial, I can tell you that,' said Mrs van Doon, dusting off her gloves. 'I bet you didn't really need me for an opinion, did you? Complete skeletonization is evident. Dr Jamieson will have to watch out for disarticulation when he removes it from the soil. But his team know what they're doing. This is not my pigeon, Inspector. I need some soft tissue. Preferably a few internal organs.'

'Yes, I know,' said Hitchens.

'Both of your victims were wrapped in heavy-duty plastic sheeting before they were buried,' said Mrs van Doon. 'It looks like the same material to me, despite the difference in the date of the burials. They were killed, bundled up in plastic, and buried.'

'We can't persuade you towards suicide then, Doctor?' asked Hitchens.

The pathologist gave him a glacial look, but didn't bother to reply.

Hitchens sighed. 'Pity.'

The DI was beginning to look worn down. Fry suspected he was starting to reflect on whether his initial decisions had been the right ones. Maybe there should have been a bigger operation from the start, an assumption that they were dealing with murder.

Hitchens looked up and saw Wayne Abbott passing by with a Quickstep ladder over his shoulder and called him over.

'We're going to have to dig the rest of this place up,' he said. 'There might be more bodies.'

'Dig it up? Do you know how long that would take?'

'I think it will have to be done, Wayne.'

Abbott put his ladder down. 'Ground-penetrating radar – that's your answer. It's not much use in woodland or on sloping ground, but we can try it here.'

'Is it effective?'

'All it does is use the electrical properties of the soil to identify disturbances in the ground. It's a lot better than sticking a probe in. You need proper training to use those probes, really. If there *is* a body, and you go too deep, you can poke the end right in. It doesn't please the pathologist, I can tell you. I heard of one probe injury that was identified at the PM as the entrance wound of a bullet.'

Fry looked around the farmyard – all those nooks and crannies, corners and gateways, paddocks and overgrown gardens.

'Where would we start?'

Abbott consulted his watch, as if the time of day might make a difference, or perhaps he had something more important to do. Christmas presents to buy, the turkey to pick up.

'We could mark out the site and look for depressions,' he said.

'Depressions,' said Hitchens. 'I think I might be getting one of those.'

118

'You and me both,' said Abbott. 'Especially since you started talking about digging the whole place up. You do know it's nearly Christmas?'

'Why depressions, Wayne?' asked Fry.

'Look, a body takes up a major amount of space when it's buried, so there's nearly always surplus soil displaced around it. When the internal organs start to decompose, the soil above it sinks, creating a depression.' He demonstrated with his hands. 'Eventually, the entire area will sink as the soil settles. And here's where the weather becomes an advantage. Depressions will collect water and form large pools when it rains.'

'Look for the puddles, then?'

'Essentially. I can't promise you ground-penetrating radar until after Christmas, anyway.' Abbott hefted the ladder back on his shoulder. 'At least we can dig the place up without irate householders having fits about the damage to their garden. Do you remember that case we had in Dronfield? You'd think we'd just turned up to vandalize the woman's property. And all she had was a few old rose bushes and a bit of lawn.'

'Thanks for your help,' said Hitchens.

'I'd say it was a pleasure, but . . .'

Hitchens didn't look any happier.

'There's no one here to object,' he said to Fry. 'That's part of the problem.'

If Fry had thought it couldn't get any worse, she'd have been wrong. What would normally have been the front door to the farmhouse was almost inaccessible through the muck and rubble in the yard. From a glance into the porch, Cooper thought it looked unlikely that the door would open, even if they could reach it. There was almost as much debris inside as there was outside.

'What in God's name happened here, Ben? Did somebody drive a herd of buffalo through, or what?'

119

'Not the front door, Diane. Don't you know that yet?'

Like many houses in these parts, the occupants of Pity Wood Farm must have come and gone mostly through the back door. Neighbours would know never to call at the front of the house, and the postman had his own routine. Only strangers and DEFRA officials would try to approach the front door. When you realized that, the obstacle course of foul-smelling rubbish might start to look like a message.

For a moment, Fry seemed determined to get in anyway, as if she couldn't accept that things weren't done in a logical way.

'Hold your noses. It's like entering a kind of hell,' said Wayne Abbott as he passed a few yards away.

'Why is he always around?' said Fry.

'It's his job,' pointed out Cooper.

'It's not his job to annoy me.'

They walked round the house and Cooper led her inside through the back door, passing the cleared rooms and entering the hallway.

'They left everything. Look, they even left the family Bible on the hall table,' said Cooper.

'So one of them found God, do you think?'

'It happens.'

'It must have been Raymond. He sounds the type.'

'Do you think there's a type, Diane?'

'Yes – those who show some signs of having a conscience in the first place. No, wait. There's another type – the ones who're already disturbed, hovering close to the edge. We see it all the time among convicted criminals. They get hold of some delusion that they interpret as a spiritual revelation, and suddenly they're born again. They think they're one of God's chosen representatives on earth, redeemed from their sins for some special purpose that He has in mind for them. And, hey presto, they don't have to feel guilty about their crimes any more.'

120

Cooper nodded, but reluctantly. He no longer went to church regularly himself, but he did at least feel guilty about not going. The way Fry talked about other people's religious beliefs made him uncomfortable. The worst thing was that he couldn't tell her how he felt, because he knew she'd take it as a sign of weakness.

'Actually, there's a third type, isn't there?' he said.

'Oh, is there?' Fry watched him expectantly.

'There are those who *pretend* to have found religion, because they think it will help them get parole.'

'Yes, it's common enough. But it's a tough act to keep up, especially when you get on the outside.'

'I suppose so.'

Fry looked at the Bible, prominently displayed on the hall table. 'I mean, if someone is genuinely religious, you'd expect to find some sign of it in their house, in private – not just for public show.'

She began to walk back towards the next room, and Cooper followed her. They moved cautiously about the house, looking for anything that resembled an office where the farm records might have been kept. But they ended up in the kitchen.

'We might as well start here,' said Cooper.

There were still no cats. Not even the signs of their food bowls or a litter tray. Wasn't a cat the Celtic equivalent of the dog Cerberus, the guardian at the entrance to the Underworld? If this was a kind of hell, where were the guardians?

Cooper hoped the farm cats had taken themselves off into the woods and fields to find their own food. He didn't like to think of them becoming roadkill. Their deaths would never be reported, if that was the case. Like the body in the excavated grave, they would never be missed, or even become a statistic.

He saw a *Daily Express* that lay folded on the kitchen table, gathering dust.

'This newspaper is nearly nine months old.'

121

'Is Winston Churchill still Prime Minister?' asked Fry.

'No, but someone's landed on the Moon.'

They went through all the drawers they could find in the kitchen, the sitting room, and a small parlour. Eventually, their search turned up a large, leather-bound book like a ledger, and sheaves of paperwork left loose or stuffed into boxfiles. Cooper lifted out the book and freed it from the papers.

'Farm accounts?' asked Fry.

'Yes, I think so.'

'Bag everything, Ben, and make sure it's all logged as evidence. We'll look at it when we get back to the office.'

'Fair enough.'

Cooper did as he was told, then continued to poke around in the kitchen cupboards, curious about what the Suttons might have left behind that gave an insight into their lives.

'This is interesting, Diane.'

'What have you found?'

'A Sani Bag.'

'A what?'

'A sanitary-towel disposal bag. This one is from a Novotel. They provide them in their bathrooms for guests.'

Cooper turned the bag over in his hand. He'd never looked at one closely before. It was made of a strong, shiny white plastic, overprinted with blue text in four languages, and it could be sealed by peeling off an adhesive strip and folding down the flap, the way some envelopes were sealed. A set of symbols on the back made it clear that the bag should be disposed of in the bin, not in the toilet bowl. For some reason, these instructions were given in six languages, rather than four.

'There's a Novotel in Sheffield,' he said. 'On Arundel Gate, near Hallam University. That's the nearest one I can think of.'

'There's another at Long Eaton, near Junction 25 of the M1.'

'The M1? Well, that would be convenient, too. I suppose it's the sort of thing you might take away with you from a hotel, like those little bars of soap, and hand towels.'

'Yes,' said Fry. 'But only if you're female.'

'So we've found evidence to suggest that at least one female was living at Pity Wood Farm. One of our victims, Diane?'

'Impossible to say, until we have an ID.'

'We need to get SOCOs into this kitchen,' said Cooper. 'If violence was committed, this is a likely place for it to have happened.'

'Yes, I suppose we might hit lucky – old bloodstains on one of those knives, or in between the tiles of the floor.'

'Or poisons in the fridge.'

Cooper opened the door of the Electrolux and let her have a glimpse of the jars with their unidentifiable crystallized residues.

'Jesus. Did people really live in this house?' said Fry. 'Or did they just turn it over to the animals?'

'If we can establish a primary crime scene, Diane, it would change everything.'

'Yes, you're right. I'll suggest it as a priority.'

Fry stood in the middle of the room and turned slowly on the spot, examining the kitchen – its stained walls, its old armchairs, its cast-iron range, and even the still dripping tap in the sink.

'What do you think, Diane?' asked Cooper.

'To be honest, I think you must be Doctor Who, and you've just zipped us off to another place and time in your Tardis.'

'I do know where there's a police box,' he said helpfully. 'But it hasn't moved for years, to my knowledge.'

'Ben, I don't recognize this world. These people are an alien species to me. I feel like an anthropologist examining the remains of a vanished civilization.'

'I know what you mean.'

Fry stepped over a heap of muddy straw on the kitchen floor. 'Actually, "civilization" is putting it a bit strong.'

She was trying to make a joke of it, but Fry really did feel out of her own place and time. The sensation was very

123

disturbing, as if the time machine had left her travel sick and nauseous.

And she had the suspicion that it wasn't the Suttons who were the aliens around here.

Just as she was thinking about aliens, Wayne Abbott put his head round the door. His shaved head bristled aggressively.

'Oh, there you are,' he said. 'I was just wondering whether you'd knocked off and gone home. I thought you might like to know – there's an extensive burnt area behind the poultry sheds. Do you want us to start sifting through it?'

'How large an area?' asked Fry.

'Like the size of several bonfires. It could have been an entire building that went up, if it was made of wood. But there's no sign of a concrete or brick base. I'd guess someone was burning rubbish, and used accelerant to make a good job of it. The ash is several inches deep in places.'

'I suppose you'll need more resources for that job?'

'You bet.'

'Contain it for now, and we'll let you know.'

'No problem. Oh, and the builders' foreman is here. The Polish bloke. He says you wanted him.'

Nikolai Dudzik nodded cautiously, sensing from Fry's manner that he was in a difficult position. Instead of his yellow hard hat, he was wearing a shapeless woollen cap, indicating that was he was off duty.

'Bones,' he said. 'A few bones, that was all.'

'Yes, bones, Mr Dudzik.'

'The skeleton of an animal, yes? It's a farm, after all. There must have been lots of animals buried here, I think.'

'So you got the men to fill the hole in again and cover it up?'

'Yes.'

'For God's sake, why?'

124

Dudzik raised his hands apologetically.

'I knew there would be a lot of fuss if we reported it, Sergeant. It would have delayed the job too much. We're already behind schedule, you see. Because of the weather.'

'The skeleton of an animal wouldn't have delayed anything,' said Fry. 'You knew it was human.'

'History,' he said. 'They send in the scientists. They don't let you build for weeks, for months.'

'You're saying you thought the discovery would involve archaeologists coming here to dig up an ancient graveyard?'

'Yes, exactly.'

Fry could see the second body tent in the background. The thought of an entire graveyard at Pity Wood Farm made her skin go cold.

'But this isn't history, Mr Dudzik.'

'I'm sorry. We thought we were doing the right thing.'

'Jamie Ward seems to be the only one who wasn't let in on it.'

'No, we didn't trust him. He was different, he would want to speak to the authorities.'

'Thank goodness he was around. *He* was the one who did the right thing.'

Fry sighed. It was still too late, wasn't it? The grave had already been disturbed, and crucial evidence could have been lost.

'Am I in trouble, Sergeant?' asked Dudzik, anxious now to get away.

She looked at him thoughtfully.

'We could sort it out, if you're co-operative, sir.'

'Anything I can do to help. I'm at your disposal.'

'Your workmen – they must sometimes pick up small items for themselves. Things they find, that look as though they aren't wanted by anyone.'

'Ah, yes. They do like these old places, particularly. Sometimes they find little bits of treasure.'

'I'm looking for a specific bit of treasure.'

'Oh?'

Fry told him about the broken cross that Jamie Ward had dug out of the first grave, which hadn't turned up in the skip with the rest of the debris. He'd described it as a cheap crucifix on a chain, with part of the base chipped away.

'Whoever has it, Mr Dudzik, I want it returned,' she said. Dudzik pulled his cap back on.

'Leave it with me, Sergeant,' he said. 'I'll find it for you.'

When he finally got back to his desk in Edendale, Cooper took a return call from his contact in Norfolk, where the horticulture business was totally reliant on transient workers.

'You don't need as much accommodation for illegals as you might think, Ben,' he said. 'Most gang masters practise a hot-bedding system.'

'Two men sharing the same bed, working and sleeping in shifts?'

'Right. It's incredibly difficult and time consuming to check them all for forged documents. Some are very good forgeries, in any case. There's nothing special about those IND documents they're supposed to produce for employers.'

'Hold on – IND? It's a Home Office department, I know, but I don't have my acronym dictionary to hand.'

'Immigration and Nationality Directorate.'

'Right.'

'King's Lynn is the hub for East Anglia. We have at least two thousand illegals here, at last count. They sleep in sheds and garages, as well as any houses they can find to rent. They're charged for accommodation and transport, and some-times up to twenty thousand pounds for a false passport. They're promised that they'll earn three or four hundred pounds a week when they get to Britain, but they're lucky if they get half that, in reality. They're told they have to work to pay off their fees, and the gang master takes a cut.'

'I described it to my DS as like being sold into slavery,' said Cooper.

'You're right. Yes, it *is* like being sold into slavery. Many illegals don't earn more than two pounds or two pounds fifty an hour, even if the employer pays the legal minimum wage. So workers are trapped – they have to carry on sending money home to pay their debt. Even if they get regular work, that takes about five years.'

'And from the employers' point of view, it's all about convenience, I suppose.'

'Of course. Farmers simply ask for a certain amount of labour on a certain day and turn a blind eye to where it comes from. When farmers or growers employ illegal workers, it's because they can't get legal workers locally, and then they have to rely on a third party to provide them, or lose the crop.'

'So do you have anything specific for me?'

'I checked the intelligence when you emailed, Ben. Sorry, mate – there's nothing in your area. I thought it was all sheep in the Peak District, anyway?'

'Not quite.'

'Well, if you want to take it any further, you'll probably have to tackle the Immigration and Nationality Directorate in Croydon. They'll have an Enforcement and Removals team that operates in your region.'

'Thanks.'

'Oh, and Ben?'

'Yes?'

'Watch out for anyone called Ernest Xavier Ample.'

Half an hour later, Fry stood with Hitchens at the tape marking off the freshly excavated patch of ground, now covered by its own tent. Pity Wood Farm was starting to look like a campsite for tourists with strange tastes in sleeping arrangements. Inside the tent, Dr Pat Jamieson was humming to himself, like a mechanic under a dodgy Ford Escort.

Forensic anthropologists were conservative by nature, especially when asked to report on the biological profile of a victim. Jamieson was one of the most conservative of all, likely to suck his teeth and shake his head without committing himself to an opinion.

'You know I can't address cause of death, Inspector,' said Dr Jamieson, his bald head gleaming briefly in the light. 'That's a medical determination, for the pathologist to make. An assessment of age, sex, stature and ancestry, yes. Time since death, possibly. But beyond that, well . . .'

While Hitchens was fidgeting impatiently, Fry took a call from Murfin on her mobile.

'Bad news, Diane. We've lost a couple of those builders.'

'What?'

'Two of the East Europeans have done a bunk from their B&B, and the agency has had no word of them since Thursday. They suggest they might just have gone off for a long weekend.'

'A long weekend doing what?'

'Boozing probably,' said Murfin. 'I can't blame them, personally. We might have to wait until Monday and see if they turn up again.'

'Damn. Did we check on their status?'

'You said it could wait,' pointed out Murfin.

'No, Mr Hitchens did.' Fry couldn't disguise the small surge of relief. 'Which two are missing?'

'A Slovak and a Czech. I'd give you the names, but I can't pronounce them.'

'I'll get Ben Cooper on to it. He has some contacts.'

Fry ended the call and switched her attention again.

'The pathologist's preliminary report on the first victim said there were no signs of major trauma,' Hitchens was saying to the anthropologist.

'Oh, well – there's your other difference, then,' said Dr Jamieson, with a patronizing smile. 'Apart from the age of the burial, that is.'

'What difference is that, Doctor?'

'The bodies might appear to be intact and free of major trauma as far as the torso, but beyond the upper vertebrae we're in quite different territory.'

'Injuries? A cause of death?' said Hitchens hopefully.

'Not necessarily. But your second body is definitely different, Inspector. This one is missing a head.'

12

There was plenty of work for SOCOs and the photographic unit to do now. Before it could be moved, any item of physical evidence would be photographed in situ from several angles with a ruler for scale, and a sketch containing accurate dimensions with locations and measurements of all objects would have to be made.

'Well, I can only give my view if the pathologist requests it,' said Dr Jamieson. 'And most of them think anthropologists are charlatans when it comes to the manner of death.'

'But the missing head –?' said Hitchens.

'– wasn't necessarily the cause of death. Not that I can pronounce on the subject.'

'Removing someone's head is a sure way of causing death. Even I can pronounce on that.'

The anthropologist shook his head. 'Postmortem removal. Do I need to say more?'

'Oh.'

'I understand you're bringing in ground-penetrating radar to examine the site for more burials?' said Jamieson. 'I'll be here if you need me.'

'Thank you, Doctor.'

'You're welcome.'

'Postmortem removal,' said Hitchens to his detectives, when they were out of earshot of the anthropologist.

'Somebody removed the victim's head after she was dead,' said Fry.

'Yes, I know what it means, Diane. Well, I know what the word means. But what's the significance of the act? Who would take a head from a dead body?'

'Collectors?' suggested Murfin. 'There are people who collect anything.'

'Oh, yes. I bet it'll be worth a fortune on eBay.'

'Do you want me to check?'

'No, Gavin. We'll leave that for later.'

'Serial killers love dismemberment,' said Fry. 'The psychologists say that taking body parts from their victims as trophies gives them a feeling of control, a sense of achievement previously lacking in their lives.'

'We're not dealing with a serial killer,' said Hitchens firmly. 'Don't even joke about it. This is Edendale, not Ipswich.'

'We have two bodies already,' pointed out Fry.

'Two doesn't make a series.'

'Well, perhaps . . .'

'I'm serious here. The last thing we want is to start a scare. Besides, there might be no connection between these two victims, apart from the fact that they were buried a few yards apart. Heck, we don't even know they were murdered. They might be accidental deaths, or they might be suicides. So let's have no talk about serial killers. There's absolutely no justification. Understood?'

'Yes, sir.'

Hitchens relaxed a little. 'We don't want our new detective superintendent arriving in Edendale and finding us panicking unnecessarily. Now, do we?'

'No, of course not,' said Fry.

She looked at Cooper, who had been silent so far. But he lowered his head, refusing to respond. No doubt he had his own theories. She'd get them out of him later.

'Actually, we're calling our second victim "she", but we won't get confirmation of gender for a while yet,' said Hitchens. 'So no assumptions, OK?'

'No assumptions,' said Fry.

That taste was in her mouth again. She didn't know where it came from, or why. It was like a pregnancy craving, but she wasn't pregnant, thank God. No chance of that.

'Are you all right, Diane?'

She became aware of Cooper standing nearby, watching her with concern written all over his face, as if he had stumbled across someone who was ill.

'Of course I'm all right. What are you staring at?'

'I just thought –'

'Ben, were you thinking of hanging around here until the rain stops? We both have work to do back at the office.'

Cooper shuffled his feet in the mud. 'They've found a shoe, about ten feet from the second body, just under the surface of the soil.'

'A woman's shoe?'

'Yes, size four.'

'Can they get a shoe size from a skeleton?' asked Fry.

'I don't know, Diane.'

Fry paced back towards the house, skirting the crime scene tape. But then her feet slowed as if the weight of the mud was drawing her to a halt, and she stopped.

'If Raymond Sutton knew those two bodies were buried in the yard, would he have been willing to sell the farm? He must have known there was a good chance a new owner would start digging the place up, if it was going to be developed.'

'Perhaps he didn't know it was going to be developed,' said Cooper.

'What do you mean?'

'Well, I'm thinking about all the vehicles and equipment that were left behind. Apart from the livestock, nothing seems to have been sold off at all – not even the furniture in the house. I wonder if Raymond Sutton was under the impression that the farm was being sold as a going concern.'

'Sold to another farmer, you mean?'

Cooper nodded. 'If Mr Sutton thought Pity Wood was going to continue as a dairy farm, he might not have worried about the bodies. Farmers have more to keep them occupied than building patios, especially if they're starting a new herd from scratch.'

'Did you ever speak to the auctioneers?'

'No, I never got round to it. It didn't seem all that important.'

'Perhaps you'd better do it now,' said Fry.

'OK, I will.' Cooper turned. 'You talked to the new owner, didn't you? Goodwin, is that the name?'

'Yes, I spoke to him on the phone. Why?'

'Did he seem like someone who'd make a convincing dairy farmer?'

Fry thought for a moment. 'Not to me, he didn't. I'd say he sounded more like a moderately successful provincial solicitor. You know – divorces and boundary disputes, that sort of lawyer. Steady business, but nothing that demands too much in the way of brains.'

'And he lives in Manchester somewhere?'

'Yes.'

'Mmm. Dropping out of the rat race, maybe?'

'Downshifting, they call it.'

'I suppose that's pretty much what you did, Diane. Moving from the big city into the country. It was a bit of a leap, wasn't it?'

Mrs van Doon had the first body on the table in the mortuary. When Fry entered, suited and masked, the pathologist was trying to separate the skin from the mummified hand, easing it off the desiccated fingers like a glove. She would be hoping that someone could get usable fingerprints from it once it was clear of the corpse.

'Can you estimate a time of death yet?' asked Fry.

'Ooh, time of death. That's a favourite question, isn't it? Well, by far the best indications of time of death are rigor mortis and body temperature. Anybody want to guess why those aren't helpful in this case?'

Fry looked at the remains on the table, was about to speak, then realized the pathologist was probably making a joke.

'That's right. Because they're both useless once you get past about thirty-six hours. Here, we're well past that by a factor, of . . . oh, I'd say about three hundred or so. The only possibility you're left with in this case is finding some evidence of the last time your victim was seen, or the last time anyone had contact with her.'

'A factor of three hundred would make it about a year,' pointed out Fry.

'Oops, did I let slip an opinion? It was unintentional, I assure you.'

'But appreciated, all the same. We need anything we can get.'

'Well, there's one thing I've never seen before,' said Mrs van Doon. 'There seems to be an extraordinary amount of tooth decay for an individual of this age. Quite excessive. I propose to consult the forensic odontologist for a specialist opinion.'

'If the victim had some unusual medical condition, that might help us tremendously.'

'Yes . . .' The pathologist hesitated, as if about to say something else. 'Well, we'll see. No point in speculating *too* much, is there? I know we're as one on that point, Detective Sergeant.'

Cooper settled himself back at his desk in Edendale and opened the records book carefully. The bound ledger only went back to the 1980s, presumably to the time when the brothers had first taken over the farm from their father. Their names were inscribed inside the front cover, with the date the book had been started.

He was pleased to see that whoever was responsible for the neat, copperplate handwriting had taken the trouble to record the stocking rates and cropping rotas on the farm, as well as adding up the accounts. DEFRA would have been proud of them.

At the time the ledger was started, the main enterprise on the farm had been a flock of Swaledale ewes – four hundred head of them, either bred pure or crossed to a Bluefaced Leicester ram to give mule lambs for sale. It seemed that all the purebred Swale ewe lambs were retained as flock replacements, and sent into Lincolnshire for their first winter, while the males were sold as stores through Bakewell market. It was still standard practice on many sheep farms in the Peak District.

A few years later, a small herd of Belted Galloway cattle had been tried. Cooper nodded approval. That was a good idea of someone's. Galloways were hardy cattle, and that was important because there was little space for in-wintering cattle at Pity Wood Farm, and the breed would have been capable of making use of the coarser grasses.

Flicking through the records, Cooper began to see the evidence of falling prices and rising costs as the years went by and Pity Wood entered the 1990s. The thriving enterprise that Raymond and Derek had inherited from their father was gradually, inexorably, getting into trouble. He tried to imagine the brothers discussing their financial problems by the fireside in the evenings, but he couldn't manage it. An anxious silence filled his head, both brothers reluctant to talk about what was worrying them, perhaps even more reluctant to admit there was anything wrong. Optimism in the future, that was the keyword in those days.

And then, in 1999, he saw the first attempts at diversification. That was already too late. The writing had been on the wall for a decade by then. After the arrival of Tom Farnham, there had been other failed enterprises – a farm shop, a campsite, holiday lets, rare breeds of sheep.

There was diversification, and there was diversification. If you had half a million pounds to spare, you could buy into the buffalo meat business with your own hundred-strong breeding herd, including butchery and storage equipment and stalls at farmers' markets. Cooper had seen it advertised quite recently. A water buffalo enterprise over at Chatsworth, and thriving by all accounts.

But sheep? There were already half a million sheep in the national park alone. They were a feature of the landscape, those white, woolly blobs scattered across the hillsides like snow. They were a driving hazard on the unfenced roads, especially on the high passes of the Dark Peak at night, when they were drawn to the tarmac for warmth and their eyes gleamed suddenly in a driver's headlights as he rounded a bend.

Yes, many people would say there were already too many sheep in the Peak District.

When Fry returned from the mortuary, Cooper was unfolding a map attached to some legal documents.

'You know, Tom Farnham said they used to park farm trailers on that bit of ground where the first grave was found.'

'Yes?' said Fry.

'Well, I've been going through the deeds, and there was a copy of a map drawn up for the conveyance between the Suttons and the previous owners. It clearly shows a building on that part of the property.'

'Are you sure?'

'Yes, and it's a pretty big building. It looks as though it ran from the corner of the paddock almost to the first gate, right along that wall.'

136

'Does it specify what the building was?'

'No, it just says "outbuildings".'

Fry looked at the map. 'It might just have been re-drawn from an old document. They don't bother to come out and re-map a property every time it's sold, do they? So this map probably shows the way the farm looked at the time of an earlier purchase.'

'Possibly,' said Cooper.

'Farms change appearance all the time, don't they? Farmers knock old buildings down and put up new ones, willy-nilly. They're not subject to the same planning regulations as the rest of us.'

'That's true. But a building this size . . . well, it wasn't just some old pigsty they didn't need any more.' Cooper shook his head. 'It's a shame there aren't any photos of Pity Wood from that time.'

'We should be so lucky.'

He put the map back into the document wallet where he'd found it.

'You know that area should never have been disturbed?' said Fry. 'Not by the building contractors, anyway. Jamie Ward was digging a completely unnecessary trench when he came across the first body.'

'The new owner might have been planning on calling in some landscape gardeners later on, or he might have wanted to tackle the garden himself.'

'This is the Manchester solicitor, Goodwin?'

'Right.'

'Is he a keen gardener?'

'I have no idea, Diane.'

'I do wonder why he bought that farm,' said Fry.

'Didn't he say he wanted to move out into the country for some peace and quiet? You called it downshifting, didn't you?'

'I meant, why *that* farm? Why Pity Wood? The place is a

complete mess. There must be lots of more attractive propositions within commuting distance of Manchester.'

'Of course. But probably it was a question of price. This property would have been a lot cheaper than most. You just need deep pockets for the modernization work.'

'What if he had another reason for choosing that particular property? A more pressing reason?'

Cooper thought about it for a moment. 'You mean he might have known there were two bodies buried on the farm and couldn't risk anyone else buying it, in case they discovered the graves?'

'Well?'

'It's possible,' said Cooper. 'It might explain the hurry.'

'Was there a hurry?'

'They didn't take the time for an equipment sale.'

'Oh, that. Well, all that stuff is starting to make a bit of sense now. I think I'll give Mr Goodwin a call and ask him why he chose Pity Wood.'

'You've no evidence for this theory, Diane.'

'Somebody has to use a bit of initiative.'

Cooper raised an eyebrow. He thought he could see Fry already starting to respond to the imminent arrival of the new superintendent. No doubt she believed she'd do better under a female boss. He didn't think that DCI Kessen or DI Hitchens had ever shown any bias for or against her, and had never avoided giving Diane responsibility because she was a woman. But perhaps he wasn't in the right place to notice. From Diane's point of view, the situation might look completely different. It was possible that she observed lots of little things, small signs of favour or disfavour that no one else saw or would know how to interpret.

'By the way, was there anything interesting from the post-mortem?' asked Cooper.

'A vague stab at twelve months since time of death, and an excessive amount of tooth decay.'

'Was Mrs van Doon in an unhelpful mood?'

Fry sighed. 'No, not really. She just has an impossible job, like everyone else.'

Watching Fry walk back to her own desk to phone Mr Goodwin, Cooper remembered how ambitious she was, how often she talked about moving up or moving on. At one time, he'd thought that Fry's sister, Angie, would be enough to keep her in the area, but now he wasn't so sure.

The relationship between the two sisters had always baffled him, and still did. The odd thing was that Diane had seemed to feel closer to Angie when she was missing than she did now that her sister was very much around. It didn't fit with Cooper's own ideas about family at all. But was his experience necessarily the way things ought to be?

Cooper rubbed the tiredness from his eyes and returned to the farm records. In seconds, he was back in the past, living a mouth-to-mouth existence at Pity Wood Farm.

13

Aaron Goodwin was between clients. Nevertheless, he gave Fry the impression that he'd charge her by the hour if she took more than five minutes of his time.

'Why did we buy the farm?' he said. 'I can answer that in one word. Horses.'

Fry didn't know what Mr Goodwin looked like, but she was enjoying a mental image of him arriving at Pity Wood Farm in its present condition. She pictured him wincing at the mud, the abandoned builders' equipment, the police tape protecting the grave sites.

'My wife and my daughters are mad about horses,' he explained. 'They've plagued me for years to find a house in the country where we could have our own stables and paddocks, a ménage, somewhere to park a couple of horse boxes. As soon as we had enough money, it was just a question of locating the right property.'

'And Pity Wood was it?' asked Fry, barely able to keep the incredulity out of her voice.

Goodwin paused, as if checking his watch. 'It was a bit of a stretch, admittedly, considering all the work that needs doing to the place. The cost of the alterations and renovation is almost as much as the purchase price, to be honest. I really hope it's going to be worth it.'

'Well, you're certainly going to be in the country,' said Fry. 'Have you any experience of rural life?'

'Not at all. We're strictly city people.'

'Then I'm afraid some things might come as a bit of a shock, sir.'

As a city girl herself, Fry might have felt a degree of kinship with the solicitor, if it weren't for the fact that he was moving to the countryside voluntarily. He was bringing it all on himself, and it diluted her sympathy. But perhaps she ought to enlighten him a bit.

'Country people can seem like an alien race, you know. They're very, er . . . conservative, in some ways. In others, their activities are way out on the edge. Their lives seem to revolve around the church and the village pub.'

'Rather than the office and the bistro, you mean?' said Goodwin.

'And a lot of them really do like shooting things, I've found.'

'We have that in Manchester, except they shoot people instead of foxes and grouse. But at least they make you feel part of a community out there, don't they?'

'You haven't visited Rakedale, then?' asked Fry.

Goodwin paused. 'We didn't make the decision lightly. There are some questions you have to ask yourself before you move to the country.'

'Oh, yes. Like whether you can cope with mud and the stink of a freshly fertilized field.'

'I was thinking of whether you'll be able to survive without theatres and nightclubs. But perhaps you never had to ask yourself those questions, Detective Sergeant.'

'Not really.'

There was a moment's silence, and Fry had a suspicion that

141

the solicitor was only half listening, perhaps taking the chance to read a file before his next client arrived.

'Mr Goodwin, are you at all aware of the history of Pity Wood Farm?'

'Its history? What do you mean? The estate agent's details mentioned the date the house was built. Late eighteenth century, I believe.'

'You must know something about the previous owners. Did you ever meet them?'

'No, never. The property was already empty when we viewed it.'

'Are you sure? What about Mr Raymond Sutton?'

'Sutton is the name on the deeds, that's all I know. Why do you ask?'

'I wondered if you'd visited Pity Wood some time previously.'

'Oh?'

'I thought you might have had your eye on it as a suitable property if it ever came up for sale. It's the sort of thing people do when they have a plan, like yours for keeping horses. They see the ideal place, and they keep it in mind for the future.'

'Yes, I suppose they do. But that wasn't so in our case. To be honest, Sergeant, I'm not all that familiar with the Peak District, let alone Rakedale.'

Fry had to accept that it sounded like the truth. 'Thank you, sir.'

'Now that you mention the farm's history, though . . .' said Goodwin.

'Yes?'

'This murder case gives it rather an interesting history, doesn't it? Bodies buried in the farmyard and all that.'

'We don't actually know for certain –' began Fry.

'No, no, of course. But it's rather a selling point.'

'A selling point? It won't put you off the place, then?'

'Not at all. It adds a macabre charm. Something to tell our friends when they come to visit.'

'You're really looking forward to living at Pity Wood Farm, aren't you?' said Fry. 'You really are.'

'You sound as though you're trying to put me off.' Goodwin chuckled. 'You know, some people told us once that, when we move to the country, we'll have to keep quiet for at least five years. Don't go poking your nose in, they said. No organizing things, or making changes. It's considered interfering. You're an outsider and you have to serve an apprenticeship, until you're accepted.'

'And I suppose you don't think that will apply to you?' said Fry. 'Well, Mr Goodwin, you don't know the half of it.'

Cooper was discovering that there could be a whole social history buried in farm records. It was possible to trace the changes that had taken place in farming over the decades through the day-to-day details of income and expenditure.

For example, until the 1980s, government grant schemes had been committed only to increasing food production, which meant they often supported plans to improve rough pasture or increase grazing levels, which damaged conservation interests. But for some years now, grants had been moving towards environmentally friendly land management and biodiversity. There was the Countryside Stewardship Scheme of the early 1990s. Then the reform of CAP and environmental stewardship, encouraging farmers to manage land in a way that enhanced the landscape and conserved wildlife.

Somehow, though, the Suttons and Pity Wood Farm had fallen between two stools. It seemed as though they'd been too slow to change. Perhaps they'd been confused by the conflicting pressures, baffled by the fact that practices encouraged in their younger days were now considered almost criminal. Their farm records showed that their attempts at diversification had been half-hearted at best, and misguided at worst.

Cooper felt a twinge of sympathy for them. The Suttons

weren't alone in failing to grasp that conservation was now more important than the production of food.

There was an irony in the pattern the Suttons had followed. By the mid-1990s, the brothers could have got a decent price for Pity Wood Farm, if they'd decided to sell. But, like so many farmers, they probably thought they could get through the bad times and things would improve.

So they'd missed their chance to capitalize on the myth of the countryside idyll, which had been widespread in the 1990s. Living in the countryside had become the city dweller's dream. Features in the Sunday supplements suggested the country-side could provide the space to be yourself, to have the freedom to live your life without close neighbours, busy roads, the daily struggle to get to work. Nobody spoke of the down-sides – the isolation, inadequate services, having to walk a mile to the nearest bus stop, if there were any buses. No one pointed out that within a few years there'd be no shops or hospitals, nor even a post office.

Feeling weary, Cooper got up to fetch himself a coffee. It had been a long day already, and he wasn't finished yet. When Fry returned, she'd want hard facts, not some gloomy reflec-tion on the state of the countryside.

He gazed out of the window while he drank his coffee and rubbed his weary eyes. The past fifteen years had dispelled that myth of the countryside idyll. People in rural areas lived shorter lives, had fewer medical facilities, and were more likely to get depressed and kill themselves. One in four people in the countryside lived below the poverty line, just as in urban areas. Their children were injured on the roads more often, it took a lot longer to get to a hospital if you suffered a heart attack, and if you used a mobile phone you were more likely to suffer from brain tumours than someone in a city. There wasn't quite such a rush into the country any more.

Cooper went back to the records. The only big surprise was that Pity Wood had survived into the middle of the first decade of the twenty-first century. It had already been an anachronism by then, dead on its feet, sinking into debt.

He knew from the articles in *Farmers Weekly* that Matt showed him what the situation was. Farm incomes in the national park had fallen by seventy-five per cent over ten years. The potential return from livestock farming had ceased to match the investment of time and capital. Without subsidies, only a few dairy farms in the Peak District would be making any money now – a ludicrous average of four or five thousand pounds a year, as long as there was no allowance made for paying the farmer and his family. For beef and sheep farms, it was even worse. Their bottom line would be a minus figure.

So what had the Suttons done to try to escape this looming disaster? All the wrong things, it seemed to Cooper. A poultry enterprise had been the major decision in recent years. He remembered the old poultry sheds, empty of birds but still smelling powerfully of ammonia. No battery cages, but deep bedding, so there had been some attempt at humane treatment of the chickens, at least.

Cooper searched the records in vain for purchases of any major equipment, such as a straw spreader. It looked as though the Suttons hadn't been able to find six thousand pounds or so to spend on such a luxury item, so presumably the straw in the poultry houses had been spread by hand.

The fields had still been cut for silage in the last few years, though there were no ruminants left at Pity Wood to eat it. No cattle or sheep to get through the winter. The Suttons must have intended to sell it to their neighbours – and, indeed, there were some records of earlier sales. But Cooper had seen this year's cut of silage himself, still sitting in its bags in the yard.

When Fry returned to the office, Cooper was surrounded by papers that spread across two desks. He was holding a glossy four-page brochure, unable to control the expression of amazement on his face.

'What have you got there, Ben?'

'The estate agent's details for the sale of Pity Wood Farm. The photographs make it look quite attractive. Somebody managed to find a sunny day. And they used a camera with a wide-angle lens. But not so wide that it showed the mud.'

'"*A rare opportunity to purchase a farm holding with superb potential in a most sought-after area,*"' read Cooper. '"*Traditional farmhouse and adjoining barns with further buildings and grassland extending to ninety-five acres. Pity Wood Farm comprises a delightfully situated south-facing property in an unrivalled position. A range of stone outbuildings provide scope to extend to convert into holiday lets, subject to obtaining planning consent. The farmhouse requires some refurbishment, modernization and general upgrading . . .*"'

'You can say that again.'

'"*. . . but once complete will create a truly enviable residence in an idyllic rural location.*"'

'Funny how people use that word "idyllic" to mean "primitive".'

Cooper didn't reply. He was concentrating on trying to make all the buildings listed by the estate agent fit the map on the old conveyance and his memory of Pity Wood Farm. *To the front of the property is a walled garden area and patio.* That must be the overgrown patch where the old caravan was parked.

He made a quick note. Had Scenes of Crime got round to the caravan yet? Who had been living in there? He bet it had been overlooked, amid all the other excitement and conflicting priorities.

Three-bay general-purpose building of block construction, two corrugated-tin-sheet sheds, timber-framed slatted house with feed barriers and a slurry store, monopitch block-built shed, *timber-framed cowshed, implement sheds, useful six-bay general-purpose building* . . . The list seemed endless, yet some of those buildings must be in ruins. Well, the estate agent did mention renovation.

'"*A mains water supply is available*,"' said Cooper out loud.

'A mains water supply,' said Fry. 'That's a selling point, is it?'

'In this area, yes.'

'So what have you got from the farm records, Ben? What exactly were they doing at Pity Wood Farm to earn money – I mean, enough to make it profitable? And was Raymond relying on the sale of the farm to meet the cost of his residential care for the rest of his life?'

'Apparently not. They brought Tom Farnham in to introduce some new enterprises. They could see that Pity Wood would never survive as a livestock farm alone. That was quite perceptive of them, you know. I mean, it's obvious to everyone now, but in those days a lot of the old farmers were just crossing their fingers and hoping things would pick up. Most of them couldn't face the idea of changing their way of life. A farm like Pity Wood, that's been in the same family for generations – well, it would take someone very forward-looking to see what was necessary at such an early stage. From what I've heard of Raymond Sutton, he doesn't seem that sort of person. He's very traditional.'

'It would have to be Derek, then. He was the younger brother, after all.'

'Maybe,' said Cooper. 'How old would Derek have been at the time?'

Fry did a quick calculation. 'Fifty-six when Tom Farnham came into the business.'

'Mmm. I think we should ask Farnham how he met the Suttons. Did they invite him into the business, or did he do a sales pitch on them?'

'You think he might be some kind of con man?' asked Fry.

'I think the Sutton brothers might have been an easy target for a clever talker.'

'Would that fit your assessment of him?'

'Possibly,' said Cooper.

'By the way, did you get anything from the IND?'

'Hold on, let me check my notes.' Cooper flicked back through his notebook. 'OK, Section 8 of the Asylum and Immigration Act. The law makes it a criminal offence to employ a person who is subject to immigration controls and has no permission to work in the UK. The only statutory defence is if the employer can show that they carried out checks on the documents of potential employees. The confusing area seems to be the A8 countries, Diane.'

'The accession states.'

'Yes. The Czech Republic, Lithuania, Estonia, Poland, Hungary, Slovakia, Latvia and Slovenia. Individuals from those countries are entitled to come to the UK and work, but they have to register with the Home Office. Once you've been working legally in the UK for twelve months you have full rights of free movement and you no longer need to be on the Worker Registration Scheme.'

'Twelve months?'

'It's a critical time period, isn't it?'

'Absolutely.'

'The thing is, some employees don't bother. It works well for the larger firms, but not for the smaller ones who employ a couple of people. And this isn't exactly Bernard Matthews.'

'The turkey man?'

'My contact says Bernard Matthews employs a thousand Portuguese workers in Great Yarmouth. But that's a different kettle of fish. There are translators, bi-lingual trainers, everything done right. Small-scale employers are the problem. The paperwork is too much trouble for them, not to mention the cost. I imagine a lot of small farmers might think they can get away without paying seventy pounds to apply for a certificate.

Besides, there's the forgery issue. A worker brings along a standard letter from the Immigration Service and a forged passport, and a small employer doesn't look twice. I was told to watch out for Ernest Xavier Ample.'

'Who on earth is Ernest Xavier Ample?'

'E.X. Ample,' said Cooper. 'It's the made-up name the forgers take off sample work permits. No imagination, some people. Or perhaps they think it's a normal English name.'

'For heaven's sake. So we could be looking at a procession of Slovaks, Lithuanians and Latvians passing through Pity Wood?'

'Something like that,' said Cooper. 'Many of them might have gone on to be legit later, though, if they changed employers.'

'Are there any gaps in the farm records? Periods that aren't accounted for?'

'No, but the accounts don't come right up to date, of course. They end nine months ago. There was a period of time after Raymond Sutton gave up the farm and before the builders moved in. Only a few months, but it might just be in our time frame.'

'And the farm was empty for that time?' asked Fry.

'Yes, and I bet there were plenty of people around Rakedale who knew it.'

'Damn it, that doesn't help us at all. Unless forensics can give us some evidence to narrow down the time of death, we're going to have to concentrate on identifying the victims and establishing a link between them.'

'Anyway, the most recent enterprise at Pity Wood seems to have been a poultry business,' said Cooper. 'That can be quite viable, I believe. But it's no wonder the Suttons' enterprise failed. They weren't producing enough birds to make a realistic profit. It was hardly worth their while running the sheds.'

'Is there much expense involved in raising poultry?'

'A lot of overheads when the birds are housed indoors – heating, bedding, all their feed and antibiotics. But the main

149

cost here seems to have been the wage bill. The way the Suttons ran the enterprise must have been pretty labour intensive. No capital to invest in machinery, I suppose.'

'Or the way Tom Farnham ran it.'

'Yes.'

'So what about the wages? There must be a list of employees' names?'

'No, damn it,' said Cooper. 'Just initials. No indication of who they were, what they did, whether they were male or female. The only fact I can work out is that they seem to have employed a dozen people at any one time. But the initials change quite often, so the turnover of staff must have been quite high. It was unpleasant work, I suppose – killing, plucking and gutting.'

Cooper gazed out of the window, trying to make the facts fit. How did the number of workers represented by these wage bills correlate with the output from the poultry production units? Well, the answer was that it didn't. Those workers must either have been sitting around doing nothing for a large part of their time – or they must have been doing something else entirely.

14

By the middle of the afternoon, the low sun was painting more colour into the landscape. As Cooper left West Street and drove down the hill into the centre of Edendale, the clouds over the eastern hills were developing yellow and pink tinges, and the moors were no longer such a dingy brown.

Friday was market day in Edendale. There were crowds doing their pre-Christmas shopping among the market stalls. Stout men with ruddy faces and waistcoats, tall men with long white sideburns, women in tweed skirts and headscarves – the sort of people you never saw at any other time, even in Edendale. It was almost as if they were employed by the council to give an authentic Dickensian flavour to the town for the festive season. Or perhaps they were members of some esoteric club, the Pickwick Papers Re-enactment Society.

But Cooper knew that was his new, town-dwelling self speaking. He knew who they were – these were the small hill farmers, the inhabitants of the more isolated homesteads, who travelled into town for market day.

By the time he reached the market square, it was already nearly four o'clock, and the market was being packed up for the end of the day. A procession of Ford Transits and Renault Trafics squeezed through the side streets, blocking every access

151

while they loaded. Some of the stalls were clearing rapidly, their owners anxious to get home to their fires. Others took longer, stallholders staggering backwards and forwards in green and red Santa hats, shouting banter to each other. 'I can manage on my own, don't worry about me, I'll be all right. You're too old to be carrying these heavy boxes.'

Cooper found an empty slot to park the Toyota, thinking smugly that it wouldn't have been quite so easy if he'd arrived in town an hour earlier. From here, he could easily walk the half mile to The Oaks.

He passed the town hall, its façade boasting four decorative pillars. The building had been edged with stones carved in a wavy pattern, and there were so many of them that local people had nicknamed their town hall 'The Wavy House'.

His feet tangled for a second in the tattered remains of some party poppers discarded on the pavement. Office parties would be going everywhere tonight, as they had been last night – and would be tomorrow night too, of course. By the morning, council workers could expect to have far more than a few party poppers to clear up.

Within minutes of him arriving, the streetlights were coming on, and it was dark in the corners of the market square. Workers were stripping the awnings and dismantling the tubular steel stalls, clanging and chattering, wheeling racks of clothes over the cobbles. The dipped headlights of cars swept by from the roundabout. A tractor came towards him with a yellow warning light flashing, towing a trailer to collect the dismantled stalls.

When he entered the lounge at The Oaks to see Raymond Sutton, the other residents fell silent, watching him. He supposed they thought he was just a visitor. Perhaps they took him for Raymond's grandson or something. They'd be asking Raymond questions about him as soon as he left. With a sinking certainty, Cooper thought it was probably that some of these old dears never got a visitor of their own from one year to the next.

The Oaks reminded him of the Old Vicarage, the nursing home his own mother had been in towards the end. On the surface, there weren't all that many similarities. Residents of The Oaks were just old and needed some help with their day-to-day living. They were the frail and forgetful, the tired and confused, the ones who just couldn't cope and had no one to look after them. They probably went on outings and had bingo evenings and sing-songs. Isabel Cooper had never had any need for those things.

'We've had a bit of an issue with Raymond this afternoon,' said the care assistant, Elaine, when she let him in. 'He got a bit upset.'

'What was wrong?'

'It's difficult to say. We have a couple of care workers here who are from Lithuania. They're nice girls, but Raymond doesn't like it when they speak to him. I think it's because he doesn't understand them properly. It must be awful not to understand what's going on.'

'I feel like that myself sometimes.'

'He's all right now, anyway. He soon calms down.'

'Does Mr Sutton have any old photo albums, do you know?' asked Cooper. 'Photos from his time at the farm?'

'Not that I know of. Only women keep photo albums, don't they? I can't see Raymond sitting around in the evening sticking pictures of family weddings and christenings into an album.'

Now that he looked at Raymond Sutton more closely in the light, Cooper could see that the old man's skin was dry, and faintly yellow. He was reminded of the kitchen at Pity Wood Farm, the tint of the walls and the smoky stains on the ceiling. Mr Sutton would have fitted into the Yellow Room naturally, almost as if he'd decorated it in his own image.

Perhaps some kind of liver problem had caused this unhealthy colour. He made a note to ask one of the staff about Mr Sutton's physical health. Heartless as it might seem, no investigation team wanted their chief witness dying before he could provide a full statement.

Chief witness? Raymond Sutton might yet turn out to be the principal suspect. All the more reason to be concerned about his health.

'Do you remember me, sir? I'm Detective Constable Cooper, from Edendale Police. I came to see you the other day, with my inspector.'

'I don't get many visitors, lad,' said Sutton. 'How would I forget?'

Cooper mentally crossed his fingers that Mr Sutton was having a good spell. If he believed he couldn't forget, that was a positive sign, wasn't it?

'Don't you have any family left, Mr Sutton?'

'Some cousins in Stoke. They might get my money when I go, but they won't get the farm, will they?'

'No, you've already sold the farm.'

Cooper sat alongside him.

'Your brother died, didn't he? Derek?'

'Aye. He's gone over, has Derek.'

'That was before you sold the farm, Mr Sutton.'

The old man nodded slowly. 'We could see he was tappy already by then.'

'Tappy?' repeated Cooper.

'Approaching his end.'

Cooper searched his memory for the word, and came up with an image of a wounded animal going to ground in the woods to die.

'Sir, did anyone else die at the farm? Women?'

'Women?'

'Did some women die?'

Sutton looked at him closely. 'Are you a Christian?'

'Yes, of course.'

'A proper Christian?'

154

'Yes, sir.'

He genuinely felt it was true. But Cooper hoped he wouldn't be asked when he last went to church on a Sunday. Like many people he knew, he'd got out of the habit. Weddings, funerals and christenings – that was about it these days. His mother had been the one keen on church attendance, so he and Matt and Claire had always gone to St Aidan's regularly as children. Sunday school, too. Bible stories and choir practice, Whit walks and visits by the Church Army with their free badges. But he suspected that had been as much because it was the respectable thing to do, rather than on account of any particular devoutness on his mother's part.

It was probably that factor that led him to be a bit facetious sometimes when other people's beliefs seemed to be just *too* extreme.

'So you know that Hell burns,' said Sutton. 'Hell burns with an agony like no other.'

'Yes, sir. And there's no butter in Hell.'

Sutton stared at him, failing to smile at the joke, failing even to get the allusion. Cooper immediately wished he could take the words back. He felt embarrassed, realizing that Raymond Sutton might never have been the type for reading books, except one. Certainly not shamefully disrespectful parodies like *Cold Comfort Farm*.

Still, his brain kept throwing up images from the Gibbons book. The preacher, Amos Starkadder, hectoring the Church of the Quivering Brethren – '*Ye're all damned!*' And Brother Ambleforth, whose job was to lead the quivering, conducting the congregation with a poker to put them all in mind of hellfire.

Cooper wondered irreverently whether Raymond Sutton might get into the role on Christmas Day, if asked to pull a cracker by one of the female residents. '*Hush, woman . . . Tempt me not wi' motters and paper caps. Hell is paved wi' such.*'

155

'So you're like me, and you don't believe in evil spirits?' asked Sutton suddenly.

'What? Ghosts, you mean?'

'Not ghosts so much. More of . . . well, perhaps a presence in the atmosphere of the house.'

'I'm not sure. Perhaps, in certain circumstances.'

'When something dreadful has happened.'

'Yes.'

'Have you been to the old house?'

'Yes, Mr Sutton.'

'I always swore I wouldn't take anything away from the place. I wanted it all burned, destroyed. I wanted someone to come in with a bulldozer and a big bloody skip, and cart it all off. It was cursed.'

'Yes, sir.'

Sutton looked at him, working his mouth nervously. 'There was one thing, though. There was the good book. Our family Bible.'

'I saw it,' said Cooper.

The old man gripped his arm. 'Is it still there?'

'Do you want me to see if I can get it for you?'

'Yes.' His grip relaxed, to Cooper's relief. 'Can you do that?'

'I'll have to ask my supervisor. But I'm sure it's still safe.'

'Thank you. You're a good lad, coming to see me.'

'Mr Sutton, I need to ask you about any employees you had on the farm in the last four years.'

'Employees?'

'You had a poultry production business. Do you remember the birds?'

Cooper noticed his voice rising, the way people's voices did when they were talking to someone who was deaf or stupid, or foreign. Was Raymond Sutton deaf? There was no sign of a hearing aid, but that proved nothing. Small items like hearing aids and spectacles went missing very easily in residential care homes. False teeth too, sometimes.

'We raised poultry, yes. We had thousands in the big sheds,' said Sutton. 'Did you want to buy some birds? You're too late. We got rid of them. All the lot.'

'No, I want to ask you about your employees. Can you remember the names of anyone who worked for you at the farm during that time? During the last four years?'

Sutton hummed quietly. It occurred to Cooper that he might not actually know what year it was now, so the question might be meaningless.

'I brought the farm records book,' he said. 'It might bring back memories. See if you can think of a few names to go with these initials, look.'

Sutton glanced at the book for a moment, and sighed. 'The service round here is terrible. I'd kill for a cup of tea.'

As he signed himself out at the door a few minutes later, Elaine smiled at him.

'Was Raymond a bit better?'

'Yes, a bit. I was trying to jog his memory.'

'It works sometimes. He's a bit unpredictable. It depends how tired he is.'

Cooper looked at the collection of old ladies on their chairs in front of the TV set.

'Some of the residents will be going home to their families for Christmas, I suppose?' he asked her.

'Yes, some. But not all.'

'Are a few of them too ill to leave?'

'Yes, and then there are those who don't have families. Well, not families who want to see them at Christmas, anyway.'

'I see.'

Cooper stood outside for a few minutes, looking at the windows of The Oaks. He had no idea when family and community had started to fall apart, but he had a feeling his grandparents wouldn't have recognized society the way it was now. In their time, old folk had been looked after, instead of being allowed to spend their final years abandoned and alone. He had known, deep down, that the disintegration of family life was happening everywhere – not just in the big cities, but right here in the villages that had always relied so much on a sense of community.

Of course, he saw the results every day among the people he had to deal with in his job. Children running out of control on the streets, young people walking away from home to lives full of drugs and destitution. Single mothers everywhere, trying to raise families on their own. Mentally disturbed individuals who either lived outside society, or ended up in prison. Old people dying, neglected, their deaths unnoticed for months by their family or neighbours, or even by the postman. It would never have happened at one time, he was sure.

Of course, people had died for quite different reasons back then.

Back in the town centre, the streets were full of light – the white bulbs of the Christmas trees attached to the buildings, the occasional orange streetlamp, the light from shop windows falling on the pavements. Beneath the lights, the last stragglers were on their way to the car parks, some of them setting off across the county after a day at the cattle market. School children were hanging around outside the chip shops with their friends, celebrating the last day of term.

The hotel on the square had a stream of smoke drifting from one of its chimneys, and a flashing tree in an upper window. It was a better display than the official tree in the park across the way. A yellow Sixes bus went by, the slogan 'Be a dirty stop-out' on the back.

It was really going cold now, and Cooper thought he felt the first touch of rain.

That night, Matt took his brother to their local pub, the Queen Anne. It was one of the oldest pubs in the Peak District, dating back to the early seventeenth century, it was said, and reputedly haunted by the friendly ghost of a landlord who died in the cellar tending his ales. But all the best pubs had at least one ghost, didn't they?

The wooden bar was stained black, and a line of stools stood in front of it. The food at the Queen Anne was traditional enough to satisfy even Matt – home-made steak-and-ale pie, haddock and chips, chicken and chips, T-bone steak. There was practically dancing in the streets when T-bone steak came back on the menu after the BSE scare. The doom mongers had predicted it was gone for ever – eating meat off the bone being considered far too risky for men who spent their days operating high-powered machinery with sharp blades and handling bad-tempered animals that could kill with a single kick.

Ales were served on a rotation basis, and tonight the bar boasted Barnsley Bitter, Ale Force from the Storm Brewery at Macclesfield, and Towns of Chesterfield. Even a cask-strength whisky. Enough to drown your sorrows, whatever they might be. But a pint of Towns would suit, for now. It was good to get out of the rain.

'I'll get the first round in,' Matt said.

'I won't argue.'

Cooper noticed they'd introduced lamb Madras to the menu at the Queen Anne. There were two bars, one that had been a smoking area until the ban came in. Like himself, Matt had never smoked, but would probably have liked to see the smoking bar retained. Tradition again? Or a stubborn fondness for dangerous activities?

Ben remembered their great uncle, who had farmed all his life, explaining that a farmer's life and the lives of his animals followed an annual cycle that moved with the seasons and was influenced by natural elements, such as the weather.

'Not these days,' said Matt sourly, when he was reminded

159

of it. 'More like influenced by the price of milk and the latest EU regulations.'

An old milk churn stood near the doorway under an ancient stone lintel, and log fires burned in both bars. In the summer they often preferred to sit outside at one of the picnic tables in the garden, admiring the hills or watching the gliders pass overhead. But Matt wasn't in a mood to notice the scenery, even if it had been daylight.

'Some of the people who live in these villages now are on a different planet from what we are. If you meet people down at the postbox or in the pub, they don't relate to what you're doing at all. Their work and life experiences are so different from ours. They think we're either mad or quaint.'

That night, the pub was filled with people in various stages of saturation and evaporation. It was like a Turkish bath where everyone had forgotten to take their clothes off. You couldn't get near the fire for piles of drenched cagoules and plastic over-trousers.

'It's sheer ignorance. They think we're all either grain barons or peasants.'

The smell of cooked food mingled with the steam from drying clothes, like the aroma from the kitchens of some exotic restaurant. If he closed his eyes, Cooper could imagine a genuine curry being prepared in the background, hot with cayenne and spiced with interesting herbs.

'You know Geoff Weeks at One Ash? He has Right to Roam over part of his farm. Some ramblers complained about finding a dead sheep on his land the other day. They rang the police, even – can you believe it?'

Ben wanted to say that, yes, he could believe it. You only had to spend half an hour in the Call Reception Centre to get an idea of the complaints from the public that call handlers had to deal with. Three thousand of them a day. Litter on the pavement, birds stuck up trees. A dead sheep was nothing.

160

Sometimes the actual nature of the incident wasn't clear until response officers arrived at the scene.

But he said nothing, preferring not to interrupt Matt when he was getting things off his chest.

'If you've got five hundred ewes,' said Matt, 'and you run them until they're seven or eight crop, the way Geoff does, then a certain percentage of them are going to die. It's a fact of life, isn't it?'

Ben nodded. Yes, death was certainly a fact of life in the countryside. It was one of the things that urban dwellers didn't appreciate. These days, they ran special coach trips from the cities to give townies a chance to smell the difference between a cow and sheep. But you didn't know about the omnipresence of death until you lived here.

Usually, a mention of the word 'diversification' was enough to spark a rant on its own. Tonight, Matt was abnormally subdued.

'I don't know if you remember Jack Firth, over near Chapel. It turns out he'd been running a nice little sideline, killing and burying unwanted greyhounds on his land. The rules say unwanted dogs should be euthanized by a vet, but breeders and trainers find that too expensive. It was much cheaper to use Jack's services.'

'What's your point, Matt?'

'He was meeting a demand, you see. It's what the government wants us to do, find new ways of exploiting our assets, and providing services the public actually wants. Jack told me there are twenty-five thousand unwanted dogs produced every year by the greyhound racing business – dogs at the end of their racing lives, or that have never been particularly good in the first place. The rescue centres could never cope with that number, so Jack had found a niche market. His business would have been safe for years to come.'

'Was he found out?'

'Yes. But there was no evidence of cruel or inhumane

treatment of the animals. Even when he was arrested, he could only be charged with failing to obtain the proper licences. He didn't fill in the forms for the bureaucrats. So now he's a criminal.'

It wasn't quite what Ben had expected. But he could see that Matt had found an example of diversification that he'd be using for years to come, as a warning to others. Best to change the subject a bit.

'Can you see a future for the girls?' he asked. 'They'll want to go off and do their own thing when they grow up, won't they?'

'Well, I'd like at least one of them to be involved in farming. Our family have been farmers since the year dot.'

'I know, Matt.'

'I should think it's ever since farming has existed. All right, the younger brothers and sisters have always had other jobs, like you. But if they haven't had a farm themselves they've always been involved in some way. There's got to be a couple of cows or a few sheep – it's just a way of life. But young people need to believe they can make a living from farming, and they want to get some respect. Farmers feel like they're regarded as the dregs. We can't do anything right.' He paused to take a long swig of beer. 'And there are the marts.'

'You mean Ashbourne?'

Ben knew the closure of Ashbourne cattle mart had been a blow for local farmers, though there was still Bakewell, and even Uttoxeter over the border in Staffordshire.

'That's just the latest,' said Matt. 'Those farmers in isolated locations look forward to market as a chance for a trip out, to meet people with similar problems. The only other person we talk to much is the bank manager. When the rest of the local marts go, that'll be it, Ben. That'll be it for livestock farming in this county.'

'Oh, come on, Matt.'

'No, I'm telling you the truth. In ten years' time, I'll either still be farming, or drawing the social, and that's a fact. There was an article in the *Farmers Guardian* a while ago that said we'd see the end of small farms by 2010.'

'There are still a few left, though.'

'Aye, a few.'

Cooper was silent for a moment, savouring his Towns, letting its flavour wash away the strange chemical taste that seemed to have settled at the back of his throat since he'd first visited Pity Wood Farm.

'Do you really think it will happen, Matt?' he asked.

'I'm damn certain it will. I think it's all planned out some-where. In London or in Brussels, I don't know. But I reckon there's a dossier sitting in some bureaucrat's desk drawer right now, showing the target date for the closure of the last small hill farm. They've got our fate worked out, and there'll be nothing we can do about it.'

'Nothing? You could start planning for it now, couldn't you?'

'Oh, yes? You try coming in exhausted after a long day and sitting down to do the government's bloody paperwork. Then see how much time you have to start planning your future. Not to mention trying to spend a bit of time with your family. You see, that's the trouble with us farmers. We've got this suicidal urge to farm. If we were sane, we'd have said "sod it" by now.'

Cooper felt a familiar niggle of worry about his brother surface at the back of his mind. He'd suffered severe spells of despondency himself, and he knew what it was like when things looked really black and the future held no hope. There was such a temptation to consider the easy way out, the one that would take all those burdens off your shoulders in an instant.

He could only hope and pray that the tendency wasn't present in his brother, at least not to any greater degree. Matt had seen this happen to people he knew – too many of them, over the years. The highest rates of suicide in the UK were among farmers. They became very attached to their patch of land and could find it hard to cope, particularly when a problem such as foot and mouth occurred.

It was one of the saving factors about farming that you were always looking to the future – anticipating the next harvest, or the next lambing season. The work you did today would bear fruit in five months' time. It was quite different from living on a day-to-day basis, when every week was the same and nothing was likely to change.

But if that optimism about the future was taken away, then farmers like Matt would have nothing to keep them going.

'Are we going to have another drink?'

Matt thumped his empty glass down. 'Why not?'

Ben drained his Towns and got up to go to the bar. After a day like this, he did start to wonder who the sane ones were. Maybe, in the end, it was the likes of Diane Fry who could see the future most clearly, and had it all worked out. Fry's attitude was the real sanity. Well, perhaps.

With mounting, irrational rage, Fry stared at the contents of the box she'd lifted from beneath the loose floorboard. Diamorphine hydrochloride. Pharmaceutically prepared heroin, freeze dried in glass ampoules for injection into the wrist.

She'd heard about this use of diamorphine. Low-profile trial schemes had been taking place around the country for some time. Because it came in measured doses, you knew exactly how much you were taking, and you could function perfectly well. That was the theory, anyway. It was heroin on the NHS. And at a cost to the taxpayer, she'd heard, of about ten thousand pounds a year per addict.

Fry knew there were very few pure, one-drug addicts. Heroin users took crack, and vice versa. No one had suggested prescribing crack on the NHS yet, but she supposed it could happen. On the street, women could earn between a hundred and two hundred pounds a night. And in many cases, it all went on gear. A heroin habit took a lot of feeding.

She sat down suddenly on the bed, feeling a powerful surge of guilt at having invaded her sister's privacy. She wanted to weep at the destructiveness of the emotions that had driven her to do it. Jealousy, bitterness, and fear. Their relationship couldn't be founded solely on a shared set of genes, could it? There had to be more to family than this endless anger and suspicion.

But Fry looked at the boxes on the floor. And immediately the fury swept over her again in a stomach-churning tide, too powerful to resist.

To her certain knowledge, there was no diamorphine trial taking place in Edendale for local addicts. So where had her sister been going? Where was Angie obtaining her supplies?

15

Cooper knew it wasn't going to be a good day as soon as he entered the CID room and set eyes on Gavin Murfin. Somehow, Murfin was able to arrange his features into a picture of abject misery. Martyrdom and gloom were written all over him this morning. It was enough to shrivel the tinsel.

'What's the matter, Gavin?'

'I've been put down for duty over Christmas. All thanks to this job at Rakedale. I'm really going to be in the dog house, I can tell you.'

Cooper took off his jacket and sat down at his desk. 'I'll swap with you.'

Murfin looked up. 'What?'

'I'll swap duties with you, Gavin. No one will mind. As long as someone's around to deal with anything that crops up. Then you can have Christmas at home with your family, and everyone's happy, right?'

'But what about you?'

Cooper shrugged. 'It's not so important for me. I don't have kids.'

'Even so. They'll be expecting you at Bridge End on Christmas Day. Your lot always have a big family get-together,

166

don't they? You've told me about it often enough. Brothers and sisters and aunts and uncles, and hordes of little nephews and nieces.'

'There aren't that many, Gavin. Besides, it'll be different this year. It's the first year Mum won't be there.'

'Oh, right. Yeah, that could be a bit tough, I suppose. So you'd rather come into the office than be at the farm, would you? Sure?'

'I'll be all right. I won't mind being busy.'

Murfin studied him for a moment. 'Hang on, though. What about Liz?'

'She's going home to her own family in Stoke.'

'And you're not invited?'

Cooper felt himself starting to get a bit irritated by Murfin's selflessness. 'It's OK, Gavin, really. I want to swap. I'll do Christmas duty.'

'Well, all right. Will you tell Miss, or shall I?'

'I'd better do it, I think. By the way, what are you buying your kids for Christmas, Gavin?'

'The eldest is really into computer games.'

'I like The Sims,' said Cooper.

'I'm a bit worried about that one, in case the wife gets hold of it.'

'Sorry?'

'Well, they say there's the thing about women who play The Sims. They use it to exercise their cruel streak, and have fun tormenting small, helpless creatures. They make them live in houses with no toilets. They lock them in rooms with no doors and windows and see how long it takes them to go mad.'

'Is that so?'

'If I didn't know better, I'd think it was designed by our DS.'

No matter how long the morning briefing had been allowed to run on, it would not have been capable of providing a

167

satisfactory conclusion. There was no lucid narrative to the deaths of the two victims at Pity Wood Farm, no story of their lives to give them an identity. Apart from confirmation that they were both female, they still had no humanity.

Every officer present in the room was conscious of the lack of information, the gaping hole in their enquiry, the blockage that was stalling it before it had even got going. No IDs.

Cooper always felt a particular sense of despair at these cases. Of course, there were many people who lived transient lives. They put down their roots in shallow soil. Unnoticed when they arrived, and unmissed when they left.

'First of all, there's no evidence of major trauma, no broken bones,' said Hitchens, getting straight to the main issue. 'Some poisons might show up in the hair mat that had sloughed off the first victim. But if death was due to injury to the soft tissues, we're right out of luck.'

'Parts of the first body looked almost . . . mummified,' said someone.

'That's adipocere. We don't see mummified body parts very often in this part of the world – you need a dry, arid climate for that.'

The list of potential evidence dug out by the forensic anthropology team was impressive. During the excavation, they'd packaged up forty-four bones, two dirt samples, twenty-nine bags labelled 'unknown debris', fifteen bags of clothing fragments, and seventeen teeth.

'Yes, they've been dead for about a year and four years respectively, we're told, but neither of them was necessarily killed where they were found,' said Hitchens. 'Or even buried there when they first died. Apparently, the scene is right on a geological boundary – the clay on the south side of Pity Wood Farm doesn't extend into the fields to the north or east. It's probably why the place was built there in the first place. Historically, I imagine there was a brickworks, or a clay pit.'

'It's almost certainly how the farm got its name,' said Cooper.

'Pity Wood, because there were several clay pits here, in the woods. Obviously, most of the trees have gone now, too. They would have needed the wood for firing kilns.'

'What about dental records, sir?' asked Fry.

'OK, we have good dentition remaining on the more recent of the two bodies. Enough to confirm an identity from dental records. If we had a potential identity to confirm, of course. But at the moment we haven't a clue who she is.'

'Mrs van Doon said there was an unusual amount of decay to the victim's teeth.'

'Yes. When I said "good dentition", I didn't mean to suggest her teeth were in good condition. I mean we have a good profile of her teeth, and any dental work, plus the unusual condition. This gives us a better chance of making a positive identification.'

'Understood.'

'As for the second victim, this individual is also female. What more can I tell you?'

'There was a shoe,' said Cooper. 'That could give us a lead, at least.'

'But the shoe wasn't found *on* the victim, it was lying in the soil about five yards away from the body. Without a direct connection to the victim, it isn't a known piece of evidence. It could have landed up there some other way.'

Hitchens looked around the group. 'Now I'm going to hand over to our consultant forensic anthropologist, Dr Pat Jamieson, who is going to fill us in on some of the details.'

Murfin groaned dramatically, as if he'd been shot. Despite himself, Cooper couldn't help laughing.

'Superintendent Branagh has expressed a firm view on this,' said Hitchens, as if he'd anticipated resistance. 'She thinks we should be fully briefed by the forensic specialists. We ought to make full use of their expertise while we have them on the payroll, so to speak. The superintendent believes we'll all benefit from the insight.'

Murfin was making noises as though he was going to be sick. Hitchens looked at him.

'And she emphasized that it should be the *whole* team.'

When Dr Jamieson entered, he looked as surprised as anyone to be sitting in a meeting room with a bunch of DCs who thought they had better things to do. Cooper wondered who had twisted his arm. The mysterious Superintendent Branagh, perhaps?

Jamieson rallied bravely, despite the chilly atmosphere. He became professional after he'd set up his laptop and screen, and began his presentation.

'Well, there are four things we might hope to establish from decomposed or skeletalized remains,' he said. 'Sex, race, age and stature.'

'And cause of death?' suggested someone hopefully.

Jamieson turned to Hitchens. 'Inspector, you know I can't address –'

'Yes, I know. Carry on, Doctor.'

The anthropologist hesitated. 'I see. Well, let's press on. First comes sex.'

He seemed to notice Gavin Murfin's expression out of the corner of his eye and hastily amended his words.

'Ah . . . first comes gender. As a rule, it's easy to determine gender in adults if the remains include the pelvic bones. The pelvis of a woman is generally broader than that of a man. It has to be wider in females because it surrounds the birth canal, and a baby's head has to pass between the bones of the pubis. Without the pubis, the probability of making a correct identification of gender declines. Generally it comes down to size differences, but there's a certain amount of overlap in the middle. There are approximately ten per cent of individuals who confuse the middle ground.'

'We do have some very large young women walking around Edendale.'

'It's not a question of obesity,' said Jamieson, 'but of height, the width of the shoulders, the density of the bone . . .'

'And in this case . . .'

'In both cases, the pelvis was clearly female. It was obvious even in the field. For both Victim A and Victim B, the pelvis is broader at the hips, with a raised sacro-iliac joint, a wide sciatic notch, a greater sub-pubic angle. All part of the geometry of birth. The skull can also be a help, but of course . . .'

'We don't have two skulls.'

'Not for Victim B. No, we don't.'

Jamieson paused, allowing for more questions. 'Now, race is a question we're often asked to pronounce on. But it's getting more difficult. Some characteristics of particular populations are evident in the skeleton, but there's a lot of variation, even within groups that are historically pure. In the case of Victim A, we have the hair mat, which had sloughed off the skull. As you can see from the first picture, it's very dark brown and slightly wavy. That, plus the shape of the teeth, mark the victim as white, where the discoloured skin might have been misleading.'

'And Victim . . . I mean, the second woman?' said Fry.

'We can't be sure, Sergeant. Completely skeletalized remains, and the absence of a skull – well, I'm sorry, but . . .'

'OK.'

'Now, age. By the time a person reaches the age of twenty, most bone growth is complete, the epiphyses are united and most teeth are fully calcified. So we look at several different structures: skull sutures, clavicles, pelvis.'

Jamieson presented another series of photographs on the screen.

'In Victim A, the bones of the pelvis were dense and smooth, with a marked absence of grain; the bones of a mature but young woman. Her clavicles had not fully matured, and the basilar structure in the skull was only partly fused, an indicator that she was not yet twenty-five. Factoring all the indicators together, I'm confident that Victim A was somewhere between twenty and twenty-five.

Victim B is a little older, fully matured. Without the skull, it's difficult, but I'd say between twenty-five and thirty.'

'Height, Doctor?'

'To estimate height, we turn to bone measurements and regression equations.' He seemed to sense the shuffling and muttering. 'Yes, I know it sounds like scientific jargon. What it means is that we can predict stature from the length of the femur, for example. Multiply by one number, add another, and bingo. For Victim A, length of the left femur is forty-four centimetres. Using the stature calculation formulas, we estimate she stood between five feet one and a half inches and five feet four and a half.'

A few officers were at least making notes, having detected some facts in the doctor's presentation.

'And the skeleton?' someone asked.

'Yes, Victim B. You'd think we could just lay a skeleton out and measure it to get the victim's height. But cartilage decays and shrinks after death, sometimes by several inches. In Victim B's case, the femur is forty-eight centimetres, giving a height of between five feet six and a half inches and five feet nine and a half inches.'

'How accurate are these ages and measurements, Doctor?'

'I'm confident the estimates are accurate, within the parameters I've given you. But I'd like to urge the police officers present to be careful with their missing person reports when trying to make a match. Don't assume any degree of accuracy there.'

'Why not?'

'Well, a lot of people don't actually know how tall they are. Or they lie about it. Some would like to be a few inches taller, others a bit less tall. And of course, they don't realize that their height changes when they age, so they can be giving the wrong height for themselves for years without knowing it. Besides, if you're looking at a missing person report, ask yourself who provided the information? A spouse, a friend? Some of those figures could just be a wild guess.'

Jamieson took advantage of the silence he'd created to press on hurriedly with his final point.

'And how long have the remains been buried, you'll ask me. Well, an unembalmed adult body buried unprotected in ordinary soil will normally take ten to twelve years to decompose down to a skeleton. Burial depth and soil temperature might vary the decomposition rate. A body in air decomposes eight times faster than when buried.' He looked up from his laptop. 'Like Detective Constable Cooper's dead sheep.'

Gavin Murfin laughed, but no one else seemed to understand the joke. The anthropologist moved on rapidly.

'When bodies are exposed to cool, moist soil, the soft tissues can decay quite slowly and turn into adipocere. Adipocere is a soapy, greasy substance that forms when body fat decomposes in a damp environment. It's sometimes called grave wax. Adipocere is the cheesy greyish-white mass you can see in this photograph.'

Yes, they could see it quite clearly on the photographs. Some of the officers looked away for a moment, but forced themselves to turn back. Jamieson left the most revolting photograph on screen while he finished off.

'Adipocere inhibits putrefying bacteria, so when a body reaches this state of decomposition it might stay that way for several years before it decomposes any further. There was a large quantity of adipocere beneath the chest and abdominal regions in the case of Victim A. So I would say you have the cold, wet soil of Rakedale to thank for the relatively intact condition of this body. If I might offer a very non-scientific comment, it's almost as though Victim A has been waiting in her half-decomposed state for someone to find her.'

Jamieson smiled as he diverged from his professional approach for a moment. He waited for comments, but none came.

'Finally, then,' he said. 'There was no sign of trauma on either victim – no fractures, cut marks, or signs of perimortem damage on any of the bones we've recovered. But we don't

173

have every bone for Victim B. As we've already mentioned, there is no skull. And, before any of us run away with assumptions, I should mention that it's very common for the head to come off when a body disarticulates. With the skull, we have one of the heaviest parts of the skeletal structure, supported by one of the most fragile.'

The anthropologist finished with a flourish, closing his laptop and waving his arms in a graphic gesture.

'To put it plainly, ladies and gentlemen, if you left a body out on a slope to decompose – the head might just roll away.'

Cooper had been considering the anthropologist's presentation as the rest of the team dispersed and went about their tasks for the day.

'Diane, do you think we could analyse the chemical content of the bones to get an angle on her origins?' he said. 'I've heard that it's possible.'

'You know we don't have facilities for anything like that, Ben.'

'But the FSS might. Or a university somewhere.'

'It would take months and months. And besides –'

'– it would cost a lot of money. I know.'

'Think budgets, Ben. The fact is, this will probably remain an unsolved case.'

'No. You're joking.'

'If there were any leads at all, any sure indication of a cause of death that suggested murder, or even a confirmed ID that we could work with . . . But, as it is, we have nothing. We could faff around here for months and still have nothing.'

'We can't just leave it, with these two women unidentified.'

'We might have to,' said Fry.

'No.'

'Look, how many cases have you got on your desk at the moment, Ben?'

'Well . . .'

'Five, six? A dozen? Wouldn't you stand more chance of getting results if you spent your time on some of those? I bet there are people shouting for statements and case files.'

'Yes, there are. There *always* are. You know that.'

'Well, then.'

Cooper was silent. He could see that Fry thought she'd won the argument by sheer, unassailable logic. Budgets, and case loads. Who could argue with those? It wouldn't be prudent to say what he was thinking right now.

Half an hour later, Gavin Murfin was able to spring a surprise on his colleagues in the CID room.

'By the way,' he said. 'I see Derek Sutton had a criminal record. I found him on the PNC.'

Fry sat up with sudden interest. 'Oh?'

'Illegal fuel. He was using laundered red diesel.'

'A typical rural crime.'

Cooper walked over to Murfin's desk and looked at the file.

'A prosecution was brought against Derek Sutton by HM Customs and Excise, following a spot check at the cattle market in Ashbourne. A hefty fine. That was an expensive day out for him.'

Red diesel was normally used in farm machinery, and it was illegal to use it in road vehicles, because it wasn't taxed. To evade detection, the more enterprising removed the red dye, producing what was called laundered diesel. The Customs and Excise checks would show that up. But Sutton had only been charged with use, not with laundering. He must have known of a source somewhere. Probably everyone did.

'The Hydrocarbon Oil Duties Act,' said Fry. '"*Certain vehicles are exempt from normal fuel duties as they are primarily used off-road and normal road use is only incidental.*"'

As always, Cooper was impressed by the efficiency of her mental filing cabinet. He'd almost heard the correct drawer clicking open.

'Well remembered.'

'It's another subsidy for farmers,' she said. 'Enshrined in the law, no less. They pay less tax for their fuel than ordinary mortals.'

'Well, not really. If their farm vehicles never go on the road, they don't contribute to wear and tear, do they? And they don't use other facilities on the roads. So why should they be taxed for their maintenance and repair?'

'You won't convince me that they don't go on the roads. I've got trapped behind enough farm vehicles to know differently.'

Cooper shrugged. 'If I recollect the intelligence, Customs have suspected that a diesel-laundering plant might be operating in this area. Do you remember the operation that was closed down in Northern Ireland? It was being run from a converted hay shed at a remote farm.'

'Like I said, a typical rural crime. These people think they can get away with anything because nobody is watching over them.'

'You've really got it in for farmers at the moment, haven't you?' said Cooper. 'What's brought this on?'

'Spending time in Rakedale,' said Fry. 'It's enough to make anyone bitter and twisted.'

Cooper shook his head in despair. Fry was almost a lost cause. He would have to introduce her to Matt some time, and see what happened. The results would be interesting, if nothing else. Two jaundiced personalities clashing head-on. The thought was enough to make him shudder.

Tractors were the main agricultural vehicles to fall under the 'exempted' definition of the Act. The duty rate for rebated red diesel was about a tenth of the duty for normal road vehicles. In the Northern Ireland case, twelve large tanks had been used to take dye from red diesel and convert it into white diesel that could be used by motorists. The price difference was about two pounds per gallon, and forty thousand litres of fuel had been contained in storage tanks at that laundering unit on the farm in Northern Ireland. Good money to be made, then.

But it wasn't advisable from the motorist's point of view. Apart from the risk of prosecution, the acids used in the laundering process would wreck the fuel pumps in diesel engines, so buyers of cheap fuel ran the risk of causing long-term damage to their vehicles.

Much closer to home, Customs and Excise had dipped most of the tanks of people attending a horsey event at Chatsworth a while ago. They were looking for anyone 'running red'. C&E were wise to dual tanks and every other trick. They would also sample the fuel at the injectors and relied on chemical tracers. The dye could be removed with absorbents, but the tracers couldn't. And, if they caught you, the fines were big.

A few gallons in the four-by-four, or a few miles on the road to take some cattle to market in the pick-up now and then. They seemed like no big deal. But it would still mean a large fine if you were caught.

Cooper searched for details of the Irish case. From the farm, the raid had also recovered a generator, pumps, and storage equipment. In addition, thirty-seven tonnes of toxic contaminated sludge, the hazardous chemical residue of the laundering process, were cleared from the site, which had livestock and an inhabited farm dwelling nearby. Subsequent warnings had been issued about the damage caused by contamination to arable land and our water and rivers.

For some reason, Cooper was reminded of Raymond Sutton. *Hell burns. Hell burns with an agony like no other.*

'Diane,' he said, 'there was a Bible on the table in the farmhouse.'

'Yes?'

'Could it be released? Raymond Sutton was asking for it.'

'I can't see any problem with that. Make sure you record it.'

'Of course.'

177

Fry looked at him quizzically. 'So, are you starting to feel any kinship to these people at Rakedale yet?'

'What do you mean?'

'I know what you're like, Ben. Before long, you'll start feeling sorry for someone, and you'll end up making promises you can't keep. It's a mistake to promise anything to a member of the public, you know. Don't let them know your sympathies at all. Keep your feelings to yourself.'

'I know, I know.'

'You might know the theory, but it's the practice you find difficult, isn't it?'

Cooper bit his lip and moved back to his desk. Fry spotted the flier in his out tray, advertising the carol concert by the male voice choir, which would be followed by a children's party. There were going to be mince pies and mulled wine, and even a visit by Santa.

'Doing good work for the community again? Very commendable. You're not going to play Father Christmas yourself are you, Ben?'

'No, I've asked Gavin to do it.'

'*Gavin?* You've asked *Gavin* to be Father Christmas?'

'He's about the right shape. He won't need much padding to fit the costume.'

'Yes, but won't the kids be expecting a bit of jollity and a certain amount of ho-ho-ho-ing? Not someone who kicks them out of the way to get at the mince pies?'

'Actually, Gavin is very good with children. You should see him at home – he makes a great dad. He just puts an act on at work for the sake of his image.'

'His image? Now I've heard everything. DC Murfin has an image.'

Murfin looked unruffled. 'Hey, Diane, the new choir is always on the look-out for new members. Isn't that right, Ben?'

'Well . . .'

'You don't need to have done any public singing before.

There are about twenty performances a year, and practice sessions in a church hall at Allestree. You'd do that for a charitable cause, wouldn't you, Diane?'

Fry looked at his smiling face suspiciously. 'I thought this was a male voice choir? Surely a requirement for membership would be that you had testicles to drop?'

Murfin grinned more widely. 'That's right,' he said. 'Spot on.'

Fry's phone rang – the DI calling her into his office to hear the latest news from the forensics team.

'It's really quite odd,' said Dr Jamieson when Fry joined them. 'The evidence might almost be called contradictory. I didn't mention it in the presentation earlier for that very reason. Because I can't explain it, scientifically.'

'What do you mean, Doctor?' asked Hitchens. 'We'll need it in simple terms.'

'Well, we can tell from the pattern of decomposition and the disarticulation of the body that Victim B was dug up and re-buried some time after death.'

'So the victim was killed somewhere else, then moved to Pity Wood as a permanent place of concealment? That's pretty much what we expected.'

'Well, no – that's not a legitimate conclusion, I'm afraid,' said Jamieson.

'No? But you just said –'

'I said the body was dug up and re-buried. But we found no samples of soil or vegetation that might be considered inconsistent with the site where the body was found. Normally, you see, we'd expect to sift out some clues about the original burial site – traces of a different soil type, for example. Variations in chemical composition, vegetable fibres that don't belong.'

'I understand,' said Hitchens.

The anthropologist threw up his hands in frustration. 'But there's nothing in this case. Absolutely nothing. On the contrary, the remains of Victim B showed every sign of never having been moved, at least from a geological and botanical point of view.'

'The builders unearthed the skeleton and covered it over again,' pointed out Fry. 'They were worried about delaying the building work.'

'No, no. This didn't happen recently.'

Hitchens frowned. 'Doctor, I thought I was following you at first, but now you've lost me. What are you trying to say exactly?'

'Inspector, I'm saying that some time ago your victim was dug up and re-interred, but never actually moved. On the second occasion, the body was re-buried in exactly the same spot.'

16

In Cooper's copy of the forensic anthropologist's report, the dead woman had been assigned a reference number. This was her biological identity, all that was officially known about the person she'd once been. A Caucasian female aged twenty to twenty-five years, about five feet three inches tall, with dark brown hair. The condition of her teeth was the only peculiarity. There might be useful dental records, if she'd ever called on a dentist in the UK.

'Diane, we're going to have to talk to the neighbours in Rakedale again, aren't we?'

'The Three Wise Monkeys, you mean? They not only heard, saw and spoke no evil, they couldn't believe anyone else would either.'

'That's touching.'

'Touching? I asked one woman whether she'd ever invited the Suttons round when she was having her garden parties and barbecues in the summer. Do you know what she said? "That lot? They never accepted invitations, except to funerals."'

'We really need to dig out their memories, Diane.'

'Well, we'd better requisition an excavator. That place isn't a village – just a series of stone walls. Literally and metaphorically. They clammed up like traps as soon as they knew we were from the police. And I mean every one of them, young and old. Mr Brindley was right. I don't know how news of our arrival got around so fast – they must use thought transference. Does that come with in-breeding?'

Cooper didn't answer. It was true that there was only a narrow range of names on the electoral register for Rakedale, the same ones cropping up several times over. Blands, Tinsleys and Dains seemed to be everywhere.

'Anyway, they probably know each other inside out,' said Fry. 'But these people we're asking about were itinerant workers. They were passing through, not planning to settle down and raise families. I don't suppose there were any women for them to marry, anyway. Not in this place.'

Cooper nodded thoughtfully. 'So they would probably never mix in, never visit anyone, and never join anything.'

'Not if they were familiar with village life. These men would know only too well that they were incomers – and always would be, for as long as they were likely to stay here.'

'Well, there's one part of village life I can almost guarantee they took part in,' said Cooper. 'I bet they went to the pub.'

'Do you mean the Dog Inn? The pub at the end of the universe?'

'It's the only place to go.'

'All right,' conceded Fry. 'But *you* can try it this time. When I went in there, I felt as though I was in a scene from *Deliverance*.'

Following the minimal success of house-to-house on Friday morning, someone had decided to try parking the mobile police office in Rakedale for a few days, to encourage people to come forward with information. Intelligence-led policing at its finest.

When Cooper arrived, he waved to a couple of officers who sat in lonely isolation in a corner of the Dog Inn car park, watching customers come and go to the pub. They looked miserable and could hardly raise the enthusiasm to wave back. Rakedale did that to you.

Some of the pub's exterior decorations had blown off in the wind, and the hanging baskets were definitely not at their best. Rendering was coming away where the down spouts met the wall. Here, too, the porch had been added later. Cooper wondered whether people in this area had become less tough over the years, less able to withstand the Pennine gales without those little stone extensions to deflect the weather. He didn't think the weather had got worse over the centuries, but maybe these buildings let in the wind more as they grew ancient and their stones cracked and separated.

Yes, the Dog Inn was unprepossessing, even for a non-tourist village like Rakedale. Closed at lunchtimes during the week, of course – and not too sure whether it really wanted to be open at other times, either. Catering for the public was all a bit too much trouble, even for the front door, which scraped reluctantly against the raised edge of a flagstone when Cooper tried to push it open.

Strands of tinsel glittered over his head as he passed through the door into the bar, expecting one of those silences that descended whenever a stranger walked into the saloon in a Western film. In here, Fry would have been pretty much a woman with two heads. He bet everyone had stared at her, but no one would have been willing to catch her eye. There were some situations where her approach didn't necessarily work.

The men in the bar were quiet as Cooper walked in. He greeted the sheepdog, which was the only one to acknowledge him, and went to the bar. At least there was a nice open fire, which was useful while he observed the customary wait. At his feet was a brick step up to the bar, and a bowl of water for customers' dogs.

Cooper always looked at the beer pumps in a pub – they could tell you so much about the customers. Real ale or keg, lager or Guinness? Here, they had Black Sheep, Ruddles, and Baboushka spiced ale from one of the Derbyshire breweries, Thornbridge. There was also M & B Mild, a drink that was definitely out of fashion in the trendy bars back in town.

'Cooper, did you say?' asked Ned Dain.

'Yes, DC Cooper, from Edendale.'

'And you work with that woman sergeant that came in the other day?'

'Yes.'

'Was your dad a bobby?'

'Yes, he was.'

'OK, I get it now.'

Dain laughed as he moved along the bar to serve a customer. It was a slightly disturbing laugh that he had, a sound like the deep, wet gurgle from one of his own beer pumps.

'Oh, and tell that sergeant from me there's no Billy,' called Dain. In the corner, a man with a beard laughed.

'Billy?' said Cooper.

'Just our joke. There never was any such person as Billy Sutton.'

Puzzled, Cooper opened his mouth to put another question, but the landlord interrupted him.

'You ought to talk to the old lady,' said Dain. 'My mother. She'll remember the stuff you want to ask about.'

'How do you know what I want to ask about?' said Cooper.

'Talk to the old lady,' repeated Dain. 'You'll find her through there. And shut the door behind you.'

The old lady seemed to have her own sitting room off the kitchen, where she could supervise what was going on through the open door without taking her eyes off the TV for too long. Cooper entered her lair respectfully, conscious that he was being studied critically. The first impression he made might be crucial, the one factor that could make Mrs Dain decide whether to open up to him or keep her mouth firmly shut, the way so many people in Rakedale were doing.

184

When he introduced himself and told her what he had come to talk to her about, he could see her bending her head forward to listen closely to his words. He suspected she was not just hearing what he said, but listening to his accent, judging whether he was local, assessing from his manner whether he was worth talking to.

To his surprise, she lit a cigarette and blew a cloud of smoke. So the door to the bar was kept closed for Health and Safety reasons. No one would realize that there was a free passage of air into the kitchen.

'Who else have you spoken to?' she said eagerly, when Cooper told her the purpose of his visit.

'Oh, Mr Palfreyman. Mr Farnham.'

'Tom Farnham? Did you ask him about his wife?'

'He's a widower, isn't he?'

'Yes, but you know what they say – a widower by choice.'

'Sorry?'

'Well, it's only gossip, I suppose. It's just what people were saying at the time.'

'Are you suggesting that Mr Farnham killed his wife?'

'Not me. It's what I heard, that's all.'

'He was never charged with anything. The inquest verdict was accidental death.'

'Well, they never found any evidence. It doesn't mean he didn't kill her, does it? The perfect murder is the one they can't prove you committed.'

'It's a point of view,' said Cooper.

Privately, he wanted to agree with Mrs Dain. There were plenty of cases where the police believed they knew the perpetrators of crimes, but were never able to prove their guilt in court. It was a mistake to believe that their aim was to achieve justice. Most effort was concentrated on putting together a strong enough case for a prosecution. Without sufficient evidence, and without a rigid adherence to procedures in gathering and presenting it, the concept of justice became academic.

It was an interpretation of the criminal justice system that wasn't normally shared with members of the public.

'I know how easily these rumours get around,' said Cooper. 'But it's unwise to repeat them, Mrs Dain.'

'Oh, I wouldn't repeat it to anybody else,' said the old lady hastily. 'But I thought it would be all right in your case. I mean – you know what it's like, don't you?'

When the kitchen door opened again, Cooper caught the sound and smell of sizzling onion rings. He was starting to feel hungry. Cutlery rattled and a girl emerged from the kitchen and went into the bar with two plates of food. Proper countryside portions, too – the plates were laden. Cooper inhaled as the onion rings passed by.

'It would be about five years ago. Your husband was the licensee then.'

'His name was over the door. But I ran the pub.'

Cooper smiled. 'Yes, that's what I heard.'

'You heard right.'

'At that time, there were some itinerant workers employed at Pity Wood Farm.'

'Pity Wood? The Suttons?'

'Yes.'

'It was a shame about those boys. I knew them when they were young men. They were a few years older than me, of course, but as a girl I took quite an interest in them. I always thought Derek was rather dashing. He was the one I fancied, anyway.'

She looked at Cooper with a hint of a twinkle, and he knew she'd been won over.

'And Raymond?' he asked.

'Raymond wasn't too bad, but he was a bit dour – especially later on, when he got all Bible and black suit.'

'You mean when he took to religion?'

'Aye. That was a bit of a shock. He thought we all ought to be as miserable as he was, told us we were going to Hell

186

for enjoying ourselves. We never saw him in the pub after that, of course. Derek had to come in on his own. Sometimes he had a mite too much to drink. I couldn't blame him, if all he had to go home to was that brother of his. But I bet there were a few rows at home over his drinking.'

Cooper thought of his early image of Raymond and Derek Sutton sitting in their armchairs in silence. He had barely known their names then, but they'd been clear in his mind already.

'I'm not so sure about that.'

'And then, of course . . .' Mrs Dain began to struggle out of her chair, and Cooper leaned forward to offer a hand to help her up. 'There are some photographs here somewhere. I keep them in the drawer.'

'Photographs of the Suttons?'

Mrs Dain pulled out a set of photographic envelopes and began to sort through them very slowly, pausing occasionally, as if for private recollection.

'Have you found anything?' said Cooper.

The old lady looked offended to be hurried, or perhaps Cooper had said something wrong. Whatever the reason, she changed her mind.

'No. Now that I recall, I gave some photos to the new heritage centre for their exhibition.'

'That's a shame.'

'I'm sure there was a photograph of the brothers. Decent lads. I was never quite sure about their mother, though. I always had a suspicion she was of the Old Religion.'

For a moment, the faint murmur of conversation from the bar and the clatter of cutlery from the kitchen were the only sounds. In the little sitting room, there was silence. Cooper sat quite still, holding himself in, hoping the old lady would explain. From the way she said 'Old Religion', he could tell the words had capital letters. But if he was too impatient again, or said the wrong thing, he knew he would never find

187

out what she meant. She would become one of Fry's 'Three Monkeys' in an instant.

So he waited. But instead of explaining, Mrs Dain slid the photographs back in the drawer with an air of finality, and picked up her cigarette from the ashtray. She put it to her lips, sucked, blew, coughed, and had to sit down suddenly.

'The Old Religion,' said Cooper. 'What do you mean by that?'

But it was no good. The moment had drifted by.

'It's all in the past,' said Mrs Dain. 'Beatrice Sutton is long dead. Things like that don't exist any more, so there's no point in talking about it.'

'I'd be interested to hear –'

'There's no point,' said the old lady firmly, 'in talking about it.'

Cooper raised the palms of his hands in a placatory gesture. He didn't want to antagonize her, not when he'd been doing so well. Mrs Dain had accepted him into her world, and he'd made good progress with her. She would tell him the rest of it when she was ready.

Fry took delivery of a small envelope that had been left for her at the front desk in West Street. It was a grubby white envelope, with her named scrawled on it in felt-tipped pen and her rank spelled wrongly.

She pulled on a pair of gloves before she opened it. You couldn't be too careful. She was pretty sure it wasn't a letter bomb, but there were plenty of people who might think of sending her other unpleasant items by way of greeting.

But inside the envelope she found only one thing – a small, cheap crucifix with part of the base chipped away.

Fry let out a breath she hadn't realized she was holding.

'Thank you, Nikolai,' she said.

Cooper took the opportunity to take a toilet break, and discovered that the toilets at the Dog Inn were reached through a series of winding stone passages that seemed to lead almost into the next village.

When he returned to the bar, it was as if Ned Dain had been given some kind of signal by his mother, or maybe it was just the fact that she'd agreed to speak with Cooper for so long that had given the official seal of approval. Whatever the reason, Dain sidled up to him before he left the pub and whispered in a conspiratorial manner.

'I thought you ought to know, there was a foreigner in here last night, asking questions.'

Cooper stopped. 'Oh? What sort of questions?'

'He wanted to know what all the police activity was. What was going on up at that old farm? He wasn't very subtle about it. His English wasn't too good, but we could see what he was after. Nosing about, wanting the gossip.'

'Could you get an idea of his nationality?'

Dain shook his head and flapped the moisture out of a bar cloth. 'Not really. He looked like you or me. Not totally dark or anything, I mean. Not that kind of foreigner. He sounded like some of those blokes that have been doing the building work at Pity Wood.'

'East European?'

'Probably. I couldn't be sure. A few of those builders came in here on Thursday, chattering away to each other. He sounded like them.'

'Can you describe him? Age? Height? How was he dressed?'

'Hold on, that's too many questions all at once. I suppose he'd be about twenty-five or twenty-six, not above average height. Oh, and I do remember he was wearing a sort of black padded coat. You know, you see asylum seekers wearing them when they get pulled off the EuroStar.'

'And you didn't find anything else out about him?' asked Cooper, sure that the landlord must have tried.

Dain wiped an imaginary spill off the bar counter with his cloth. 'Close-mouthed, he was. I'd go so far as to say ignorant. I can't do with folk like that, who come in here and don't know how to make conversation. They take offence if you ask them an innocent question or two.'

'Funny, that,' said Cooper.

17

'Bloody man. He never mentioned to me that his mother was still alive,' said Fry when Cooper reported on his visit to the Dog Inn.

'He probably thought she wouldn't want to talk to you.'

'Well, why –? Oh, never mind. It sounds as though you did well, Ben.'

'Thanks,' said Cooper, knowing that he hadn't yet learned how to keep the note of surprise out of his voice on the rare occasion that she said something complimentary to him. 'It's a shame Mrs Dain didn't have any photographs she could show me. I might try to make time to call at the heritage centre and see what they've got.'

'Put it on your list,' said Fry.

'What's next, then?'

Fry smiled. 'I think I'd like to have a chat with your PC Palfreyman.'

'Ex-PC.'

'Whatever. Do you fancy a trip out?'

'He'll be absolutely delighted to see us,' said Cooper.

David Palfreyman emerged from his kitchen to answer the door. Although he was in the house, he was still wearing his floppy hat. When a man wore a hat all the time, it usually meant that he was completely bald. But Cooper knew that Palfreyman still had some hair. Perhaps it was all those years of wearing a helmet that made his head feel naked.

'Do you live on your own, Mr Palfreyman?' said Cooper. 'I never thought to ask you last time.'

'I'm divorced. You know what it's like – they can only stand the job for so long.'

'Of course. It happens a lot.'

Cooper refrained from saying that he thought what police officers' partners couldn't stand wasn't the job, it was coming second to the job. If he ever got married himself, he'd make sure it didn't happen. Not to the point of divorce, anyway.

'So no woman in the house, then?'

Palfreyman looked at Fry. 'Not until now.'

When they were seated in the lounge, Fry stepped in and took over the conversation.

'Mr Palfreyman, DC Cooper tells me you know pretty much everything and everyone in Rakedale.'

The ex-bobby's eyes flickered sideways to Cooper. 'Yes, pretty much. What do you want to know?'

'We need to know everything about the Sutton brothers at Pity Wood Farm,' said Fry.

'Of course you do. I've watched the news and read the papers. Two unidentified bodies now, isn't it? Unless there have been more since the last news bulletin . . .?' He raised an enquiring eyebrow at Fry. 'But, of course, you came here to get information, not to provide it.'

'You must have visited Pity Wood Farm occasionally when you were on the force.'

'Yes, a few times. Courtesy calls, that's all. I don't suppose you do that any more? No, I thought not. You wait until a crime has been reported before you meet the law-abiding public. And then it's already too late to form a proper relationship.'

'We didn't come here for a critique of modern policing methods,' said Fry.

Palfreyman sighed. 'My views are of no interest to you. I understand, Sergeant. I'm just an irrelevant old dinosaur. I can't possibly know anything about policing now that I'm retired.'

'Pity Wood Farm . . .?' said Fry.

'I was never called to an incident there. I never heard of any other officers attending an incident either. There were certainly no missing persons reports during my time. None made from the farm, none that led to enquiries at the farm. But you must know that; you'll have checked.'

'Of course. But during your courtesy visits, did you meet any of the itinerant workers employed there? Did you have any reason to wonder what had happened to any of them?'

'You're presumably thinking of the women? You don't say so, but it's obvious. Your theory is that one of the workers was killed during her employment there and buried on the farm. No – two of them?' Palfreyman's eyes twinkled. 'Interesting theory. Two murders, both of which went undetected. And three years apart, if the media have it right.'

'Approximately,' said Fry, through audibly gritted teeth.

'Careful, Sergeant, you're almost revealing information. Not quite, but it *was* confirmation.'

Cooper could sense that Fry was likely to stop playing the game soon. She wasn't long on patience, and Palfreyman was pushing her close to the limit. The ex-bobby wouldn't like it if he saw her other side.

'I can't remember whether you asked me how long ago I retired,' he said, in a more conciliatory tone. Perhaps he, too, was able to recognize that look in Fry's eye. 'I'll tell you anyway – I hit my thirty just over four years ago. Celebrations all round, kind words from the chief, a bunch of the lads getting pissed at the pub. And then I was out of the door, with my pension in my pocket. And no one ever thought of

Dave Palfreyman again. I was history as soon as I handed in my warrant card.'

'Your point is . . .?'

'I wasn't in the job when your murders happened, Sergeant. If they *were* murders. Do you have direct evidence?'

'You're not my DI,' said Fry.

'No.'

'Well, stop talking to me as if you are.'

Palfreyman inclined his head. 'I apologize. Sergeant.'

An uneasy silence developed. Cooper shifted uncomfortably in his chair, desperately wanting to say something to break the silence, but afraid of wrecking Fry's strategy. Presuming she had a strategy. But she could keep silent as long as she needed to, and it was Palfreyman who broke the mood.

'You went to see the Brindleys over at Shaw Farm yesterday, didn't you?' he said.

'Very observant. You know them?'

Palfreyman nodded. 'Yes, I know them. Alex and Jo. They have two teenage kids, Chrissie and Evan. The parents are kind of snobbish, academically speaking.'

'They're a bit fussy who their children mix with?'

'Fussy? Any kid who wants to visit their house has to take an entrance exam. Stand-offish, the Brindleys are. Stuck up. You probably noticed.'

Fry didn't smile. 'You seem to know a lot more about them than they do about you.'

Palfreyman shrugged. 'That's the way it is. That's the way I like it, if the truth be known.'

'They're not local people, are they? I mean, they haven't been in Rakedale very long?'

'I know what you mean.' Palfreyman eased himself into his armchair, like an old dog settled into its basket. 'Well, they've lived in the village since they were married. And the oldest kid, Evan, is eighteen. So they must have been here twenty years or so. Not very long, as Rakedale goes.'

'Twenty years?'

'As a family, that is.'

He looked at her expectantly, inviting her to ask the next question. No, that wasn't what she was getting from his expression. He was *challenging* her. Challenging her to ask the right questions, if she wanted the answers.

'One of them was here in the village before they married?' she said. 'Alex or Jo?'

'Jo. She was Joanne Stubbs before she married. And that house they live in is hers – she inherited it from an aunt. She was only a lass when she first came to Rakedale, hardly into her twenties. I remember it well. Bit of a hippy, she was. All crystals and meditation. God knows where she picked that stuff up from. It certainly wasn't from her aunt, or any of the other Stubbs family round here. They were all chapel-goers.'

'So Jo actually is a village person. She said she wasn't.'

'Well, she's right,' said Palfreyman. 'Joanne Stubbs has never fit in, and never will. She knows that perfectly well.'

Fry was trying to play along with the ex-PC's game. 'There's some kind of history here. What has Jo done to upset the village?'

'Well, when she first came to Rakedale, some of the local people thought she was a bit strange. They didn't really take to her tarot cards and joss sticks, all that rubbish. Not to mention the stuff she kept trying to force on to people if she thought they showed signs of being ill. Herbal remedies, she called them. Me, I reckon they were mostly based on cannabis, but I never took any action on that suspicion. I never knew anyone accept her remedies, or it might have been different. I suppose you think I was wrong in that?'

Neither Cooper nor Fry reacted. He looked slightly disappointed, but went back to his story.

'And there were all those cats she had, as well. Too many cats to be natural. A woman living out there on her own? You can imagine what the gossips were saying about her.'

195

'Only too well,' said Cooper.

'Anyway, one day she came home from doing her shopping in Bakewell, and her house had been broken into. It looked as though nothing had been stolen. But she thought the intruders must still be in the house, because she could hear noises somewhere. Not voices exactly. She described what she called surreptitious bumps and whisperings, scraping sounds and scratches. Sensibly, she called the police and got herself back outside the house to wait. When the FOAs went upstairs, they found three crows flapping about in her bedroom.'

Cooper shivered. He knew what that meant. It was the old warning against witches. Until now, he thought it had died out in the eighteenth century. Someone in Rakedale had a long, long memory to remember that custom. And an even deeper well of superstition to consider putting it into practice.

'What did you do?' he asked. 'I mean, I take it you were one of those officers responding to the emergency call?'

'Aye. And a young lad who turned up from Edendale to assist. He was a bit wet behind the ears, but he had a bit of sense. He knew enough to leave everything to me.'

'Like a good young copper.'

'Like some, anyway,' said Palfreyman, giving him a sly look.

'And so . . .?'

'We got rid of the crows without much damage. Just a few splodges of shit on the carpet, and she soon got that cleaned up. Then we checked over the house to see it was secure, and we left. Called it in as a false alarm. Listed as NFA.'

'No further action?'

'Not officially. Well, there aren't many folk who have the know-how and the wherewithal to catch a set of crows, not to mention the nerve to turn them loose in someone's house. I called and had a few words. It never happened again.'

'But didn't Mrs Brindley want to report the break-in?'

'Look, you have to understand something about the

eighties,' said Palfreyman. 'We were allowed to use our discretion then, and no one asked any questions, provided you got the job done. It meant we did things you would never dare do. You'd be too afraid of getting your arse kicked and losing your pension.' He glanced sideways at Fry. 'Or not getting that promotion you want so badly, eh?'

'All right, it was different back then. We get the message.'

'Well, just don't judge me on your own terms. In those days, we always knew who needed a quiet word in the ear, and who needed something a bit more . . . robust.'

'You're living in a dream world,' said Cooper. 'Those days have been over a long time. You joined the force in – when was it, 1972?'

'That's right. The blokes who taught me the job were old school. But they'd all gone by the time I retired.'

'That old-fashioned coppering had already disappeared in the eighties. My dad complained about it often enough.'

Palfreyman smiled slyly. 'Oh, aye – your dad. Sergeant Joe Cooper. Did you think I didn't know who you were? Joe Cooper was my shift supervisor for a while.'

Cooper felt the anger rising, and knew he was changing colour, the red flush rising uncontrollably into his cheeks.

'He would never have tolerated a copper like you on his shift,' he said.

Palfreyman smirked. 'That's what you think.'

Fry put her hand on Cooper's arm. 'Ben,' she said, warningly. She was probably just in time.

Palfreyman shook his head. 'Anyway, Joanne wanted to go on living there, didn't she? It wouldn't have done her any good with the neighbours to kick off a burglary enquiry. Someone might have been arrested and charged, and she'd never have lived easy in Rakedale after that. As it was, she was left alone with her cats and her herbs, thanks to me. Nobody talked to her much, of course. But if you've seen some of the characters round here, you'd reckon that was a blessing.'

'But she's been here more than twenty years now.'

'Aye. She's married and she has children, and they're all considered respectable enough. Alex Brindley seems to have done very well for himself. But don't think that means people forget.'

'Mr Farnham, now – he seems quite a different individual.'

'You've talked to Tom Farnham as well, eh?'

'Yes.'

For a moment, Palfreyman weighed her up, as if taking her seriously for the first time.

'I hope you know how to tell when someone is lying, Sergeant,' he said.

'Of course. We're trained these days.'

Palfreyman rolled his eyes. 'Psychology seminars? Body-language recognition techniques? I thought so. Well, *we* didn't need training. In my day, any good copper learned to develop an instinct for when someone was telling the truth.' He slapped his stomach. 'My gut always told me when I was hearing a lie. It was never wrong.'

'If your instinct was never proved wrong, it was only because you were allowed to hide your mistakes,' said Fry.

Palfreyman tried to laugh, but couldn't get the right shape to his mouth.

'What do *you* know? You know nothing. You don't belong to this part of the world, and you don't belong in the job, if the truth be known. I bet you were a graduate entrant – am I right?'

'I'm not ashamed of that.'

Cooper watched Fry and Palfreyman as they faced each other across the room, with the light from the window falling on them both equally. Fry looked slight and brittle, perched on the edge of her chair in an attitude that was both tense and belligerent. In contrast, PC Palfreyman was enormous – twice Fry's size at least, but soft and heavy, his weight crushing the sofa in a more passively hostile manner.

198

From where he sat, Cooper could see the outside world going on beyond them: birds flicking across the sky, lorries moving slowly up the hill into Rakedale. He was struck by how different these two were, the former village bobby and the ambitious DS. Not only physically different, but psychologically and technically, and in the way they'd been trained. Well, different in every way he could think of, in fact. Watching them was like seeing the past and future facing each other across a green rug and an IKEA coffee table.

There was no question that policing had changed. It had been transformed in the few years since Palfreyman retired, and it was changing still. There weren't any beat bobbies any more. In fact, there weren't any beats, except under a different name. In Derbyshire, they were called Safer Neighbourhood police teams – a combination of police officers, special constables, PCSOs and local authority wardens, even some Neighbourhood Watch volunteers.

Meanwhile, just across the border, Nottinghamshire had become the first force in the UK to have armed officers on routine patrol. In parts of Nottingham, officers were issued with Walther P99 pistols, just like the one James Bond used, and had Heckler and Koch semi-automatic carbines in their patrol cars for back-up.

And that was before September eleventh and July seventh, and all the other landmark dates of terrorism. Cooper found the development worrying, an ominous sign for the future of policing in this country. But he couldn't ally himself with the Palfreymans of the world, either.

'Yes, I *do* have the training to spot a liar,' said Fry as they walked back down Palfreyman's drive to the car.

'I'm sure you do, Diane,' said Cooper.

'I know all the indications to watch for.'

'You don't need to tell me. You know David Palfreyman was just trying to wind you up back there, don't you?'

'Bastard.'

Cooper looked across the road. 'Hold on a minute, Diane. I won't be long.'

'Where are you going?'

'There's a Range Rover parked at the Brindleys' house. Is it theirs?'

'Yes, I think it's Mr Brindley's. Why?'

'It's a TD model.'

'So? You're not that interested in cars, Ben.'

'Do you know what TD stands for, Diane? It means Turbo Diesel. I want to ask Mr Brindley if he's ever been offered cheap illegal fuel.'

When Cooper came back, Fry was sitting in the car, still fuming.

'They're called the Ten Signs,' she said. 'Lack of eye contact, a change in the pitch of the voice, clearing the throat. And then there's the body language – tapping the foot, fidgeting with the hands, blinking too much.'

Cooper got behind the wheel. 'Turning the head or body away, changing the subject, attempting to deflect questions using humour or sarcasm.'

Fry looked at him. 'Have you done the same course?'

'Er, I sort of picked it up on the job,' he said, trying not to sound too much like Palfreyman.

'What did Mr Brindley say?'

'He'd never even heard of illegal diesel.'

Fry watched the landscape going by as Cooper drove over the plateau towards Edendale. On the highest points, the drizzle and mist became almost indistinguishable from low cloud, and Cooper had to put the headlights on. Spray from passing lorries made visibility even worse.

'Ten Signs,' said Fry. 'Put all those techniques together, and only a really good actor can get away with an undetected lie. And PC David Palfreyman is *not* that good an actor.'

*　　*　　*

Back at the office, they found DCI Kessen in the CID room with Hitchens. He had put in an appearance from his other major enquiry and was catching up on progress.

Kessen studied Fry as she entered the room.

'Ah, DS Fry, glad you could join us.'

Fry seemed to go stiff and awkward, as if she'd been caught out doing something she shouldn't. But that wasn't the case, was it? She'd been following a reasonable line of enquiry that might have produced some useful information. Cooper wanted to speak up in her defence, but no one would have appreciated that, least of all Fry.

'Your DI has brought me up to speed on the Rakedale enquiry. You did a good job recovering the crucifix from the grave site.'

'Thank you, sir.'

Hitchens held up the evidence bag containing the cross. 'Examination reveals scratch marks on the back, near where the arms and the upright meet. They're probably initials, Diane. We think they look like an "N" and possibly an "H".'

'The owner's initials?'

'Could be. They do match a set of initials from the list of employees at Pity Wood, but unfortunately that doesn't help us to make an identification. Not yet, anyway.'

'But it might do,' said Fry.

'Let's hope so.'

Kessen nodded. 'Yes, that's very helpful. As I said, a good piece of work. However, DS Fry, we've agreed your energies would be best employed from this point on exploring the missing persons angle. It's being neglected at the moment.'

'Missing persons? But, sir, I think I could be more productive pursuing some other lines –'

'No, DS Fry, I think I'd prefer you to concentrate on the missing persons check.'

Fry hesitated too long before she responded, and Kessen registered it.

'Of course, sir.'

Cooper looked across at her, but she refused to meet his eye. Was it just coincidence that he'd been thinking only yesterday about the DCI's apparent even-handedness? Was that why he'd noticed this little incident? Or was it that Kessen's attitude had changed since the arrival of a new superintendent over his head?

Cooper didn't know how to interpret what he'd witnessed, but he was sure that Diane would be filing the incident away in that very efficient mental filing cabinet she carried around inside her head. He pictured it as the equivalent of one of those old-fashioned green cabinets, heavy and fire-proof, with drawers that slid out on strong, steel hinges.

For a moment, he wondered what was written in his own file – the one pushed to the back of the bottom drawer, slightly dog-eared and crushed out of shape by the more important information in front of it. Nothing he'd want to read about himself, probably.

18

'SOCOs collected a lot of samples from the kitchen at the farm,' said Hitchens, assembling the team when the DCI had left. 'Some old blood traces that the lab is working on, and lots of other stuff, the kind that you might expect in a kitchen. But analysis also found substantial traces of a chemical compound, KNO_3. Potassium nitrate.'

'Potassium nitrate?' asked Fry. 'What is that used for?'

'The lab thought we might want to know that. Killing tree stumps, for a start. You can get it in most garden centres, or hardware shops. It's an ingredient of some fertilizers. Also toothpastes that are formulated for sensitive teeth. And gunpowder.'

'Versatile stuff, then.'

'Wait – you haven't heard the best one. Potassium nitrate was considered for many years to be an anaphrodisiac.'

'A what?'

'They thought it suppressed sexual desire. It was added to food in all-male institutions. Did you ever see *One Flew Over the Cuckoo's Nest?*'

'The film with Jack Nicholson?'

'Right. Well, in the film, Nicholson's character mentions that's he's afraid of being "slipped" potassium nitrate in the mental institution where he's committed. It was a common practice at the time, a way of controlling the behaviour of patients.'

'Cool. But I'm not sure it helps us.'

'Is potassium nitrate a natural product, or artificially manufactured?' asked Cooper.

'It's a naturally occurring mineral,' explained Hitchens. 'Traditionally, the major sources were the deposits crystallizing on cave walls, or the drainings from dung heaps. Ammonia from the decomposition of urea – you know.'

'We get the picture,' said Fry.

'But it can also be manufactured. The old method was to mix manure, wood ash, earth and organic materials such as straw.'

Cooper nodded. 'A compost heap, in fact.'

'Exactly. But they were known as nitre beds, which sounds nicer, I suppose. A heap was kept moist with urine in the, er . . . traditional manner, and turned to accelerate decomposition. After a year, it was leached with water, and the resulting liquid was rich with nitrates, which could then be converted to potassium nitrate, crystallized and used in gunpowder.'

'Potassium nitrate is an explosive, then?' said Fry.

'Not on its own. It does have another useful property, though, particularly for fireworks manufacturers. A mixture of potassium nitrate and sugar produces a smoke cloud six hundred times its own volume. Just great for smoke bombs.'

'How does it kill tree stumps?'

'It doesn't really kill them. You have to kill the stump first – then the potassium nitrate makes it decompose faster.'

'Wait a minute,' said Cooper. 'Those compost heaps – did you say they were called "nitre beds"?'

'That's right. One of the common non-scientific names for potassium nitrate is –'

'– saltpetre?'

'Correct.'

Cooper found that he wasn't in the least surprised. It seemed to fit so naturally with what he'd learned already of the owners of Pity Wood Farm, and the other residents of Rakedale.

'Potassium nitrate is used in Edgar Allan Poe's story "The Cask of Amontillado" as the lining of the crypt where Montresor buries Fortunato alive. It's why he has so much trouble with his breathing in his last moments. *"For the love of God, Montresor!"'*

'Didn't the IRA use saltpetre in their bomb-making operations at one time?' said Fry. 'I had a feeling it had been put on a restricted list, not available for sale to the general public.'

Hitchens laughed. 'You can make bombs from sugar and fertilizer, so why would anyone worry about saltpetre?'

'Also, it's been implicated in having carcinogenic properties.'

'I don't think anyone was worrying about getting cancer or making bombs,' said Cooper.

'Oh?'

'This other stuff in the kitchen. Did it include sesame seeds, by any chance?'

'Yes, it did,' said Hitchens. 'How on earth did you know that, Ben?'

He'd have to ask Amy for the exact wording, but Cooper thought he could remember the recipe pretty well.

Squeeze out the blood. Embalm it in a shroud and steep it in a solution of saltpetre, salt and pepper for two weeks, then dry in the sun. The candles are made from a hanged man's fat, wax and Lapland sesame.

'I'd like to make a prediction,' he said. 'I predict that if we find another body at Pity Wood Farm, it will be missing a hand.'

Within a few minutes, and thanks to the internet, Cooper knew how to make potassium nitrate himself. The practical part was simple. You could either dissolve solid fertilizer in boiling water, or boil down a liquid fertilizer until crystals started to form. When the solution had cooled to room temperature, it was placed in a fridge. The white crystalline precipitate was mainly KNO_3. Garden products tended to contain ammonium nitrate, too, which contaminated the KNO_3.

'We should have picked this up earlier,' said Hitchens. 'Potassium nitrate can cause eye and skin irritations. Breathing it in can irritate the nose and throat, causing sneezing and coughing. High levels can interfere with the ability of the blood to carry oxygen, causing headaches, fatigue, dizziness and a blue colour to the skin and lips. Even higher levels can cause trouble breathing, collapse and death. Long term, potassium nitrate may affect the kidneys and cause anaemia. Chronic long-term health effects can occur some time after exposure and can last for months or years.'

'Is this really something you ought to keep in your fridge?' asked Murfin.

'No, Gavin.'

'And what was it that Derek Sutton died from, did you say?'

'Heart failure.'

'That appears on so many death certificates. It's what doctors write in when they can't see any other cause of death but don't want to put the family through the ordeal of a postmortem.'

'Obviously, no one would have suspected potassium nitrate poisoning at the time, so there wouldn't have been any toxicology done, even if there had been a PM,' said Fry.

'Well, it's academic, since there wasn't a postmortem,' said Hitchens. 'Derek Sutton was signed off, certificated and cremated within a week.'

'It would be cremation, of course. So no chance of getting an exhumation order.'

'You say that no one would have suspected potassium nitrate poisoning,' said Cooper. 'But his brother Raymond might have suspected it, if he knew what Derek was up to.'

Hitchens shook his head. 'That old man? How would he have known the effects of potassium nitrate? Who knows what saltpetre is exactly? I didn't, until just now.'

206

'Even so, he must have wondered what was wrong. You don't just drop suddenly without any other symptoms, do you?'

Hitchens checked the report. 'Eye and skin irritations, sneezing and coughing, headaches, fatigue, dizziness, a blue colour to the skin and lips, trouble breathing.'

'I found several sites on the internet where I could order food-grade saltpetre. Lots more where it's listed as an ingredient in garden chemicals.'

'OK.'

He'd also found a method for treating skin infections that had supposedly been passed from father to son over many generations in farming. If you got bitten or scratched and it looked as though the wound was getting infected, you should bathe the area in a solution of hot water and saltpetre. It inhibited the growth of organisms associated with skin infections. Clostridium, Streptococcus and Staphylococcus. It made sense. He was just surprised that he'd never heard of it in his own family. Father to son over generations? Maybe Matt used the treatment on the quiet.

'Ben – this thing about a hand of glory,' said Fry, interrupting his reading. 'You don't think you're letting the superstition business get to you too much?'

'Not me. I think it had got to Derek Sutton, though.'

'You really think there's a body without a hand somewhere?'

'Yes.'

'Prepared to bet on it?'

'I'm not really a betting man,' said Cooper.

'Ha-ha.'

Potassium nitrate had a smell reminiscent of burnt gunpowder. That rang a bell with Cooper. For a while, supplies of fertilizer had been stored in a breeze-block extension to the main barn at Bridge End. The inside always had a heavy smell of potassium nitrate fertilizer. Burnt gunpowder was right – it had always made him think of Bonfire Night and firework displays.

207

He would probably never be able to go to a garden centre without being reminded of it these days. Not without being reminded of poor Derek Sutton, preparing his saltpetre recipe in the kitchen at Pity Wood.

Fry was seething quietly at her desk when Hitchens appeared at her side, his face creased with discomfort.

'Diane, have you got a minute?'

'Sir?' said Fry, automatically responding to the tone of his voice. It was a management tone, the kind of voice people used when you were being summoned into their office for a reprimand. Or to get bad news. 'Is something wrong?'

'Let's just step into my office, shall we?'

They moved out of earshot of the team in the CID room and Hitchens shut the door of his office with a deliberate slam.

'I shouldn't be telling you this,' he said. 'But we've worked together for a while now, and I think you ought to know as soon as possible. Sit down, won't you?'

Reluctantly, Fry sat. She preferred to stay on her feet when they were discussing an enquiry. Sitting in the chair across from his desk felt too much like a disciplinary interview, the recalcitrant pupil called to the headmaster's room.

'There was a meeting of the CID management team this morning,' he said.

Fry nodded. Of course, everyone knew that. Word had gone round the CID room like the wind. DIs and above were in a meeting with the new superintendent. Something was afoot, they said. Changes were going to be made. The End of the World was nigh.

'Detective Superintendent Branagh has been studying the department carefully before she takes up her new role,' said Hitchens. 'She's gone into everything very thoroughly – detection rates, targets, staff records. As Mr Jepson said, she's very thorough. Very thorough indeed.'

'A ferociously efficient administrator. That's what he called her.'

'Oh, yes. Well, that was accurate, too.'

Hitchens seemed to be gathering his thoughts. A uniformed PC knocked on the door and stuck his head in, but Hitchens waved him away with an abrupt gesture.

'Superintendent Branagh asked for copies of all the PDRs for everyone. All of us. Me, too. She doesn't believe in people getting stale and falling into a routine. She says an officer who gets into a rut is an officer going nowhere.'

So perhaps the doom mongers were right. Fry pictured some of the older CID officers, such as Gavin Murfin or DS Rennie. A shake-up would come as a shock to some of them.

'Has she got some changes in mind?' she asked.

Hitchens nodded. 'She's going to produce a set of proposals for the department. But it's safe to say that some moves are on the cards.'

'Moves?'

'Transfers. A few shifts in areas of responsibility. Maybe a promotion or two, Diane.'

He was trying hard to sound positive, but Fry could see through it. She wasn't fooled by flannel, and her DI should know it by now.

'I take it there was something specific about me?' she said. 'You were talking about me during this meeting?'

'Well, you were mentioned,' admitted Hitchens, his eyes flickering nervously like a guilty suspect in an interview room. He looked as though he was starting to regret sending the PC away, after all.

'And what did Detective Superintendent Branagh make of my Personal Development Review? Has she got something in mind for my future? Will I actually be allowed to know what's being said about me some time?'

'There will be individual interviews, of course. Everything

will be discussed with you fully. You'll have an opportunity to have your say at that time.'

'But . . .?' said Fry.

'It's all still up in the air, Diane. There's nothing absolutely definite . . .'

'But . . .?'

Hitchens sighed. 'Superintendent Branagh was asking – did I really think you fitted in here? She wondered if you might be more suited to another division. I'm sorry, Diane.'

Cooper consulted his notes, reminding himself of what he'd missed doing. Time seemed to be going by so fast, what with one thing and another.

He saw that he hadn't suggested a search of the old caravan at Pity Wood Farm yet, as he'd meant to do. Maybe that wasn't too urgent, because the forensics team probably wouldn't get round to it for days anyway. He added a note to fit in a visit to the heritage centre some time, to see if they had anything on Pity Wood. Old photos could reveal such a lot.

Then Cooper noticed that he'd never spoken to anyone at the auctioneers, Pilkington's, to ask them whether they'd been approached about a farm equipment sale. There must be something planned for the disposal of all that machinery and the other stuff at Pity Wood. It wouldn't all fit into the skip.

Cooper thought about the interior of the house, the few items they'd recovered that might be of relevance. The farm records, some jars of crystallized saltpetre, a single Sani Bag. And he supposed the family Bible should be included. But might there be something important that was no longer present, so they just weren't seeing it? The impression of a *Marie Celeste*, abandoned intact, could be quite misleading.

He looked at his phone. Fry had been called in to see the DI, and neither of them had looked too happy. Besides, she was supposed to be chasing mispers now, so he supposed he was a free agent for a while. Initiative was called for. He reached for the handset.

'Mr Goodwin, did you ever meet the previous owners of Pity Wood Farm?' asked Cooper, when he managed to get through to the Manchester solicitor.

'Oh, no. It was all done through the estate agent. The farm was already unoccupied when we visited for a viewing. I know they were called Sutton, but we had no personal contact. Just the usual exchange of contracts.'

'Mr Sutton didn't take much away with him, did he?' said Cooper.

'Not much,' said Goodwin. 'Just a few personal things. There's an awful lot of rubbish to clear out, as you've probably seen. It won't be a quick job. But that was the deal – it was one of the reasons I got the property at a good price. It was sold "as is". I understand the owner was in care, so everything had to be disposed of anyway.'

'Can you recall anything that was removed, sir? Anything out of the ordinary? There must have been a few items that were present when you viewed the property, but which had gone when you took possession.'

The solicitor was silent for a moment, except for a thoughtful mumbling.

'Nothing that seemed to be of any value,' he said. 'It's not exactly the sort of place you'd expect to be stuffed with antique furniture, is it? Or, if it ever was, they sold anything of value years ago. I gathered the farm had been failing for some time.'

'Yes, I believe so.'

'Then there was nothing, really, Detective Constable. Nothing that I wouldn't have wanted to get rid of, anyway.'

Then he began to laugh, and Cooper looked at the phone as if it had done something weird. 'Would you like to share the joke, sir?'

'Well, I'm sure this can't be what you mean,' said Goodwin, still chuckling. 'But obviously, they took the severed head.'

19

Fry took a moment to steady her breathing, shocked by the unexpected surge of panic that had turned her stomach over for a few seconds. It was a totally irrational feeling. She'd thought the same herself many times, hadn't she? She was like a fish out of water in E Division. In Derbyshire, come to that. Her home was back in the city, away from these people she would never understand and couldn't tolerate.

It was just hearing the sentiment put into someone else's words that had hit her like a blow to the solar plexus. It was a statement of the obvious. Yet she loathed the idea that Detective Superintendent Branagh had sat in a meeting this morning and expressed the thought to her managers. She hated the intrusion of someone like Branagh reading her file and summing her up so easily. It was illogical, of course. But no less hurtful for that.

'Oh, no need to be sorry, sir,' she said quietly. 'No need for *you* to be sorry at all.'

That fear of being an outsider had haunted her all her life. At school, in her various homes in the Black Country, and even when she'd studied for her Criminal Justice and Policing course at UCE. As a child, she hadn't realized that everyone dreaded finding themselves on the outside, not a part of the gang. She thought it was her own particular weakness of character that drove her to seek acceptance from her peers.

It made her wince now to think of her teenage self, hanging around in the corridors of her comprehensive school, trying to attach herself to a group. It was only as an adult that she'd learned it was the same for most kids of her age. Some were so desperate to belong that it became a question of any gang that would have them.

Being a member of the herd was a primal instinct – probably the deepest, most powerful instinct of them all.

'If you do go, Diane,' said Hitchens, 'we'll miss you.'

'They called him Billy,' said Cooper, the moment Fry entered the CID room. 'Screaming Billy Sutton. But of course he probably wasn't a Sutton. He could have been anybody. Anybody at all, Diane.'

Fry jumped as if she'd been shot. 'What the hell are you talking about, Ben?'

'The landlord of the Dog Inn said something about a Billy. At first, I thought he might have meant another brother, or a son. But there's no indication of a William Sutton. So this must be him.'

She had never seen him so animated. He was running around the office like an excited puppy, yapping at anyone who would listen. But what *was* he yapping about?

'Ben, slow down. Explain yourself properly.'

Cooper looked hot and breathless, as if he'd been running. 'It's like Dickie of Tunstead, you see. There's a place called Tunstead Farm, up in the north of the county near Chapel-en-le-Frith. Now, *that* one is quite famous. There's some doubt whether it's male or female, but locally it's always been known as Dickie. A previous owner of the farm was murdered in his bed in an ownership dispute –'

He paused to take a breath, and Fry held up a hand like a traffic officer, speaking louder to drown him out.

'Ben, stop.'

'The Suttons must have managed to keep this one quiet, though,' he said. 'It was known about locally, but everyone seems to have been reluctant to discuss it. Superstition, of course. Careless talk, the Scottish play, all that sort of stuff.'

'For God's sake, will you just stop? Stop!'

'Screaming Billy was supposed to . . .' Cooper finally ground to a halt and looked at her in amazement. 'Why are you shouting at me, Diane?'

Fry took his arm. 'Ben, sit down and shut up for a minute. Take a few deep breaths.'

He opened his mouth to speak, but she snarled at him, and he closed it again quickly. He sat down.

'All right, that's better,' she said.

'Can I speak yet?'

'Just collect your thoughts first. I'm getting the impression you have something to tell me that you think is important. But so far you haven't managed a word of sense. Not a word.'

'Oh. Are you sure?'

'There was somebody called Billy, and somebody called Dickie, and one of them was screaming. That's all I got. The rest of it was gibberish.'

Cooper wiped a hand across his forehead. 'I'd better start again.'

'I'll fetch you some water. And I suggest when you do start again, you start from the beginning.'

When Fry came back from the cooler with a cup of water, Cooper was looking much calmer, but he was still fidgeting in his seat, impatient to pass on his information.

Fry found she couldn't stay irritated with him, after witnessing his burst of enthusiasm. It took years off him, made him seem like that eager young DC she'd encountered when she first arrived in Edendale. That had been her initial impression of him. He'd changed a lot since then. The mark of what life had thrown at him, she supposed.

For just one second, a disorientating second, Fry felt the two of them might actually have something in common. But it was so little that they shared. Far too little.

Fry watched him take a drink of water. 'All right, go ahead.'

'I'd better explain Dickie of Tunstead first,' said Cooper. 'I suppose you've never heard of him.'

'You suppose right.' Fry pulled up her chair. 'I'm sitting comfortably.'

'Tunstead Farm is in a village called Tunstead Milton near Chapel-en-le-Frith, over in B Division. Local legend says that an owner of the farm was murdered in his bed during an ownership dispute with a cousin who'd taken the place over while the real owner was away fighting in the wars.'

'And this was a very recent event, I suppose? Like, seventeenth century or something?'

'Sixteenth.'

'Of course.'

'But the point is, they still have his skull. His head was preserved and kept at the farm. It's what's known as a "screaming skull". You've never heard of them?'

'No again,' said Fry. 'But you're starting to interest me now.'

'Dickie of Tunstead is quite celebrated. He's been written about often. These days, no one is sure whether it's a male or female skull, but locally it's always been known as Dickie, so that's the name it goes under still. There are others around the country, in rural places, where people have believed in the power of the screaming skull.'

'Don't start losing me, Ben. Stay in the realms of sanity.'

'I'll try.' Cooper took another drink. 'Well, the belief is that removing Dickie's skull from Tunstead will bring bad luck. They say it's been removed three times over the years – as a result, crops failed, a barn collapsed, livestock died, the house was damaged in a storm. The skull has been thrown in the river, buried in the churchyard, and stolen by thieves.

The thieves were so disturbed by things that started to happen to them that they returned the skull to Tunstead.'

'And this thing really is just a skull?'

'I've seen photos of it. It's just a yellowing old skull, holed and fragmented at the back as if it had been struck with a hammer at some time.'

'We can establish cause of death in that case, then,' said Fry. 'Pity we can't do it for more recent deaths.'

'Dickie of Tunstead possesses supernatural powers to prevent anyone moving him out of his home,' said Cooper, with a note of awe in his voice. 'When the skull is left in place, everything goes right at the farm. He even acts as a guardian, warning when strangers approach. His real claim to fame was getting the course of the railway altered.'

'Oh, come on. Railways are fairly solid and practical,' said Fry.

'It was in the nineteenth century, when they were building the Buxton to Stockport line. There was a compulsory purchase order for land belonging to Tunstead Farm. The railway company wanted to build a bridge and embankment on the land, but building work collapsed, and men and animals were injured. Engineers said the ground was unstable, but local people credited Dickie. In the end, the company diverted the line, and the new bridge was named after him. It's still there, Diane. The bridge is real, and so is the skull.'

'All right. And there was one of these skulls at Pity Wood Farm?'

'Mr Goodwin says so. He was shown it, when he viewed the property. But it was one of the few things that had been taken away when he completed the purchase.'

'A severed head inside the farmhouse.'

'Yes, Diane.'

'And this poor, gullible Manchester solicitor was told some ghostly legend about it, to keep him quiet?'

'Well, there was definitely a skull,' said Cooper.

'So does Mr Goodwin know where the head went?' asked Fry. 'Has Raymond Sutton got it?'

'In the bottom of his wardrobe at the care home? Hardly, Diane.'

'Where, then?'

'Mr Goodwin says the man who took it away claimed to be the farm manager.'

'Tom Farnham?'

'The very same.'

'Let's go, then.'

'Right. Oh, Diane – aren't you supposed to be on missing persons?' said Cooper.

'Sod missing persons. They can stay missing.'

Cooper had forgotten that there were areas in this part of the Peak where the viability of farming was already borderline even before the fall in prices, before foot and mouth even. It was obvious when you drove through. Many of the dry-stone walls were badly maintained, farms had scrap heaps of old machinery standing in their yards, and there was a generally unkempt feel to the landscape. Foot and mouth had shown how much tourism and farming depended on each other in a place like this. A rural way of life that had disappeared from most of England had survived here until quite recently.

Cooper recalled his father telling him about farms out this way that didn't have electricity or running water until maybe twenty years ago. The 1980s, the decade of prosperity.

He bet most of the country wouldn't have believed how people lived their lives, here on the fringes of the Pennines. 'It's not as if we're living in a Third World country,' they'd say. 'There are cities only a few miles away, for goodness' sake. You can practically see Manchester over that hill. Hi-tech industries and café society, a huge airport sending jet liners all around the world. How can anyone be living without electricity?'

217

But these local communities were conscious of the changes taking place around them. More conscious than most, he guessed.

Fairies and elves, spells and charms had been an integral part of life of the countryman, who wouldn't have understood the causes and effects of droughts and floods, crop failures, or sickness in his livestock. Witches were blamed for evil in the Middle Ages, Celts had worshipped the head.

Lost in his own thoughts, Cooper only became aware of the nature of the silence when they were halfway to Rakedale.

'What's wrong, Diane?'

'Nothing,' she said.

He hated it when she said 'nothing' like that. Her tone of voice meant anything but 'nothing'. It told him that he damn well ought to know what was wrong, without him having to ask her.

'Come on, what's the matter?'

'I told you. Nothing.'

Well, at least that meant it wasn't his fault. She'd never been shy about telling him when he'd done something wrong. Quite the opposite. So someone else had upset her.

'This business with the skulls – is it what Mrs Dain meant about "the old religion"?' asked Fry eventually.

'That would be Old Religion – capital "O", capital "R".'

'I doubt it's in my dictionary, Ben, all the same.'

'Actually, I think she might have been referring to a series of TV programmes that were made back in the seventies. The producers claimed to have found a community in the Dark Peak who still worshipped the old gods.'

'Just a minute – I suppose that would be Old Gods, capital "O", capital "G"? Are we talking Paganism here?'

'Not exactly,' said Cooper. 'In fact, the people involved were mostly practising Christians, I think. No, it was said to be a sort of respect for traditional beliefs that didn't conflict with their Christian practices. They believed in the old Celtic

218

gods, but never mentioned them. The programme interviewed someone who called herself a "guardian". She talked about a scattered community who still believed in the old ways. They didn't name the small mill town she came from – but most local people could have a good guess.'

'That's nearly thirty years ago. The world has changed a lot since then.'

'Yes, even in . . . well, even in the Peak District.'

He turned on to the A515 towards Newhaven. Not far away from here was Arbor Low – a sort of flattened version of Stonehenge, a circle of megaliths laid out like a clock face. When he'd walked up there on a school trip once, Cooper had thought the stones looked as though they'd been blown down by the wind. But their teacher said it was more likely they'd been deliberately knocked over by Christian zealots who disapproved of the stones' religious significance.

Religious significance? Arbor Low was built more than four thousand years ago, wasn't it? Now, that was the *real* Old Religion.

'Do you think Raymond Sutton knew about the bodies buried on his farm?' asked Fry. 'You've talked to him, Ben, what do you think?'

'I think he might have had a suspicion,' said Cooper. 'But no more than that – just a suspicion that something bad had happened.'

'Involving his brother?'

'I don't know. He talks about Hell a lot. Somebody is going to be damned.'

'So here's a scenario,' said Fry. 'One or both of the Sutton brothers killed these women, either during some barking mad pagan rituals in Derek's case, or out of religious mania in Raymond's case, because they were damned and needed to be punished and sent to Hell.'

'Well . . .'

'Whatever. I'm vague on the details yet. But word got out

219

in the area – as it was bound to do round here. Rumour, rumour. Gossip, gossip.'

'And then people just kept quiet?'

'Well, in my scenario, Dixon of Dock Green turns up at the farm to see what's what.'

'PC Palfreyman?'

'Yes, PC Bloody Palfreyman. "Evening, all," he says. "What's this I hear about you two lads committing a couple of nasty murders? We can't be having that, you know. I might have to give you a clip round the ear for being naughty boys."'

'It could only have been one murder,' said Cooper reasonably. 'The second victim died three years after Mr Palfreyman retired.'

'True. But the principle is the same.'

'You really think he might have known all about what went on at Pity Wood Farm, and covered up for the Suttons?'

'Why not? "I called and had a few words. It never happened again."'

Cooper shook his head. 'I can't see it. Granted, Palfreyman has his own ideas about justice, like so many of the old coppers did. But he wouldn't cover up a murder, let alone two. That couldn't be considered justice, not in anyone's book. Could it?'

'Well, actually, it might depend,' said Fry, 'on who those women were.'

'Might it?'

Cooper considered that idea, and gradually realized what she was hinting at. There was one category of women who were considered not only dispensable, but sometimes undesirable.

'Do you mean street girls?' he said.

'"Street girls" isn't really a suitable euphemism out here,' pointed out Fry. 'Shall we call them sex workers?'

'Prostitutes, if you like. But where would they do business?'

'Wherever there are numbers of men with nothing much else to do.'

Cooper pictured Pity Wood Farm. 'Targeting itinerant farm-workers, for example?'

'Who else?'

At first, he thought it was a rhetorical question. But the tone had been wrong, and Fry seemed to be waiting for an answer.

'Yes, who else?' said Cooper, regarding her curiously.

'All right. I was thinking about old-fashioned police officers who operate under their own discretion and run their own patch, with no questions asked.'

'That old thing?' said Tom Farnham. 'Who would want that? It's just an old skull. Some damn superstition of Derek Sutton's. Mad bugger, he was.'

Farnham fidgeted with the spray can he'd been using to touch up a dent on the lawnmower. Its repair was nearly complete now. Its working parts gleamed with oil, and its paintwork had been cleaned and polished.

'But you do have it, sir?'

Farnham sighed. 'Don't you need a warrant or something?'

'Only if you don't agree to help us. But why would you want to prevent us seeing this skull if it's worthless?'

'Why indeed? Screaming Billy, that's what the old fool called it. Supposed to protect the farm from bad luck, or something. Raymond didn't see eye to eye with him on that, not at all. He wanted it out of the house when the place was sold. Said he wouldn't curse the new owners with it. Raymond, he didn't care about anything else – he was glad to get shut of the place in the end. It was just that skull he had a bee in his bonnet about. He rang and asked me to get rid of it before the new bloke took over the farm. So I did him a favour, see? For old times' sake, and all that.'

'Very loyal of you, sir. And it's still here?'

'Yes, it's still here.'

Farnham moved across to his work bench and took a key from his pocket. He unlocked a cupboard under the bench and withdrew a cardboard box packed with old newspaper. In the middle of the newspaper, something smooth and yellow nestled.

Cooper took the box from him and pulled on a pair of latex gloves. He carefully lifted the skull free and placed it in a plastic evidence bag. The bone was faintly yellow, like paper that had been left in the sun.

'You couldn't sell it, then?' said Fry.

'What?'

'That's what you were hoping for, I imagine.'

'Oh, for Christ's sake. Raymond couldn't have cared less. He just wanted it out of Pity Wood. He's never mentioned it to me since, so why shouldn't I sell it? I got nothing out of all the time I spent working with the Suttons, you know. Look at me, I'm broke. I try to make a living repairing other folks' lawnmowers. A few quid would have helped me out a bit.'

'But you had no luck?'

'There were a few collectors interested. But it's not good enough quality, they said. Too damaged.'

'Damaged?'

'A bit of bashing about. Look, at the back there. But that's to be expected, when it's so old. I mean, it had been in the farmhouse for, I don't know – centuries, I suppose.'

'Are you sure of that, sir?'

'How do you mean?'

'Can you tell whether this is an old skull, or a more recent one?'

'More recent one?'

Farnham stared at her, then snorted and began shaking his head vigorously. 'Oh, no. You're not going to pin something like that on me. You're trying to tie me in with those bodies you found at the farm, aren't you?'

Cooper tensed. The fact that the head had been removed from one of the bodies had not been released to the media, so Farnham shouldn't know that. But had he really made an admission? Or was he just putting two and two together, and making a clever guess?

'You've confirmed that you were working at the farm during the relevant period,' said Fry. 'You must have known who else was working there. If you want to help us, you should suggest some names. That would be your most sensible move, Mr Farnham.'

He looked at the skull Cooper was holding in its new evidence bag. Several teeth were missing from the jaw, and the skull grinned horribly, as if at some private joke of its own.

'You know, they were mostly workers who came for a few weeks or a few days, then moved on. You can't expect me to remember their names. I hardly got the chance to know some of them to speak to.'

'So where did these individuals come from?'

'They were contracted in. See, that was the way it was at Pity Wood in those days. We didn't employ any workers ourselves. We had a contract for labour, and when we asked for them, they turned up. Sometimes we wanted people on a regular basis, but other times we just needed a gang in for a few days. It depended on what we were doing. It changed every year at Pity Wood. Every season.' He looked at Cooper. 'You understand, don't you?'

'All your failed enterprises,' said Cooper. 'None of them lasted more than a year or two.'

'Yes. Well, like I said, it wasn't my fault they failed. Times were difficult. We had a lot of bad luck.'

'We'll need to know who sub-contracted your labour. Who was the gang master?'

'Look, do I have to?' said Farnham. 'I want to help, really I do. But dumping on someone else is not good.'

'Well, we could arrest you, Mr Farnham, and take you into custody in Edendale. And then we could search your house, as well as taking your fingerprints and your DNA. And we'll see what that ties you to.'

Farnham groaned. 'His name was Rourke.'

'Rourke?'

'Martin Rourke, yes. He was the man, you know – the fixer.'

'Is he local?'

'No, not him. I think he lived in Chesterfield at that time, but he was Irish. I haven't seen him around for a year or so. I can give you the phone number we used for him, if it's any help.'

'Yes, please. And what about the women, sir?'

'Women?' said Farnham. 'Which women do you mean?'

'Which women? Were there a lot of them?'

Farnham began to look shifty again. For a few minutes, he'd been telling the truth, but now his eyes were roving around the workshop, his hand went to cover his mouth, as if to keep the words from escaping.

'Well, there isn't much entertainment out here, you know. Just the pub in Rakedale, which doesn't satisfy all of a man's needs, if you know what I mean. And a lot of the blokes didn't want to go to the pub anyway. If they were dossing on the farm for a week or two, they needed something to keep them happy.'

'So women came to the farm?'

'Now and then.'

'Now and then? What does that mean? Once a week, once a month? A special treat on someone's birthday? What?'

'Most weekends, I suppose. But only in those seasons, you know – when there were gangs on the farm to get the harvest in, or to get an order out. You want to talk to Rourke – he was the one who organized it all. He always seemed to have the right sort of contacts.'

'Are you sure you don't know where Mr Rourke is now?'

'Nah. He could be anywhere. He might be working in agriculture, or the building trade. Rourke was the sort who could turn his hand to anything, I reckon. Always good at talking himself up, you know? He might have gone back to

224

Ireland, of course. They say there's a lot of jobs over there now. No need for the paddies to come to England for work any more.'

'The Celtic Tiger.'

Farnham rallied enough to make a joke. 'Yes, I suppose you might call him that.'

Fry never responded to interviewees who tried to be funny or make light of the subject. She regarded Farnham sourly until he stopped smiling.

'We suspect that Pity Wood Farm was being used for some kind of illegal activity, Mr Farnham,' she said. 'We think this was happening during your period there as a partner or farm manager, whatever you want to call yourself.'

'If anything was happening, you can't prove I was involved.'

'The circumstances look very suspicious.'

'Well, I'm afraid I'm going to have to leave you to your speculation. I congratulate you on your imagination, Sergeant. But I don't have much time for flights of fancy myself.'

'The evidence is there at Pity Wood, Mr Farnham. Once we have a tight enough case against you, we'll be back.'

'Look, I'm not so stupid that I'd leave evidence lying around, if I'd committed a crime, now, am I? So if there *was* evidence left lying around, that proves that I didn't do it, right? That is clearly the action of somebody with much less ability for planning ahead and foreseeing all eventualities than I am. So it's psychologically wrong, don't you see?'

'Mr Farnham, we only deal with the facts, not with psychological theories.'

'OK, you do that. You won't find any evidence that connects to me. It just isn't possible.'

Fry was frowning as they left Farnham's house. Within a mile or two, her frown had turned to an expression of outrage, and she turned on Cooper.

'Imagination?' she said. 'Imagination? *Moi?*'

225

'So how do we go about finding Martin Rourke?' asked Cooper.

'Check the PNC and pray for an accurate address?'

Cooper ran the check when they got back to the office. The PNC could give him convictions, distinguishing marks, place of birth. But that wasn't enough. He logged into the criminal intelligence system and looked for aliases, changes of address or known associates. No sign of Martin Rourke.

That left only one option. He put a call in to liaison and got a contact for the Garda Síochána in Dublin. Oh, yes, said the officer. They'd do everything in their power to help their colleagues in Derbyshire locate Mr Martin Rourke.

Cooper thanked him, and rang off. Oh, yes? Well, it would take the luck of the Irish.

20

That afternoon, the yellow skull recovered from Tom Farnham's garage was packed up and sent off to Sheffield University for the anthropology team to examine. Dr Jamieson would report on its provenance, in due course. But this was Saturday, so Fry knew she couldn't expect any results for a few days.

She looked across the CID room, where Cooper was at his desk.

'You know, this is a case that *has* to be all about the victims,' she said.

'Isn't every case about the victims, Diane?'

'Of course,' said Fry, waving a hand impatiently. 'But, in this instance, the identity of the victims is crucial. We not only have to find out who they were, but how they were connected to each other – and we need to do both of those things before we can even begin to focus on any suspects. How did these women come to be at Pity Wood Farm? If we can start to build up a picture of them, Ben, we're halfway there. Damn it, if we can do that, we're almost *all* the way there.'

Cooper looked thoughtful. It was the one thing Fry could say about him – he always listened and considered what she said, even if he then went off and did something entirely different.

'In a way, it feels as though there ought to be a third victim,' he said.

'What?'

'A third victim. One who came in between these two, perhaps. I don't know. But a victim that would fill in the gaps and make the connection. The ones we've found might not be Victims A and B at all, but A and C. It could be the absence of the real Victim B that's making them look as though they're not part of a sequence.'

'Explain yourself, Ben.'

Cooper got up and began to pace in frustration, as if he was struggling to articulate in plain words some nagging but elusive idea that had been slithering at the back of his mind.

'What I mean is, there might have been a third person who had connections to these other two. If there was a middle victim, the pieces could fall together. At the moment, it's like there's a black hole, a missing section where all the links have been broken.'

'But there isn't a third victim.'

'Not that we've found, Diane.'

Fry thought of the excavated farmyard. 'Well, not at Pity Wood. There isn't a third victim *there*. We'd have found her by now, Ben.'

'Has anyone checked that old caravan?'

'The search team gave it an initial sweep. The SOCOs haven't got round to it yet, but there's certainly no body in it, if that's what you're thinking. Not even any personal possessions that might lead to an ID.'

'No, but there might be some trace evidence,' said Cooper. 'It was almost certainly being used to house itinerant workers.'

'I'll suggest making it a higher priority. OK?'

But Cooper continued to pace, unsatisfied. 'These victims didn't go missing at the same time,' he said. 'There'd have been a major enquiry, if there had been three. We'd still be looking for them now. There must be a connection between them, though.'

'I repeat, we haven't found three bodies. It sounds ridiculous to say "only" two, but . . .'

'But you're right. We need to look more closely. Extend the area of search. You know, I was thinking about the Fred and Rosemary West case. Those girls who were offered cheap accommodation in the Wests' house, and never left. If I remember right, not all the bodies were found at the house. There was a second burial site, at some property connected with the Wests.'

'I remember. Any ideas, then?'

Cooper sat down, looking suddenly tired. 'Well, I'll need to go through the files again, Diane.'

'Do that. If there *is* a third victim, she might be the one who makes the connection with all the others.'

'It's another Catch-22. We need to make the connections first to find her. And we need to find her to make the connections.'

Mentioning it to no one, least of all Ben Cooper, Fry took half an hour to visit Edendale Museum for herself. She had to show her warrant card to get admission, because the museum was closing for the night.

'The hand of glory, Sergeant?' said the attendant. 'One of our most popular exhibits. The kids love it. Little ghouls, most of them.'

'Is this a real human hand?'

'Certainly, certainly. I'll show you.'

Fry followed the attendant to the display case. So Cooper thought she would never have heard of such a thing as a hand of glory, did he? Well, there he was wrong, for once. She was from the Black Country, and the area had its own mummified hand of glory, so called. That one had been taken from inside the chimney of a pub when it was being renovated. The White Hart at Caldmore Green.

Everyone knew the White Hart in the Black Country. Back in the sixties, the A34 Murderer had been caught because he was overheard asking a victim the way to 'Karma Green'. Until then, police had thought he was a Brummie, from the neighbouring city of Birmingham. But only Black Country folk pronounced Caldmore as 'Karma'. A killer's origins had given him away.

Once, Fry had seen the object itself in Walsall Museum, above the central library on Lichfield Street. It had been just one artefact among the scold's bridles and Second World War gas masks, a historic collection of iron locks, and some gaucho spurs and stirrups. She'd heard that the museum had taken it off public display at one time because it was frightening the children too much, but you could still see it if you asked. It had become a sort of under-the-counter hand of glory.

'This is one of Edendale Museum's most popular exhibits,' said the attendant. 'Well, one of the most viewed, anyway. Not everyone approves of it.'

'A bit controversial, is it?'

'Let's say the reactions to it vary considerably. There are many people who refuse to believe that it's actually a real hand. Even when we explain the whole thing to them, they still don't believe us. They go away thinking it's a plastic reproduction, which it isn't.'

Of course, the White Hart at Caldmore Green had a ghost or two of its own. There had allegedly been a death in the attic where the 'hand' was found, the suicide of a servant girl. A previous landlord had reported hearing sobs coming from the attic room, and an investigation found nothing but the mysterious handprint of a child in the dust.

Whether the White Hart hand of glory had ever belonged to the servant girl was doubtful, though. Fry had seen it just as she was beginning her training to join the police and had already started her course at UCE in Perry Barr. Even if she hadn't already picked up a smattering of medical knowledge, it would have been obvious to her that the object in the museum was actually the severed arm of a small child, torn off right up to the scapula, then pickled in formalin.

Despite the story that had become attached to it, she was pretty sure that Walsall Museum's hand of glory was more likely to be a medical specimen from the mid-nineteenth century. If that was supposed to be a magical item used to aid burglaries, there must have been some malefactors being badly misled by their hand-of-glory supplier. How or why a medical specimen had come to be concealed in the chimney of a pub, no one was saying. Everyone preferred the stories of ghosts and magic, obviously.

'By the mysteries of the deep, by the flames of Baal, by the power of the East and the silence of the night, by the Holy Rites of Hecate, I conjure and exorcise thee.'

'Sorry?'

He pointed at a printed card inside the case. 'It's the spell you're supposed to use with the hand of glory. If you do it right, it not only protects you, but provides light that only you can see. Naturally, it was used mostly for nefarious purposes. Anything useful always is, don't you find?'

The phenomenon of general credulity on the subject baffled Fry. Fair enough, if there was something genuinely mysterious and unexplained, you might be forgiven for letting loose the imagination and coming up with your own interpretation. But when the scientific facts were staring them in the face, how could people ignore them and believe instead in something that flew in the face of the evidence? Some would believe that the world was flat, or that the Earth circled the Moon, just because they wanted to believe it. Others had faith in the magical powers of a pickled hand or a severed head.

Good luck to them. But if she found them putting their crazy ideas into practice, she'd be obliged to lock them up.

231

Prison or high-security psychiatric hospital, she didn't really mind. So long as colleagues like Ben Cooper didn't get in her way with some well-meaning rubbish about cultural identity.

But here, in Edendale, was a genuine hand of glory.

'The only other one that we know of is in the museum at Whitby,' said the attendant.

'Obtaining a human hand under the proper circumstances could prove to be quite difficult in this day and age,' said Fry.

'I expect so. But . . .'

'What?'

'Well, there are ways and means, aren't there? You can find people willing to do anything, for the right price.'

DCI Kessen was standing near the back of the CID room when Fry returned. Before she could get her coat off, his voice stopped her.

'Ah, DS Fry. Do we have any possibilities yet from the missing persons reports?'

Not knowing what else to do, Fry looked down at her desk. A misper report sat right there, left for her by someone while she was out.

'Yes, sir.'

'Let's have it, DS Fry.'

Fry picked up the report and read it for the first time. 'This is a local woman who was reported missing four years ago. She's five foot seven, twenty-four years old, reddish hair.'

'Red hair? Is that a match?'

'The older body is missing a head.'

'So it is.'

'But it's the closest we've got at the moment, sir.'

'Who made the report?' asked Kessen.

'A sister.'

'Is it possible she would still have some of the missing woman's possessions?'

'Something that would retain a print, you mean?'

'Exactly.'

'I don't know, sir,' said Fry.

'Well, ask her.'

Fry sat down and picked up the phone.

'Hold on, we have a miracle,' said Hitchens. 'The mobile unit in Rakedale has had success. A member of the public came in with some information. We've even got a name. Jack Elder.'

Fry put the phone down again. 'Shall we go and pick him up?' she said eagerly.

'If you like. He lives in a bungalow on Field Lane, Rakedale. But word is that he's been seen going into the village pub, and he hasn't come out yet.'

'Who's the informant, sir?'

'Mr Alex Brindley, of Shaw Farm.'

Cooper looked at Fry as they went out. 'Mr Brindley? Is he a reliable witness?'

'Yes. Well, *I* believed him – which is more than I can say for anyone else I've spoken to in Rakedale.'

The atmosphere in the Dog Inn had turned several degrees cooler, if that was possible. Nothing to do with the weather, but with the sudden ceasing of conversation and the hostile stares of the customers. Cooper looked around the bar, but saw only tense faces and deliberately turned backs. The sheepdog looked mournfully up at him from its place under the table, but didn't make a move.

'We're looking for Mr Jack Elder,' announced Fry into the silence. 'Is he here?'

Watching the reactions of the customers carefully, Cooper worked out which person they were all avoiding looking at. A man with a long, grey beard and wearing a green sweater was sitting near the dartboard, pretending to straighten the flights on a set of darts. Even from here, Cooper could see that the flights were plastic ones, which didn't need much straightening. He walked across the bar and stood in front of the table.

'Mr Elder?'

The man pulled an irritated expression and placed a finger against the point of one of his darts.

'Who's asking?'

'Police. I'm Detective Constable Cooper. This is Detective Sergeant Fry.'

Cooper produced his warrant card, but the man didn't look at it.

'We'd like to ask you a few questions, sir.'

He felt the silence in the bar shifting somehow. A shuffle of feet, the tap of a glass being drunk from and replaced on a table. Then someone sniggered.

'Go on, slap the cuffs on him. He's the one that done it, Inspector.'

There were equal amounts of curses and laughter. Elder glared along the room, but he seemed to sense that the fleeting solidarity of his drinking companions had already started to dissipate.

'Piss off!' he snarled at someone Cooper couldn't see.

'Mr Elder, perhaps we could go somewhere else for a talk.'

Elder dropped the darts on the table with a clatter, and made a great show of standing up very slowly, putting as much bravado as he could into retrieving his coat and zipping it up.

'Where's my hat?' he said. 'Has one of you buggers pinched my hat?'

There were more sniggers. But Elder's hat was clearly visible on the settle behind him. Cooper waited patiently, glad that Fry had had the sense to stay in the background for once. Since the Dog Inn's toilets were reached only through a winding series of stone passages, Elder didn't have much chance of making a bolt for it through the back door.

'All right, I'm ready.'

Elder paused in the doorway, seeming to feel that he wasn't making as good a show as he'd like to have done in front of the other regulars. He opened the door and let a squall of rain in from outside.

'I'm going out now,' he said. 'And I may be some time.'

He tried a chuckle as he looked around at his friends. But the sound died in his throat as he saw that no one else was laughing. Not even the dog.

21

That night, Cooper drove out of Edendale until he'd left the streetlamps behind and there was only the reflection of the Toyota's headlights from the cat's eyes in the road and from the rain that drifted across the bonnet. He saw few cars on the road and passed even fewer houses – just the occasional farm wrapped in its own little bowl of light.

According to the weather forecast on the BBC, there was no chance of snow this year. It would be a traditional grey Christmas. Fog was the best that Edendale could hope for in the way of seasonal weather. There'd be a blanket of it filling the valley, smothering the sound of Christmas Day traffic, hiding the flickering lights of the council decorations. And killing a few more visitors on the roads, no doubt.

The old people sometimes described the Peak District climate as 'six months of bad weather, followed by six months of winter'. But those times were past, the years when snow drifts had made the roads impassable and villages were cut off for weeks. Cooper felt a curious sense of loss.

Fry had taken on the task of interviewing Jack Elder herself, allowing Cooper to keep his date. He had no idea what had made her do that, because he didn't normally expect favours from her. Still, don't look a gift horse in the mouth, as his mother would have said.

Liz Petty lived in Bakewell, the touristy heart of the Peak District. Tonight, she felt like a change, so they opted to eat at the Australian Bar, close to the Bakewell section police station. Here, the Aussie theme had gone beyond the name and the boomerangs in the window, and had spread right through the menu.

While they shared some skinny dips, Liz got a few grumbles off her chest. Cooper had heard most of them before, around the station. Like the other SOCOs, she often complained how frustrating it was to hear police officers say there were 'no forensics'.

'Some of them *still* don't know what the word means,' she said.

The division had finally got one of the two long-wheelbase four-by-fours that Scenes of Crime had been saying they needed for years, but not the second. And the policy of automatic attendance at burglary scenes had led to some crazy situations, such as SOCOs dusting for fingerprints when the aluminium powder from their last visit to a victim's home was still visible on the window frame. There was a story doing the rounds about another burglary, where the officer dealing with the incident had entered in the command and control log: *There are no forensic possibilities for SOCO, but I have to ask them to attend.*

Dipping a deep-fried potato wedge into mayo and garlic, Cooper exercised his listening skills. It wasn't difficult in Liz's presence. She never bored him, because she never took herself too seriously. At the end of her whinge, she would gaze at him and burst out laughing. He treasured those moments, when they seemed to be connecting at some level that was beyond any words.

'We're still the forgotten department,' she said. 'The Cinderellas of the division.'

'There was only one Cinderella,' said Cooper. 'The others were Ugly Sisters.'

And Liz laughed. 'That describes my colleagues perfectly.'

Liz chose Swagman's Tucker, while Cooper passed over the Bruce Burgers and hesitated between Bondi Chicken or Dingo Dog. Waiting for him to decide, Liz took a drink of wine and gazed out of the window at Granby Road. She lived just off Fly Hill, only a few minutes' walk away, in a three-storey terraced cottage she rented from her uncle.

Cooper found himself distracted from the menu by her profile against the lights from the street outside. He would be happy just to sit and look at her for a while, listening to her talk, and forget about the Dingo Dog.

But then he realized how hungry he was, and ordered the Outback Bruce Burger after all.

'I hear you're getting a new superintendent,' said Liz.

'Yes. She arrives on Tuesday, but she's already making her presence felt.'

'Are there going to be changes?'

'You bet.'

'One of the guys said he thought Diane Fry might be leaving.'

'Did he?'

Cooper was completely taken aback. There had been several occasions when he'd thought Fry might head off into the blue. Fry had even hinted at it herself, hankering after a job in Europol, or anywhere more exciting than Edendale. But it was so odd to hear it from someone else. It made the idea sound as though it might be true.

'Well, she's ambitious,' said Liz.

'She certainly is.'

'To be honest, I think it would be a good thing if she went, Ben.'

Cooper was silent for a moment, thinking about his Bruce

Burger. He'd promised himself not to dwell on work tonight. Not the current enquiry, anyway. You had to escape from those things for a while.

'There are always changes,' he said. 'Life never stays the same. See how different it is since you came to E Division.'

He meant changes in her department. Before Liz's time, there had been a period when there were only two SOCOs in the division for eighteen months. But their performance was measured on volume crime, and no account was taken of serious crime and road traffic collision work. If Liz had grumbles, she ought to have heard the level of whining in Scenes of Crime for those few months.

But Liz took his comment quite differently, and went slightly pink. She changed the subject as their food arrived.

'Speaking of Cinderella, wasn't the pantomime great the other night?'

'Great.'

'I know it's all a bit naff, Ben. But if you take it in the right spirit, it's good fun.'

'Of course. It was great. I enjoyed it. Really.'

Liz laughed again, because she knew he was lying.

'And you're still coming with me to the baptism service tomorrow, aren't you?'

'Of course. I'll be there, with my suit on and everything.'

And, although he'd promised himself he wouldn't, Cooper found himself thinking about work. He was mentally trying to fit the residents of Rakedale into a pantomime cast. Some of them were chasing the magic genie of the lamp, while others stood around in the street cracking bad jokes, and the Emperor Ping Pong refused to let his daughter marry a poor washerwoman's son.

Cooper had a feeling he'd met Wishy Washy and Widow Twankey. Maybe even Inspector Chu. But where was the evil Abanazar?

*　　*　　*

239

Jack Elder dragged his fingers through his beard, staring in disbelief at the walls of the interview room and at the triple-deck tape recorder as the tapes started to turn, waiting for his answers to Fry's questions. He'd been waiting an hour already, while checks were made on him. It wasn't long, but it was enough for anyone to get nervous about what was going to happen next.

'Mr Elder, we have information that you've been offering supplies of cheap diesel. Would you like to tell us where you've obtained that diesel from?'

'Oh, that? Well, that's just a bit of business, you know. I work for this little haulage company as a driver. I'm a farmworker really, but you make a living any way you can round here these days, and haulage is a good business to be in, if you get your HGV licence. And I've got this mate, you see –'

'Name?'

'You what?'

'The name of your friend?'

'Now, I can't do that. You don't shop a mate, do you?'

'Well, I can understand that. But it would only be a problem if you were doing something illegal together, Mr Elder. Is that the case?'

'Well, I . . .' He stumbled, unsure now of what the right answer was.

'Where did this cheap diesel come from, sir?'

'My mate, see, he works for the same haulage company, at the depot. The company has its own diesel tanks, to keep the wagons fuelled up.'

'So this is diesel you and your friend steal from your employer?'

'No, well . . . I don't ask him how he gets hold of it, I just assume it's legitimate, you know. Surplus to requirements, or something.'

'Oh, come on.'

'I help him to sell it, that's all,' said Elder earnestly. 'He gives me a cut on sales. A bit of commission, if you like. Just to supplement my wages.'

Fry felt unreasonably disappointed that Elder was only admitting to the diesel being stolen.

'You see, the thing is, Mr Elder, we checked your record on the Police National Computer, and we discovered that you have a conviction for the use of illegal fuel.'

'Ah, well.'

'And that wasn't stolen fuel, but laundered red diesel.'

'That was just a one-off, you know. I thought I'd get away with it, just using it once, but the Excise turned up in the wrong place and they caught me out. I held my hand up for it and got a fine.'

'It's quite a common offence in these parts, it seems,' said Fry.

'I wouldn't know about that.'

'Red diesel is sold to farmers and people like them for use in off-road vehicles. Tractors and so on. As a farmworker by trade, I expect you know lots of farmers.'

'Yes, I do. But –'

'Tell me, Mr Elder, isn't it the truth that the diesel you're helping your friend to sell isn't from the haulage firm at all, but red diesel that is being laundered somewhere for sale to motorists?'

'I can't answer that.'

'There's a huge mark-up, I believe. Plenty of commission on sales, if there's a sizeable operation going on somewhere. We need you to tell us where that laundering operation is, Mr Elder.'

'I can't.'

'Have you ever been to Pity Wood Farm, sir?'

'Oh – Pity Wood?'

'Pity Wood Farm. It was the home of the Sutton family until recently. I'm sure you know it. Have you ever been there?'

'No, I haven't,' said Elder, dropping his gaze to the table and fiddling with his beard.

'Are you quite sure?'

'Sure.'

'Only, we do have a witness who says he's seen you going in and out of the farm in your lorry many times.'

'Well, he's lying,' said Elder. 'Whoever he is, he's lying. I know the Suttons, of course I do. But I only ever met them in the pub. I was never at that farm.'

'You know your answer is being recorded, Mr Elder?'

'Yes. Well, I mean . . . I think I should have a solicitor.'

'You'll get one,' said Fry. 'But it might take some time. It's nearly Christmas, you know.'

An officer knocked on the door. Fry paused the interview and went out. He passed her a message.

'Oh, interesting.'

She went back in, and found Elder watching her hopefully in a vain expectation that she might be coming back to tell him it was all a big mistake and he could leave.

'On quite another matter, Mr Elder,' she said, 'do you know a place called Godfrey's Rough?'

Elder looked confused by the change in the direction of questioning.

'Where?'

'Godfrey's Rough picnic site. I believe it's a well-known dogging area.'

'Sorry?' Elder cocked his head as if he had misheard and thought his ear might have suddenly become blocked. 'Did you say "dogging"? Are you talking about people walking their dogs? But they do that everywhere.'

'Walking their dogs? Hardly.'

Elder looked even more puzzled.

'It's one of those modern expressions, I suppose,' he said. 'Something to do with the internet? Or mountain bikes. Or those skateboarding things. They have their own languages, the young people. I can't understand a word they're saying sometimes.'

'The fact is, Mr Elder, couples park up in some of these out-of-the-way places at night for the purpose of having sex in their cars.'

'Oh, is that all?' said Elder.

'Not quite. Sometimes there are people there who watch them doing it.'

'Those are peeping toms,' said Elder. 'Voyeurs, you might call them. Well, that's not new. We've always had them. We had sex in my day, too, you know – just not so much of it, and more discreet. In those days, peeping toms had a hard job of it, so to speak.'

Elder smiled. Fry felt that familiar frustration of trying to get through to people who seemed to talk a different language from her own. Most of all, she hated those secret little smiles and nods of understanding that sometimes passed between Ben Cooper and people like this Elder. It was as if the fact they were born within a few miles of each other gave them some hidden means of communication that no one else could ever learn. She was glad she'd let Cooper go.

'You don't understand, Mr Elder,' she said. 'This is watching by arrangement. It's part of the thrill, apparently.'

Elder's eyes popped. 'They want folk watching them while they're doing it?' He considered the prospect, didn't find it appealing, and shook his head. 'No, I can't see it. I'd call it perverted. But I suppose things are different now. Is that really what they get up to at night?'

'And not just at night either. Lunchtimes, even. During their breaks from work. Sometimes it's at a date and time fixed up in advance. Sometimes they just go along to a well-known dogging spot like Godfrey's Rough and see what turns up. The people who do the watching are the ones called doggers.'

Elder was quiet, trying to imagine the scene in the woods.

'I suppose this is shocking you, Mr Elder?'

243

'It's a new idea, that's all. And it's a bit too late for me to learn, maybe?'

'I think not, sir.'

'Happen they're not doing any harm, anyway,' said Elder. 'Have you thought of that?'

'The point is,' said Fry, 'things can sometimes go wrong. Doggers have been known to fall out with each other. People try to join in when they're not wanted . . . Well, you can imagine. It's fraught with dangers.'

Elder nodded slowly. 'That's bound to happen,' he said. 'Folks are always the same. But these'll be city folks, no doubt. Students and such.'

'Some of the keenest doggers,' said Fry, 'are lorry drivers.'

'Eh?'

'Lorry drivers. Truckers. They have favourite places where they like to park up for the night. I suppose they get bored just watching the telly in the back of the cab and eating microwaved chips. So they get together sometimes, have a few cans of beer, and go dogging. A bunch of big, hairy truckers can be a bit intimidating, and not quite what people are expecting. Things can get out of hand.'

'Those will be long-distance drivers,' said Elder. 'Blokes doing a haul up to Scotland or somewhere. They're miles away from home, you see. They have to stop where they can. Most of them are from the Continent these days – Germans and French and Italians. I saw one the other day from a place called Azerbaijan. I don't even know where that is. I couldn't find it on the map. A damn great Mercedes he was driving, too. Just think of it. Miles away from home. Miles and miles and miles.'

'Not all of them are from the Continent, Mr Elder,' said Fry. 'Some of them aren't far away from home at all.'

'I don't know what you mean.'

'See this make and registration?' said Fry, showing the note. 'This DAF was recorded by one of our patrols as being parked at Godfrey's Rough. It's a local registration, Mr Elder. This

244

lorry doesn't belong to any Frenchman or Azerbaijani. It belongs to you.'

Fry paused the interview tapes again. Jack Elder was developing the classic breathless, bewildered look of the guilty person suddenly finding himself smothered under the weight of evidence that he'd either overlooked or had never imagined could exist.

'We'll take a break, shall we, Mr Elder? You can settle into your cell while we wait for the duty solicitor to arrive. It will probably be tomorrow when we can talk again. I hope you didn't have plans for Christmas.'

Tom Farnham was only thirty-eight years old. He jogged a couple of miles through the woods whenever he had time, and he visited the gym about once a month. He was as fit as he wanted to be, for his age. Though he was struggling financially right now, he had lots of plans for future enterprises, when the time was right. Tom Farnham liked money.

When Farnham went out to his workshop that night, the wind had risen. He could hear a continuous rustling in the woods, as if the trees were whispering to each other, whispering secrets that ought to be kept quiet. It was still raining, and the trees were sodden. In these woods, the sound of dripping water could be mistaken for footsteps after a while.

As usual, he'd left the door of the garage open to disperse the petrol fumes. The lawnmower was pretty much finished, and he just wanted to see how the newly sprayed paint was drying. Those detectives had interrupted him, and he wasn't sure whether he'd made as good a job of it as he'd have liked.

In a way, it was a relief to have rid of that skull from his property. He'd never liked the thing, and anything that couldn't make him money was a waste of space, in the end. All the stuff about it bringing luck and protecting you was nonsense, of course. Ridiculous superstition that only the likes of Derek Sutton believed in.

245

While he was bending over the lawnmower, Farnham sensed that the quality of the light had changed, and realized that his security light had come on outside. That wasn't unusual. Wild animals strayed out of the woods sometimes and got into his garden. Foxes, badgers, even a small deer occasionally. It was surprising what lurked in Pity Wood.

It was only when he heard the crash of his garage door thrown back and the thump of boots on concrete that Farnham began to rise. He had barely straightened up when the first of the dark figures burst into the light, meeting the turn of his shoulder with the impact of a baseball bat.

Fry was a good driver, trained in the West Midlands force driving school to handle pursuit cars. But she spent most of the drive home distracted from the road. She was trying to avoid Christmas songs on the radio, flicking from station to station until she found something unseasonal. She ended up listening to 'Crosstown Traffic' from Jimi Hendrix's *Electric Ladyland* – the only rock song she could think of that featured a kazoo. Nothing Christmassy about that.

For the past few hours, Fry had been trying to keep the conversation with DI Hitchens out of her mind. But that was only possible during the day, when she was working. The Pity Wood Farm enquiry provided enough to occupy her mind and take her full concentration. It wasn't the case when she left the station in West Street and headed out towards her flat in Grosvenor Avenue. The concentration started to slip, despite her best efforts.

Fry knew that she ought to have gone south, to London. They always needed officers in the Met, and it would have suited her much better in a big city where nobody cared who you were or what you did with your life. By now, she would have been well established, fast-tracking to promotion, instead of dickering about in this rural force.

Turning her Peugeot into Castleton Road, Fry stopped at

the little corner shop run by an Asian family. The young couple had always been pleasant to her, even when she hadn't been in a mood to reciprocate. A friendly greeting could be welcome at times.

She wasn't really hungry, but she bought enough supplies to keep body and soul together for another twenty-four hours. Cheese and toast would satisfy her. Anything else would sit uncomfortably on that tight, anxious knot in her stomach. She passed over the cakes and chocolate displays, and instead picked up a yogurt. And not just any yogurt, but an organic bio-live luscious low-fat fruit yogurt, raspberry and cranberry flavour. She felt strangely virtuous.

Groups of young men and women tottered or staggered around the pubs on the corner of Grosvenor Avenue, some of them with tinsel in their hair or reindeer antlers on their heads. It was Saturday night, of course. She'd forgotten that. At weekends, some of her fellow flat-dwellers lived dangerous and unpredictable private lives. Not her concern when she was off duty, though.

'Just stay out of my way, or I'll run you over,' she muttered at a drunk who stumbled off the kerb into the path of her car. What difference would another dead body make?

But a fresh body was a different matter from aged remains. Pity Wood Farm was a classic historical case. Fry knew that most of the evidence in any historical investigation was found in the form of layers. It didn't matter whether you were researching your family history, or hunting for a serial killer. There would be layers on top of each other – different levels of meaning and significance. Over the years, meanings distorted and accumulated irrelevant associations. An enquiry had to dig down to the lowest level to find the one that was most accurate, the most free of irrelevant material. A good bit of digging, that was what she needed. But psychological digging, not the knee-deep-in-mud type.

She was aware that the lorry driver, Jack Elder, might turn

out to be a complete red herring. But it was comforting to have someone in custody. Anyone. At least there would be charges at some point.

But somewhere, waiting to be dug up, were the identities of the two victims at Pity Wood Farm. They couldn't remain Victim A and Victim B, a couple of reference numbers in the anthropologist's report, and a Forensic Science Service case-work enquiries code. They had been human beings once, and they were owed a proper identity.

The body that Jamie Ward discovered had made the message clear. Fry wouldn't forget that grey hand, bent in a pathetic summons, coaxing her towards the grave, and ensuring that she could never turn her back on it.

Of course, once an ID was established, that was really only the beginning. These young women had families – partners, parents, perhaps even children – who were wondering where they'd gone, and waiting to hear from them.

There was an astonishing statistic that Fry had once been given. Something like ninety-eight per cent of couples who lost a son or daughter through murder would separate within a couple of years of the crime. It was because the loss of a child was an experience that destroyed your life, and put such a strain on a relationship that the damage might never be repaired.

Ninety-eight per cent. That was a really bad statistic. When a victim had been a teenager or young woman when she went missing, the parents would no longer be together, almost certainly. She would be looking for people whose lives had already been wrecked. She'd be turning up on their doorstep to tell them a body had been discovered, and she thought it was probably their daughter. Could they come along and confirm that? Oh, and Merry Christmas, by the way.

Fry finally pulled up at number twelve and walked up to her flat on the first floor. Angie was out, of course, but her clothes were still here. Outside, the noise of drunken revellers would go on for hours yet, and the rain wouldn't stop them.

It had been dark since before she called at the museum to see the hand of glory. But that was the nature of late December.

Rain and dark nights. Ideal for festive jollity.

Farnham's clothes were soaking wet now, and his shoes slithered in the mud as he dodged from tree to tree, stumbling over roots. His breath was ragged against the sound of rain and the whip of branches hitting his face. The noise of his breathing went ahead of him through the woods. But it was the sound of a man whose life was already over.

For a second, he stopped and leaned against the trunk of an oak tree. He shook his head, spraying rain, sweat and mud from his face. His jacket was streaked with dirt, and fragments of vegetation clung to his jeans where he had charged through the undergrowth. Ahead of him were more trees, and the bank of a fast-running stream, brown water surging noisily in the night.

His wheezing concealed any noises from behind him, except for one soft footstep. There was a moment of silence. Birds rustled their damp wings in the branches, and a small shower of water fell on his face. As his breath blew out painfully into the air, he knew it might be his last.

'You don't want to do this,' he called. 'Stop it, now.'

He heard his own voice shaking with fear, and became angry at the humiliation he was being forced to suffer.

'You're making a mistake. You know that? A big mistake.'

A bullet whistled over his head and shredded a branch before burying itself in the trunk of a tree. It was no more than a bit of foreplay, though. Farnham heard the cocking of a hammer.

He began to run again, dodging left and right, slithering in the mud between the trees. He was almost back at his house, desperately trying to reach a phone, when the second bullet entered the back of his thigh, just above the knee. It snapped a tendon, punched a hole out of the femur and pierced the full thickness of his thigh muscle. The bullet emerged from a rip in his jeans and buried itself in the earth as he fell forward on to his face.

Farnham tried to get up again, but found his right leg refused to support his weight. He was crying as he flopped helplessly on the ground, terrified of the footsteps moving slowly towards him – a deliberate, skating tread which barely disturbed the wet leaves. He heard a rustling, and then a voice, quiet and low.

'We all make mistakes,' it said.

And Farnham never even noticed the third bullet.

When they'd finished what they came to do, the two men dragged Tom Farnham's body back into the workshop and closed the door. Then they vanished as quickly as they'd come, slipping away into the darkness among the trees.

They left nothing behind them that moved. Nothing, except a thin, red ribbon of blood, meandering slowly across the concrete floor.

22

Sunday

All Saints parish church in Edendale was unusually full for the Sunday-morning service. There was nothing like a baptism or a wedding to attract the sort of congregation you'd never normally get on a Sunday.

Cooper felt uncomfortable in his suit. He must have put a bit of weight on since he last wore it. Liz looked great, though. She'd broken out a dress from her wardrobe, put on shoes with heels and brushed back her hair. Cooper was unduly proud to be seen with her. She scrubbed up really well, as the saying went around here.

Across the aisle, Liz's friend and her family were squeezed into the front three pews. Mums and grandmas had come in their best hats, and dads coughed uneasily, glancing at their watches, wondering whether they'd be free before the pubs opened. The baby herself was there somewhere, clutched by her mother in a long, trailing christening gown. She was a remarkably well-behaved baby, who hadn't cried once yet.

When everyone was settled, the vicar began performing the introduction.

'*Here we are washed by the Holy Spirit and made clean.*

Here we are clothed with Christ, dying to sin that we may live his risen life.'

With mounting horror, Cooper realized that he was thinking of the pantomime from a couple of nights before. There was a startling similarity between the priest in his vestments intoning the opening lines of the service and the Pedlar stepping out on to the stage at the Royal Theatre for the first scene of *Aladdin*.

Oh, I'm a man from a distant land,
A place where camels roam
And if they don't like your face, they'll cut off your
*   hand . . .*

Liz gave him a warning look. Maybe he'd let a smile show, or twitched in the wrong way. Cooper took a breath and tried to control himself. This was not the way to behave in church.

After a couple of hymns, the vicar lit a candle and called for 'The Decision'. Raggedly, the congregation answered his questions, reading the replies from their order of service.

'To follow Christ means dying to sin and rising to new life with him. Do you reject the Devil and all rebellion against God?'

Cooper found himself mentally drifting away from the church. His mouth was still moving as if he was giving the replies with everyone else. But his mind was a mile away, in the lounge at The Oaks care home, where the staff would be serving a glass of sherry soon and the residents would be looking forward to their lunch.

'Do you renounce the deceit and corruption of evil? Do you repent of the sins that separate us from God and neighbour?'

He felt sure those words would really mean something to Raymond Sutton. Far more than they meant to him, or to any of the people squirming impatiently in their pews.

Sins that separate us from God and neighbour.

What sins were committed at Pity Wood Farm that had separated the Suttons from their neighbours, and from God?

Cooper suddenly had a terrible intuition of the torment that Raymond Sutton must have been going through all this time. Whatever had happened at Pity Wood, he'd either been a part of it, or he'd acted as a passive witness. It was surely impossible for him to have lived at the farm and not been aware of what went on. Raymond must have known every inch of that place like the back of his hand, as anyone would who'd lived on a farm his entire life.

Liz nudged him hard, and Cooper realized that the congregation was about to go into another hymn, and he was clutching the wrong book, his eyes distant, his mind wandering.

'Pay attention,' she said.

'Sorry.'

As the organ music began, Cooper recalled one of the sheepdogs at Bridge End dying when he was child. His great uncle had buried the dog behind the barn, out of sight. But Ben had known something was wrong the instant he arrived home from school. He'd prowled the farm buildings until he found the disturbed ground. He'd never needed to ask anyone. The very soil and air had talked to him and told him all he needed to know.

Cooper murmured under his breath. '*Raymond, there's no way you could forget that. You know exactly what happened.*'

The parents and godparents of the child had finally gathered around the font at the back of the church for the climax of the service.

'*We thank you, Father, for the water of baptism. In it we are buried with Christ in his death.*'

And the baby, who had been so quiet and well behaved throughout the service, began to scream as the water hit her face.

It looked as though residents in the care home had been having a good time at their Christmas party. Cooper found Raymond Sutton sitting in the lounge wearing a paper party hat, the kind that came out of a cracker and only lasted an hour or so before it fell off or got ripped. Mr Sutton's hat was green. His fellow residents had got the red and yellow ones.

'We have the party before Christmas because some of the residents spend the day itself with their families,' explained Elaine. 'It means all the staff can come in, too.'

'Mr Sutton won't be going anywhere on Christmas Day, I presume?' said Cooper.

'I don't know. Does he have any family locally?'

'Not that I'm aware of. But I'd be interested to hear if he gets any visitors.'

'I'll let you know. But you come here so often yourself, Detective Constable Cooper, that you're already his most frequent visitor.'

Cooper smiled at her, noticing her properly for the first time. 'I'm sorry if I'm being a nuisance, Elaine.'

'Not at all. In fact . . .'

'Yes?'

'I wondered what you'd be doing after work?'

'More work, probably.'

She gave him a quizzical smile. 'They must let you have some time off? But never mind.'

In the lounge, Cooper allowed an old lady to persuade him to pull a cracker with her. She read him the joke, and he laughed to please her. But he drew the line at wearing the paper hat, and she went away in disgust.

'You never had any children, did you, Mr Sutton?'

'No, I was never married.'

'I understand marriage isn't necessary any more, sir.'

'A child out of wedlock? It would be shameful.'

'No one would care these days, you know. Not in the least.'

'So they tell me. But I've never understood it. When was it that decent behaviour went out of fashion?'

'I don't think it went out of fashion exactly, sir. It's just stopped being compulsory these days.'

Sutton scowled. 'Well, I don't live in "these days", do I? I live in the past. That's what everyone always tells me. And why not? Maybe the past was a better time, and a better place.'

'Even when evil things happened?'

Cooper felt the old man's glare becoming more angry and more aggressive.

'You're trying to trap me,' he said.

'No, sir. I just want to understand what happened at the farm. Two women died, and that's wrong. I think you know who was responsible. Don't you want to see justice done?'

'Follow justice and justice alone, so that you may live and possess the land the Lord your God is giving you. Cursed is the man who withholds justice from the alien, the fatherless or the widow. Then all the people shall say, "Amen!"'

Sutton's words faded away into a tired squeak, and his head began to nod. Within moments, he was asleep in his chair.

Cooper shook his head in defeat. Raymond Sutton was like a man who'd been parachuted in from another century. He might have learned to accept cars and television, but he still clung to his set of Victorian beliefs as if they were a life raft. Even his voice seemed to have rusted over from neglect.

Only Mr Brindley was at home today, not the rest of the family. There must be a second car if his wife was out, because the Range Rover still stood, gleaming, on the drive.

'Well, we'd been talking about it between ourselves the night before, turning it over in our minds,' said Brindley when Fry asked him about his information on Elder. 'And when we saw the temporary police office in the village, we felt obliged to call in, as good citizens. I hope it was the right thing to do.'

'Certainly. That's what it was sited there for, sir. I'm glad you felt able to come forward. Not many people in Rakedale have.'

'Well, I'm not surprised. I suppose the village people are

rather clannish, aren't they? They want to stand by their own. But we're already outsiders, you see, so it doesn't matter what we do or say. It will hardly make any difference to our relations with our neighbours, will it?'

'I wouldn't be too sure, you know,' said Fry, thinking of the incident of the crows in the bedroom. That had been in this very house, hadn't it? She couldn't know whether Jo Brindley had told her husband about it, so she didn't mention it.

'What do you mean, Sergeant?'

'It might be advisable to check your security measures. Just in case word gets out and somebody takes exception.'

He looked concerned. 'Oh, I suppose you're right. They've never really been aggressive to us before. Rude, yes. We've had some unpleasant comments made to us in the pub from time to time, when we've called in. But outright aggression, no. I wonder if we did the right thing, after all.'

'Yes, of course you did. If you'd kept information like that to yourself, you'd be as bad as they are, wouldn't you?'

'Ah. And I wouldn't want that, would I? A good point, Sergeant, well made.'

'Could you just explain to me what your connection is with Mr Jack Elder? I know you've been through it before, but –'

'No, that's all right.' Brindley steepled his hands. 'It must have been a few years ago that I first came across him. I can't be sure how long exactly. It was one of those occasions that we'd been into the pub, Jo and I.'

'This would be the Dog Inn?'

'In Rakedale, yes. We do call in from time to time, to try and show our faces. We've done our best to mix in, Sergeant, really we have. But the locals always seem very hostile. They whisper among themselves – and, even worse, some of them make quite outrageous comments out loud. Elder was one of those. He always seemed to be in the same corner of the pub whenever we went in, and we came to dread seeing him there. That's why we stopped calling. Personally, I hated to stop, because it looked like cowardice. But Jo would get upset, so I went along with her.'

'And then there was an encounter with Mr Elder away from the pub, I understand?'

'Yes. Well, I used to see him many times away from the pub. But there was one specific occasion I recalled for the officers in Rakedale. Elder actually came here, to the house, once. Fortunately, no one else was home at the time, except for me. I often work from home, you see. That day, I couldn't believe it when I saw Jack Elder park his lorry in my gateway and come up to the house. I was ready for an unpleasant scene, I can tell you.'

'And what happened?'

'Well, I answered the door, and he stood there, grinning at me through that awful beard. At first, I couldn't understand what he wanted. But eventually it became clear that he was trying to sell me cheap fuel. He kept pointing at my car and saying, "Look, mate, it's diesel, in't it?", or something like that. He got very aggressive after a while, and started making comments about Jo. Obviously, I shut the door and he went away again. I'm ashamed to say I was a bit shaken by the incident.'

'But you didn't report it?'

'No. Well, it would only cause more trouble in the village. I'm thinking about the welfare of Jo and the children.'

'So what made you change your mind now?'

'The murders,' said Brindley. 'That's what they are, aren't they? The two bodies at Pity Wood Farm? If Jack Elder is connected in any way to those, I couldn't possibly keep quiet any longer.'

'But what makes you think he might be connected?'

Brindley leaned forward. 'I said I'd seen him many times away from the pub. Perhaps I didn't make it clear that the place I used to see him most often was coming and going from Pity Wood Farm with his lorry.'

Fry made a note in her notebook, listening to the quietness in the house.

'Is your wife not at home, sir?'

'No,' said Brindley, relaxing again. 'She's at extra rehearsals in Edendale today. Some panic over a few changes to the dance routines for the chorus.'

'A Christmas production of some kind?' asked Fry, recalling that theatres came into the Brindleys' lifestyle, along with restaurants and shopping.

'Yes. I can tell you where she's rehearsing, if you want to speak to her. I must warn you, she might be a bit distracted, though. She really gets into character, you know.'

Brindley laughed, showing a perfect set of teeth. Fry smiled politely, but she didn't get the joke. Well, not until later.

While Fry was on the way back to Edendale, Murfin rang her mobile with a message. He sounded muffled, as though he'd started eating mince pies early. Fry fully expected to find the office carpet scattered with crumbs next time she went in.

'Diane, there was a call for Ben Cooper,' he said. 'But he isn't here, so I thought you ought to know about it.'

'What, Gavin?'

'The Garda Síochána have traced Martin Rourke.'

'The Garda? So he's back in Ireland then, just as Farnham thought he might be.'

'Yes, he's back on his home patch in Dublin. Running a souvenir business, apparently. Seems he's given up manual labour and gone into the tourist industry.'

'It's where the money tends to be these days,' said Fry. 'It's true here, and I'm sure it's true in Ireland.'

As he was leaving The Oaks, Cooper found a small, elderly lady standing in the doorway of the dining room, supporting herself on a walking stick. She smiled at him as he passed.

'Had a nice visit?'

'Yes. Thank you.'

'You came to see Raymond.'

'That's right.'

Cooper was about to move away when he heard a voice in the back of his mind saying: 'Talk to the old lady.' And he stopped, and smiled.

'I'm Mrs Greatorex,' she said. 'Annie Greatorex.'

'Hello, Mrs Greatorex. Nice to meet you.'

'He's gone a bit ga-ga, hasn't he? Raymond?'

'Well . . .'

'It's no surprise. His brother went the same way. Well, not the same way – a bit different, I suppose. The result is the same. The place we all end up.'

She winked at Cooper and edged a bit closer, scraping the rubber end of her stick on the carpet. When she was near enough, she touched his sleeve. He noticed a faintly mischievous gleam in her eye, behind the harmless smile.

Diane Fry would have told him that he had work to do back at the office, and not to waste his time with batty old women just because he felt sorry for them. But there was something more than that about Mrs Greatorex. The glitter in her eye suggested that she wasn't really batty at all. And old ladies . . . well, old ladies knew things that other people didn't.

'I lived near the Suttons before I came in here, you know,' she said.

'Did you? At Rakedale?'

'One of the cottages on Main Street is mine. The one with the green door.'

'I think I know it.'

Cooper decided not to tell her that the cottage was standing empty and the paintwork of the door could barely be called green any more. He guessed she hadn't been home for a long time.

259

'I know them all in that village. Have you met the family at the pub, the Dains?'

'Yes, I have.'

'Ada Dain is a friend of mine.'

'It's the Suttons I'm really interested in,' said Cooper. 'The Suttons of Pity Wood Farm.'

'Pity Wood. Oh, aye.'

The old lady glanced to one side and clutched his arm a bit more tightly. 'I could tell you a few things about the Suttons,' she said.

'Could you?' said Cooper. 'Could you really? Shall we have a sit down in the sun lounge for a moment?'

23

Fry hadn't been in a theatre for a long time. She thought it had probably been the Birmingham Rep, and it was a smart new theatre then, all glass and white walls. Nothing like the Royal Theatre, Edendale. This place looked as though it had hardly been designed to accommodate the public at all. The access was via narrow corridors, and flight after flight of shallow, plush-covered steps.

She found Jo Brindley in a makeshift dressing room, waiting for her call to go on stage for a rehearsal. There were four or five other women there, but they left when Fry arrived and stood outside in the corridor, chattering.

'We thought we had it all off perfectly, but the director and choreographer decided to make some changes after the first couple of nights,' said Mrs Brindley. 'It's putting all the girls into a bit of a tizz. They'll be nervous when we go on again. Sometimes it's better just to leave things alone, don't you think?'

'I couldn't really comment,' said Fry, staring at the woman's outfit and make-up. 'So you're a dancer, rather than an actress?'

'Well, a bit of everything. The little group of us are a sort of comic turn, you see. We don't dance exactly, but we do things together, so we have to be choreographed.'

'I see. I came to ask you about the information you and

your husband gave to the mobile police unit in Rakedale. About a Mr Jack Elder.'

'Yes, Alex phoned to say that you'd called at the house. I don't know what I can tell you that you don't already know from my husband. It was Alex who spoke to this man, not me.'

Over their heads, music began. Feet thumped on wooden boards. Fry had to raise her voice over the noise.

'Mrs Brindley, I know you've been in Rakedale longer than your husband – you inherited the house from an aunt, didn't you?'

'Yes, that's right.'

'So you must know more about the sort of beliefs and superstitions people in a place like Rakedale have. I've heard talk of something called the "Old Religion".'

'Oh, I remember the old people talking about things like that. I mean, the people who were already old when I was a child – my grandmothers, and their generation. But it doesn't still go on now, does it? I'm sure it can't do, Sergeant. Not in this age of TV and computers and mobile phones. I can't credit that people still believe in those things.'

'But there was an incident when you first moved to Rakedale, wasn't there? A rather unpleasant incident, involving you personally.'

'Oh. So someone has been talking, have they?' Mrs Brindley gave a brittle laugh, causing the stage make-up on her face to crack and fall in a small shower on her costume. 'I wonder who that could have been? As if I didn't know.'

'PC Palfreyman dealt with it at the time, in his own way. But you must have been disturbed by it.'

'Yes, of course. To be honest, I've never forgotten it. It wasn't the birds so much as the few minutes when I thought there was an intruder in my house. A real, human intruder.'

'Well, there must have been a real intruder in the first place. Did Mr Palfreyman ever tell you who he suspected?'

262

'No. And I agreed with him that it was best not to know. I would have found it difficult to behave normally with them, if I'd found out. And then it would have been me who was being odd and refusing to be friendly.'

Fry knew from PC Palfreyman's story that Joanne Stubbs, as she then was, had already been considered odd in the extreme by the villagers of Rakedale. But there were subtle and peculiar dynamics in rural relationships that had to be respected. There was certainly some kind of unspoken code that she didn't understand. Probably that was why she had never been accepted the way that Joanne Stubbs finally had. It was because she refused to acknowledge the code.

'A bit of a Catch-22 situation, Mrs Brindley.'

Joanne tugged at her costume. It was only a short tunic, and she was wearing nothing but tights below it.

'I got over it. There's no need to drag it all up again now. It's in the past, as far as I'm concerned.'

'Do you think the person responsible might have been Jack Elder?'

She sighed. 'Yes, it's possible.'

'Have you mentioned this to your husband?'

'As I said, it's in the past.'

In Fry's experience, the people who said '*It's in the past*' most often were those who couldn't wipe out the memory of a traumatic experience. Repeating the mantra seemed to give them some degree of reassurance, like licking an open wound. They used the words as a defence against recollection.

Yes, those bad memories could be a killer.

Cooper had left Liz waiting in the car for him while he talked to Raymond Sutton. She was very tolerant, but by the time he came out of The Oaks, she was starting to sulk a bit. Understandably. He was neglecting her badly.

Cooper apologized as best he could. 'I came to the reception after the baptism,' he said. 'I ate some sandwiches and sausage rolls, because you said you had to stay for a while. Now this was something *I* had to do.'

'All right. It's the job. And did you speak to the old man?'

'Briefly. They were having a Christmas party.'

'I hope you stayed away from the mistletoe.'

'I tried.'

'So what's next, Ben?'

He hesitated, conscious of dangerous ground in front of him, but too late to avoid putting his foot right in it.

'I've got to phone Diane Fry.'

Liz was silent for a few moments, staring out of the window. Cooper watched her, fingering his mobile phone, wondering when it would be safe to start dialling. Though her face was turned away from him, he could practically see the conflict going on in Liz's mind. It was visible in the tenseness of her shoulders, in the way she fiddled with the buttons of her coat, in the ragged breaths that steamed up the damp window. She knew it was the job, and she was aware of its importance to him. But even so . . .

Finally, she turned back to him.

'As long as we can go and sit in the pub while you do it, Ben,' she said. 'Then at least I won't have to sit here twiddling my thumbs.'

Fry was back in the office when she took Cooper's call. While picking mince pie crumbs from the carpet next to her desk, she listened carefully to his account of his visit to The Oaks.

'And what was it that made you go there this morning, Ben? I didn't quite understand that part.'

'It was the baptism service, Diane. "*To follow Christ means dying to sin.*"'

'I'm not big on the Bible, Ben. I've read it, of course. But I always tended to skip the miracles and go for the begetting, and the killing of the first born.'

'That wasn't what I meant.'

264

Fry decided to leave it at that. Some things were always going to be inexplicable. It was the nature of communication between human beings. Or between her and Ben Cooper, anyway.

'So what did this sweet old lady tell you?' she asked.

'A lot of stuff that wasn't relevant,' admitted Cooper.

'Oh, surprise me.'

'But I think there were a few snippets that might be of interest. I'll need to check them out, of course. Get some corroboration.'

'In case Granny is just wandering in her mind, as I warned you.'

'I don't think she was. She seemed quite lucid, though a bit too talkative.'

There was a burst of noise in the background – laughter, female. Fry tried to picture the scene, but couldn't quite fill it in. She could see Cooper himself, sitting perhaps with a drink in front of him, casual and relaxed, surrounded by his friends. In Fry's mind, the friends were many, but vague and faceless.

'Go on, then, Ben.'

'Well, according to Mrs Greatorex, there was more going on at Pity Wood Farm than farming. She said there were often too many people there – far more than there should be on a farm, and not always at harvest time. It would confirm the impression I got from the farm accounts. And they weren't always men, she says. Mrs Greatorex claims everybody knew this.'

'So the Three Wise Monkeys are exactly what I thought, then.'

'See no evil, hear no evil, speak no evil?'

'Yes . . .' Fry hesitated. 'No – that isn't quite right, is it? They're just sticking to the third part.'

'Meaning they must have seen and heard things. They're just not willing to talk about them.'

265

'Right. That's the way people are around here, isn't it?'

Somebody seemed to be speaking to him now, distracting him from the call. Fry had the impression that he might have put his hand over the mouthpiece for a moment to muffle the conversation with his friends.

Of course, these people might not be what Cooper himself would call friends, but just acquaintances, the sort of people he sat with in the pub. Familiar enough to spend time with during his off-duty hours, without having to know anything about them, except what they drank when it was his turn to get a round. That kind of relationship was very shallow, wasn't it? Not something to regret that she didn't have herself.

'Perhaps,' said Cooper. 'But that saying is originally from a carving in a Japanese shrine. The three wise monkeys represent the principle *"If we do not hear, see, or speak evil, we ourselves shall be spared all evil."* It's a play on the Japanese word for monkey. But sometimes there's a fourth part to the saying: *"Do no evil."* Most people seem to miss that one off.'

Cooper glanced across the pub to see where Liz had got to. She'd found some friends and was chatting happily to them at another table. He felt a momentary spurt of jealousy. But that was completely irrational. She'd left him alone to make his phone call in peace, which was exactly what he'd wanted her to do, wasn't it?

Fry was very quiet at the other end of the phone. And that was odd, too. Cooper felt she ought to be interrupting his thoughts by now and telling him what to do next.

'Are you all right, Diane? Shall I come into the office this afternoon and we can talk it through?'

'I've got a new assignment, Ben,' she said.

'A new –?' Cooper wasn't quite sure what she meant.

'You won't be seeing me for a little while. I'm going on a trip. Mr Kessen wants me to fly to Dublin to interview Martin Rourke. I have to liaise with the Garda Síochána.'

'Ireland? Well, that's great.'

'Is it?'

'You ought to be delighted, Diane. Anyone else in the department would give their right arm to be off on a trip to Ireland. When do you fly?'

'Tomorrow. I'll be away until Wednesday probably. So you won't see me around the office for a couple of days.'

'We'll manage without you for a while,' said Cooper, trying to lighten the tone of the conversation without understanding why it was taking a downbeat note.

'You know what's happening on Tuesday?' said Fry, a trifle impatiently.

'Er . . .'

'Our new detective superintendent is putting in an appearance. In person. She'll be meeting the troops for the first time. Except, she won't be meeting me, because I'll be in bloody Dublin.'

'But, Diane, that doesn't mean anything,' protested Cooper.

'It doesn't mean anything to *you*, Ben,' she said. 'But that's because you never see what's really going on.'

When Cooper finished the call, he took a drink and wondered what he should do. The realization that even Diane Fry was worried about her position made him uneasy. This was one of those moments when anyone could be forgiven for covering their backs. He ought to take stock of the things he'd neglected to do, in case he was challenged on them some time.

He looked at Liz. She met his eye, and stood up. Cooper wondered if there was something on his list that wouldn't seem too much like work. If so, he might just get away with doing it today.

As Liz came over to his table, he remembered. Time for a visit to a nice heritage centre, perhaps.

24

Two hours later, and the day had been disrupted for everyone. Units were arriving rapidly at Tom Farnham's house near Newhaven. Cars rattled over the cattle grid, officers were taping off the breeze-block garage, the flash of a digital camera burst intermittently from behind the half-open doors.

Cooper could see that the chiefs were out in force for this one. And on a Sunday afternoon, too. DCI Kessen and DI Hitchens stood conferring with the crime scene manager, Wayne Abbott, in the doorway of the garage workshop. The discovery of Tom Farnham's body had been reported by one of his customers, calling to pick up a repaired lawnmower.

'A totally senseless crime,' said Fry. 'Apparently, they didn't get away with a thing.'

'There's no sign that they were disturbed in a burglary,' said Cooper.

'Apart from the deceased body of the householder lying covered in blood on the floor, you mean?'

'I mean, what were they hoping to steal from the workshop?'

Fry looked around. 'Lawnmowers? There's a good market for them, I'm told.'

'Yes, there is. But they haven't touched them. You can see none of them has been moved an inch. And who would beat the householder to death when they were only out to nick an old lawnmower?'

'Like I said, totally senseless.'

Cooper thought Fry had been much too quick to jump to conclusions about the attack on Tom Farnham. But he didn't really blame her for it. Senseless crimes were all around them these days – there were stories in the papers every day. People didn't understand the reasons for them, but they no longer doubted that such things happened. It was almost a first assumption.

'There could be some other motive. It's more than a coincidence, Diane.'

'Oh, right. They were followers of the Old Religion, of course. And Tom Farnham had broken the faith.'

Hitchens came towards them. 'All hands on deck, chaps. The medical examiner says that the victim wasn't just beaten to death, he was shot. His attackers used something like a nine-millimetre pistol. They gave him a beating first, then finished him off with a couple of bullets.'

'Bullets?' said Cooper. 'Firearms, not a shotgun?'

'No, Ben. There's blood splatter in the woods, and a trail across the drive where they dragged him back.'

The search of Farnham's house gave fragmentary glimpses into his lifestyle. His interests had run to anything mechanical or technical, from the innards of old garden machinery to simple computer programs. His PC system boasted a number of peripheral devices – scanner, colour printer, webcam, and some that Cooper didn't recognize. Money had been spent on this system. Surely more money than could be earned by repairing lawnmowers.

In the study, Cooper found a cork board on one wall of the bedroom, covered in photos. All of them showed Tom Farnham himself, smiling that hesitant smile in a variety of locations around the world. But these were no holiday snaps.

There was one of Farnham dancing with Marilyn Monroe, another of Farnham shaking hands with Winston Churchill, and one of him standing behind Stalin on the balcony of the Kremlin. Over here, Tom was sharing a joke with Roosevelt, and in the bottom corner he had his arm around Frank Sinatra, like a previously unknown member of the Rat Pack.

Cooper studied them more closely. 'Mr Farnham was very skilled with Photoshop, Diane. But then, it looks as though he had a lot of practice.'

Fry peered over his shoulder. 'You mean he put himself into all these photos? Why would he do that?'

'Some kind of celebrity obsession? He was never likely to meet these people in real life, but he could look at the photos and pretend he had.'

'They're all dead, Ben. Dead before he was born, in most cases.'

'OK, an obsession with dead celebrities.'

'Very sad.'

'We all find our own ways of getting through life.'

'Sinatra, Churchill, Monroe?' said Fry. 'I don't suppose there's a pattern?'

'Not that I can see. It's like a quiz question – what do all these people have in common?'

'I don't like questions without answers,' said Fry.

'It looks as though Farnham was on the dole,' said Cooper. 'There's a calendar here, but all it shows are the dates of his giro cheques, once a fortnight.'

'But he was making money on the side, wasn't he?'

'Illegally, of course.'

'I'm betting his visitors last night were some criminal friends of his that he fell out with.'

'Friends with nine millimetres in their pockets? They sound like some kind of street gang from Manchester or something.'

Fry laughed. 'Who do we know from Manchester that has a connection to this case?'

270

'Mr Goodwin, the solicitor? Surely not?'

'Stranger things have been known,' said Fry.

The kitchen reminded Fry of Pity Wood Farm, though only in its amount of clutter. Gavin Murfin had found another door on the far side.

'Where does that lead, Gavin?'

'I don't know, it's too dark to see.'

Murfin fumbled for a switch on the wall. 'Ah. Let there be light.'

'A utility room of some kind.'

The chest freezer in Farnham's utility room was full of neatly wrapped packages. Fry lifted a few out and fingered their contents. She knew the shape of a joint of meat, or a packet of frozen sausages. But these were strangely sharp and lumpy. She put on a pair of latex gloves and unwrapped the nearest freezer bag. Even before she'd peeled off the final layer, she could see a line of exposed teeth grinning through the film. A second later, she uncovered a single, dark eye.

'Jesus. What's this?'

Cooper came to stand at her shoulder, and watched as she slowly exposed the frozen object. Patches of fur had darkened and stiffened around the head. A pair of tiny, clawed feet were held rigid, close to the chest.

'A rat,' said Fry. 'What sort of person would keep a dead rat in the freezer?'

'No,' said Cooper. 'It's a squirrel.'

Fry's hands shook a little as she placed the frozen body on top of a plastic Wall's ice cream box. She covered the animal's eyes, though she knew it was a mad notion to be afraid that it might turn its head and stare at her accusingly for disturbing its rest.

'Oh, sorry,' she said. 'There I was, thinking there might be something odd about having a rat in the freezer. But keeping a frozen *squirrel* among your pork chops – that's perfectly normal, of course. Doesn't everybody do it?'

'Well, it depends what it's for, Diane.'

'Oh, yes?'

'Mr Farnham probably knew a taxidermist. There's one quite near here, in Bakewell. They're always on the lookout for well-preserved animals.'

The DCI entered the house and watched them working for a few moments, not being critical but assessing their performance.

'I understand you have a suspect in custody, DS Fry,' said Kessen at last.

'Yes, sir. Mr Jack Elder. But he's being questioned on allegations of the sale of illegal fuel, and his vehicle was logged by patrols monitoring a dogging site near Sheldon. He has no connection with Tom Farnham that we know of.'

'He does now,' said Kessen. 'We ran the registration number of Farnham's Subaru pick-up through the intelligence system. One of the other vehicles monitored at the dogging site was his. Mr Farnham and your suspect were present at the same time.'

A few minutes later, Fry and Cooper were heading north towards Sheldon. Cooper didn't know Godfrey's Rough, but he had a vague idea where it was, somewhere near the White Peak village of Sheldon.

'The monitoring patrols recorded Farnham's pick-up and Elder's lorry at this Godfrey's Rough at the same time, but there were no other vehicles present,' said Fry when she finally came off the phone.

'So much for the idea that they were out dogging, then,' said Cooper. 'I think you need a few more participants, don't you?'

'Exactly. And it's the wrong time of year anyway.'

'What do you think they were up to?'

'I wish I knew, Ben. But now that Elder has a confirmed connection with Tom Farnham, he's involved in a murder enquiry. We've got to dig out what his involvement is.'

Cooper shook his head. 'If they were just meeting at Godfrey's Rough, we won't be any the wiser.'

'They were a long time, according to the log,' said Fry. 'The patrol logged their registration numbers at six twenty-five p.m., and again at eight fifteen. That's more than just a quick chat.'

The car was constantly ploughing through seas of muddy water. Not floods exactly, just a general consequence of wet weather, the result of rain pouring down from the hillsides on to the roads. Here, the dry-stone walls were held together by a sheath of green moss.

A hundred yards in front of them was an Arla Foods milk tanker, heading for one of the dairies at Manchester or Ashby de la Zouch after its daily farm collections. Cooper felt these limestone areas of the White Peak were a more friendly landscape than the moors further north. It felt lived in, shaped by human activity. The White Peak was a particularly satisfying landscape, somehow. Psychologically satisfying.

'But what else is there at Godfrey's Rough?' asked Fry. 'What would have taken the two of them there for so long?'

'I don't know,' said Cooper. 'We'll have a look round when we get there.'

Seeing that his tank was getting close to empty, Cooper took a diversion through Hartington and pulled into a little filling station – old-fashioned personal service, and just two pumps to choose from, unleaded or diesel.

When he was getting his wallet out to pay for the petrol, Cooper found an envelope in his inside pocket that he'd forgotten about.

'Oh, by the way, Diane, with all the excitement, I didn't get round to showing you this.'

'What is it? A photograph?'

Cooper got back behind the wheel and drove out of Hartington, glad that he was familiar with the locations of remote filling stations in this area.

'I borrowed it from the heritage centre,' he said.

Fry studied the photo. 'I can see three men standing in a farmyard. Is that Pity Wood?'

'Yes. It was taken in the 1960s. When I went to the heritage centre, I wasn't really looking for anything that old, but still . . . It was a bonus.'

'Why?'

'There's a caption on the back. Names and a date – I wish more people did that. Here on the right is Raymond Sutton, standing in the doorway of the barn. See him?'

'Yes.'

'He's changed a lot, but I can just about recognize him. There's a look around the eyes and the shape of the jaw. It's quite distinctive. A Sutton chin. I think there are Sutton ears, as well. A little bit protruding.'

'They're like jug handles,' said Fry bluntly. 'But the hair cut doesn't help, I suppose. I've heard rumours of those short back and sides.'

'Right. The man sitting on the tractor is Derek Sutton, who died twelve months ago.'

'Yes, I can see the ears. He was the superstitious one.'

'That's right. He was a few years younger than Raymond, but he seems to have gone a bit strange over the years.'

'He never married, did he?'

'No. Nor Raymond, either.'

'Old bachelors living together. They were bound to go a bit funny, as you call it. Especially at Pity Wood Farm.'

'His older brother didn't have much influence over him anyway, so far as I can gather. In fact, Derek's superstitious beliefs seem to have been a kind of rebellion against Raymond's piety. It suggests to me that Raymond was a sort of father figure – their real dad died when they were only boys, you know. Old Mr Sutton was killed in the Second World War, serving with the Sherwood Foresters in North Africa. I suppose Alan wouldn't even remember his father at all.'

Fry looked up. 'Alan?'

274

'Alan Sutton.'

'Who?'

'There were three brothers. Alan was the youngest.'

Cooper took one hand off the steering wheel and put his finger on the photograph. 'He's here, behind the tractor. Unfortunately, we can't see him very well, because he's standing in a shadow from the barn. It was summer – you can tell that from the way they're dressed, even if the date hadn't been on the back. August 1968. I bet they were about to start the harvesting.'

'Why has no one mentioned a third brother? And where is Alan now?'

'I phoned Ned Dain while I was at the heritage centre. He was very evasive, and when I pressed him he had to go away to consult his mother. But they finally agreed that Alan Sutton just upped and left the village one day, seven or eight years ago. They reckoned he couldn't bear living with the other two. The Dains hinted that they treated him badly.'

'Why have they been so shifty about mentioning a third brother? They could have come straight out with that information when we first visited the Dog Inn.'

'Yes, they could.'

'But Dain was deliberately vague and misleading when I spoke to him,' said Fry, starting to sound angry. 'I know damn well he and his mother haven't just suddenly remembered this Alan Sutton. In a place the size of Rakedale, it's inconceivable that they wouldn't know exactly who was in the family at Pity Wood. So what have they been trying to hide?'

'I don't think they've been trying to hide anything really,' said Cooper. 'I think they were protecting him, in their own way.'

'Protecting Alan Sutton? From what? Interest by the police?'

'Possibly. Or from being found by his brothers.'

Fry considered it, her mouth tight with irritation. 'You think the Dains took sides in some sort of dispute between the

275

Suttons? Maybe they know where Alan is, and they've made a promise not to tell anyone.'

'It would explain their behaviour. They would have been worried that we'd go off and find him.'

'On the other hand, they might be taking Raymond's side.'

'How so?'

'Well, Raymond seems to have sold the farm without any reference to his younger brother. Shouldn't Alan be due a share of the proceeds? But if he's disappeared to the other side of the world and lost touch, Raymond could be hoping that he never gets to hear of the sale – or at least, not until it's too late.'

'That's a theory, too,' said Cooper.

Fry was silent for a while as they drove, but Cooper knew she wasn't going to let the question drop. He could almost hear the calculations going on in her mind as she gazed at the photograph of the three brothers.

'So what really happened to Alan Sutton?' she said at last.

Cooper looked at her. 'What makes you think something happened to him?'

'Well, given the recent history of the family, it seems a good bet.'

'I don't know. You could be right. But all we really know is that Alan went away. I had a quick check through the records – there was no report of him missing at the time.'

'But who was likely to put in a misper report?'

'His brothers.'

Cooper thought of the plan of Pity Wood Farm, with the grave sites cleared marked on the eastern boundary. Fry might be right in her suggestion. If one of the victims they'd found had been male, he could have a guess at the identity, too.

'But if Alan Sutton met an unpleasant end somewhere, it wasn't at the farm,' he said. 'The search would have turned him up by now, wouldn't it?'

'We could try to find him, wherever he's got to. But it

would take an awful lot of work. A common name like Sutton . . . And if he hasn't been around at the farm for nearly ten years, he's out of the time frame, anyway.'

'I don't think anybody actually saw him leave,' said Cooper. 'The Dains were full of dark hints, especially the old lady.'

'Mr Dain didn't even lower himself to a hint when I spoke to him. But I knew there was something he wasn't saying. He must have thought I was a fool because I didn't know there were three Sutton brothers. And he made no attempt to enlighten me.'

Cooper nodded. 'He told no lies when he was asked a direct question, but he didn't volunteer information either. It's the way a lot of people are, I'm afraid.'

'And why hasn't anyone else mentioned Alan Sutton?' said Fry. 'Palfreyman, for example.'

'I don't know,' admitted Cooper. 'It *is* a bit odd.'

'In a place the size of Rakedale, everyone must have known him, or at least have been aware that there were three brothers at Pity Wood, no matter how much they kept themselves to themselves.'

'I wonder if they've been protecting someone,' said Cooper thoughtfully.

'Protecting who?'

'I couldn't say. It just makes me think of one of those family tragedies or misfortunes that no one talks about. It might not be for the protection of anyone living, even. It might be out of respect for the mother, old Beatrice Sutton.'

'But she's been dead a long time, surely?'

Cooper shrugged. 'It doesn't mean that people in Rakedale won't still respect her memory.'

'It must be great to have such caring neighbours,' said Fry.

'I suppose the best option is to ask Raymond directly about Alan, and see what reaction we get.'

'Old people,' said Fry. 'Even when they aren't in the early stages of Alzheimer's like Raymond Sutton, they don't always talk sense, you know. Their minds wander, and their memories let them down. Because they know that perfectly well, they make things up. They don't really intend to lie, they just want to keep the conversation going, they desperately want to be interesting. It's because they're lonely.'

'I'm aware of that. But I don't think it's true of all old people, Diane.'

'I'm just suggesting,' said Fry, 'that if you're at the care home again, take anything you're told with a pinch of salt. Whether it's something you're told by Raymond Sutton, or anyone else.'

'Old ladies are useful sources of information,' said Cooper. 'Old ladies know things that other people don't. Look at old Mrs Dain. Her memory goes back a long, long way.'

'Ben, I'm fully aware that you don't take a blind bit of notice of any advice I give you. But I'm warning you that if you go off and do your own thing regardless one more time, you mustn't be surprised if I say "I told you so" in no uncertain terms. *And* if I record it on your Personal Development Review next April.'

'OK, OK. I get the message.'

He could feel Fry staring at him until he started to flush, but he wasn't going to rise to her baiting.

'Have you noticed,' he said, 'how quickly Pity Wood Farm went on the market after Derek Sutton died? Raymond must have phoned the estate agents at the same time he called in the funeral directors.'

'He wanted to be busy,' suggested Fry. 'One of the main reasons we have funerals is to give bereaved people something to do. The way it was explained to me, you have to continue doing things that are in the present tense, otherwise your life would just stop when a loved one dies.'

'We were told that, too, when Mum went. But it's funny that Raymond didn't really do that when Derek died. Well, not for long. He seems to have had the farm up for sale pretty

278

quick, doesn't he? That was certainly a "past tense" action, if you like. It brought everything to a stop. The whole of the life that he and his brother had been living at Pity Wood for decades – it was just ripped up and thrown in a skip by a Polish builder.'

'Yes, it does sound very final, when you put it like that. But he might have had reasons.'

Cooper finally remembered what else was near Godfrey's Rough when they were still more than half a mile away. He could see it, standing gaunt and eerie on the skyline, framed by skeletal trees. Stone ruins like the keep of a medieval castle. Steel winding gear like a rusted scaffold. Deep shafts that drove eight hundred feet into the ice-cold water below the limestone.

'Magpie Mine,' he said. 'Beware of the widows' curse.'

25

Minerals had been a key element in the wealth of the Peak District for centuries. The remnants of the lead-mining industry were widespread, their impact on the landscape had been so dramatic that it would be many centuries yet before their traces disappeared.

Magpie Mine was the best preserved of the hundreds of lead mines that had once been visible everywhere, rumpling the surface into bumps and hollows, piercing it with hidden shafts, scattering it with centuries of miners' spoil. Its heyday was in the nineteenth century, but it had finally closed in the 1950s, and it was heritage now, one of the youngest protected sites in the national park.

'I don't think it was the picnic site that interested Farnham and Elder,' said Cooper. 'I think it was this.'

'Why, Ben?'

'A remote location, easy to access, and unlikely to be disturbed for development, because it's a protected site. Yet look at these spoil heaps from the old mine workings, Diane. Heaps? They're small mountains. You could bury anything here, and no one would notice any disturbance. Half of the remaining structures are underground anyway.'

A cloud of starlings swept across the road, twisting and

turning, dipping until they almost skimmed the tarmac before settling all at once in a ploughed field. They immediately vanished, camouflaged against the brown earth. When Cooper parked and got out of the Toyota, the wind rattled the buckle of his seat belt against the side of the car. Ash keys hung in damp clumps from the branches of a tree, too wet even to rattle in the wind.

They stepped carefully over the bars of a cattle grid. Beneath the bars, the pit was filled with a black sludge of leaves and stagnant pools of water. Past the cattle grid, the sheep pellets scattered on the ground changed to cow pats, though Cooper couldn't see any cows.

The wind scything across the plateau felt cold enough to slice off an ear if you turned the wrong way. As they walked on to the site, loose sheets of corrugated iron could be heard banging incessantly in the wind.

The former agent's house was the first building, now a field centre for the mine's historical society. Beyond the agent's house, the old mine buildings crowded in suddenly, clustering on either side and looming overhead on a high mound.

Even in the sun, the wind was too cold to stand still in for long, too cold to leave your hands uncovered if you didn't want your fingers to go numb.

Fry shivered. 'What did you mean about the widows' curse?' she said.

'Can you feel it, Diane?'

'Feel it? I can't even feel my fingers. It's bloody freezing out here, Ben.'

'They were the widows of the Red Soil men,' said Cooper. 'You see, there were originally two separate mines on this site, governed by the rules of the old Barmote Court. But Magpie miners broke through into the Great Red Soil vein, and there was a long-running dispute between the two mines. The Magpie men lit fires from straw and tar to smoke out their rivals, and three Red Soil miners were killed in the shaft,

281

suffocated by the fumes. Ten men were tried for their murder at Derby, but they were found not guilty. Conflicting evidence, and a lack of intent. It could be difficult to get a successful prosecution, even in those days.'

'Was that justice?'

'Local people didn't think so. It was one of those disputes that was bound to happen. Red Soil was being worked by local men, but the Magpie was being mined by labour imported from Cornwall. Anyway, it's said that the widows of the murdered men put a curse on the mine. It never made money again.'

There were two tall chimneys surviving on the site, a round one and an older square chimney. At the base of the round chimney, Cooper found a large iron grille set into the ground. He tugged at it, and found the grille was loose and could be lifted off its bolts. It was heavy, but he had no trouble raising one side and letting it fall back on to the ground, leaving the entrance to a tunnel clear. In one direction, it seemed to lead into the base of the chimney. The other way, he guessed it must enter the engine house.

On the floor of the tunnel he could see a disposable lighter, crumpled yogurt pots, and an empty John West tuna sachet. Left-overs from someone's picnic that could be forced through the bars of the grille.

The main mine shaft was supposed to be more than seven hundred feet deep, though the bottom fifth of it was always flooded. On a bright day, they said, you could see the water if you peered through the grille. But there was no brightness today, just the grey cloud and drizzle cloaking the skeletal trees.

Cooper stood over one of the smaller shafts. Ferns peeping through the grille were dying and blackened by frost. But below them, a couple of feet into the shelter of the shaft, he glimpsed the glossy green fronds of some plant he didn't recognize, still thriving in the gloom, even in December. Whatever it was, it looked much too healthy, considering the lack of light and the cold wind whistling overhead.

A couple of old millstones lay abandoned on the ground, one of them broken into three pieces. The walls of the engine house ran with water on the inside. Drops of water fell from the arch and the lintels of the windows. Cooper craned his head back and watched a drop falling towards him. Before it reached him, it was caught by the wind and veered off suddenly, elongating like a tear drop as it accelerated.

The water above the flooded level of the shaft was drained by the Magpie Sough, which ran into the River Wye, away to the north below Great Shacklow Wood. That was one of the longest soughs in the Peak District, more than a mile and a quarter of it, and its construction had practically ruined the mines' shareholders.

'My hands are completely numb now,' said Fry. 'Why is it so much colder here than in Edendale?'

'We're completely exposed,' said Cooper. 'Imagine what it was like working here.'

'I don't want to.'

'And imagine,' he said, 'how easy it would be to bury a murder victim here.'

Fry took a call on her mobile. 'That was the DI,' she said. 'They're setting up a HOLMES incident room for the Farnham killing.'

'I suppose that's no surprise.'

'No. A high-profile shooting takes immediate priority over our old remains at Pity Wood. So all the expertise will be arriving from Ripley, even as we speak. At least that means a lot more resources – there'll be separate teams concentrating on the new lines of enquiry.'

'Pity Wood is ours, then?' said Cooper.

'Pretty much. So we'd better get back to the farm.'

A few minutes later, as they got close to Pity Wood, Cooper saw a solitary figure walking along the edge of the road, trying

283

to stay off the muddy verge. A young man in his twenties, dark hair, medium height. A black padded jacket. '*You know, you see asylum seekers wearing them when they get pulled off the EuroStar.*'

'I'm going to pull up. Let's check this guy out.'

When he heard the car slowing down, the man looked as though he was about to start running. But he slipped on the mud, thought better of it, and slowed to a walking pace again.

He didn't look round to see who was in the car until it stopped just ahead of him, and Cooper got out.

'Police, sir. DC Cooper, from Edendale CID. Don't worry, you're not in trouble, but could you tell me your name?'

'My name is Mikulas Halak.'

'Where are you from?'

'Slovakia.'

The young man was carrying a small rucksack over his shoulders, and his skin was a shade or two darker than most Derbyshire folk. In some places, that would be enough to put him under suspicion. Fry got out of the car and came to stand on the other side of Halak.

'And what are you doing in Derbyshire, Mr Halak?'

'I'm doing no harm. I'm looking for my sister. She was working here, in this place.'

Cooper and Fry looked at each other.

'In Rakedale?' asked Fry. 'Your sister was working in Rakedale?'

Halak pointed out Pity Wood in the distance. Even from here, the police vehicles were visible, and one of the crime scene tents was flapping damply in the breeze.

'I believe she had work at the farm, there. I've seen it on the television. I believe Nadezda was there. Look, I have a photograph.'

'Get in the car, please, sir,' said Fry. 'We need to talk to you back at the station.'

*   *   *

When Mikulas Halak had been provided with coffee and seated in a free interview room, they checked his documents. He carried a Slovak passport, issued since the country had become a member of the European Union, and everything looked to be in order.

Once he seemed reassured and a little more relaxed, Fry produced the broken crucifix in its clear plastic evidence bag.

'Do you recognize this, sir?'

'Nadezda had one just like it,' said Halak. 'But it wasn't broken like that.'

'Would there be any way to tell whether it was hers?'

'My sister – she always put her initials on her things, in case someone tried to take them from her. She would scrape it, you know.' He mimicked using a small, sharp object like a needle on the back of his hand.

'She scratched her initials on her possessions?'

'Yes.'

Fry picked up the bag and turned it over. She held it up to the light and squinted at the back of the crucifix. The metal was flaking away and discoloured. But in the middle, where the upright and the arms of the cross met, she could see the glitter of the scratch marks.

'N.H.'

'Nadezda Halak. That is my sister's.'

The photograph Halak had produced showed a young woman with shoulder-length, dark brown hair pulled back and tied behind her head. Her eyes were a warm brown, and her brows finely arched.

She wasn't exactly pretty, though. Her skin had a faintly sallow tone, and her cheeks showed the signs of faint blemishes, the residue of some earlier illness, perhaps. And Fry thought Nadezda's jaw was wide enough to have confused the anthropologist, if that had been all he had to go on. Nadezda was wearing a white nylon jacket, unzipped to reveal a T-shirt underneath. She was smiling, but not showing her teeth.

'She was very unhappy in Slovakia,' said Halak. 'She was poor, we were all poor. But Nadezda had no hope of work. She watched the television, and she kept saying she wanted to go to England, or the USA. She had been married, but she was treated very badly by her husband. He beat her, and hurt her very much. Then she said she would get the money any way she could, and she would come to England to work. So that's what she did.'

Fry watched his face as he said 'any way she could'. She knew that many young women from Eastern Europe set off to Britain with high hopes, only to be sold into virtual slavery when they arrived at the airport, trafficked for their bodies.

'Sir, I have to ask you this,' she said. 'Was your sister a prostitute?'

Halak became distressed.

'No, no. She was a worker, an honest worker. She went where she could make money. But a prostitute? No, never.'

Before he left the station, Fry asked Mikulas Halak to agree to a buccal swab. A DNA sample would enable the lab to confirm whether he was indeed related to Victim A, and how closely.

But at last they did seem to have an identification for the first body, and she was no longer just Victim A. Now she had a name. Nadezda Halak, aged twenty-three, a Slovak from the city of Košice. About five feet three inches tall, according to her brother. Slight build, dark brown hair.

All that remained of her was that hair, and a partial set of fingerprints from her sloughed-off skin. Oh, and those inexplicably decayed teeth.

Fry briefed the DI and received the congratulations she was hoping for. But she knew she wasn't going to take the focus away from the shooting, which was currently claiming her bosses' attention.

Accommodation had been found for Mikulas in Edendale,

where he promised to make himself available if he was needed. Fry swore she would keep him informed of developments, and she meant it.

'I hope he doesn't do a runner, or anything else stupid,' she said when he'd gone.

'He doesn't seem the type, does he?' said Cooper.

'If he's concerned about his own status in this country, he might disappear again. After all, he's achieved what he came here to do and found out what happened to his sister.'

'I think he'll be interested in helping us get justice for her,' said Cooper. 'Don't you agree, Diane?'

'Yes, but I bet forged papers can weigh heavily on your mind when you're involved with the police.'

'If they *are* forged.'

Cooper really did think Mikulas Halak would want justice. But he worried about that word sometimes. It seemed to mean something different when it came from other people's mouths. Raymond Sutton, for example, had quite a contrary idea of its meaning.

26

At ten o'clock on Monday morning, with a major incident room getting into full swing at Edendale, two care assistants from The Oaks drove their minibus into Pity Wood Farm. They steered into a parking place that had been cleared for them as close to the farmhouse as possible, and they unloaded Raymond Sutton in a wheelchair via the hydraulic ramp at the rear of the vehicle.

When Sutton emerged into the light, he looked bemused by all the activity going on at his old home.

'I thought it was all dead and buried, this,' he said.

'Some things don't stay buried, Mr Sutton,' said Fry. 'Not for ever.'

'I don't know what you mean.'

When Cooper heard him say that, he started to have doubts about Raymond Sutton. It sounded too much like the script trotted out by suspects in the interview. '*To tell you the truth*' always meant '*I'm about to tell you a lie now*'. And '*To be perfectly honest*' could be translated as '*I've never been honest in my life*'.

It might be unfair, but '*I don't know what you mean*' was another of those phrases that he'd heard so often during

288

interviews. Every police officer had heard it, many times. It was a diversionary phrase, a way of avoiding answering a difficult question that had just been put.

As he watched Sutton being wheeled towards the house, Cooper was distracted by the noises around him. Everyone seemed to be sneezing and coughing at Pity Wood that morning. It sounded like the ward of an isolation hospital.

'Have you been passing your cold on, Diane?' he said.

'It's this bloody weather. The only wonder is that we haven't all got pneumonia.'

Cooper didn't suffer much from winter colds himself. He put it down to his upbringing. Being brought up in a house where there was no heating in the bedrooms or in the bathroom, and the snow sometimes lay on the inside of the window ledges. Bad weather had never kept Matt and himself indoors when they were growing up. Rain, wind, snow, fog – they had been outside in everything, and it made you hardy.

But he had to admit that he was starting to feel a bit wheezy himself. There was an irritation at the back of his throat, and a tendency for his eyes to water in the cold wind.

A police photographer hovered a few yards away, video recording Raymond Sutton's visit. It wasn't clear what DI Hitchens hoped to glean from Sutton's reactions, but they would be recorded for detailed evaluation later.

First they steered his wheelchair gingerly over the duckboards towards the tent covering the area where Jamie Ward had discovered the first body. Sutton looked around with bemused eyes. Cooper could see that he barely recognized the place. And why would he? Even before the police arrived with their vehicles and tents and began to dig up the farmyard, Nikolai Dudzik's builders had already made a start on transforming Pity Wood into that gentleman's residence.

'Yes, we had a shed that stood here,' he said, after the first question had been repeated to him. 'But it's long gone, twenty years or more. We broke up the foundations for hardcore.

Is that what you want to know? No, I know nowt of any woman.'

Fry nodded, and one of the care assistants released the brake and pushed Sutton towards the back of the house. He physically flinched at the sight of the yellow skip and the trenches dug across his former property. He began to tremble and become agitated.

'No,' he said. 'It's all wrong. There's no point in asking me these questions. You should be asking Farnham.'

'If only we could, sir,' said Fry.

'Those people who worked here, they were brought by Farnham and the other bloke, the Irishman.'

'Mr Rourke?'

'Yes. They brought people here, they worked, they went away again. I never knew who they were, or where they went. I didn't ask. I left it to Farnham. Was that wrong?'

'Who can say, sir?'

'The old caravan behind the house,' said Cooper, as the wheelchair was turned round. 'Was that used for housing some of the migrant workers?'

'Aye, now and then. Farnham and Rourke used it for themselves, too.'

'Did they? What for?'

'Nay, I don't know. And I didn't –'

'You didn't ask. Of course.'

Despite Sutton's words, his expression was tight with anxiety, his eyes close to tears, as if he was remembering more than he was telling, suffering pangs of guilt for things he'd done, or hadn't done. Or maybe for what he'd never asked.

Sutton gazed around the farm, like a man saying a last goodbye.

'When I die, this place will still be here, these hills and valleys, choose how.'

Fry looked at Cooper for a translation. 'Choose how?'

'He means "come what may".'

290

'Aye,' said Sutton. 'Choose how. Come what may. The hills and valleys, but not the farm. There are some cousins of ours over in Stoke – they can have whatever money there is when I'm gone, and welcome to it. I would never have given anyone the farm.'

'This farm must have been here for centuries, Mr Sutton.'

'Aye,' agreed Sutton. 'It's middlin' old.'

Cooper watched the old man until he seemed to be calmer.

'Mr Sutton, we found Screaming Billy,' he said.

'Billy? Aye, where is he?'

'Right now, he's in a laboratory in Sheffield.'

'Derek would have said it won't do 'em any good. It was bad luck ever to move him, Derek said.'

'But you didn't believe in that, sir?'

'No. Complete rubbish. The Lord has your fate in his hands, not some dirty old bit of bone.'

'And was Derek trying to preserve a hand?'

'A hand? I don't know of any hand.'

But Sutton looked troubled, as if it was a possibility that seemed only too likely.

'We found the materials in your kitchen for preserving a hand in saltpetre. It's an old recipe. Your brother could have learned it from the museum in Edendale.'

'I never knew what he was up to,' muttered Sutton. 'And never cared to ask, either. It would always end up in a row, and he knew it. Superstitious bastard, he was. I could never talk any sense into him.'

Cooper recalled Palfreyman's description of the two brothers sitting silently in their kitchen, failing to exchange a word all evening. He wondered when exactly Raymond had tried talking sense to his brother. It would have been much easier just to let him get on with his odd ways, wouldn't it? That was usually the way in families. Familiarity bred acceptance, and all kinds of bizarre and strange behaviour would be treated as normal within the family, no matter how

291

likely it was to attract the men in white coats if it was seen on the outside.

'Did he have any particular superstitions that bothered you, sir?'

'Bothered me? Nowt bothers me,' said Sutton. 'Nowt.'

Wrong word. Try again. 'There were some things he believed in that you disagreed with?'

'Damn well all of them. Oh, he went to chapel, but he never followed the way. He was tainted, corrupted. Right from a child, he was. Our dad showed us the right way to do things, but Derek had to be different. He took after our mother, I reckon. Folk always said she was fey.'

Fey. It was many years since Cooper had heard that word. His mother had used it of one of their neighbours at one time. It had been meant in a disparaging way, he was sure. Disapproving, certainly. But he'd always felt there was a degree of admiration in the word, too. A sense of the awe and respect that had traditionally been accorded to the wise woman, the healer, the widow people surreptitiously visited at dusk to ask for advice, or a special herbal preparation. *She's a bit fey.* Attuned to the supernatural world – he supposed that would be the nearest translation. In touch with the fairies, perhaps. Blessed with visionary or clairvoyant ability, if you really wanted to be kind. But Cooper had an inkling there was another meaning, too.

'And what about Alan?'

Sutton was suddenly silent. The tears that had been threatening to appear since he arrived at the farm started to trickle down his cheeks. Cooper immediately regretted being so blunt. And he prayed he never reached the stage in his own life where he could be made to weep so easily.

'Alan is long gone, too,' said Sutton.

'What happened to him, Mr Sutton?'

'He left. He couldn't stand living here any more.'

'Where is he now?'

Sutton gave a long, unsteady sigh. 'I don't know. Alan's gone, Derek's gone, the farm is gone. What else matters?'

Fry stood over his wheelchair. 'Is Alan still alive?' she asked.

Sutton turned away, refusing to look at her. 'We haven't heard from him for years. Eight years or more, it must be.'

Fry glanced across at Cooper, and he knew what she was thinking. An evasive answer.

But they let Sutton go with his carers, and he was helped back into the minibus for the return journey to The Oaks.

'Did you notice something about Raymond Sutton's behaviour?' said Fry when the minibus had left. 'Apart from the fact that he evaded a direct question, I mean.'

'Oh, what?' said Cooper.

'He was fine with us – well, in his own way. But he had a bad reaction to the uniforms.'

'Yes, I did notice that.'

'Interesting.'

'What are you thinking, Diane?'

'I'm thinking I'd liked to have asked Mr Sutton what he remembers of PC David Palfreyman. In particular, why he's so worried when he sees a police uniform on his farm.'

Suddenly, there was a commotion at the back of the farmhouse. Voices shouting, someone running heavily through mud, a door slamming, more shouts.

'What the heck's going on?' called Fry to a SOCO standing at the corner of the house.

'Someone got through the outer cordon. It looks like they've caught him inside that old caravan.'

'Interesting,' said Fry. 'Let's go and see what this is all about.'

By the time she and Cooper made their way to the brokendown caravan, two uniformed officers had their suspect secured and in the back of a car. One of the officers had slipped during the chase and was vainly trying to wipe the mud from his trousers.

Fry walked over to the car.

'Do you see who I see, Ben?'

'Yes, an old friend of yours.'

Fry opened the door. 'Well, what are you doing here – again?'

Jamie Ward looked up at her from the car. He was a frightened boy again, white faced and dishevelled. The same young labourer she'd met that first day on the farm when he turned up human remains.

'I wasn't doing any harm,' he said. 'I told them, but they wouldn't listen.'

'Jamie, you shouldn't be here at all. It's a crime scene.'

'I'm sorry.'

'What were you doing in the caravan?' asked Fry. 'Were you looking for something, Jamie?'

'No.'

Fry shook her head. 'Don't lie to me. I don't like it.'

Jamie turned away. 'I can't tell you. I don't want to get in trouble.'

'You're already in trouble.' Fry turned to the mud-spattered officer. 'Has he been searched?'

'Yes, Sergeant. Nothing on him but a few personal items.'

Fry regarded Jamie Ward sadly. 'We'd better search the caravan then, hadn't we? It was going to be done anyway, before long. I'm sure you realized that, Jamie.'

The young man groaned. 'Oh, look – it's only a bit of pot. It's no big deal. I used to sneak into the caravan for a quick smoke in my break, when the other blokes weren't looking. It was the only thing that made working here tolerable.'

'Jamie, you're a silly boy if you left your drugs lying around for anyone to find.'

'Christ, it's only a bit of pot. I couldn't take it home with me, in case my mum found it.'

'So is that all we'll find when we search the caravan?'

Jamie wriggled uncomfortably, but didn't answer.

'It would be better if you told me now,' said Fry, 'rather

than having to answer questions under caution down at the station.'

He hung his head. 'All the blokes did it,' he said. 'They all took things from the site. They said if things had been left lying around, it was because no one wanted them. Nikolai said it himself. He was right, wasn't he? It's not really stealing.'

'What did you take, Jamie?'

'It's in the drawer under the sink. None of the others ever went into the caravan, so I thought it would be safe.'

At Fry's nod, Cooper pulled on a pair of latex gloves and went into the caravan.

'It smells bad in here. And it's not just the scent of cannabis being smoked, either.'

'The drawer, Ben.'

'OK, got it.'

Fry waited patiently. She was trying not to anticipate what Cooper would find in the drawer. But she couldn't help images coming into her mind – visions of Derek Sutton lurking in the kitchen of Pity Wood Farm, bending over the sink, cooking up saltpetre for the preservation of a grisly relic.

But the object that Cooper was holding when he emerged was the wrong shape to match her mental image. It was a box covered in felt. When he opened it, she could see that it contained a medal on a purple-and-green ribbon.

'Awarded to Private Raymond Sutton, 1st Battalion Sherwood Foresters,' said Cooper.

'Mr Sutton served in the war?'

'Not the Second World War, he's a bit too young. This is a General Service Medal, and the bar says Malaya. He must have been fighting Communists in the 1950s.'

'So he really did leave his past behind.' Fry looked at Jamie Ward again. 'Don't tell me – eBay?'

'I've seen them going for fifty or sixty quid,' he said. 'I need the money.'

'To help your studies? Or to buy more pot?'

'I'm sorry.'

Jamie looked so ashamed of himself that Fry sighed. 'You can go. But if I see you round here, Jamie, I'll make sure you're locked up.'

27

Later that morning, Cooper looked up the word 'fey' in a copy of the *Collins English Dictionary*. He'd borrowed the book a few weeks ago from his landlady, Mrs Shelley. She loved loaning him her books – she thought she was helping with his education, her tenant being an ignorant but well-meaning police constable and all.

He'd brought the dictionary to the office one day, and it had stayed in his desk drawer ever since. He really must remember to return it. He hated it when people borrowed his own books or CDs and never gave them back.

Yes, there *was* another meaning to 'fey'. Fated to die, or doomed. From the Old English *faege*, marked for death. Tappy, in fact. Cooper nodded. Old Mrs Sutton had been tappy. And so had Derek Sutton. But who else at Pity Wood had been tappy or fey? Two young women, at least. Victim A and Victim B. They had certainly been fated to die.

This morning, E Division headquarters was the focus of activity. HOLMES staff had been arriving from Ripley and equipment was being set up. Detectives had been drafted in from other divisions and were being assigned their actions. Some teams were already out, chasing down associates of Tom Farnham's, pursuing sightings of vehicles in the area at the time of his shooting, checking on the whereabouts of suspects in previous shootings. It had the look of a professional job, after all.

All the activity was making Cooper feel a bit left out. Even the identification of one of the bodies at Pity Wood Farm no longer appeared quite such a breakthrough as it had at the time. They knew who she was, but not how she'd died. No signs of major trauma – that's what the postmortem said. Establishing how she'd met her fate was going to need a much bigger stroke of luck.

And they were still no nearer identifying any of the other migrant workers who'd been employed at Pity Wood Farm. Enquiries with agencies had drawn a complete blank. Gavin Murfin had just crossed the last one off the list this morning. Tom Farnham wasn't going to be any further use – which left Fry's trip to Ireland to interview Martin Rourke as the last hope, reluctant though she was to go.

'Well, your nose might have been accurate, Ben,' said Fry, striding into the office with a file and perching on the edge of a desk between his and Gavin's. 'According to the initial report from the chemist's lab at the Forensic Science Service, there were a number of chemical traces found in the soil at Pity Wood Farm – and inside some of the buildings, too. Nothing out of the ordinary for a farm, so far as I can see.'

'You have no idea what's normal on a farm,' protested Cooper.

Fry raised an eyebrow, but took it well. 'Fair point. I've got a copy of the report here, so let's run through the results, then. Gavin, are you listening?'

'All ears,' said Murfin, though, as far as Cooper could see, he was concentrating on a chocolate bar he'd found somewhere. Not one that had disappeared from the packed lunches the other day, was it?

'First of all, hydrogen peroxide,' said Fry. 'That's basically plain water with an extra oxygen atom, according to the chemist. I didn't know that.'

298

'Hair bleach?'

'I'm thinking peroxide blondes,' said Murfin. 'Jean Harlow, Marilyn Monroe.'

'Yes, back in the fifties and sixties, that was the popular way to dye your hair at home.'

'Do people still use it?' asked Cooper. 'I heard it turns your hair orange.'

Fry gave him a challenging look. 'How would I know, Ben?'

'I've no idea. Sorry.'

'Isn't it used as a fuel, too?' suggested Murfin. 'I think it was leaking hydrogen peroxide that blew up that Russian submarine a few years ago.'

'The *Kursk*, yes. How did you know that, Gavin?'

'I've got a teenage lad. He's interested in things like that, so I get lectured about them at the dinner table.'

'The chemist's report says that about half of hydrogen peroxide produced is used to bleach wood pulp or paper, as an alternative to chlorine-based bleaches. He also suggests mouthwash, contact-lens cleaning solutions, and dental-bleaching gels.'

'More to the point,' said Cooper, 'it's added to animal feed sometimes, to help fibre digestion. And it's in some fertilizers, too. I think you can even use hydrogen peroxide in septic tank systems. It oxidizes the slime.'

'Lovely. So no surprise to find it on a farm, then?'

'What else is there in the report?' persisted Cooper.

Fry sighed. 'Dilute hydrochloric acid, also known as muriatic acid. Bricklayers use it to clean mortar off bricks, because the acid dissolves the lime in mortar. It's used for cleaning concrete, too. It doesn't take a big leap of the imagination to figure out where that came from. The builders have been at Pity Wood Farm for weeks.'

'Isn't hydrochloric acid dangerous?' said Murfin. 'It *sounds* dangerous.'

'In the concentrated form, yes – you'd get a pretty severe

burn without protective gear. But this is a commercial solution, and less dangerous. I'd still wear gloves and a face mask, though, if I were you.'

'Next?' asked Cooper.

'Potassium hydroxide, also known as lye.'

'Drain cleaner.'

'Problems with the drains at Pity Wood? I should say so. What about you, Ben?'

'OK.'

Fry turned to the second page of the report. 'Iodine tincture.'

Cooper had used that himself many times, spraying it on to the umbilical cords of new-born lambs and calves as a disinfectant. There were always cans of iodine aerosol standing around at home.

Fry looked up for a comment, but got none. She was smiling now, feeling that she'd been proved right. She was on the home stretch if Cooper wasn't even commenting.

'Methanol,' she said. 'Even I know that's anti-freeze. Everyone has it, if they own a car. I've got some myself.' There was a continued silence, and she pressed on quickly. 'Last couple now. Propan-2-ol. Isopropyl alcohol. Any takers?'

'Rubbing alcohol,' said Cooper. 'It's an antiseptic and cleaner.'

'And in everyone's first-aid box,' said Fry cheerfully. 'Even farmers who cut themselves use it, I bet.'

'Unless they drink the stuff,' said Murfin.

'Really?'

'Well, just something I've heard.'

Fry shook her head, but didn't seem downhearted. 'And finally . . . something called pseudoephedrine.' She stumbled over the last word and tried again, shifting the emphasis on the syllables. 'Pseudoephedrine.'

'What the heck is that?'

'It says here it's the active ingredient in proprietary decongestants, such as Sudafed. But there seems to be an awful lot of it.'

'Someone had sinus problems at Pity Wood,' suggested Murfin. 'I'm not surprised. I reckon you'd be permanently bunged up with a cold, if you lived there. I was sneezing myself when I was up at the farm yesterday.'

Fry stared at him for a moment, as if horrified at the idea of Murfin with a head cold. Cooper could practically see her mind working, pieces falling into place in that efficient, clock-work way her brain had. There were no leaps of intuition with Fry, just the logical adding of one item of information with another, to come up with a final answer, already checked and validated.

At that moment, DI Hitchens entered the CID room with an envelope in his hand. He handed it to Fry with a slightly sheepish look.

'Diane, here are your tickets for Dublin. I hope you've got your passport.'

Fry put the chemist's report down. 'I'm ready, sir.'

'Good. Your flight leaves at one twenty-five.'

They'd booked her on a cheap Ryanair flight, of course. The fare to Dublin was less than it would have cost her to catch a bus to Sheffield and back. Robin Hood Airport, too – which meant she had to drive right over to Doncaster to catch her flight.

Fry checked in, went through security, and decided to have a drink at the airside bar. And then she had to sit and wait. An hour's flight to Dublin, and an hour twiddling her thumbs. She watched her fellow passengers waiting patiently near the gate for boarding. Most of them seemed to have books or magazines, mindless stuff to while away the time. If only she could sit still and turn her brain off for an hour, the way these people were able to do.

When she'd finished her drink, Fry began to prowl the departure lounge, feeling restless and uneasy. She noted that ThomsonFly operated flights to Prague from this airport. That

301

would have been handy for Nadezda Halak, she supposed, the Czech Republic being right next door to Slovakia. In fact, they used to be one country, didn't they, before parts of Eastern Europe began to break up? But had Czechoslovakia separated before, or after, Nadezda arrived in the UK?

Fry found she had no idea. She couldn't even guess. In fact, she knew nothing else about Slovakia, except that it was where the photocopier paper was made that they used in the office. It said so on the packaging.

She hated being so ignorant of important facts. And this *could* be an important one, since it made a difference to the nationality of the victim. Damn. It was an overlooked detail, and she didn't like them. The wrong loose end could unravel a case completely.

She took her notebook out of her bag and jotted down a reminder to herself. She supposed she could call someone back in Edendale on her mobile, but she didn't want to seem like a pest, some sad character who couldn't leave her desk behind. Everyone else in the office seemed to be convinced that she was the lucky one to be flying to Ireland. A day off, they called it. A jaunt, a little jolly. She'd been conscious of envious glances, as if she was the teacher's pet. '*Don't drink too much Guinness, Diane. And watch out for those leprechauns.*'

Fry became aware that she was getting a headache. And she hadn't brought her Lemsip capsules with her, so it was guaranteed that an hour in the recycled air of an economy class cabin would make her cold twice as bad. It had been lurking around for days now, barely suppressed by the medication, irritating her nose and throat. If she didn't do something, she would arrive in Dublin with a sore throat, barely able to speak.

Well, she still had twenty minutes to spare before boarding, and there were some shops airside. No Boots the Chemist at a small regional airport like Robin Hood, but at least there was a World News. All the essentials for the happy traveller.

302

Keeping an ear out for announcements, Fry browsed the small range of pharmaceutical products on offer. She picked up a packet of Lemsip and some Paracetamol, then noticed the Sudafed. She wasn't congested, not yet. But that was the worst symptom of a bad cold, and you couldn't be too careful.

Out of habit, she turned each packet over to read the ingredients and contra-indications. She wasn't a hypochondriac, but if she ever had an allergic reaction, she wanted to know exactly what she was allergic to.

Her eyes were drawn to the active ingredient in Sudafed. Pseudoephedrine. That word had been bothering her since she'd gone over the chemist's report earlier in the day. There had been traces of the chemical found at Pity Wood Farm, scattered through the outbuildings and even in the soil surrounding them.

What else had there been on the list? Hydrogen peroxide, dilute hydrochloric acid, drain cleaner, iodine, anti-freeze, rubbing alcohol. And pseudoephedrine. A lot of pseudoephedrine. There was something she was missing, a loose end nagging at her here.

The first call came over the PA system for boarding Ryanair flight FR-1969. It was time to go. Fry grimaced, irritated by another detail that she wasn't going to be able to pin down.

Fumbling for her money, she took one last look at the ingredients on her purchases. Sudafed, Paracetamol and Lemsip. Well, that should sort out her cold, all right. In fact, you could get really high on that lot.

'Oh, my God.'

Fry froze at the counter, causing the assistant to stare at her as if she was mad. Then Fry turned and barged aside a queue of customers in her hurry to get out of the shop. She dragged her phone out of her bag as she ran and dialled a number. It was lucky she had it on speed dial, because her fingers were shaking with urgency. She tried to steady her voice, aware of her heart pounding in her chest and her breathing ragged with the surge of excitement and fear.

DI Hitchens came on the phone just as the final call for boarding was made and the last few passengers began to trickle through the gate for Dublin.

'Sir, it's DS Fry. Listen – I don't have much time. We need to get everyone clear of Pity Wood Farm immediately. Yes, all of them. I suggest we establish a safe perimeter and pull everything back. We've got to get them out of that place – *now!*'

28

Meth, speed, crystal, ice, glass, crank, tweak, yaba. Cooper knew it would have taken him longer than Fry to put the pieces together, but he might have managed it, given time. Everyone had heard the reports of an incident a few months ago, not many miles from here.

'Muriatic acid, iodine tincture, hydrogen peroxide. It's quite a list. Oh, God. And there was all that other stuff lying around,' he said. 'Plastic Coke bottles, tubing, aluminium foil, mason jars. There were even some coffee filters.'

DI Hitchens nodded. 'They weren't just rubbish, as we all thought. They were the tools of the trade. Someone has been operating a crystal meth lab at Pity Wood Farm.'

'It must have been the first of its kind in this area.'

'But not the last, of course,' said Hitchens with a sigh. 'They're much more professional operations now. This lot at Rakedale seem as though they might just have downloaded the instructions from the internet or something. It's a wonder they didn't have any major accidents.'

All the officers and civilian staff who'd been at Pity Wood Farm during the last few days had been ordered to present themselves for health checks this afternoon. While Cooper waited for his turn, he read the intelligence reports that had been copied and distributed throughout the department since Fry's conclusions had been confirmed.

And the reports made disturbing reading. He hadn't felt ill before, but Cooper was more than ready to be sick by the time he'd finished.

Meth, speed, crystal, ice, glass, crank, tweak, yaba. Call it whatever you liked, methamphetamine was highly addictive, producing a high that could last from twelve hours to a few days. The latest assessments warned that it had the potential to rival crack cocaine as the most dangerous drug in the country.

Only this year, methamphetamine had been upgraded from a Class B substance to Class A, which meant that anyone caught dealing it could receive a life sentence, and even possession got you seven years. On the street, it was generally found as an odourless, white, bitter-tasting powder, though it could also turn up in the form of pills, capsules and large crystals. Frequently snorted, but also used orally, smoked, and injected.

Methamphetamine was being manufactured in Britain as well as imported by a Filipino criminal network. It had begun to spread throughout the UK and was thought to be available in almost every city, according to the intelligence. It was increasingly popular among clubbers, and had started to enter mainstream drug use within the last few years. Hence, a rising demand that created a lucrative industry for unscrupulous entrepreneurs with access to the right sort of location.

Cooper watched Gavin Murfin dragging his heels towards the door as he was summoned to see the doctor. He wasn't sure what order they were being called in. Reverse alphabetical, maybe. Or the oldest first. He'd have a while to wait yet, anyway.

'Good luck, Gavin,' he called.

'Yeah, thanks.'

The right sort of location. That was the heart of the matter. Cooper had speculated about the laundering of red diesel going on somewhere like Pity Wood Farm, but crystal meth production required a remote location, too. Clandestine labs were often run in rural places because noxious smells could dissipate unnoticed.

The advice said that one of the more obvious signs of a methamphetamine production lab in operation was an odour similar to that of cat urine. Well, yes – the smell had been obvious. But he'd been too stupid to think of anything apart from the presence of cats.

Cooper's blood ran cold when he read the next paragraph. Meth labs also gave off other noxious fumes, such as phosphine gas, mercury vapours, lead, solvent fumes such as chloroform, iodine vapours and white phosphorus.

The back of his throat constricted at the thought. Cooper wondered about the fate of the forensics teams who had been digging up the yard for several days, sifting through the rubbish and searching the contents of the kitchen. He thought about Liz, and prayed she was safe.

And then there was the toxic waste. For every pound of meth manufactured, five or six pounds of toxic waste were produced, and it was usually disposed of in the yard or surrounding area. The toxic waste and fumes produced can seep into ground water as well as run off into fields. Anyone living near where meth manufacturing had occurred could suffer serious illnesses related to chemical toxicity. Chemicals permeated into the water, ground, carpeting, walls in the home, and into the air.

And the really bad news for Aaron Goodwin, the Manchester solicitor, was that once a home had been exposed to the toxic chemicals from methamphetamine production, it had to be condemned, and the clean-up costs were tremendous. Mr Goodwin would need deeper pockets than he'd imagined, if he was ever going to be able to live his rural dream, with horses in the paddock and a swimming pool in the yard.

So what about the workers? Users of methamphetamine put themselves at enough of a risk, but tweaking crystal meth was as dangerous as manufacturing it in the first place. Makeshift laboratories put their operators at risk of death or injury from explosions and the poisonous fumes produced during the cooking process.

The list of ingredients was totally horrifying. The chemicals used to make methamphetamine included iodine, drain cleaner, paint thinner, battery acid, anti-freeze, and cat litter. Some of those substances were akin to nerve agents. And not forgetting one of the vital elements in the recipe – pseudoephedrine, the active ingredient from several over-the-counter cold remedies.

Today, specialists were being sent in to Pity Wood Farm wearing protective clothing and breathing apparatus. Officers in white coveralls, green gloves and overshoes, carrying oxygen tanks had replaced the SOCOs and the anthropology team, not to mention the CID officers protected by nothing more than a pair of latex gloves. Warnings had been set up that the site was extremely hazardous. Exposure to some of the volatile toxic chemicals that had been found could have carcinogenic effects.

And DI Hitchens was right – like everything else, the instructions for methamphetamine production were readily available on the internet.

The meth factory at Pity Wood had already closed before the drug had been re-classified to a Class A substance. Not that the threat of a life sentence was much of a deterrent to the people who ran meth factories. They relied on not getting caught, and the amount of money they could make justified the risks – especially as the risk was mostly to other people, ignorant workers who just did as they were told. And, of course, they hadn't been caught. Not yet.

Cooper looked up and saw Hitchens pacing the room. Instead of retreating to his own office, the DI was fretting about every member of his team who might have been exposed to risk.

'The women buried at Pity Wood Farm, sir?' said Cooper. 'Nadezda Halak, and the other woman who died – how might they fit into the scenario?'

'If their bodies had been found sooner, Ben, toxicology might have established whether they were crystal meth users. But at the moment, we can't say one way or the other.'

'They were most likely working there, don't you think? Producing the methamphetamine.'

'Slave labour of some kind, yes. The gangs who run these operations are ruthless.'

'Are we talking about the same people who shot Tom Farnham, do you think, sir?' asked Cooper.

'Well, Ben, when these people have a dispute they don't go to court. They have their own ways of sorting things out.'

Cooper turned to the last page of the intelligence bulletin, which was headed 'Common Side Effects'. Again, his brain could hardly take them all in. Diarrhoea, nausea, loss of appetite, insomnia, tremors, irritability, weight loss, depression. The list was endless. Why would you risk doing all these different kinds of damage to your body? An overdose could cause brain damage, hallucinations, paranoia, kidney damage and something called formication, described as the sensation of your flesh crawling with insects.

But Cooper's eyes were drawn to the most peculiar symptom of chronic methamphetamine use of them all. The report referred to a dry mouth, excessive thirst triggering frequent consumption of high-sugar drinks, tooth grinding and the decreased production of acid-fighting saliva. Together, they caused the symptoms of rapid tooth decay. Sometimes known as 'meth mouth'.

One way or another, methamphetamine had killed Nadezda Halak.

Without her phone for about an hour and a half, Fry felt lost. She stared out of the window of the plane at the Irish Sea passing below. It looked grey, and very wet. She hoped that Ireland itself would be more welcoming. Break out the Guinness and the shamrock, we've got a visitor. Oh, yes, that's how it would be.

Well, it couldn't be worse than Rakedale. If she'd been forced to spend another day in that place, she would probably have gone mad, even without the effects of the toxic chemicals on her body.

For a moment, Fry wondered whether she could sue Derbyshire Constabulary for not providing her with proper protective equipment to do her job. Yes, probably. Health and Safety regulations called for a risk assessment, which hadn't been carried out, so far as she was aware.

But all she had was this damn cold to show for it. And no doubt she'd discover that the officer who ought to have carried out the risk assessment was her.

But Rakedale was definitely her idea of one of the outer circles of Hell. The people who lived there were slightly less than human, dead to normal standards of civilized behaviour.

Fry had once heard of a rare medical condition that destroyed the sense of touch. When you had the condition, it became impossible to tell sandpaper from silk, leather from stone, or water from oil. Impossible to feel anything at all.

They said that touch was already present as a sense in the foetus. At eight weeks after conception, it started in the lips and spread to the rest of the body. So how was it possible to lose this sense, of all the senses? A man who talked about his condition described wanting to stroke the family dog, but not being able to feel it, unless the dog had been out in the sun and was warm, or had been caught in the rain and was cold. Beyond that, there seemed to be nothing for him to touch.

She felt like that when she was in Rakedale. As a police officer, she'd learned to be sensitive to the smallest signals that people unconsciously gave out, the gestures and facial expressions that revealed their real thoughts, the body language and lack of eye contact that gave away a lie.

But there, she was unable to detect any normal responses. Those people were recognizable only at the extremes of emotion. They were either hot or cold, but in between there was a gap where human emotions seemed to cease to exist. In that state, they were out of reach of her senses, beyond her ability to touch.

As the plane began its descent towards Dublin Airport, Fry recalled David Palfreyman asking her whether she was able to tell when someone was a liar. Palfreyman's mockery of modern techniques was in itself a classic distraction tactic. She decided to focus her techniques on Palfreyman next time she met him. She felt sure he would fail the body language test.

Oh, don't worry, Mr Palfreyman – DS Fry certainly had the training to spot a liar. There were ten major signs that someone was lying. And Fry had seen every one of them during her time in Rakedale.

DCI Kessen was being interviewed on TV for the news bulletin. Cooper wondered if he would still have that job when Superintendent Branagh had settled in. It was high profile, and it didn't suit everyone. Would Branagh be better in front of a TV camera than she was in the photographer's studio?

'The chemicals used in the production of this drug are volatile and dangerous if inhaled, so officers have to be extremely cautious during their examination of the premises at Rakedale,' Kessen was saying. 'We were initially concerned that some of the toxic chemicals used in the production of methamphetamine might have been dumped in the local woods, but we have checked the area and we believe it is safe.

'This is likely to be a long investigation,' he warned, 'as we're having to take great care not to put our officers or the public at unnecessary risk from these toxic chemicals. The

311

production of methamphetamine can be very dangerous for anyone involved.'

Terrific. A long investigation. If that was true, Christmas was starting to look very unlikely. Perhaps they should cancel it altogether, and celebrate it in February instead.

Kessen finished by deflecting the question that everyone was bound to be asking.

'We're not able to say at this stage whether the death of Mr Thomas Farnham in a shooting incident is related. But all possible lines of enquiry are being followed up.'

Thinking of Christmas, Cooper remembered that Jack Elder was still in custody, and he would have to be either charged or released soon. Fry had left him her interview notes and her copy of the tape. Cooper went through to familiarize himself with Elder's answers, then he called down to ask the custody sergeant to put Elder in an interview room.

Elder's long grey beard did make him look a little bit like Santa Claus, though a Santa who'd been down too many chimneys and drunk too much of the sherry.

'I'm sure we'll have this sorted out soon, sir,' said Cooper, sitting across the interview-room table. 'There are just a couple more questions I'd like to ask you. One or two things that we're not clear about.'

'What's that, then?' said Elder.

'Well, for example, you said in your previous interview with DS Fry that you had never been to Pity Wood Farm. Is that correct?'

'Yes. I was never at the place. I saw the Suttons in the pub, and that was all. I stayed away from their old farm.'

'And my colleague put to you a statement from a witness who claims to have seen you going in and out of the farm many times with your lorry.'

Elder shook his head. 'Not me. They were wrong.'

'You see,' said Cooper, in his best kindly manner, 'since we had to arrest you, Mr Elder, we took your fingerprints and

312

a sample of your DNA when you arrived in custody, as you know. That's standard procedure, and it's not significant in itself. But it does mean that we can compare your prints, and your DNA profile, with any that we have on file. Those will include samples that have been collected from crime scenes over several decades.'

'Oh?'

'It's amazing what technology can do now. We're clearing up an awful lot of old crimes, just by comparing DNA samples to the database.'

'What has that got to do with me?'

'Well, it's like this,' said Cooper. 'How shall I explain it? If you told us you'd been at Pity Wood Farm, then there would be no problem. But since you've insisted twice now that you've never been there, it means that, should we happen to find your fingerprints, or some DNA evidence that does put you at the scene, then . . . well, we know you've been lying to us. And that looks very suspicious, doesn't it?'

Elder licked his lips and twisted a finger in his beard. 'Suspicious?'

'We'd have to draw certain conclusions from the fact that you were lying. Especially since we're engaged in a murder enquiry here. Probably a double murder, Mr Elder.'

'Even if I *was* there, it doesn't mean I was part of any murder,' said Elder.

'Surely it would have to be something as serious as a murder to make you sit here and lie about whether you'd visited Pity Wood,' said Cooper reasonably. 'I mean, what other reason would you have to do that?'

He could see Elder was starting to get anxious. His fingers twisted tighter and tighter until they must have hurt. Cooper let him think about it for a few moments longer before he asked again.

'So, what do you say? Shall we put your previous answers

behind us, and I'll give you a chance to answer again? Have you ever been to Pity Wood Farm, Mr Elder?'

''Course I bloody have,' blurted Elder. 'You know damn well I have, loads of times. You and your fingerprints and your DNA, trying to catch me out. If you find my blood at Pity Wood Farm, it'll be because of that bastard Derek Sutton. Mad as a weasel, he was. He would have killed me, if his brother hadn't pulled him off. And just because I had a bit of a joke with him.'

'A joke?'

'I used to do some vermin control when I was in farming. I still turn my hand to it now and again. That day, I'd been clearing some Larsen traps. Do you know what I mean?'

'Yes, they're used to catch carrion crows.'

'Aye. Well, I kept one bird in a trap, and I had it with me when I went up to Pity Wood. I slipped it into the cab of Derek's Land Rover when he wasn't looking. By God, he went berserk when he found it flapping around inside there, shitting on his seats.'

'Hold on, who else was there when this happened?'

'As well as me and Derek? Just his brother, Raymond.'

'What about Alan?'

Elder hesitated. 'Alan?'

'We do know about Alan, the third brother,' said Cooper.

'Ah, well, I never really knew that one. He was gone by the time this happened. They always said he couldn't stand living with the other two, and you can see why.'

'All right. So Derek was angry about the bird in his car?'

'Angry? I've never seen a bloke so mad in all my life. Like a wild thing, he was. Smashed his fist right through my jaw.'

'He broke your jaw?' said Cooper.

'Aye. Why do you think I have this beard? They took days putting my face back together.'

'So what happened? Was there a charge of assault against Derek Sutton? It would be grievous bodily harm, surely?'

Elder went suddenly quiet, his eyes wary. 'No, nothing like that.'

'But you did report the assault, Mr Elder?'

'Raymond did. It was him that called the police, and the ambulance. But there were never any charges.'

Watching his manner change, Cooper guessed the answer to his next question.

'What was the name of the police officer who dealt with the incident?'

Elder stared at him, a question of his own clear in his eyes. But he evidently read what he wanted from Cooper's face, and realized he wasn't giving away any information that Cooper didn't already know.

'PC Palfreyman turned up. He said he'd sort it out himself, the way he always did.'

29

Cooper had no choice but to go to his DI with the results of his interview. Hitchens had just received the results of the postmortem on Tom Farnham, and he was ready to hear some good news.

'Blunt-force trauma from a severe beating,' he said. 'Blows to the arms and legs produced contusions and haematomas, and the radius of the left arm was fractured. Further blows to the chest caused extensive bruising, and an injury to the abdomen had damaged the spleen. And that's before we get on to the penetrating trauma from two bullet wounds, one of which was actually what killed him.'

'They wanted to make a proper job of it,' said Cooper.

'More than that. They didn't just kill him, Ben, they were sending a message.'

'Yes, I see.'

'And I bet everyone in Rakedale has received the message loud and clear. Not that they needed any encouragement to keep their mouths shut, by all accounts.'

'No, sir,' said Cooper. 'Except . . .'

Hollowbrook Cottage was low lying enough to avoid the hill mist that was clinging to the plateau now that the rain had stopped. Palfreyman was raking dead leaves from his path, and heaping the damp, black mass into a compost bin. He dropped his rake when the car turned into his drive and came forward to meet them. He led them into the house with hardly a word.

'Mr Palfreyman,' said Hitchens, opening the conversation, 'you've told my officers that you visited Pity Wood Farm on several occasions while the Sutton brothers lived there.'

'In the line of duty, yes.'

Palfreyman already sounded on the defensive. Of course, he wasn't stupid, and he had experience of the job. A third interview, and the presence of the DI himself, would suggest that someone didn't believe what he'd been telling them, or thought he had information he was keeping back.

'That's right. But according to other witnesses we've talked to, you actually became quite friendly with the Suttons. You were often seen drinking with them at the Dog Inn.'

Palfreyman smiled. 'Now, that would be *off* duty, of course.'

'Was that a regular occurrence?'

'A regular occurrence? What sort of language do they teach you these days?' Palfreyman gave a small sigh. 'I used to go to the Dog regularly for a pint or two in those days. I still do, though not so often. I can't really afford it. But Raymond and Derek were regulars there, too. It's the only pub you can get to without driving a few miles.'

'So you met them in the pub often?'

'Obviously.'

'And they bought you drinks? Or did *you* buy them drinks?'

Palfreyman began to get annoyed. 'Look, there's something you probably don't understand, Inspector. I can see you haven't been in the job all that long yourself. In those days, the local bobby wasn't just some bloke in a car who might, or might not, turn up when your house got burgled. He was part of the community. It was his job to know everyone, to be aware of what was going on around his patch.'

'Yes, sir. I know that.'

'Well, that was me – I was part of the community here, and folk liked to see me in the pub, or in the post office, when we had one. I was never exactly off duty, you see. They could talk to me about anything that was bothering them, whenever they saw me around the village. They could even come to my house, and I would try to help them. And, yes, if they felt the urge to buy me a drink occasionally, that was fine, too. That's because they knew I was on their side, and they trusted me. They *liked* me. I don't suppose you get that much, do you?'

He glanced at Cooper, as if seeking support. But, looking at the retired officer, Cooper couldn't see what it was that people had liked so much.

Hitchens let a small silence follow the outburst, perhaps hoping to embarrass Palfreyman with the lack of response.

'Mr Palfreyman, were you aware of any illegal activities taking place at Pity Wood Farm?'

'Illegal activities? Blimey, there are so many laws now, there must be something to cover the way the Suttons lived. Let's see. Breach of Health and Safety regulations? An EU directive on the standards of domestic hygiene? Control of Stinking Mud Act?'

'I was thinking specifically of the manufacture of Class A drugs,' said Hitchens.

Palfreyman was halted in mid-flow. 'Drugs? At Pity Wood? Not on my watch.'

'Are you sure?'

'It's ridiculous. I never saw any drugs on my patch, either supply or using. Oh, there might be one or two stuck-up folk who smoke a bit of cannabis in their own home, but nothing that troubles anyone else. Who are you suggesting was involved in manufacturing drugs?'

'Possibly Tom Farnham.'

Palfreyman shook his head. 'No, you've got that wrong.'

318

'We suspect his involvement in the production of methamphetamine at Pity Wood Farm.'

It was then Cooper noticed the ex-PC's huge hands. They were clenched tightly on the arms of his chair, their blue veins standing out like ropes. Those hands were almost the only sign of a tremendous tension that seemed to have gripped him. When Cooper became aware of it, he looked for other indications. After a moment, he saw that Palfreyman's entire body was quivering, as if a great volcano of emotion was being suppressed, a hot vat of lava that might burst at any moment. Yet Palfreyman's face remained impassive in response to the DI's questions.

Hitchens must have thought he just hadn't understood.

'Methamphetamine. That's a Class A substance known as crystal meth.'

'Impossible,' said Palfreyman bluntly. 'I would have . . .' He stopped, and gritted his teeth. 'Well, I would have known.'

Then the DI gave Cooper a look, inviting him to have a go at the subject.

'Mr Palfreyman, today I interviewed a Mr Jack Elder, from Rakedale. Do you know him?'

'I know everyone,' said Palfreyman, a trifle sullenly.

'I'd like to ask you about an incident that Mr Elder says took place at Pity Wood Farm, between him and Derek Sutton.'

'Incident?'

'I'm sure you remember. You remember everything that happens in Rakedale, don't you?'

Palfreyman gazed out of his window for a while. The grey mist hung in the woods half a mile away, but it hadn't reached his property. Not yet.

'Yes, I got the call to that,' he said. 'I had a young probationer with me, showing him the ropes. We responded to a 999, and we blue-lighted to the scene. Got there way ahead of the ambulance. We found Jack Elder bleeding all over the place, and you could see his jaw was broken. Derek had calmed down by then, but Raymond was in a right state. When we arrived, he was pacing up and down the yard, swearing violently. Honestly, he was like Ahab cursing Moby Dick. Sin and damnation, and I don't know what else.'

'What did you do?' asked Cooper.

'I did the right thing. I had a word with all three of them, then got on to the radio to Control and told them it was a farm accident. We loaded Jack into the ambulance when it came, and he got fixed up. It was the probationer who took the most sorting out, but he did what I told him.'

'Did that really seem like the best way of dealing with it?'

'Yes. The thing is, you don't want a long enquiry and a court case hanging over you, when you've got other things to do. Think of all that blasted paperwork, the time you have to spend hanging around outside a courtroom. What's the point? Is it any better now? No, I can see from your faces that it isn't. Worse, maybe? I bet you know exactly what it's like. Once your collar number is on a job, it'll be round your neck for months, or years.'

'Derek Sutton committed an assault. What about punishment for his crime? What about the concept of justice?'

'That's exactly what it was,' said Palfreyman. 'Jack Elder got the justice he deserved.'

'Was it him who was responsible for the incident with Jo Brindley, too?'

'Yes, of course. Nasty bugger, Jack. Derek Sutton did us all a favour.'

'Are you sure Derek was responsible for the assault?' asked Hitchens.

'Yes, he admitted it.'

'Did he have injuries? Scraped knuckles? Blood on his clothes?'

'Why does it matter?'

'I just like to get the details accurate, sir.'

'Yes, we all have to deal with liars, don't we?'

Hitchens looked up, surprised. 'Sorry?'

'You're asking me all these details to try to catch me out in a lie. I know the technique. That female DS you sent the other day, she bragged about being trained these days. But don't you find it difficult to have to go through life assuming that everyone is lying to you? Don't you ever experience trust? Can't you tell when someone knows what the right thing is to do?'

Neither Hitchens nor Cooper could answer the question. It was rhetorical, surely? Cooper couldn't think how you would know that. Everyone's ideas of 'right' were different, just as their concepts of justice varied.

Palfreyman sighed at their expressions.

'God help us. Let me tell you something. There was an incident when I was a young bobby, only two years in, so I was just qualified. You know, nothing actually marked the passing of your two years' service then. It was supposed to be such a milestone for a new copper, but all I got was a pep talk from the commander, and a quick handshake. The only celebration I can remember is having to buy cakes for the rest of the section. Then we got this misper report. You've been working through missing persons on this case, I dare say?'

'Of course.'

'Aye. Well, this was a small child that was missing. Three years old, she was, and the parents were screaming the place down. We were FOAs, me and my mate. While he talked to the parents, I made a floorboard check, like you're supposed to do when you're sent to a misper report. Especially as it was a child.'

'In case a member of the family had killed her and hidden her body?' said Cooper.

'It happens,' said Palfreyman. 'A space under the floorboards, the bottom of a wardrobe, a cupboard below the stairs. Just somewhere to stash the body until the coppers have been and gone. It gives them time to decide how to dispose of her permanently.'

'Did you find anything?'

'No. The bosses turned up – and your lot, CID. They decided she was a genuine case of suspicious circumstances. They pulled out all the stops for a while.'

Cooper looked at him. 'You didn't agree with that assessment?'

'It didn't matter what I thought. I was just a young response bobby, wet behind the ears.' Palfreyman shrugged. 'I had no evidence anyway, just a bit of an odd feeling about the parents. The way they reacted seemed off, somehow. They were bothered about the wrong things – asking where we were going to look, when we'd be coming back to talk to them again, that sort of thing. Do you know what I mean?'

'You had a gut instinct,' said Cooper.

'Right.'

'And what happened to the child?'

'Oh, they found her, six months later. She was unrecognizable by then, though. The father thought he'd suffocated her in her sleep, and they both panicked. So they waited until we'd gone, and they buried her under the garden shed. I always wondered if she might still have been alive when we first arrived.'

'There's no way you could tell that.'

Palfreyman watched his visitors for some reaction, and seemed disappointed. 'A gut instinct doesn't count for much these days, does it? Some of the old school might have listened to me back then, but not the SIO who was put on the case. He was too full of himself. Done all the courses, got all the certificates. If I'd said anything to him, I'd just have made a fool of myself. I still had hopes of promotion then, you see.'

'I understand,' said Cooper.

Palfreyman laughed. 'Sad, isn't it?'

'No.'

'Yes it is. Those are the decisions that come back to haunt you years later, you know. The ones where you chickened out, bottled it, or betrayed your own beliefs.' He looked more closely at Cooper. 'Has it happened to you yet, lad? Don't let it, if it's not too late already. Be true to yourself. Say what you think.' He nodded at Hitchens. 'Don't play their game. You'll regret it later, if you do.'

'I'll remember that,' said Cooper.

But Palfreyman leaned across and gripped his arm. 'It's important. You know there are lots of coppers who feel like I do. They just daren't say so.'

As they were leaving Hollowbrook Cottage, Palfreyman held Cooper back for a moment until he was out of earshot of his DI.

'You know, back then, if you'd visited Rakedale, you could have depended on finding people with a bit of self-reliance – they were known across Derbyshire for a streak of independence. It was an independent spirit forged by hardship, all right. But that made them all the better as people, I reckon.'

'I think I know what you mean,' said Cooper.

'Well, you've met some of the people who live in Rakedale now. Would you say that describes them?'

'Perhaps not, sir.'

'Don't be so namby-pamby, lad. You can see perfectly well they're not like that any more. They're defeated. Their spirit has gone.'

Cooper wasn't sure about Palfreyman's verdict on the people of Rakedale. His contempt had sounded more like a judgement on himself.

There seemed to be building going on everywhere in Dublin – new offices, new housing estates, new roads. Fry saw signs claiming that some of the projects had been funded by the European Union. So that's where her taxes had been going. She'd often wondered.

Detective Garda Tony Lenaghan had greeted her in the

arrivals hall at the crowded airport. He was a cheerful-looking man in his thirties, relaxed and talkative. He gave Fry such a genuine smile of welcome that she almost hugged him on the spot. She hadn't felt like doing that to anyone for years.

'Sergeant Fry, welcome to An Garda Síochána.'

He loaded her bag into his car and asked where she was staying. It was only a short drive from the airport at Swords to Coolock, which turned out to be an area of north Dublin, lying somewhere between the M1 urban motorway and the northern arc of Dublin Bay.

'Croke Park is just down the road here,' said Lenaghan. 'We were all on duty at Croke, back in February. The rugby, you know? England versus Ireland. Your boys had never been allowed to play at Croke before, for obvious reasons.'

Fry frowned, thinking she was missing some arcane fact about the game of rugby.

'Obvious?'

'Because of the Black and Tans.'

After a few seconds, Lenaghan rightly interpreted her silence.

'You do know about the Black and Tans? The massacre in 1920?'

'Sorry.'

Lenaghan stared at her in amazement. In fact, he stared for so long that Fry started to worry about his car drifting danger-ously across the carriageway.

'Thirteen spectators and one player were killed during the match between Dublin and Tipperary. Shot by the Black and Tans. It was the original Bloody Sunday massacre. Surely they teach you about that at school in England, Sergeant?'

'No. These Black and Tans – were they English, then?'

Lenaghan shook his head in despair. 'Eight hundred years of suppression, and you just forget.'

They'd booked her a room in a place called the Flyover B&B, a place with pine dressers and cast-iron fireplaces.

Its name exactly described its location, right under Junction 1 of the motorway, where it met the Upper Drumcondra Road.

Fry made arrangements to meet up with Lenaghan in the morning, and she unpacked in her room. Then she switched on the TV, more for some background noise than because she wanted to watch anything.

Finally, she got out her phone. It had switched automatically to a local service provider in Ireland, but there were no messages that she'd missed. She put it on the table by the bed. But for the rest of the evening, her phone did not ring.

Cooper was sitting in his flat in Welbeck Street. He was watching the news on the telly, with his cat Randy purring on his knee and his mobile phone pressed to his ear.

'So what do you want to do tonight?' he asked.

'I want to go shopping,' said Liz. 'I've still got some last-minute stuff to buy.'

'Really? I thought you were more organized than that. I imagined you were the sort of person who had everything put away months ago. Drawers full of carefully wrapped and labelled presents for everybody you could think of.'

'Presents, yes. But there are a few other things I need to take home with me for Christmas Day.'

'And you want to do it tonight?'

'Yes, Ben.'

Cooper exchanged glances with his cat, Randy. He'd never understood the appeal of shopping, but shopping on a Monday night seemed downright perverse.

'OK, then. Where do you want to go?'

'Meadowhall. We can be there in half an hour or so, and it's open until nine o'clock tonight.'

'Meadowhall? A week before Christmas? You're kidding. Think of the crowds – it'll be bedlam.'

325

'It's all right if you don't want to come, Ben.'

Cooper sighed. 'No. I'm sure it'll be an experience.'

David Palfreyman opened the cupboard and took out the bottle of whisky. Glenfiddich, and it was still half full. He smiled for the first time that day.

'There is a God, after all.'

It had been quite a day, and he deserved a drink. The police asking him more questions, a visit from Mel. It had been quite a week, actually, with the news from Pity Wood Farm that had gone round the village like wildfire, and the murder of Tom Farnham. But he'd resisted the bottle until now, hadn't even peeped in the cupboard. But a large whisky was called for. A *very* large whisky, why not?

He poured a good-sized tumbler and held it up to the light, admiring the colour of the Glenfiddich. Peaty brown, with a hint of gold. Gorgeous. He could look at it for hours.

Palfreyman had done quite a lot of drinking when he was in the force. It was what had helped him relax when he came home at night, or in the early hours of the morning, whenever his shift ended. Sometimes he'd sat drinking on his own, when everyone else in the world was asleep, or just stumbling out of bed to get their breakfast, listening for the milkman whistling outside, turning on the radio to get the morning's news. He'd drunk while the sun came up and the birds started singing. He'd drunk to ease the stress and dull the memories.

He'd only been eighteen months into the job when he was sent to a serious multiple fatal RTC. He'd been first on scene for that one. Over the years, he'd learned to handle the dead, but it had always been the living he'd had problems dealing with. He still had problems with them, even now. At that RTC, the poor woman whose husband had just died was so distressed that when he left her, he'd been close to bursting into tears himself. A big, strapping copper, left an emotional wreck. What a joke.

Later, he'd developed a sick sense of humour, pretty much like everyone else in those days. He'd viewed a fatal as a bonus. If the victim was dead, it meant one less statement to take. You had to be hard, didn't you? You had to be thick skinned. You'd go mad if you weren't.

He felt sorry for those in the job now. That detective sergeant – what was her name? Fry, of course. His memory wasn't letting him down, not quite yet. And the other – her DC. Cooper, of course. No chance of forgetting that one.

These modern police officers had it worse than he did, no doubt about it. They couldn't relieve the tension the same way he always had. No sick jokes – it wouldn't be sensitive. Or, God help them, politically correct. And drinking was probably frowned on these days, too. Poor bastards.

Palfreyman took a sip of whisky, and found the glass was nearly empty. He wasn't sure how that had happened. He mustn't have been paying attention. He eased himself out of his chair and went back to the cupboard to top it up. There was plenty left in the bottle yet.

Some memories were very clear, even now. The first sudden death he went to. It had come over the radio just after he'd finished his supper. Chicken Korma, he could remember the taste of it. His stomach had knotted at the thought when they got the call. Most reports were false alarms, they'd told him. But he knew this one was going to be genuine. He knew it from the taste in his mouth. Chicken spiced with fear.

It had been a late winter's evening, much like this one tonight. December, yes. A couple of weeks before Christmas. When they got to the house, there were no lights on and it was really cold. They'd shouted through the letter box, but got no reply. His partner had used a rammit on the door, and they'd gone in.

The occupant of the house was in the sitting room. He'd been a regular newspaper reader. They could judge how long he'd been there by the date on the newspaper he was holding.

It had been about three weeks. Palfreyman remembered hearing the radio on in the background, some music playing, and the man lying on the sofa where he'd died holding his chest.

With a gesture of defiance, he finished the last of the whisky. It had been a few minutes before training kicked in on that occasion, but there was always duty to be done. Things to be sorted out.

Yes, even the dead demanded justice.

30

Garda Lenaghan took Fry first to Coolock garda station in
Oscar Traynor Road and introduced her to his inspector. It
was only when the garda took off his jacket in the office that
she noticed he was armed.

'Is that usual?' she asked him.

'The weapon? It's my moral authority.'

Outside the garda station, there was a smell hanging in the
air that made Fry feel a familiar craving. When they turned
the corner in Lenaghan's car, she noticed a huge Cadbury's
factory across the road. So that was where the smell came
from. How did people stand it? If she worked in Coolock,
she'd be a wreck within a few weeks.

Unlike most Irish people, in Fry's experience, Lenaghan
seemed comfortable with silence.

'You have a couple of unidentified bodies, I gather?' he said,
after a while.

'Just one now. We managed to get an ID on the first. A
Slovakian migrant worker.'

'Ah.'

Lenaghan nodded thoughtfully for a few minutes. 'I don't
suppose we can make a match?' he said.

329

'I beg your pardon?'

'I wondered if we could match up your body with our missing persons file. We have a few to choose from. There's a Kosovan who's been missing since January 2004. Would she suit you? Here she is, look – thirty-three years old, five feet nine inches tall, slight build, long dark hair, brown eyes. Name of Lilijana. Last seen wearing a dark jacket, black jumper, navy trousers and brown suede boots.'

'Too old, and too tall,' said Fry.

'OK. Well, we've got a twenty-eight-year-old from County Mayo, missing since December 2000. Only five feet, this one. Small, slim build, short brown hair with red highlights. Black trousers, maroon polo-neck jumper, beige sleeveless jacket. None of them were exactly fashion icons, you understand.'

'Do you have a lot of missing persons?' said Fry.

'Oh, yes. Going back to about 1991. We don't bother much beyond that. But it would be nice to tie one up. Are you sure you wouldn't like Lilijana?'

'Sorry, I don't think I can help you. But I'll let you know.'

Lenaghan sighed. 'Oh, well. They were probably killed locally, anyway. It's the murder capital of the country here, Sergeant. Did you know that?'

'No, I didn't.'

'Dublin is awash with hand guns these days. You can buy one for two hundred euros, if you know which bar to go in.'

They passed something called the Starlight Club Memorial, which was setting off another echo in Fry. She was sure it was something she ought to recognize, but she daren't ask about it, for fear of showing her ignorance again.

'Look at this factory here,' said Lenaghan, pointing at a huge building by the road. 'It's the old Tayto Crisps plant. When I was growing up, I always used to wind the window down as we passed it. The smell of the crisps cooking would waft beautifully into the car.'

Fry laughed as Lenaghan pretended to inhale a smell, like a Bisto Kid. He joined in her laughter cheerily.

'Ah, but there's no waft to be had today, Sergeant,' he said. 'They closed the Tayto factory two years ago. Outsourcing production, they call it.'

Martin Rourke's house was in a street behind Bunratty Road, near the Northside Shopping Centre. The gardai already had Rourke in custody at Oscar Traynor Road, so Fry and Lenaghan were free to search his house.

Fry moved through the rooms, finding nothing of interest until she came to the bedrooms. The first one was a small room, still decorated with nursery wallpaper. Mr Happy and Little Miss Giggles.

'Are young children still into the Mr Men these days?' asked Fry.

'Pre-school age, I think, yes.'

'So Rourke has a pre-school-age child?'

'Ah, I don't think she's with him any more,' said Lenaghan. 'The mother took the child away, I gather.'

A single bed stood against one wall, neatly made up, with folded pyjamas on the pillow. The only other furniture consisted of a chest of drawers painted pink, a TV set, and a white melamine wardrobe. Lenaghan opened the curtains and peered through the sash window on to the yard below.

To Fry, the bedroom felt cold and empty. It was strange how quickly a room began to feel that way, once its occupant was no longer there. She'd been in bedrooms where a child had been missing for only a few hours, but the feeling was unmistakable. As if the room itself knew that its occupant was never coming back.

Lenaghan pulled out the bed to make certain there was nothing underneath it, then opened the wardrobe. A few items of clothing swung from plastic hangers. On the floor were shoes and a pile of children's books.

Fry had gone to the chest of drawers and was searching through more clothes, T-shirts neatly folded, pairs of socks rolled into balls.

'Anything?' asked Lenaghan.

'Nothing obvious.'

But Fry had a nagging buzz at the back of her brain, an irritation telling her that something was missing, but she couldn't think what it was.

Cautiously, Lenaghan shifted the wardrobe away from the wall. 'Sergeant, come and look at this. Your visit to Dublin could be worthwhile.'

Detective Superintendent Hazel Branagh sat at the head of the room with DCI Kessen and surveyed the assembled CID team, waiting for the chattering to settle down.

'Do I have your attention, DC Murfin?'

'Yes, ma'am,' said Murfin, sitting up straight at the sound of her voice. Cooper had never seen him react quite like that before. It was almost as if someone had shoved a steel spike up his backside.

The fact that she knew Murfin's name and picked him out from a room full of officers was impressive in itself. So far, she hadn't been introduced to anyone in CID below inspector rank, yet she seemed to know who everyone was.

'Good morning. You might already be aware who I am, but for those of you who were asleep, I'm Detective Superintendent Branagh.'

There was a ragged chorus of 'Good morning, ma'am', mouthed rather than spoken too loudly, for fear of attracting attention. Cooper was reminded of the chorus at the pantomime, amateur singers coming together for the first time to practise sounding like one.

'I'm fully aware that you have a major enquiry on your hands, and I want to assure you I'm not going to get in the way. DCI Kessen will remain SIO while I settle in and get my feet under the table. However, I do want to get to know everyone personally as soon as I can, so don't be surprised if you find me hanging around in the CID room asking what you're doing.'

Cooper shivered at the hint of a threat in the last sentence. He sneaked a glance at Murfin, who was still looking stricken at having been singled out.

'The shooting is taking precedence at the moment, and it's attracting quite a lot of media attention – as is the discovery of the abandoned crystal meth lab. Fortunately, I've managed to negotiate extra resources, and the drugs squad are working with us. Rest assured, we're pulling out all the stops.' Branagh turned to the DCI sitting alongside her. 'But the human remains at the farm, Stewart – is this a cold case?'

'It looks like it,' said Kessen. 'Twelve months in one instance, anyway. Four years in the other.'

'There isn't still an open enquiry on either of the victims?'

'Not that we're aware of. But since we haven't actually managed to establish an identity on the second . . .'

'Witnesses?'

Kessen gritted his teeth. 'None. As far as we know, the only eyewitness was Thomas Farnham.'

'I understand the former owner of the farm is still alive?'

'Yes, Mr Sutton. But he's very elderly, and borderline senile. So far, we haven't been able to obtain much useful information from him.'

'Push him harder,' said Branagh.

'We can do that, but . . .'

'Good. And there's a suspect still in custody, I believe.'

'Oh, yes,' said Kessen. 'Jack Elder.'

'And what's the position on Mr Elder?'

'The CPS say we have enough evidence to charge him with some minor offences, but there's nothing to substantiate anything more serious.'

'Let's go for a charge, then, and release him.' Branagh looked around the room. 'And then perhaps DC Murfin can suggest a few new lines of enquiry. From what I've heard, he seems like an officer with some unusual ideas.'

'Thank you, ma'am,' said Murfin.

'It wasn't meant as a compliment.'

The CID room was quiet without Diane Fry. Particularly hushed after the first meeting with Superintendent Branagh. But Murfin wasn't going to be kept quiet for long.

'Actually, I *have* got a theory, Ben,' he said suddenly.

'Oh? I hope you're not going to try showing off for the new Super, Gavin. I'd be careful, mate.'

'It's about this Raymond Sutton bloke,' said Murfin, waving aside Cooper's advice. 'He sounds like a bit of a Holy Joe, right?'

'Yes, I suppose so.'

'Do you think he could have killed the woman in some drug-crazed religious ritual that went wrong?'

'Raymond Sutton is a Methodist,' said Cooper. 'From what I've heard, Methodists don't drink or swear, or take drugs.'

'Or fart, I suppose,' said Murfin.

'Sceptical, Gavin?'

'In my experience, every bugger in the world has the same evil thoughts and dirty habits. Some just *pretend* they don't.'

Cooper laughed. Methodism made him think of the Tolpuddle Martyrs and the temperance movement. Apart from that, they were a bit of an alien sect, with mysterious ways of behaving.

Thinking of mysterious behaviour, he had to admit it was a bit strange for DCI Kessen to confine Fry to mispers, then suddenly decide to send her to Ireland. But he was sure it didn't mean anything sinister. Fry was being too thin-skinned. He supposed it came with the keenness of her ambition. Not the slightest little thing should get in her way. Not a hint of being passed over or left out when something was happening.

Murfin answered the phone, disappeared for a few minutes, then came back into the room.

'You haven't been presenting your new theory, have you, Gavin?' said Cooper.

'I decided it needed a bit more work. No, there's a girl in reception. She says she's David Palfreyman's granddaughter.'

'Really? What is she like?'

'Well, for a start, she seems to be wearing more tattoos than clothes. That blue ink must have some sort of insulating quality. Do you reckon?'

'How old is she?'

'Late teens. She describes herself as a student, but she doesn't seem to be studying very much. As far as I can tell, she's re-taking her gap year. But she's banging on about her brother being killed in a car crash years ago, and I can't make any sense of it.'

'I'll talk to her, if you like.'

'Thanks, Ben. You're a pal.'

Cooper got up and put his jacket on before he met a member of the public.

'Hey, by the way, Ben,' said Murfin. 'Is Diane Fry leaving?'

'What?'

'Haven't you heard anything?'

'No. Have you, Gavin?'

'It was just something that the DI said.'

'No, she's only gone to Ireland. She's been sent to interview Martin Rourke.'

'Oh.' Murfin tapped his teeth with a pen, in a way that made Cooper pause before he went down to reception.

'You're always getting things slightly wrong, Gavin. Did you know that?'

Murfin looked at his computer suddenly, and his face went pale. 'Oh, God.'

'What's the matter now?'

'I've got an email, Ben. From Detective Superintendent

Branagh. She says I'm first in for a personal interview with her tomorrow morning.'

Cooper didn't notice the girl's tattoos so much. Instead, he noticed her eyes. They were big, brown eyes, like a veal calf's. In shadow, she looked like a weary Madonna – pale and worried, dark hair hanging around her face. But when she turned to greet him, the light of the grey December afternoon did nothing for her appearance. Before the tattoos, she'd been an ordinary teenage girl with nice hair, but really bad acne.

'You're the granddaughter of Mr David Palfreyman at Hollowbrook Cottage, Rakedale?'

'Yes, my name is Mel Palfreyman. It's short for Melanie, but I never really liked that name.'

Cooper could have guessed it. It was much too feminine and girly for a teenager who wanted to rebel.

'Are you close to your grandfather?'

'Yes, closer than I am to my mum and dad. I visit him all the time in Rakedale. In fact, he's like a real dad to me. Tells me off, disapproves of my boyfriend. You know the sort of thing. But, yes, we get on fine. I was always Granddad's favourite, whereas Ian was my parents'.'

'Ian?'

'My brother?'

'You told my colleague that your brother died.'

'In a car accident. When he was fourteen. Granddad refers to it as the RTA.'

Cooper nodded. Even the use of acronyms dated Palfreyman. No one referred to a Road Traffic Accident any more. It had to be called an RTC – a Road Traffic Collision. If it was an 'accident', then no one could be charged with responsibility for it. And in twenty-first-century Britain, there always had to be someone to blame.

'How did it happen, Mel?'

'We were both in the car, in fact,' she said. 'We were with

our grandparents on a day out. We were going to Sheffield to do some shopping. Granny and Granddad wanted to buy us some new clothes. Our birthdays were quite close together, as it happened.

'Granddad was driving. He made a mistake pulling out on to the A6 near Bakewell. The road was very busy, a lot of heavy lorries. It was near Ashford in the Water. You know the place I mean?'

'Yes.'

'We had to wait a long time at the junction to pull out. Cars were queuing behind us, drivers were getting irritable. Ian was impatient, too. I remember hearing him say, "Come on – go for it, Granddad." But Ian was sitting in the back seat, with me. How could he have known whether it was safe to pull out? He couldn't, could he? But Granddad pulled out anyway. If he'd been a bit quicker on the accelerator pedal, we might have been all right, even then. But there was a lorry – and it couldn't avoid us.'

Mel touched the scar on her forehead. It was more noticeable now than it had been before. The memory was making it flare red, like a fresh wound.

'That's when I got this,' she said. 'I hit the back of the headrest on Granny's seat.'

'And your brother was killed?'

'Yes. Granny and Granddad weren't badly hurt, but emotionally they were devastated, of course. We were in their care, after all. They never got over the guilt of that, especially Granddad.'

'It's understandable.'

'But they weren't as upset as Dad.'

Cooper waited.

'Mum, Granny, Granddad – they were all grateful for the fact that I survived, and they were so concerned about my recovery. Head injuries can be a lot more serious than they seem at first, you know. But Dad –'

337

'Yes.'

'Well, I think Dad always believed the wrong child died in that crash. He showed no interest in whether I survived or not. His beloved son had been killed. And, somehow, that was *my* fault.'

'Why did you want to tell me this, Mel?'

'So that you understand a bit more about my granddad. I know how he likes to come across. He thinks he's still in the police sometimes. He loved that job so much, he can't accept that he's retired. It makes him feel lonely and useless. So he gets cross and bad-tempered about it whenever anyone mentions it. I bet you found him like that.'

'To be honest, yes.'

'Also, he always says the modern police have no idea how to do the job that he did. Proper policing, he calls it. I don't know what he means, exactly, but he's very disrespectful.'

'Ye-es.'

Mel laughed at his expression. 'In fact, I'm surprised he hasn't tried to solve your case for you by now. Or, at least, told you how to do it.'

'Well, I don't think Mr Palfreyman has done that,' said Cooper.

To be fair, he had no idea what the former PC had got up to after he and Fry left his house. If, by some miracle, Palfreyman actually did solve the case of the two dead women at Pity Wood Farm, he wouldn't be complaining. But he bet Diane Fry would be.

'Mel, I still don't really understand why you thought it was so important to come into Edendale and tell us this.'

Mel Palfreyman pushed back her hair and stroked the tattoo on her neck. Black-painted fingernails followed the shape of a Celtic knot etched in blue ink.

'My granddad thinks you're trying to set him up as a suspect for these murders at Pity Wood. Are you?'

Cooper couldn't hide his surprise. 'And why would we do that?'

Mel began to laugh again. 'You know, Granddad gave me a lecture once, all about how you can tell if a person is lying. He thought it would be useful to me when I started going out with boys. He said one sign to look for is when someone answers a question with another question. It's an attempt to divert your attention, instead of giving a direct answer. I think that was the gist of what he said.'

'That was pretty good advice,' admitted Cooper, trying hard to hide the expression in his eyes. He supposed that would show, too. He hoped he wouldn't blush, or start stammering.

'Yes, I thought so.'

'We don't set people up, anyway. It's just not something we would get away with. Not these days.'

She studied him closely, and seemed to accept what she saw. 'I don't know. It's what Granddad thinks, though. To be honest, I reckon it's because it was the way things were done in his day. The way he saw things being done.'

'I can promise you it's not like that any more,' said Cooper, tempted to cross his fingers behind his back as he said it.

'So you haven't been digging out people who'll say things against him? You haven't been gathering circumstantial evidence that would make a case against him, just because he's a convenient suspect?'

'No, of course not. Though there are certain circumstances that . . .'

'That what?'

'Well, that might need a bit of explaining.'

'So Granddad will be questioned again?'

'Almost certainly, I should think.'

'I see.'

'But that doesn't mean he has anything to worry about. He won't necessarily be arrested.'

'Necessarily?'

'I don't make these decisions,' said Cooper apologetically.

339

'It'll be decided at a higher level, by a senior officer in discussion with the CPS.'

'Will you be there when it happens, at least?'

'I can't say. I'm sorry.'

Cooper knew that he'd failed to reassure her. But there was nothing else he could say, without going into details of the evidence, which was against all the rules. Of course, he didn't feel confident enough in the outcome himself, and he couldn't tell her things he didn't believe in, could he?

He showed her back to reception and watched her leave the station, pulling up the collar of her jacket when she got outside. Thankfully, there was one thing that Mel Palfreyman hadn't asked him at all – whether she was likely to be questioned herself.

DI Hitchens caught Cooper as he arrived back upstairs. Cooper could sense that something was up, from the DI's manner.

'Oh, Ben, you'll want to know this. I realize you've been involved quite heavily with this aspect of the enquiry.'

'Sir?'

'We've decided to stop pussy-footing around, and we've brought Raymond Sutton in for questioning.'

'Here? You've put that old man in a cell?'

'No, he's not under arrest. We've put him in an interview room,' said Hitchens defensively.

Cooper didn't need to ask, he could guess whose decision this had been. Superintendent Branagh was making her presence felt.

'Are you sure he's well enough to be interviewed?' said Cooper. 'Sir?'

'We've had him checked over by a doctor, of course. But he's been passed fit, so we're about to start questioning.'

'I'm not happy about it.'

'Tell you what, Ben,' said Hitchens, with a placatory gesture. 'You can sit in, and make sure you're comfortable with it.'

'Thank you, sir.'

But as soon as he'd said it, Cooper wondered whether he should really be thanking Hitchens. Who was going to take the blame if this all went wrong?

Raymond Sutton looked at the two detectives with resignation as they sat down at the table in the interview room.

'You're going to be asking me about the woman,' he said directly.

'The woman?' said Cooper. 'Do you mean Nadezda Halak, sir?'

'I had no connection with her at all,' said Sutton. 'Except that I witnessed her death.'

31

Martin Rourke was one of the least attractive men Fry had ever seen, and that was saying something. His head was badly shaved, leaving a short, patchy fuzz all over his skull, like an old tennis ball that had been chewed by the dog.

'But I know nothing about those women,' he said.

'We have evidence that you knew them, Mr Rourke. You can't deny it.'

'I don't mean that. I'm not trying to deny that I knew them. Of course, they were around a lot. But I don't know what happened to them. I had nothing to do with that. As far as I was concerned, they just disappeared.'

'We'll see what the Crown Prosecution Service has to say. If they think there's enough evidence, you'll be charged with two murders.'

'That won't happen. It can't.'

Rourke stared at her, his face suggesting that he might have said the wrong thing already.

'What was the involvement of the Sutton brothers in your operation?'

'The two old guys? We kept them out of the way as much as possible. Tom Farnham had them under his influence well enough. He could twist them round his little finger, could Farnham. He'd got himself well in there, all neat and tidy.'

'Were you laundering red diesel at any point during this time?'

'No. That was what we told the old guys,' said Rourke. 'They never questioned it, the idiots. Well, why should they? They were already implicated, because they'd used it themselves as a way of saving money. They were guilty before I ever got to work on them. In fact, Tom Farnham got a guy he knew to process a few gallons for them to use, so they'd have no trouble persuading themselves to believe it. But the bottom had gone out of the diesel business by then. Farmers got too scared of the Excise.'

'But why there? Why Pity Wood Farm?'

'Farnham was the man who came up with the idea. And, I have to give him his due, Pity Wood was a perfect set-up for what we wanted. A remote farm, where no one would notice the smell. Lots of smells on a farm, eh? And plenty of empty sheds, plus space to bury the waste. Perfect. All we needed was labour. Well, labour that didn't ask any questions. That was where Martin Rourke came in. It was my speciality. I had the contacts with people in the import business.' He grinned. 'Human imports, I mean. Obviously.'

'Cheap imported labour.'

'But so what? It's only like getting your telly from China, or your clothes made in India. The whole world runs on cheap labour now. It's a fact of twenty-first-century economics. The only difference is that people don't care as long as they can't see it happening. Sweat shops in Asia are fine, but let someone like me employ a few economic migrants and the law comes down on me like a ton of bricks.'

'I think the correct term would be illegal immigrant.'

'Whatever. It's the same, no matter what you call them. But if it happens here, some entrepreneur like me taking advantage of cheap labour to run a going concern, then people get all outraged. What a scandal, they say. It's practically slavery.

343

All that sort of crap. But those workers live a lot better here than they do in Bangladesh, you know.'

'Or Slovakia.'

'Slovakia?'

'Don't you remember a woman called Nadezda Halak? She was from Slovakia.'

He shook his head. 'I don't remember their names, for heaven's sake. They got their wages in cash, and we provided accommodation, but that's as far as our obligations went. They didn't stay around for long, any of them. They'd get a toe-hold in this country, or in the UK, and off they'd go to work in a sandwich factory or something. We were providing a service, really. The government ought to have been giving us a grant.'

'You were using these people to manufacture illegal drugs, at great risk to themselves,' pointed out Fry. 'There's no way you can even attempt to justify that.'

'We all take risks in life,' said Rourke. 'If we think it's worth it. Don't *you* take risks, in your job?'

'The difference,' said Fry, 'is that I *know* what risks I'm taking.'

With the tapes turning slowly, Raymond Sutton talked. He didn't appear to be talking to Hitchens and Cooper, or even to the tape recorder, but to some voice inside his own head – a voice which seemed to be answering him at times.

'When you're young, you don't think you're ever going to die,' he said. 'But sometimes, when you're old, it can't come too soon.'

Cooper leaned towards Sutton. 'Your brother, Derek – you remember we talked about his superstitions?'

'Eh?'

'Derek had some funny beliefs, didn't he? You said he was a bit *fey*, like your mother.'

'You never knew our mother.'

'You told me, Mr Sutton. Remember?'

Cooper wanted to take hold of his arm and shake it until the old man remembered. Though he held himself under tight control, Sutton seemed to read the shadow of a threat in his face and flinched away.

'All kinds of bad luck came along. But it was only to be expected. It was what I warned them all about.'

'What do you mean?'

Sutton stared at him. 'The bad luck. All those disasters. Derek said there would be bad luck when Billy left the farm. He said it had been known for generations. There was a terrible row when I chucked Billy out.'

'You got rid of the skull?'

'Yes. Damned thing. It was damning us all. I told Derek, it was an evil thing, and it had to go. The house was cursed, cursed by the Devil, and my brother was one of his dupes. It had to go.'

'There must have been arguments.'

'Arguments, aye. Blazing rows. Derek wouldn't hear of it, and we stopped speaking of the thing altogether after a while. One night, when he was asleep, I took it out of the wall, and I smashed it up and I burned it in the incinerator, and I scraped out the ash and I drove out to Carsington Reservoir, and I tipped it in the water. And Billy was gone. *For he that is dead is freed from sin.*'

'How did your brother respond when he found out?'

'He was raving. He was never stable, Derek. Never followed God. He'd strayed off the path. God rest his soul, but he was a lost cause.'

'We found traces of potassium nitrate in your kitchen – that's saltpetre. And other ingredients used in a recipe for a Hand of Glory. Have you heard of it?'

'Ah, he was always on with his messing. Meddling with things he knew nothing about. Tempting the Devil, I called it. I wouldn't have none of it. I threw his stuff out if I found it, or chucked it down the sink. He started trying to hide

345

things from me, but I smelled him out. The stink of evil is never forgotten.'

Cooper remembered the kitchen at Pity Wood Farm, the dripping sink and the unidentifiable jars in the fridge sitting next to the builders' milk. There had certainly been a stink that he might never forget. Whether it was the stink of evil he supposed was open to interpretation.

'I don't know what you want,' said Sutton, suddenly agitated. 'What is it you want?'

'Mr Sutton, it was the head, wasn't it? It had nothing to do with a Hand of Glory. After you threw Billy out, your brother wanted a head.'

Sutton focused on him nervously, his eyes watering now, and Cooper thought he would lose him altogether in the next few moments.

'I believe in what I believe. But Derek's faith lay elsewhere. If you believe in something – *really* believe it – you're prepared to take your belief to the extreme.'

'What are you saying, sir?'

'She was dead already. Dead as can be. Derek said it wouldn't hurt her. The body is only the shell, when the soul has moved on to a better place.'

'And so you dug her up and removed her head?' said Hitchens, aghast. 'I can't believe it.'

'No, no. Well, it was already . . . detached, more or less.'

Cooper recalled stories of riots at gallows sites, when the families of hanged criminals fought the anatomists' men for corpses. People had different reasons for wanting possession of a body, or parts of it.

'Derek said we needed another one,' said the old man finally. 'But he was wrong. It never worked, did it?'

And Cooper sat back, suddenly exhausted. He hadn't realized how tense he'd been, the amount of nervous energy he'd been expending on willing the old man to speak, to stay aware for the amount of time he needed him to.

'No, Mr Sutton,' he said wearily. 'It didn't work.'

Raymond Sutton looked around the room, his eyes becoming vague as they met the light from the window. Tears glinted in his lashes and settled slowly on to his cheeks.

'I want you to go away now,' he said. 'I want everyone to go away.'

Cooper caught himself shaking uncontrollably by the time he left the interview room. He couldn't face the idea of crossing the car park from the custody suite and walking back up to the CID room to transcribe his notes, as if everything was perfectly normal. So he sat for a few minutes in his car instead.

He couldn't conceal the fact that he'd found the interview with Raymond Sutton unbearably upsetting. But at least he knew why – and it wasn't just some pathetic tendency to sympathize with the underdog, as Diane Fry would have suggested. Raymond Sutton's rambling about his home being cursed had reminded him too strongly of his own mother at the height of her illness.

Specifically, it reminded him of one traumatic incident that had taken place just before the family had faced up to the fact that Isabel Cooper had deteriorated to the point where they could no longer keep her at home.

Above all, Cooper found that he was remembering the smell. It was as if it had seeped into his car silently and rapidly, like a lethal leak from his exhaust.

There had been a stink in the room worse than anything he had ever smelt on a farm. No cesspit, no slurry tank, no innards from a freshly gutted rabbit or pheasant had ever smelt as bad as the entirely human stench that filled the room. There was excrement daubed across the wallpaper, and on the bedclothes piled on the floor. A pool of urine was drying into a sticky pool on the carpet near to where similar puddles had been scrubbed clean with disinfectant, leaving pale patches like the remnants of some virulent skin disease. A chair lay on the rug with one leg missing. A curtain had been torn off its rail, and the pages of books and magazines were scattered like dead leaves on every surface. A pink slipper sat ludicrously in a wooden fruit bowl on the chest of drawers, and a thin trickle of blood ran across the top drawer, splitting into two forks across the wooden handle. The drawers and the wardrobe had been emptied of their contents, which were heaped at random on the bed.

It was from beneath the heap of clothes that the noise came, monotonous and inhuman, a low, desperate wailing. When he moved towards the bed, the mound stirred and the keening turned to a fearful whimper. Cooper knew that the crisis was over, for now. But this had been the worst so far, no doubt about it. The evidence was all around him.

He leaned closer to a coat with an imitation fur collar, but was careful not to touch the bed, for fear of sparking off a violent reaction. The coat was drenched in a familiar scent that brought a painful lump to his throat. A white hand was visible briefly as it clutched for a sleeve and the edge of a skirt to pull them closer for concealment. The fingers withdrew again into the darkness like a crab retreating into its shell. The whimpering stopped.

'It was the Devil,' said a small voice from deep in the pile of clothes. 'The Devil made me do it.'

The mingled odours of stale scent, sweat and excrement and urine made Cooper feel he was about to be sick. He swallowed and forced himself to keep his voice steady.

'The Devil's gone away. You can come out now, Mum. The Devil's gone away.'

When Fry went back in to interview Martin Rourke for a second time, he'd been allowed to consult a lawyer. She was expecting a string of 'no comments', and a frustrating end to her trip to Dublin. But maybe things were different here.

'Of course I remember her,' said Rourke straight away. 'I want to be honest with you.'

'Remember who?'

'Nadezda, the Slovak. She couldn't resist trying out the crank herself. Stupid bitch. It made her careless. She was bound to kill herself sooner or later.'

'Kill herself? You're suggesting that Nadezda Halak died in an accident?'

'That's exactly what happened. It was accidental death, brought on by her own carelessness. That would be a factor, all right.'

Fry glanced at Lenaghan, who gave her a nod to go ahead.

'Mr Rourke, tell us exactly what happened, in your own words.'

'Well, there's nothing much to tell. There was an explosion in the shed one day. None of us knew the chemicals were so dangerous. Nada had been standing closest to the equipment when it blew up.'

'Nada is . . .?'

'The woman you said. Halak. Nada is what we called her, for short.'

'And she was killed by the explosion?'

'Dead as you like. It was lucky she was the only one so near. There were other folk about, but they only got a few cuts, one or two acid burns. Nothing serious.'

'So what did you do?'

'Some of the workers started to panic, but Tom Farnham quietened them down. He said there was plenty of room on the farm to dispose of a body where no one would ever find it. And who would come looking for her? Like I said, those people move on all the time. They *want* to be untraceable.'

'So you buried her on the farm?'

'Yes.'

'And the Sutton brothers didn't object to this?'

Rourke snorted. 'How could they? They'd done exactly the same thing themselves, three years before.'

Cooper had never felt so bad about questioning a witness. Though they'd achieved what they set out to do, there was no sense of satisfaction in getting Raymond Sutton to confirm what he suspected. It had been a knowledge that he didn't really want to have to share, but now he couldn't keep it to himself any longer.

In a way, he supposed he'd been hoping, deep down, that Sutton would deny it, that he'd be able to prove somehow that it had never happened. Well, it might have been better if he'd never asked. But then he would have had to live with the doubt. Cooper knew there had been no way of winning in this situation.

And there was certainly no way of achieving justice – not justice in the terms of the law, nor justice in any subjective sense. Even if Derek Sutton had still been alive, what would have been the point of punishing him? His brother was an accessory to the crime, of course. After the fact, if not before. No matter how contemptuous he'd been, no matter how many disapproving silences he'd indulged in over the kitchen table, Raymond had gone along with his brother's superstitions, and had told no one about the skull.

Well, of course he hadn't. Sharing a house with a crazy brother was one thing. Watching that brother get carted off to spend the rest of his life in a psychiatric institution while you were left to cope entirely on your own – that was a different thing altogether. The decision wouldn't have been an easy one for most families, let alone the Suttons of Pity Wood Farm. In fact, there was no decision involved. Blood was blood, and you stood by your own. End of story.

Cooper finished his report and stood up. Yes, it *would* have been the end of the story. If only Raymond Sutton had died himself before the farm was dug up. That had been his plan, Cooper was sure.

But The Oaks had looked after him too well. Their care had prolonged his life longer than he'd expected. Physically, he was probably in better condition now than when he was looking after himself at home. So Raymond had sat in his room at The Oaks, watching the seasons change over the hills, while the sale of the farm went through, the paperwork was completed, and the builders moved in. From that moment, he must have been expecting every day to hear the news that something had been found. Each morning he must have looked for the newspapers to read the headlines, every evening he must have been the first in front of the TV for the start of *East Midlands Today*. And every day he must have lived in expectation of the footsteps in the hallway of his care home, the voices of strangers speaking his name.

When Raymond Sutton abandoned the farm and sold up immediately after the death of his brother, he hadn't expected to live very long. A matter of days or weeks, perhaps. But then he'd done a terrible thing. He'd survived.

Raymond had thought he was tappy, just like his brother. Approaching his end, preparing to meet his maker. All those other euphemisms for dying. But in the end he'd lived too long to escape being called to account for his actions. How ironic that Raymond was also the only member of his family who expected to be punished for eternity.

To follow Christ means dying to sin. Raymond Sutton would die twice over.

Fry produced a series of evidence bags. They contained the items they'd found at the house in Bunratty Road, hidden behind the wardrobe in the bedroom of Martin Rourke's daughter.

'Was this the woman they buried four years ago?' asked

Fry. 'Her name is Orla Doyle, an Irish national. Black hair. She would be thirty-two years old by now.'

'I don't know who she was,' said Rourke.

He was starting to sweat now, Fry could see. He hadn't felt guilty for the death of Nadezda Halak, but Orla Doyle was a name a bit closer to home.

'You were too greedy, Mr Rourke,' said Fry. 'This is Orla Doyle's passport, found in your house this morning, so you can't try to tell us you had no connection with her. I suppose you realized from dealing with illegal immigrants that there was a lucrative market for passports? And not forged ones, either, but genuine passports, taken from dead people. Is there a premium on them in the human import business, Mr Rourke?'

'I'm not answering that.'

'In fact, it must be even better if the person involved is not only dead, but has never been reported missing.'

Rourke just shook his head. His face was closing up now, and she wouldn't get much more from him. But she still had evidence to confront him with.

Fry help up a second bag. 'This is a Slovakian passport, sir. Discovered in the same hiding place, behind your daughter's wardrobe. Not as much call for a Slovak identity in Ireland, I suppose, even now? This one is for Nadezda Halak, from the city of Košice. Nadezda would be twenty-four by now, if she was still alive. Would you like to see what's actually left of her, sir? I can arrange for that to happen.'

Rourke shook his head, resorting to a silence that was no good for the tapes. Fry nodded at Lenaghan.

'Interview suspended.'

Fry couldn't wait to make the call to her DI and tell him that she'd not only established how Nadezda Halak died, but had also confirmed the identity of the second body at Pity Wood Farm. She was buzzing with satisfaction, and at the end of the conversation with Hitchens, she still felt she hadn't talked enough, so she rang Ben Cooper and told her story all over again.

'That's brilliant, Diane,' he said. 'So the trip to Ireland was really worthwhile, after all.'

'Yes, it was.'

Then Fry remembered it was Tuesday, the day she'd been afraid of being away from Edendale, and her excitement began to ebb away.

'So what's going on back home?' she said cautiously.

'Oh, the new superintendent has arrived.'

'Making an impression, is she?'

'You might say that. There's no doubt who's in charge. She's already taking the credit.'

'But she hasn't done anything,' said Fry. 'She can't have. Not yet.'

'Maybe. It's hard to tell what's been going on behind the scenes.'

Fry sighed. 'Has she done anything I need to know about?'

'Put Gavin in his place with a firm hand.'

'Oh, well . . .'

'And Jack Elder is being released.'

'Elder? He was my prisoner.'

'Not after tomorrow,' said Cooper. 'He'll be in court in the morning, then he'll get bail and walk away.'

'Damnation.'

'The superintendent is right, though, Diane – we don't have any evidence to connect Mr Elder with a serious offence. He's not a credible murder suspect.'

'No, but he's a link,' said Fry. 'I'm sure of it.'

'It's a pity you're not here to put your case to Branagh.'

'Yes, isn't it?'

'It appears Orla Doyle is one of our missing persons,' said Lenaghan when he'd escorted Rourke back to his cell. 'What a result. You can come here again, Detective Sergeant Fry.'

'Thank you. I think I can say it was a mutually satisfactory visit, Garda Lenaghan.'

'Tony,' he said.

'What?'

'You ought to call me Tony.'

Cooper got out the Toyota to drive into Sheffield, where he had an appointment with the forensic anthropologist, Dr Jamieson. A traffic officer he passed in the car park greeted him with a weather forecast.

'Fog.'

'That's bad news.'

'The roads are very busy, too. There'll be fatalities before nightfall.'

And Cooper thought it could be worse than that. If they cancelled flights at Robin Hood Airport, Fry might not be getting back from Dublin. Not today, anyway.

As he drove to Sheffield, Cooper tried to get everything straight in his head. But whenever he thought about the story, it began to unravel, like a tapestry with a loose stitch. If he tugged at it in the wrong place, everything changed shape, the picture twisted and distorted, figures vanishing from the scene and others coming closer together.

After a few minutes, the picture was becoming awfully grey and murky, just like the weather, like the landscape behind that belt of December rain.

'Oh, you were hoping to tie this skull in with Victim B?' said Dr Jamieson, when Cooper found him in his laboratory at the university.

'Well . . . yes, that was the assumption.'

'An assumption, eh? I don't believe in them myself. Do you find they achieve anything?'

'Well, Doctor, it does seem a logical conclusion that this skull belonged to the woman we've found with a missing head. Particularly when they both came from the same property.'

'I see,' said Jamieson. 'So where does the male victim come in?'

'Male victim?'

'The person the skull belongs to. Because this is definitely male. Look at the distinctive shape of the jaw, the size of the occipital dome. Somewhere, there's a male victim who's missing a head.'

'So this is the real Screaming Billy, after all,' said Cooper. 'Despite what Raymond Sutton said. This is the ancient skull that has been in the wall of the farmhouse.'

'Oh? What's that?'

'A local superstition, Doctor. A skull that protects the owners of the farm from bad luck. They call them screaming skulls.'

'Interesting. And how long is the skull supposed to have been in the wall of the farmhouse?'

'Centuries, according to local folklore.'

Dr Jamieson shook his head. 'Never trust folklore, then. If this came out of the wall of that farmhouse, it's a much more recent addition to the decor.'

'Are you sure?'

'Science doesn't lie, DC Cooper. Not within living memory, anyway. This skull is ten years old, at most. What I mean is – I'd estimate ten years since it was parted from its unfortunate owner.'

Cooper looked at the skull. 'But Screaming Billy is supposed to go back to the eighteenth century, at least.'

The anthropologist shrugged. 'This isn't Billy, then, I'm afraid. I suggest we refer to him as Victim C.'

32

A few minutes later, Cooper was getting back into his Toyota in the university car park. 'Not *within living memory.*' Where had he heard that phrase recently? Oh, yes. It had been used by PC Palfreyman, the first time that Cooper had visited him at Hollowbrook Cottage, as early as Friday morning.

That seemed a long time ago now. Palfreyman had been answering a question about whether there had been an argument between the Sutton brothers. '*Not within living memory.*' That was exactly what he'd said.

Well, Cooper supposed that living memory resided in the older generation, people like Raymond Sutton and Mrs Dain. But it wasn't everything, not in an area like the Peak District. When living memory died, the landscape still retained an imprint of times that had passed. The lead miners might be long gone, but their workings still shaped the contours of the hills and valleys. Their shafts and soughs survived, directly under the feet of modern visitors. Their ghosts, perhaps, still lingered where those Red Soil men had died, choking in the blackness, their lungs full of sulphurous smoke.

*   *   *

The flat at number eight Welbeck Street felt lonely that evening. Cooper was due to meet Liz later on, but the time he spent on his own was difficult to bear.

Thinking of PC Palfreyman made him turn to the framed picture that hung on the wall over his mantelpiece. Not within living memory? This picture was a part of his life that would stay in his memory for ever, even if it disappeared now. He was familiar with the face of every man on each of the rows, even with the pattern and texture of the wall behind them and the concrete yard their boots rested on.

Sergeant Joe Cooper, and the rest of Derbyshire Constabulary's Edendale section, had been lined up for an official visit, back in the 1980s. Those were the days when the police dealt with criminals and victims. In twenty-first-century policing, there were only offenders and injured parties. Worse, victims had become infected with acronym disease, and were routinely referred to as IPs.

Without looking, Cooper could have described the picture in detail, the way each officer held his arms, which of them was smiling, who looked suspicious of the photographer, and who hadn't fastened his tie properly that morning. He knew the feel of the mahogany frame, the smoothness of the edges, the slight ridge in the wood, like a necessary flaw. He could remember the scratch in the glass that was only visible when you turned the picture towards the light.

As he looked at the photograph of his father, Cooper was wondering whether, in a few years' time, he would himself have turned into one of those police officers who wanted to go back to the old days. The officers who wanted to abandon PACE, delete the Human Rights Act from UK law, and bring in mandatory jail sentences for burglars. Wanted to, but daren't say so.

Cooper was due to meet Liz in the market square, but he was early when he left the flat. So he took his time and walked down to the river to reach the town centre. Just before the Eyre Street bridge, he stopped at the weir to watch the ducks, a crowd of mallards fussing about in the darkness, splashing under the trees.

Above their noise, he thought he heard a familiar voice behind him.

'Ben?'

He turned in surprise. 'I thought you were in –?'

And then he saw that he'd been mistaken. It was Angie Fry who stood in front of him, much as she'd once stood on his doorstep in Welbeck Street. She wore the same anorak and even carried the same battered rucksack over her shoulder.

'Angie. Are you going somewhere?'

She didn't answer, perhaps thinking it a stupid question. She had never seemed to have much respect for his intelligence.

'Always the ace boy detective, Constable Cooper.'

Cooper swore at that moment that he wasn't going to let Angie Fry use him again for her own purposes.

'What do you want, Angie? I'm busy.'

'Sure. Communing with the wildlife.'

Anxiously, Cooper looked over his shoulder. The lights of the market square were just ahead, only a few yards away. He could see people passing under the illuminated Christmas trees and the flickering reindeer strung across Eyre Street.

'I won't keep you long from your date,' said Angie with a smirk.

'How did you know –?'

Angie pulled an envelope from a pocket of her anorak. 'I need to give you this.'

'What is it?'

'Information. I promise you'll find it interesting.'

'You should give it to Diane.'

'She's away.'

'Yes, in Dublin,' said Cooper. 'But she'll be back tomorrow.'

Angie just looked at him, holding out the envelope. She

358

seemed so much like her sister as she stood with her back to the light, shadows hiding the difference in her features, the anorak concealing her narrow shoulders, and the almost skeletal thinness of her arms – all the things Cooper remembered being struck by when he'd first met her.

He took her silence for communication. 'I understand. You won't be seeing Diane tomorrow, will you?'

'No.'

Reluctantly, Cooper took the envelope. 'Angie, are you going away again?'

Angie shifted the straps of her rucksack until they were more comfortable. 'You'll find information in that envelope about the current location of the crystal meth lab that supplies Sheffield. It's in your area. I believe it's operated by a group who took over supply when the lab at Rakedale closed down.'

Cooper was stunned. 'How did you get this?'

But Angie shrugged. 'I've been working with people who have this sort of information. They've been letting the lab continue to operate, for their own reasons, and I don't agree with it.'

'What people are you talking about?'

'I'm sure you don't expect me to answer that?'

'Are you talking about SOCA?' asked Cooper. 'Serious and Organized Crime? Did they recruit you as one of their undercover agents?'

'Agents? I think they're called covert human intelligence sources these days, Ben.'

'Angie, you can't just –'

But she'd already turned away and was walking into the darkness along the river bank.

'Give it to Diane, if you want,' she called. 'Tell her it's my farewell gift.'

When he eventually reached the corner of the market square where Liz was waiting, Cooper realized she'd been standing close enough to have a view of the river from the Eyre Street bridge.

'Who was that woman I saw you with?' she asked straight away.

Cooper flinched at the unfamiliar coolness in her voice. It was the sort of tone that might be used on a suspect in the interview room, when you wanted to make it clear that you thought they were guilty and you were expecting them to lie. He wondered where Liz had learned that tone. Perhaps it just came naturally. Perhaps it came naturally to all women.

'Were you spying on me?' he said, trying for a smile.

'You're avoiding the question.'

Cooper laughed, but she wasn't responding.

'Look, if you really want to know – it was Diane's sister.'

'Oh, you mean –?'

'Angie, yes.'

'I've never seen her before.'

'Well, Diane doesn't exactly bring her into work on Casual Friday,' said Cooper.

'OK, OK. I can see you're defensive about it.'

'What?'

Liz began to walk away. Stung by her unfairness, Cooper waited a moment, to make his point, before he followed her.

Garda Lenaghan insisted on celebrating that evening. Somehow, they ended up drinking Irish whiskey together in a bar in Coolock that stayed open until the early hours of the morning. Fry didn't normally drink spirits, and by the end of the night the whiskey was starting to have a peculiar effect on her.

'Tony, I need to get back to my B&B,' she said finally. 'I'm due to fly home tomorrow, you know.'

Lenaghan's face was swimming in front of her, but Fry was sure he was smiling. He wasn't as bad as she'd thought at first. He was a city man, not like the yokels back in Derbyshire.

'I'll call for a taxi,' he said.

In the early hours of the morning, Cooper found himself watching a film on TV, too tired to go to bed, and with too many thoughts buzzing around in his head.

He'd lost track of the film's plot in the first few minutes, but he noticed that it seemed to have been shot entirely in the dark. In every scene there were long camera shots, with nothing but a lit doorway or a window in the distance, and a tunnel of darkness for a character to walk through. Sometimes an actor walked towards the camera, sometimes away. But always through that darkness. Why did no one ever put the lights on? he wondered. Did the people in these stories never suspect what might be waiting for them in those shadows, when they moved beyond the rectangles of light?

But that was the whole point, wasn't it? It was all about the vicarious fear. The thrill was in anticipating the moment when a character stepped out of the safety zone. That was what riveted him to the screen, filled his mind and kept him from sleeping. It was watching a person walk into the dark.

When his phone rang, he thought at first it was part of the film. No one called him this late, unless it was bad news. When he answered, he wasn't surprised to find it was DI Hitchens.

'Sorry to bother you, Ben, but I thought you should know. Raymond Sutton has tried to hang himself in his room at The Oaks.'

33

Wednesday

Fry was already tired when she sat down at her desk next morning. She was supposed to produce a full report for the chiefs on her visit to the Garda Síochána, an analysis of the level of co-operation, and whether she'd made any useful contacts. Fry knew that any report to be read by senior management should use two positives to every negative, if it was going to give the right impression. Three was good, too. But never four – if you used four, it started to sound like sarcasm.

Well, on this occasion, a few bullet points would satisfy them. They wouldn't want to know too much about Garda Lenaghan, would they? The identification of Orla Doyle should be enough to focus the interest.

Fry had now made two positive IDs on the bodies found at Pity Wood Farm, though not without a bit of good luck. She hoped her efforts would be properly appreciated. It wasn't her fault that the skull didn't belong to Orla Doyle. Everyone in the office this morning was talking about Victim C, which was the last thing she needed.

She found a copy of a file on her desk. There were photographs, so far out of proportion that they looked huge and disorientating. The Forensic Science Service laboratory had performed wonders getting fingerprints from Nadezda Halak's hand, processing the sloughing skin sufficiently to provide a strong possibility of a match if her prints were on record. It couldn't have been easy, teasing out an identifiable print from a fragment of rotting hand. The entire thumb was gone, and so were half of the index and middle fingers. The skin that remained had been decomposing and so fragile that it had to be soaked in alcohol to toughen it up and draw out the water.

But under twenty times magnification in the scanning electron microscope, traces of damage to the bones of the hand were just about visible, along with fractures at the surface where the cartilage had been attached to the central arch. Magnified a hundred times, the damage was unmistakable – linear fractures ending in a small region of crushed bone. There were no signs of healing, which indicated that the fracture had occurred perimortem – at, or just before, death.

Instead of finishing her report, Fry phoned the Forensic Science Service and asked to speak to one of the chemists who was dealing with evidence from the abandoned meth lab at Pity Wood.

'Yes, methamphetamine production in a makeshift laboratory is a very dangerous activity, unless you have training as a chemist,' she said.

'I think we can take it that the people involved at Pity Wood didn't have that training, Doctor.'

'Well, if an operator without proper training allows the red phosphorus to overheat – due to lack of adequate ventilation, perhaps – then phosphine gas can be produced. If it's produced in large enough quantities, the gas usually explodes. Technically, the conclusion would be auto-ignition from diphosphine formation, caused by the overheating of phosphorus.'

'Thank you.'

Fry put the phone down. Training as a chemist? The idea was enough to make anyone laugh. Illegal workers like Nadezda

Halak, paid a pittance and hardly daring to go out in daylight for fear of being seen? Their instructions would have been basic, their understanding of what they were involved in even less, perhaps.

In other circumstances, Fry would have said that it was a mistake to assume innocence, just because an individual was dead. It was possible to be guilty and a victim at the same time. But she could never believe it of Nadezda and her fellow workers at Pity Wood.

Cooper came in, accompanying DI Hitchens after a visit to Edendale District General Hospital, where Raymond Sutton was being treated.

'Mr Sutton isn't in good shape,' said Cooper, chewing his lip nervously. 'They're very worried about him on the ward. He wasn't strong to start with. If one of the care assistants hadn't been passing his room, he would have been dead a few minutes later.'

'Nobody's blaming you, mate,' said Murfin.

'We gave him a bit of a hard time, put too much pressure on him. He's an old man, after all.'

'Gavin's right, Ben,' said Hitchens. 'No one is blaming you.'

'Are you sure, sir?'

'Yes, absolutely.'

As the DI left, Fry put her phone down and caught up with the news.

'Raymond Sutton? Poor bloke. I suppose this is your fault, Ben.'

Cooper slumped in his chair, crushed into silence.

'Me, I blame the scapegoats,' said Murfin. 'They're always responsible for anything that goes wrong, I find.'

'Shut up, Gavin.'

'Yes, boss.'

'So who is this Victim C that everyone's talking about?' asked Fry. 'Any theories?'

'There were undoubtedly male workers at the farm,' said Cooper.

'Another migrant who met a sticky end?'

'Well, who else?'

'The mysterious Alan,' said Fry. 'Haven't we been told that he disappeared seven or eight years ago? I know everyone tries to claim that he left home because he didn't get on with his brothers, but we have no proof of that.'

'You're right,' said Cooper.

'You know I'm right, Ben. You've known from the moment that Alan was first mentioned that he didn't just leave home. You understand these people better than me. But I remember you saying that they could be protecting someone.'

'Yes, I did say that.'

'Well, I'll ask you again: protecting who?'

Cooper hung his head. 'I don't know, Diane. Perhaps the whole family. Perhaps the village. I really don't know.'

'We ought to have been making some effort to trace Alan Sutton, don't you think?'

'It didn't seem a priority before.'

'But things change, Ben,' said Fry. 'Around here, things change all the time.'

Cooper saw Murfin wink at him as he got up to attend his personal interview with the new superintendent. He was first man over the top, and he looked like a condemned criminal on his way to the scaffold, trying to stay cheerful but knowing he was doomed.

It was a bit like the family at Pity Wood Farm. Yes, Cooper felt sure the Suttons must have thought they were doomed. Cursed, anyway. Aside from the personal problems between the brothers, plague and pestilence had followed the changes in farming over the last couple of decades. BSE, foot and mouth, and now bird flu – each one like a dark cloud on the horizon that could break into a storm at any moment and wipe an entire industry away.

Already, the threat had come very close. The foot-and-mouth outbreak of 2001 hadn't quite reached the Peak District. But there were farms a few miles south, on the border near Sudbury, where cattle and sheep had been slaughtered in the mass cull. And then along came H5N1, the strain of avian flu virus that could be carried by wild birds. Any day a poultry farmer might look up into the sky and see a flock of geese, or a skein of mallards, and wonder whether they were bringing the disease north.

Yes, there had been new enterprises at Pity Wood, but some of them were of a nature that the Suttons hadn't understood. They had no idea that the world had changed so much around them that illegal drug manufacturing was the only way for their farm to make a profit. Ironically, it could be seen as the sort of thinking the government was trying to encourage – moving away from traditional farming to new and exciting ways of exploiting the assets of their property.

Of course, the Suttons' big mistake had been inviting Tom Farnham in. He must have looked like a saviour at the time, promising all kinds of things, including a bright new future for Pity Wood Farm, new ways of earning income, enough money to put the farm back on its feet.

But Farnham had been the worm on the carcase of a dying animal. He'd exploited the still-warm flesh for his own short-term ends. The money had gone into his own pocket, not to the Suttons, or to safeguard the future of Pity Wood.

'Those poor women,' said Cooper when he heard the full story of Nadezda Halak and her co-workers from Fry. 'They were following the instructions they'd been given, without any idea of the horrendous risks they were running.'

'They certainly didn't understand what the chemicals were, or how harmful their effects could be,' said Fry. 'And why *would* they suspect? They saw a collection of ordinary household products, bought over the counter, or from the supermarket shelf. Why would they think those products could be lethal?'

'I bet they didn't care, anyway. They just knew they were paid much better for that job than for picking carrots.'

'You sound unusually cynical.'

'Well, it's another case of "Monkey See, Monkey Do".'

'What are you talking about, Ben?'

'It's a saying that refers to somebody learning a process without any understanding of how or why it works. You made me think of it before, with your thing about the Three Wise Monkeys. If something seems to work, we do it, and we don't ask why it works. It's the origin of most superstitious rituals, too.'

'Oh, I think I see. The Joneses next door killed a cow last year, and they had a good harvest. So we'll do the same.'

'And, before you know it, sacrifice has become an annual ritual. But the thing is, to most people those beliefs are just superstition. We might go through certain rituals ourselves, but we don't really believe in them. Touching wood, crossing our fingers, throwing salt over our shoulders . . .'

'Counting magpies? Horseshoes nailed to the door?'

'Exactly. It's important to find ways of warding off evil in our lives. If you get it wrong, or upset the spirits, all kinds of bad things can happen. That's what people believe.'

And screaming skulls, he thought. They could ward off evil, too – provided you treated them right. Cooper recalled touching the yellow sheath of bone at the back of the skull recovered from Tom Farnham's garage. It had been cool and smooth, worn thin by age – and by reverent handling.

Most importantly, they were supposed to be left where they belonged. You should *never* move a skull.

'None of these women seem to have stayed very long at Pity Wood,' said Fry. 'One minute they were there, the next

367

they were gone. Perhaps they didn't like sharing the house with preserved body parts. I can't blame them.'

'The Slovak, Nadezda Halak – have you got her photograph there?'

'Yes.'

'She's smiling, isn't she?' said Cooper.

'Some people do. It means nothing. You have to look more closely.'

Cooper squinted and studied the picture again. 'No. She still looks happy.'

He put the photo down on his desk, and he sat looking at it for a few minutes after Fry had left.

Yes, Nadezda Halak did look happy. So what? She'd been one of those people who managed to keep smiling through the worst times of their lives. It seemed extraordinary that someone could smile and smile, and yet be so desperate. But it happened. It was as if they feared a word of sympathy or concern would crack their world apart, and only a smile could hold it together. That smiling façade became a defence, a wall to keep out the world and prevent anyone intruding into their secret misery. But why had no one been close enough to Nadezda to see behind that smile?

Then Cooper thought of something he'd meant to ask. 'By the way, Diane, you're not leaving, are you?'

To his astonishment, she grabbed his sleeve roughly. He flinched at the sudden awareness of her potential for violence. He knew it was in her, but he saw it so rarely that he'd managed to forget.

'What do you know?' she hissed.

'Nothing. It was just something Gavin said. Gossip probably.'

'Was anything said about me while I was in Ireland?'

'No, Diane. Well, not that I'm aware of. You know I'm the last person to find out anything.'

She let go of his sleeve. 'That used to be true. I'm not sure any more.'

Cooper brushed his sleeve straight, staring at her in amazement. He had no idea what had provoked that outburst.

'What do you mean, Diane?'

She looked around the room, and leaned closer to whisper in his ear. 'This information about the operating meth lab? Did you, by any chance, get that from my sister?'

It was one of those moments when Cooper knew it was pointless trying to lie. Fry had him fixed with such a concentrated stare that she would notice even the slightest flicker of an attempt to conceal the truth.

'Yes, Diane, I did. She –'

Fry interrupted him. 'I don't want to hear the sordid details. I just want you to know that when I got home today, she was gone.'

The door opened, and Murfin came out of his interview with the new superintendent looking dazed and in need of a stiff drink or two.

Fry straightened up, trying to make everything appear normal.

'How did it go, Gavin?' she asked.

Murfin looked at her. 'How did it go? All I can say is – the goat survived, but the bishop will never be the same again.'

An hour later, Fry stood up at the conclusion of a meeting with Superintendent Branagh and the other senior officers.
At least they'd established with a fair percentage of certainty how Nadezda Halak had died. Results now available from the Forensic Science Service laboratory were consistent with damage to her soft tissues from an explosion of phosphine gas. The tiny fractures to the bones of Nadezda's hand were probably the result of a futile attempt to protect herself from the debris hurled out by the explosion.

The function of Orla Doyle at Pity Wood Farm wasn't confirmed yet. There was a general assumption that could be made from her history in Dublin. Garda records showed Orla to have been a street girl from the age of sixteen. Fry didn't like assumptions, but she had no contrary evidence to present.

There was also no evidence to show how Orla Doyle had died, at least without possession of her skull. If only the skull recovered from Tom Farnham's garage had been hers, there might have been some progress.

Fry strongly suspected that Martin Rourke had killed her, possibly when she'd tried to leave her employment. That wasn't allowed, and injury or death were occupational hazards. She would dearly like to gather enough facts to make a case for a murder charge against Rourke, but she didn't know where to turn for leads.

'Well, the tip-off that DC Cooper obtained from his informant looks credible,' said Detective Superintendent Branagh as the meeting broke up. 'That was good work on his part. I'm delighted some of the division's officers are developing useful intelligence sources.'

Fry nodded, seething inwardly, but at the same time making a mental note for herself that she'd better mention something to that effect in Cooper's PDR. Otherwise, Branagh would be on her back asking why she'd overlooked it.

'By the way, what about the future of Pity Wood Farm?' said Fry. 'I understand the amounts of toxic waste produced by the methamphetamine manufacturing process are huge. It can take months to decontaminate a site.'

'They won't be decontaminating that place,' said Superintendent Branagh.

'No? But surely, ma'am –?'

'There's no point even trying,' she said. 'The experts have examined the levels of contamination. And, yes, they're extraordinarily high – not just in the outbuildings, but in the house itself. Not to mention the land around it, where they disposed of the by-products. Decontamination is an impossible job. Pity Wood Farm would always be toxic and uninhabitable. So they'll be taking the only available option – demolition.'

370

34

'Jack Elder is in magistrates' court this afternoon,' said Fry. 'He'll be bailed, of course. Let home for Christmas.'

'I wonder if he'll be safe,' said Cooper. 'He must be aware of the possibility that the same individuals who killed Tom Farnham will come after him.'

'I wouldn't worry too much about his welfare. But I'm hoping he'll lead us to his associates. Elder is a worried man, and he'll want to get away from the area. He'll need money for that, and some help in disappearing. I think he'll make contact, and quickly.'

'But wasn't Tom Farnham his associate?'

'There's someone else,' said Fry. 'I'm certain of it. There's a brains behind the operation. Someone with the right influence, the ability to cover up and call in favours.'

'OK. So how do we act on this certainty, Diane?'

'I already have. I've got authority to put surveillance on Jack Elder.'

'We're going to follow him?'

'As soon as he leaves court and is discharged from custody.'

'Brilliant.'

Towards the end of the afternoon, Elder went home from Edendale Magistrates' Court in a taxi, which returned him

371

direct to his home in Rakedale. Fry and Cooper stayed well behind the rear lights of the cab as it approached the village and turned into Field Lane.

'Does he have a car as well as the lorry?' asked Cooper.

'Yes, a green Nissan.'

'Pity. The DAF would have been easier to follow.'

Up ahead, there was a strange blue glow in the dusk, as if a UFO had landed behind the trees. When they got closer, the glow turned out to be Jack Elder's Christmas lights. They were strung along the eaves of his bungalow and looped over his windows in festive abundance. It looked the sort of house where the Christmas tree would play you a carol if you got too near it.

They were fifty yards up the road past the house when they saw Elder's green Nissan backing out of his drive, almost before the taxi had driven away.

'What do we do?' said Cooper.

'Has he seen us?'

'No, I don't think so. He won't recognize my car, so long as he doesn't get a view of our faces . . .'

Cooper swung into a gateway and turned round to wait. When the lights of Elder's car went past, he could be seen fiddling with the touch screen of a satnav device attached to the dashboard of his Nissan.

'OK, Ben. Let's find out where he's going.'

Elder drove past Matlock to reach the A6, where the evening traffic from Derby was building up, shoppers and workers making their way home in the December darkness. He turned on to the A610, skirting Ripley and passing right by Derbyshire Constabulary headquarters before crossing into Nottinghamshire. Four miles further on, his car joined the M1 motorway at Junction 26, heading south.

'He could be going anywhere,' said Cooper. 'We don't want to end up in London for the night.'

'We'll see,' said Fry. 'I don't think he'll be going that far.'

She didn't have to wait long to be proved right. Elder's Nissan didn't even make it as far as the next junction. After a couple of miles, he started indicating left and turned into the brilliantly-lit surroundings of the service area at Trowell.

'Pass on our location, Ben,' said Fry. 'You know the drill.'

Cooper contacted the Nottinghamshire control room to alert them to the presence of Derbyshire officers conducting an operation on their territory. Meanwhile, Fry called Gavin Murfin and asked him to rendezvous at the service station. He was only a couple of miles away, keeping in touch with their location.

'Why do we need Gavin?' asked Cooper.

'We might have two vehicles to follow when we leave here.'

'I see.'

They watched Elder park up in front of the amenities building where there were some free spaces. At least the area was well lit for security, otherwise the gathering darkness would have defeated them. Cooper found a spot as near to the exit as he could get while still having the Nissan in sight. Then they sat and waited for something to happen.

'He doesn't know Gavin,' said Fry. 'So he should be able to get nearer to the Nissan when he arrives.'

Cooper looked around the parking area and the buildings beyond it. If he had to imagine a place where no one belonged and everyone was just passing through, this would be it – a motorway service area. The ultimate nowhere land.

He'd often wondered why they bothered displaying information about local attractions inside the amenities building. Surely anyone who called at a service area was on the way somewhere else, by definition. Nearby attractions were the ones that motorists were least likely to visit, since you couldn't actually get off the motorway at this point.

Well, that wasn't quite true, of course. If you were an 'authorized vehicle', there was always a local service road over at the back somewhere. But law-abiding motorists weren't supposed to know that. If they saw a sign that said 'no unauthorized vehicles past this point', they obeyed it, didn't they?

Cooper scanned the exit lanes that ran past the petrol station, and located the service road on the southbound side. According to his map, this one twisted back towards the A609, the Nottingham road.

'You're sure Elder is going to meet someone?'

'Well, he isn't doing anything else, is he?' said Fry reasonably. 'He hasn't got out of the car yet. It's my guess he's waiting, like us.'

They saw Murfin's car turn in from the motorway, then disappear from view. A moment later, Murfin himself opened the back door of the Toyota and slid in.

'Anything happening?'

'Not yet. I need you to get closer to the Nissan over there.'

As they spoke, a liveried police car cruised into the parking area, did a slow circuit, and drove out again through the petrol station forecourt, back on to the motorway.

'They didn't even stop for a piss,' said Murfin. 'What do you make of that?'

'Maybe it's a Nottinghamshire thing.'

'Aye. They don't have bodily functions over here. Like the Queen.'

Cooper watched a minibus pull in a few places away from Elder's Nissan, but a dozen laughing women scrambled out. A hen party on the way to the airport for a couple of days hitting the bars of Prague or Vilnius, probably. This was the way Eastern Europe got a taste of British culture these days.

'Speaking of having a piss –' said Murfin, opening the door again.

'Gavin, you can't.'

'I won't be a jiffy. You said there was nothing happening.'

'Well, stay away from the café, won't you?'

'That's the trouble with these places,' said Murfin. 'They design them so you can't even go for a slash without passing right between the café and the shop. There's food on all sides of you. It's a nightmare.'

'*You're* the nightmare, Gavin.'

'I'm only kidding. What do you think I am?'

'Well, make sure you've got your phone with you. If anything starts to move, I'll call you, and you'll have to get back here damn quick.'

Murfin trotted across to the amenities building, tugging at the waistband of his trousers and shaking his legs to get rid of the cramp from sitting in the car.

Cooper tapped the steering wheel and yawned. People walking back looked at them, but took no notice. Sitting at a service station was different from doing surveillance anywhere else. One person sitting in a car didn't look unusual, but two people tended to arouse suspicion, especially two men. Residents had been known to dial 999 several times a night to report a suspicious vehicle when a surveillance operation was under way.

He remembered a story Murfin had told him once, about an old lady knocking on the car window and offering him and his partner a cup of tea, because they'd been sitting there a long time and she thought they looked bored. If old ladies could recognize unmarked police cars, then surely no criminal worth his salt would have any trouble.

'Do you think he might be on to us?' asked Cooper after a while.

'Ordinary law-abiding people don't expect surveillance,' said Fry.

'But he's not an ordinary law-abiding person.'

'I bet he thinks he is.'

Murfin reappeared, and for once there were no suspicious bulges in his pockets. He got back into his car and moved the other side of Elder's Nissan so he could see into the passenger side.

Then Cooper tensed. A white van crept slowly past their position with its headlights on. Two men were sitting in the cab, looking left and right as they crawled up to the end of the line of cars and started down the next one. It was an ordinary Ford Transit with no markings, indistinguishable from thousands of others that would be seen on the M1 every day.

'Did you get the registration?' asked Fry, noticing the same thing that Cooper had.

'Yes.'

The van stopped, reversed, and drew in next to Elder's car. Now Fry and Cooper couldn't see the Nissan at all.

'Damn.' Fry dialled. 'Gavin, can you make them out?'

'Yes, I've got a good view. Two shifty-looking blokes in a white van.'

'What are they doing?'

'The headlights have gone off. Now the passenger is getting out, opening the side door of the van. They haven't spoken to Elder yet. They've hardly acknowledged each other, but it's definitely a meet.'

Cooper started the engine of the Toyota and fidgeted impatiently. Fry began to get frustrated by even a moment's silence at the other end of the phone.

'Gavin? Speak to me.'

'OK, white van man is getting something out, a package wrapped in plastic, quite long. Elder is opening his door, and the bloke has put the package on his back seat. Hardly a word spoken between them, Diane.'

'Do you recognize either of the two men?'

'No, but I've seen plenty like them,' said Murfin. 'Mostly behind bars. Hold on, they're back in the van, and the lights are back on. Yes, they're moving. Elder is starting up, too. What do you want me to do, Diane?'

'You take the Transit, Gavin, and we'll follow Elder.'

'Fair enough. I'm mobile.'

Cooper watched for the Nissan to get well past him before he pulled out. There were three vehicles in between them by the time they left the slip road and re-joined the motorway.

They were still heading south, of course, because there was no other option.

'If he's heading home, he'll either come off at Junction 25 and go west, or he'll double back the way he came,' said Cooper.

Fry got out the map. 'Let's hope he's going west, anyway.'

At least Derbyshire lay that way. If the Nissan left the M1 to the east, they could be in trouble. Close to the motorway were the sprawling outskirts of Nottingham – Bilborough, Wollaton, Aspley, circular housing estates like spiders' webs.

Elder chose Junction 25. He led them on the A52 through the lights of Derby and on towards Ashbourne. The fog began to creep in as soon as they got west of the city. At first it was visible only as grey patches lurking in the low-lying fields, but as the land rose it began to drift across the road. On the darker stretches, Cooper had to close the gap on the Nissan, in case it should take a hidden turning.

Murfin called to say that he was in Nottingham and had trailed the Transit back to an address on the St Anne's estate.

'I don't want to hang around here much longer, Diane. This is bandit country.'

'OK, Gavin. I think you can go home.'

'Thanks. Well, let me know if you need me.'

'Jack Elder is on home ground, too,' said Cooper, when they were past Ashbourne. 'It's back to Rakedale, I guess.'

But Rakedale went by in the night, invisible in the fog, and they found themselves passing through the village of Monyash. It was getting late now, and there wasn't much traffic around by the time Elder took the last turning. Cooper dropped back as far as he could. The brake lights of the Nissan winked in the fog, like a nocturnal animal on the prowl.

By now, Fry knew where they were heading. It looked gaunt and eerie on the skyline, even in the darkness and shrouded in fog. Ruins like the keep of a medieval castle. Steel winding gear like a rusted scaffold. The site of the widows' curse. It was Magpie Mine.

35

The prevailing colour was grey. A dead grey, cold and brooding. It didn't quite conceal the landscape, but made it more mysterious and distant, transforming the bumps and hollows of the old mine workings into shapes that played with the imagination. Cooper could understand why his ancestors had filled this country with myths and legends, populated the darkness with ghosts. He could almost see those ghosts now, flitting across the fields in the fog.

They'd carried on past the entrance to Magpie Mine, leaving the lights of Elder's Nissan turning into the picnic site. They knew where he was, and he surely hadn't come all this way for no reason.

Cooper had turned off the engine of the Toyota and wound the window down to listen. There was no other traffic on the road, not within half a mile or so. Whether there was a vehicle already parked at the picnic site, they couldn't tell without getting too close.

'Are we going to have to call it off, Diane?' he said.

'No chance.'

'We can't drive any nearer. They'd hear us coming.'

'Reverse into the mine entrance, and we'll walk from there. Have you got a torch?'

Cooper produced two maglites from the glove compartment, and they got out of the car. He'd driven his car on to the verge, turning swathes of dead leaves to mush under his tyres. Fry slithered her way through them on to the gravel, and they began to walk back into the remains of the mine.

Of course, the gateway and the first few yards beyond it were a quagmire. Someone had chosen to avoid the rutted track and drive across the soft, uneven ground, churning even more ruts in the process. Cooper heard Fry cursing under her breath as she slipped and squelched, trying hard to make as little noise as she could.

Somewhere in the darkness, cattle were sleeping. Cooper could hear them breathing, so loud that they could have been right next to him. Fog had that peculiar effect – it muffled distant sounds, so that noises closer to hand seemed to be amplified.

'Are you sure we should be doing this, Diane?' he said.

'Ben, for the past week people have been trying to push me to the sidelines of this enquiry. I'm not going to prove anyone right in their opinion of me by giving up now. I'm not going to give them the chance of saying that DS Fry packed up and went home because the weather was bad.'

Cooper couldn't see her face properly, but he could hear the tension in her voice and he knew she was serious. This was important to her.

'I understand,' he said.

'Good.' Fry's breath puffed out in clouds, mingling with the fog. 'Now – are you with me, Ben? Or not?'

'Of course I'm with you.'

As they picked their way carefully on to the site, the banging of corrugated-iron sheets met them again.

'God, I wish someone would fix those loose sheets,' whispered Fry, disturbed by the noise.

'I think Elder's car will be this way,' said Cooper as they passed the front of the agent's house. 'Watch your step. There's

379

an underground flue that runs between the old winding engine and the chimney, and its roof has collapsed in places. Don't fall into it.'

'Thanks. I'll try not to.'

They turned their torches off when they felt they were getting near where Elder had parked. Cooper tried to picture how the site had looked during daylight, orientating himself by the position of the main engine house, looming above him on its high mound. The top of the building, where the roof should have been, was high enough to be clear of the densest layer of fog. He could just make out the upper stonework, jagged and grey. The wheel of the winding gear appeared briefly in front of it, a steel cable glinting and dripping with moisture.

Just ahead were some abandoned pieces of machinery slowly rusting in the damp air. He remembered a small winching truck, its sides eaten away by corrosion, its tyres flat and sinking into the ground. There were iron hoppers and a huge cylindrical boiler, gradually being reduced to such a fragile state of ruin that they would crumble in the fingers.

'Go carefully,' said Cooper.

'I already am.'

The far west of the site had contained the crushing circle and the washing floor. Here, heaps of crushed stone had been dumped, creating mountains of spoil that sheltered the mine from the adjoining fields and woods. One false step could be lethal, let alone the risk of creating a noisy cascade of stone.

'It's getting too dangerous,' said Cooper. 'Don't you think so?'

'I don't know.'

Fry had begun to shiver. The damp and cold were insidious – they crept into your bones and clung to your clothes. No one in their right minds would be out here on a night like this, unless they had serious business.

'What do you want to do, Diane?'

'How far is it to the edge of the car park?'

'Not more than a few yards now. It's just past the slime ponds, where the route of the sough heads off towards the north.'

'Oh, great.'

They moved on again, with Cooper paying as much attention to what might be going on around him as to where he was putting his feet. It was because of his lack of concentration that he was the one to stumble over a mine shaft and kick a scatter of small stones that rattled on the steel grille.

He looked up guiltily, expecting figures to appear from the fog. But the only shape he could see ahead was that of a lone, stunted tree, somehow struggling to survive between the spoil heaps. Its bare branches marked the outer perimeter of the mine.

Fry stood on a heap of stones and looked down at him.

'Hurry up, Ben.'

They slid down the last few yards to the picnic area. But they were just in time to see tail lights disappearing back towards the road.

'Damnation,' said Fry.

'I'm sorry,' said Cooper. 'That was my fault.'

'No, we couldn't have got here any quicker. It was a washout, after all. We should have called it off when you said, Ben.'

Cooper could hear the disappointment in her tone. Fry had been so sure that Elder was going to provide an important link that would hand her a breakthrough in this enquiry. He struggled to find something to say that would be supportive without provoking her to bite his head off. But he failed.

'Oh, well. Back the way we came then, Diane?'

'I suppose so. But we can use the torches now.'

As they walked back towards the invisible machinery and winding house, Fry began to curse. Maybe she found the fog liberating, felt freed by the fact that she couldn't hear or see anyone. Cooper was trailing behind her, watching his step.

'What a disaster,' she said. 'It's one bloody disaster after another. Why am I wasting my life here?'

'It isn't that bad, Diane. Life can be fun, too.'

'Fun? I'm nearly thirty years old, and I haven't had sex for months.'

Cooper didn't know what to say. He was gobsmacked – and not just in a surprised way, but in the way that felt as though his brain had shut down completely and he had no control over his vocal cords. His mouth fell open, and his eyes flickered nervously until they settled on a suggestion of movement behind the winding gear. But it was only a corner of the engine house, momentarily revealed through a gap in the fog.

'Mmm, tumbleweed,' said Fry.

Cooper cleared his throat. 'Nearly thirty. Does that mean it's your birthday soon?'

'Next week.' Fry sighed. 'Yes, Christmas. I must have been some kind of miracle baby.'

Cooper became aware that the banging of corrugated-iron sheets had stopped. That could only mean the wind had dropped. He stopped and looked across the mine to the east. He couldn't see the agent's house now, or the base of the chimney, and certainly not the scaffold-like horse gin marking the site of the Red Soil shaft. The bank of fog was too dense.

'Diane, have you noticed the banging has stopped?' he said.

'Yes, thank God.'

'Didn't it occur to you that there shouldn't have been any banging in the first place?' said Cooper. 'There's no wind.'

Fry looked at the thick blanket of fog enveloping the mine. 'No, it didn't occur to me. But you're right.'

'Damn it, I should have noticed before. Damn it.'

Cooper stood quite still and listened, straining his ears for the slightest noise. After a few moments, he became convinced that he was only imagining things, creating voices where there weren't any. It was another effect of the fog, producing sounds which weren't really sounds at all but the components of silence. It seemed to him that he was hearing an echo, but without the noise that should have preceded it.

'Do you think Jack Elder is still here in the mine somewhere?' said Fry.

'If not him, then someone else that he came to meet,' said Cooper. 'That banging sounded like a signal to me.'

At that moment, a figure appeared ahead of them, catching the light from their torches and throwing a vast, distorted shadow on the wall of the engine house.

'Can you see who it is?' whispered Cooper.

'Yes,' said Fry. 'It's PC Bloody Palfreyman. And he's carrying a shotgun.'

From his position on the mound, David Palfreyman heard the voices, but couldn't locate them in the fog. He stepped quickly behind the winding gear, bringing the shotgun up ready.

Two of them, at least. That was pretty much as he'd expected. He could take two out easily, one with each barrel. And he'd be sure of killing them, if he got close enough. Or make a nice mess of them, anyway, if he couldn't.

The fog should help him. And this maze of ruined buildings and the mountains of spoil made it easy to slip out of sight at any moment.

He'd known they would come, had judged them just right. He hadn't lost his old instincts. No one came on to his patch and treated him like that. There were different forms of justice, and some were more final than others. Tonight, they would find out everything they needed to know about *his* form of justice.

It was only when the light of the torches hit him that Palfreyman realized he'd exposed his position. Had they recognized him? It didn't matter. He knew this place better than they did, and he could be among them before they got anywhere near their car.

Palfreyman laughed quietly to himself. Poor sods. They thought they were the kings around here now. Some of them thought they were pretty clever. But they'd pissed PC David Palfreyman off, and they had it coming.

He slithered down the east side of the mound and ran to the corner of the winding house. He could see them now, trying to keep low, scrambling towards a vehicle parked in front of the agent's house.

Cooper and Fry had taken cover at the base of the square chimney, where the roof of the flue had collapsed. There was no more cover left between here and the car. They would have to cross the track and yards of muddy ground churned by cattle before they got anywhere near it.

Standing, half-stooped, in the stink and gloom, Cooper felt the presence of Fry beside him, the only source of warmth in the cold night. Fry had made the call on her mobile, and back-up would be here, an armed response vehicle on its way. But the ARV had probably been cruising the M1 when its crew got the shout. They could be twenty minutes reaching Sheldon. Even the helicopter wouldn't be getting airborne from Ripley in this fog.

'We're in trouble, Diane,' whispered Cooper.

'I think I'd figured that out.'

'Are we going to make a run for the car, or what?'

'Well, he saw us, so he must know roughly where we are.'

'And if he can see the car –'

'Yes. Why didn't we leave it out of sight? Whose idea was it to bring it all the way in?'

'Yours,' said Cooper.

'Oh. Well, it would only have been further away if we hadn't.'

'I suppose.'

'At least now we know what the package was that Jack Elder brought,' said Fry. 'He must have the right contacts in Nottingham to get hold of an illegal shotgun. I wonder what influence Palfreyman has over people like Elder to make them do what he wants. Is it fear? Respect? I don't understand it.'

'Do you have any ideas about how we're going to get out of this, or are you just talking for the sake of it?' hissed Cooper.

'Are you carrying a weapon at all?'

'Just my ASP.'

'Me too.'

'Are you suggesting we wait until he gets within arm's length and take him down with a baton across the back of the head? He's got a shotgun, Diane.'

'Ben, I don't have any other ideas.'

Cooper was silent for a moment, absorbing the shock of hearing Fry admit that she didn't know what to do. It must have been painful for her to say it.

He leaned closer and whispered. 'Well, we're going to have to run for it, aren't we?'

'Yes.'

'Let's go now, before he gets a fix on our exact position.'

'Wait,' said Fry.

'What now?'

'I haven't got the right shoes on for running.'

'Tough.' Cooper peered round the corner of the chimney. 'I can't see him now. Perhaps he's gone the other way.'

'Some hopes.'

'Well, we can't wait any longer. I'd rather die in the open air than down here.'

'All right, let's go. One-two-three. Now!'

They burst from cover and raced across the open ground, stumbling and sliding but managing not to fall flat on their faces. Fry broke to the left as they reached the car, remembering that Cooper had the keys. But Cooper waited until he was close to the vehicle before pressing the button to de-activate the locks, knowing that the lights would flash and alert anyone watching. There was nothing he could do about that.

Moments later, they were both inside, gasping with exertion

and sweating despite the cold. Cooper started the car, thankful that he'd reversed into the mine.

'Thank God for that. Drive!' said Fry.

A second after she'd spoken, the butt of a shotgun crashed through the window, showering her with fragments of glass. Fry screamed as two barrels thrust through the gap, pointing straight at her head.

36

There was a long moment, frozen in time, while the fog drifted in through the car window. David Palfreyman stood quite still, his finger tensed on the trigger. Behind him, he could hear the sound of another car approaching.

Suddenly, it had become a different situation. Maybe he'd miscalculated, and made his move at the wrong time. But it wasn't beyond his abilities to sort out. None of these people were clever enough to get away from him.

'You two stay there,' he grunted. 'And don't bloody move.'

Cooper raised his head. For a second, he glimpsed Palfreyman at the shattered window, bending down to peer into the car. His shotgun was resting on the glass, both barrels pointing into the passenger seat. If it was fired at that range, in an enclosed space, he and Fry were both dead meat.

But then Palfreyman was gone, stepping away from the car and vanishing instantly into the fog.

Fry had her eyes closed, until Cooper touched her arm.

'Am I still alive?' she said.

'Yes, somehow.'

'What happened?'

'I don't know. Something spooked him.'

Fry looked at him in concern, and Cooper realized that he was shaking as much as she was.

'What the hell are you waiting for, then?' she said.

Cooper started the ignition and accelerated across the mud, not bothering with the lights. Because of that, the driver of the car coming towards him didn't see the Toyota at all, and they smashed head on into each other before Cooper could even get as far as the first gate.

'Is that our back-up?' asked Fry, shielding her eyes against the glare of the other car's headlights.

Then the doors of the Toyota were jerked open, and they both found themselves looking into the wrong end of a nine-millimetre pistol. It definitely wasn't their back-up.

A few minutes later, Fry and Cooper had been dragged out of their car and pushed into the agent's house after one of the two men in black balaclavas had shot the padlock off the door. The door was slammed, and they stood behind it, trying to hear what was going on outside.

'Friends of Palfreyman's,' said Cooper. 'Trying to decide which of them gets the privilege of shooting us.'

'I hope it takes a long time for them to make their minds up.'

'Let's face it, we were outnumbered and outgunned, even when it was just Palfreyman on his own.'

'That maniac. PC Bloody –'

'Hold on, Diane.'

Cooper was peering through the window, watching the two men moving around outside. They seemed to be trying to separate the bonnet of their car from his, and they were having trouble with the bumper. One of the men was tall and dressed in a black coat and jeans. The other was smaller and thicker set, but they both wore balaclavas that hid their faces, so even without the fog, identification would be impossible.

Or would it?

Cooper watched the taller figure. His dark outline looked

vaguely familiar, but the associations being set off in Cooper's mind were all wrong. Ridiculous, in these circumstances. He was actually thinking of the vicar at All Saints, *Here we are . . . Dying to sin . . .* And he was thinking of himself, laughing at a private joke and being glared at by Liz for sniggering in church. *And if they don't like your face, they'll cut off your hand.*

'Oh, shit,' he said.

'What?'

'Diane,' he whispered. 'Cast your mind back. Did you say Joanne Brindley was in a pantomime?'

'What on earth do you mean?'

'Think. Was it the one at the Royal Theatre? *Aladdin?*'

'Well, she was in something. I interviewed her while she was dressed in a police tunic and tights. But what has that got to do with anything?'

'And a sort of Fu Manchu moustache?'

'That's right. She said she was only in the chorus to make up the numbers, but there are some really good actors in the cast.'

'One very good actor, at least,' said Cooper. 'He plays Abanazar, a difficult role to get right. He's Mrs Brindley's husband, Alex.'

'Mr Brindley is an actor?'

'Yes. And you said yourself a good actor would be the only person who could lie without giving himself away.'

Fry joined him at the window. 'Is that him? Brindley? I don't believe it.'

'He's in character,' said Cooper.

'Alex Brindley was the only person in Rakedale I thought *wasn't* lying to me.'

'He played a good part, then. Keeping his grasp on the magic lamp.'

The two men had moved back towards the door of the house, and they were pulling their nine millimetres out of their pockets again. This was probably it, their last moments.

Cooper wondered whether he should pray. He felt ridiculously glad that he'd been to church on Sunday.

Then one of the men dropped his torch in the mud, and both of them stopped, just outside the door. For a second, before it died completely, the light of the torch caught the paleness of a face, gleaming with water. And a voice came out of the darkness.

'You should never have come on to *my* patch.'

Cooper was deafened by the boom of a shotgun fired at close range. The blast stunned his ears, and the flash made him screw his eyes tight shut, anticipating a spray of pellets entering his flesh, ripping open his face.

But the pain didn't come – only another boom as the second barrel was discharged. And then a high-pitched scream that split the air, amplified by the fog into an awful ear-bursting noise.

The smell of burnt gunpowder filled Cooper's nostrils, hot and acrid. This wasn't potassium nitrate cooking in the kitchen at Pity Wood Farm. This was the real thing, and far more deadly.

Cooper found himself spread flat on the ground, his face pressed to the concrete, trying desperately to dig himself into the floor, the taste of stone in his mouth. He became aware that Fry was close beside him, her body pushed up against his, seeking any inch of safety.

They waited, afraid to move or breathe, until they heard footsteps heading away over the spoil heap, back towards the cars. Cooper felt Fry begin to tense, as if she was going to stand up. He grabbed her arm and pulled her back down.

'Wait!'

Her face was close to his now, and he could see her eyes glinting with fear and excitement.

'Someone is being killed,' she said. 'We should do something to stop it.'

'Like what? We're not armed. Remember the first rule is

390

to protect your own life, otherwise you're no use for protecting members of the public.'

'I'm the senior officer here, Ben.'

'So? Are you going to get us both killed to prove something? That won't impress Superintendent Branagh, you know.'

'Bastard,' she hissed. But she stayed down, waiting until they finally heard a car engine start up. A vehicle passed slowly along the roadway towards the agent's house.

'OK?' she said.

'OK. But take it slow and quiet.'

When they emerged from the door, nothing was moving outside. Two bodies lay in the mud, still wearing their balaclavas. A double-barrelled shotgun had been broken open and left on the roof of Cooper's Toyota. There was no sign of David Palfreyman.

Fry and Cooper stood looking at the bodies, knowing that they shouldn't touch anything, wondering how they'd managed to survive. They looked up when more headlights swung across the mine buildings and lit up the engine house. They were ready to run again. But they saw the blue flash, and they knew it was finally their back-up.

After that, they were surrounded by a familiar chaos. More and more vehicles arrived with their lights flashing – paramedics, armed response, the duty inspector, the whole circus.

To Fry and Cooper, trying to recover from the adrenalin still surging through their bodies, it all seemed to be going on around them in a dream. DI Hitchens appeared, and Cooper thought he saw Superintendent Branagh in the fog, but she didn't speak to either of them.

From conversations he overheard, Cooper gathered that at least one of the nine-millimetre pistols had been fired. He didn't recall hearing the shot, but maybe it had been drowned out by the simultaneous discharge of Palfreyman's shotgun.

Cooper knew that someone was bound to ask him later which had come first. He was going to make a bad witness.

Within an hour or so, news came in that David Palfreyman had been picked up, and he was claiming self-defence. He wouldn't say where he'd obtained the shotgun – but then, he didn't know that Fry and Cooper had been following Jack Elder.

'They've got Elder in custody, too,' said Fry. 'I said he should never have been released in the first place.'

'He wouldn't have led us here then, would he?' said Cooper. 'Is that a bad thing?'

The second gunman with Alex Brindley was unfamiliar to Cooper. But he felt sure that he'd turn out to be on record, a bit of hired muscle available for the dirty work. There was plenty to be had, if you knew where to ask and you'd got the money. And Alex Brindley had the money, all right. It just didn't come from the kind of source you might have expected from his nice house and nice family. Dealing in Class A drugs was a lucrative business.

'No doubt they'll match the nine millimetres with the Farnham shooting,' said Cooper.

'I'd give odds on it. Brindley took Tom Farnham out before he gave away too much information, and he came here to meet Palfreyman, intending to do the same with him.'

Cooper nodded. But David Palfreyman had called in his favours and dealt out his own form of justice for the last time. The manufacture of Class A drugs on his patch had been an insult. The fact that he hadn't known about it, unforgivable.

They'd been told to sit in a car and wait until they were interviewed. But Cooper got bored and slipped out to watch the activity around Magpie Mine. The floodlights that were going up had turned the scene into a strange underwater world, figures moving around in a yellow murk as if they were swimming. Voices boomed and echoed between the stone walls.

As he stood in the fog, Cooper heard another sound drifting on the night air. It came from way over in the direction of

Monyash, or one of the villages to the north. The air was so still that the sound might have been travelling for miles before it reached him. It could have been a message crossing the light years from another planet, for all the sense he made of it.

Then some combination of notes, or a recognizable snatch of syllables, struck a chord in his memory. Carol singers. That's what he could hear – carol singers. If he wasn't mistaken, they were performing 'Once in Royal David's City'. He pictured a group of singers from a local church, probably performing outside a pub. 'Stood a lowly cattle shed' came clear through the fog. It reminded him of Pity Wood Farm, in a strange kind of way. Lowly, all right.

Somebody had once told him that Christmas had been stolen from the pagans. The twenty-fifth of December was supposed to be the birthday of Mithras, the god of blood, worshipped by Romans. Mithraic ceremonies had been held in caves, with the smell of smoke, a long knife plunged into the throat of a sacrificial bullock, and blood that fell hissing on an altar stone. Fire and blood, and the entrails of beasts. It must have been tradition.

Cooper found it unsettling to think about such things out here in the darkness, on a cold night in December, with two bodies lying almost at his feet and pools of fresh blood forming on the ground in the lingering scent of gunpowder. It was as if the singing he heard in the distance might not be carol singers at all, but the chanting of the worshippers of Mithras, deep in their caves.

Well, things went back a tidy way in these parts. Two thousand years? That was just middlin' old.

Fry had followed him from the car. Cooper looked at her, huddling in her coat against the cold, but still shivering as though she would never stop.

'Diane,' he said. 'Is it too early to wish you happy birthday?'

37

Thursday

Superintendent Branagh leaned forward across her desk, folding her hands as she regarded the two detectives.

'And did you see what happened next? What did Mr Palfreyman do?'

'I was confused for a few minutes,' said Fry. 'It was dark, and very foggy.'

'You couldn't see anything, DS Fry? You don't know who fired the first shot?'

'No.'

'DC Cooper?'

'No, ma'am. Sorry.'

Branagh gave them both a hard stare. 'I sincerely hope there are no misplaced loyalties here. Just because an individual has been in the job previously doesn't make them immune to the law, you know.'

'No, ma'am,' said Fry.

'We understand.'

The Superintendent didn't look as though she believed them, though they were both trying hard not to give away any of the signs. Maintain normal eye contact, no fidgeting, no turning away from your questioner.

Branagh looked from Fry to Cooper. Then her gaze returned to Fry and stayed there, ominous and thoughtful.

'DS Fry, you were the senior officer in this situation. Are you confident that your actions were appropriate and lawful throughout?'

Even Cooper thought he detected a slight hesitation before the reply. Fry was quick to cover it, but it might have been too late.

'Yes, ma'am.'

The superintendent looked grim. She turned to the notes on her desk and wrote a couple of sentences in small, tight, angry letters that were impossible to read, especially upside down and from this distance.

Branagh glanced up again. 'Were you aware that Mr David Palfreyman's granddaughter Melanie had formed a relationship with the Brindleys' son, Evan?' she said. 'A relationship that was disapproved of on both sides?'

There was no need to worry about looking truthful now. The news came out of the blue.

'No, ma'am.'

'We had no idea.'

Branagh nodded slowly. 'There was no love lost between Palfreyman and the Brindleys, by all accounts. Our information is that Alex Brindley came across Mr Palfreyman in the village pub and told him in no uncertain terms to get his granddaughter away from their son. Insults were uttered, angry words were exchanged. We're treating that as a possible motive for Mr Palfreyman's actions.'

The two detectives sat silently, having nothing to say. The superintendent scowled in irritation.

'Would either of you like to comment on that scenario?'

They shook their heads.

'No, ma'am,' said Fry.

'Then you'd better leave, DS Fry. We're finished here.'

*   *   *

A team of detectives had broken out their stabbies for the raid. They were piling into vehicles to meet the armed support unit at a rendezvous point close to the site of the meth lab in Staveley. Fry and Cooper walked straight into the CID room to join them, and no one objected. They'd been part of the enquiry from the beginning.

Cooper fell into step alongside Fry as they followed DI Hitchens out to the car park.

'Diane, why were you protecting David Palfreyman back there?' he said quietly.

'Why?' Fry secured her stab vest with a final, violent jerk. 'Why? How the hell do I know?'

Cooper wondered if she really did know. Not only had David Palfreyman carried out his own form of justice. But it seemed to Cooper that he had also saved their lives.

The location of the raid was a small, run-down industrial estate on the outskirts of the former pit town. A single unit had been identified as the target, rented by a man named and confirmed as a known suspect in the Sheffield drugs trade. The unit was sited towards the back of the estate, but the service road ran straight up to its rear entrance, where a white van stood parked in front of sliding steel doors.

The CID team and Scenes of Crime waited at a distance for their chance to go in. On a signal from the operational commander, the armed officers roared up the roadway in their unmarked vehicles and jumped out, shouting orders that could be heard from the street. Within a few minutes, they had contained the scene, and four suspects were on the ground with plastic cuffs on their wrists, being searched for weapons.

'Well, that was easy enough,' said DI Hitchens when the detectives moved in. 'I like it when things go well. If we find what we're looking for in this place, I'll buy you all a drink down at the pub to celebrate. Two drinks, since it's Christmas.'

They watched the SOCOs climb into their protective suits and breathing apparatus, and enter the premises. Before long, the doors of the unit slid open and they could all see inside. Long benches were filled with equipment – rubber tubing, glass jars, a row of electric cookers. Even from outside the building, the whiff of fumes was enough to make officers begin coughing and backing away towards cleaner air.

Cooper scented the stench of ammonia, much more powerful than it had been at Pity Wood Farm. He knew better now, and he didn't look around for any cats.

Hitchens gave his detectives a thumbs up, then replaced it with a two-fingered salute. Victory? Or just two drinks down at the pub?

The clear-up and removal of evidence from the industrial unit at Staveley would be a long business. Fry and Cooper left after a couple of hours' talking to the neighbouring tenants and drove back towards Edendale.

The suspects from the operation would have been processed by now and would be residing in the custody suite. But interviews wouldn't be taking place until senior officers were happy that all the facts were in place, and that might not be for twenty-four hours yet. Drinks were definitely looking a possibility.

Cooper took a hands-free call on his mobile as they were heading out of Staveley into heavy traffic through Brimington. It was the officer on con obs duty at the hospital, keeping a constant watch on Raymond Sutton in case he made another attempt on his own life.

Sutton had begun talking again, and the officer had made detailed notes. Con obs was a really boring duty.

'Raymond Sutton is claiming that his brother Alan died falling downstairs during an argument,' Cooper explained to Fry when he finished the call. 'He says he and Derek set off to put their brother into a car to take him to hospital, because it takes so long for an ambulance to get to Pity Wood. But before they got him in the car, they realized he was dead.'

'Go on.'

'Well, then they panicked, because they thought they'd be accused of murdering their brother. Their fingerprints would be on his body, his blood would be on their clothes. Raymond says they knew they wouldn't have much chance if they told the true story to the police.'

'So they buried their brother?' said Fry.

'Yes.'

'On the principle of "out of sight, out of mind", I suppose.'

'Something like that.'

Fry glared at the traffic lights that had brought them to a halt near the crematorium.

'But they didn't bury him on the farm,' she said.

'Oh, no. Not on their own patch.'

'You don't shit on your own doorstep, do you? That's a good rule.'

'Besides, it would have been too much of a reminder,' said Cooper. 'Instead, they had to find somewhere remote, and safe from being dug up.'

'Like a protected heritage site.'

'Ideal.'

'And yet it also had to be somewhere there was already a lot of disturbed ground, where no one would notice a grave.'

'Yes,' said Cooper. 'Those spoil heaps at Magpie Mine were perfect for them.'

'Has Raymond said that's where they buried the body?'

'He's given directions for the search team. They're sending a human remains dog in.'

'But, Ben, did nobody in Rakedale notice Alan was missing?'

'Raymond says they made up a story about him going off to make his living some other way, because he couldn't stand farming any more. Nobody questioned it at the time. Alan himself had said as much in the village. So it was accepted as the truth, whether anyone had any private doubts or not.'

'Just another one of those beliefs without any substance in

reality,' said Fry. 'If you accept one totally improbable thing, why not another? Especially if everyone else around you seems to take it as fact.'

'Yes. I suspect everyone in Rakedale more or less forgot about Alan Sutton after a while.'

'Except his brothers.'

'Oh, the brothers never forgot,' said Cooper. 'They lived with his ghost. I think even Raymond felt his presence, and *he* wasn't the superstitious one. What a nightmare.'

Cooper thought they probably couldn't even begin to appreciate the depth of the nightmare at this distance. What went on inside the closed circles of families was often incomprehensible to outsiders.

'The Sutton brothers were so closely bound together that they reacted against each other constantly. Raymond became more and more disapproving and censorious, and Derek's behaviour became increasingly bizarre and superstitious.'

'Was Derek being deliberately provocative?'

'I'm sure there must have been an element of that, on both sides. And once they were trapped in the cycle, it was bound to escalate.'

Cooper was steering the Toyota round the Chesterfield bypass, using the twisted spire of the parish church as a landmark while he headed for the A619.

In fact, the Sutton brothers must have spent years tormenting and annoying each other. There had been no need for words. The brothers had understood each other fully, and they had probably abandoned any hope of ever winning an argument. But, even in their silence, they would have enraged each other. A soundless, continuous friction.

'It was their way of trying to get a response from each other,' said Cooper. 'These were two old men who didn't know how to communicate in any other way. They must have loved one another very much, underneath all that.'

'Families, eh?'

'Yes, families. What a good thing they didn't have children in that household.'

'Oh, I don't know,' said Fry. 'Loving and hating someone at the same time is a good lesson for future life.'

Fry had touched a nerve there, whether she was aware of it or not. *Loving and hating someone at the same time.* Cooper saw that in himself, whenever he dared to peek into the darker corners of his mind. There was no denying or suppressing that stuff, not completely. It might be possible to control the conscious actions, like a really good liar. But there was nothing you could do to change what was in your heart and in your mind. There were some memories and instincts that clung too close to the soul to be shrugged off and walked away from.

'You know, there's just one thing missing still,' said Cooper as they crested the hill before the descent into Edendale.

'Oh?'

'Just one little thing, Diane. But we still can't get a confirmed ID on one of our victims from Pity Wood Farm without it.'

'What's that, Ben?'

'Orla Doyle's head.'

The Dog Inn was in festive mood, decorated with streamers and balloons. The lights on the tree were twinkling, an illuminated Santa flickered behind the counter. There just weren't any customers to help Mrs Dain celebrate.

'This is suspiciously like an intuition, Diane,' said Cooper, as they stood in the middle of the bar.

'Just bear with me for a while.'

'I don't know where to start looking.'

Fry smiled. 'That's because you're not from the Black Country, Ben.'

'What?'

'And you missed the signs of superstition – the horseshoe on the door, the number thirteen absent from the jukebox. I bet that's old Mrs Dain.'

'What has Mrs Dain got to do with it?'

'I think she shared some beliefs with Derek Sutton,' said Fry. 'Maybe they shared more than that when they were younger.'

'Well, the old lady did say she had a soft spot for him – and Raymond, too.'

'It's Derek I'm interested in at the moment. You see, I'm betting he had a gift for Mrs Dain. The Dog Inn needs a bit of help staying in business, by the look of it. And you don't need two of the things, do you?'

Cooper stared at her. 'Two? You mean . . .?'

A couple of officers entered the pub wearing blue boiler suits and carrying a set of tools – chisels, hammers, wrecking bars. They spread plastic sheets on the floor in front of the central fireplace.

'It's a good job the fire is out,' said Fry. 'But then, I left instructions beforehand.'

It didn't take long for the officers to remove enough bricks from the chimney breast to uncover a cavity. One of them reached in a hand and carefully eased out a package.

The skull was black and sooty. Empty eye sockets stared from between the hands of the police officer, a few fragments of teeth grinned crookedly in the jaw. Two or three years of smoke had turned the white bone to an object that was almost unrecognizable.

Fry took the skull in a gloved hand, then she held it up to the twinkling red and green lights of the Dog Inn's Christmas tree.

'Meet Orla Doyle.'

38

That afternoon, Pity Wood Farm looked more desolate than ever, surrounded by abandoned excavations and the partially dismantled buildings, tape fluttering at a safe distance from the contaminated areas.

Cooper made his way round the back of the house, through the overgrown garden. The stone steps that led up to the garden were worn away, depressions in each step full of muddy water.

Worn away. It was an apt phrase. Not just for the steps, but for the farm itself. Pity Wood was worn down, exhausted from centuries of desperately clinging to existence. If it had been an animal, someone would have called a vet to put it out of its misery.

And what of the Sutton brothers? Well, Raymond Sutton hardly seemed to have any purpose left in life, now that his brother had gone. Even if their roles had been to torment and annoy each other, at least that had been a role. But their relationship had been ground down by decades of mutual chafing, the long, weary scouring of continuous friction.

It was possible to read in the newspapers every day about immigration, illegal workers, drugs, murder, bankruptcy, mental illness, the shift of the economy away from traditional industries. It was quite a different thing to see it all summed up in the crumbling walls of Pity Wood Farm. Raymond and Derek Sutton weren't exactly the stereotypes he had in mind when he read the *Daily Mail*.

Cooper stopped to peer through a dusty window into the farmhouse. He'd come to think of the rooms at Pity Wood in terms of colours, almost like the apartments of a stately home – the Blue Room, the Yellow Room, the Brown Striped Room. Whatever their colours, it had seemed that some of those rooms contained more light than others. And it had nothing to do with the number of cracks in the boarded-up windows, or the depth of the shadows thrown by that giant shed on the walls of the house. The play of light had been an internal one, a flickering kaleidoscope of ignorance and radiance. No amount of cement and breeze block would counteract that spiritual darkness.

And he remembered another thing – it had been impossible to tell from the bedrooms at Pity Wood which had been Raymond's room, and which had belonged to Derek. There had been too much clutter to see the truth.

The words of the baptism service still echoed in his head. *God calls us out of darkness into his marvellous light. To follow Christ means dying to sin.* Had there been an equal contrast of darkness and light in the church that day – a clash of beliefs, an uneasy pact between rationality and blind faith? Cooper couldn't be sure. He would never be sure. He lacked the ability to make that leap of faith.

Now the characters walking into the darkness were acting out parts in a private DVD that was showing in his head. He couldn't prevent them moving out of the safety of the light, no matter how hard he tried. If only he knew how to find the rewind button.

It reminded him of a line from a book, something about the nature of time. If time was all one, past and present indistinguishable, then perhaps even Derek Sutton was still here somewhere. Still here, burning in an everlasting fire.

* * *

Diane Fry watched Cooper circling the farmhouse, like a dog hunting for a scent. She was trying to suppress the feeling of dissatisfaction that still niggled at the back of her mind.

Word had come in that human remains had been discovered at Magpie Mine, scooped into a depression among the spoil heaps, close to where Cooper had stumbled that night. An identity had yet to be confirmed, but who doubted that it was Alan Sutton? The clinching detail was the fact that the remains were missing a skull. Of course they were. That had been in a cupboard in Tom Farnham's workshop, waiting to find a buyer on eBay.

So the case was solved, in a way. But it was hardly a triumph of investigative skills, not one to highlight on her PDR when the time came in a few weeks. Who knew how long the bodies at Pity Wood would have lain undiscovered, if it weren't for the fact that Raymond Sutton had given up the farm and sold it for re-development?

Fry looked around the landscape, with its homesteads scattered across the hills, their lights just starting to glint in the dusk. How many more horrors were waiting for someone to discover on farms that were still unsold and undeveloped? It was impossible to tell. Did they all harbour dark histories that would one day have to be explored, a grim bequest for generations to come? Were farmers and their families even now wrapping their Christmas presents in the knowledge of some terrible secret buried a few yards away?

God knew what might have happened in some of these farms in the past. They were isolated and cut off from the world, with far too much space to bury their sins unobserved, with no risk of strangers nosing around.

All of that was falling apart now, of course, the modern world intruding in all kinds of ways, the farming families disintegrating, the farms themselves toppling like dominoes into dereliction or re-development. And not before time, in Fry's view. It was the advance of the twenty-first century, modern ideas of justice cracking open the Pandora's box, tearing apart the dusty web of old beliefs and superstitions, like the steel nozzle of a hose thrust into a crusted cesspit. Decontaminating minds, the way the clean-up crews would decontaminate Pity Wood. And that would be the end of the story.

Fry shuddered at a sudden chill. Someone walking over her grave. Wasn't that the saying?

'Diane, did you ever read a Sherlock Holmes tale called "The Copper Beeches"?' called Cooper from the back of the house.

'No. Was that the one with the giant dog?'

'No, not the one with the giant dog. This story was set in the countryside, though. Kent or Sussex – somewhere like that.'

'So?'

'There's a line in it that rang a bell with me. At one point, as they're travelling out of London, Holmes says to Doctor Watson: *"There's more evil in the smiling and beautiful countryside than in the vilest alleys of London."* Something to that effect.'

'Really?'

'His explanation was that people are able to get away with things unobserved in the country that they never would in the city, where there are always other people close by.'

'I see. Well, it was true in this case, Ben.'

'These days, it's the other way round,' said Cooper. 'It's cities where people go around unobserved. No one takes any notice of what you're doing. They don't care if you're abusing your children or making bombs in your front room. Here, though, people do actually care what their neighbours are up to.'

Fry looked at Pity Wood Farm, its diseased walls held up by scaffolding, its roof tiles slipping into holes that let in the rain, plastic sheeting rattling miserably.

'The trouble is,' she said, 'it still doesn't prevent the evil.'

She moved along the wall to keep Cooper in sight. The ground wasn't so wet now, but her feet still slipped on the bare, churned earth. Fry came across some abandoned construction work, trenches and spoil heaps left by Nikolai Dudzik and his men.

'Even after the buildings come down, it'll be a long time before this land is decontaminated,' she said.

'If it ever will,' said Cooper, as if he was referring to something else entirely.

She didn't question what he meant. Sometimes it was better not to ask, because the answers only left her more baffled than ever.

'The demolition teams can't get on site until after Christmas, of course. But it won't take them long to bring this lot down, once they get started. I'm amazed some of these walls haven't fallen down already.'

'What about the construction crew?'

'They've all packed up and left. They've got an extended break over Christmas, then their agency is sending them off to another job in Stockport. Except for Jamie Ward. I think he's lost his taste for building work.'

'I suggested he give my brother a call,' said Cooper. 'Matt will be able to find him some work for a couple of weeks until he goes back to university. Jamie has worked on a farm before, so he'll be OK with that.'

Fry checked the back door of the farmhouse to make sure it was locked. She wasn't sure whether she was responding to a concern about vandals breaking in, or an inexplicable instinct to prevent anything getting out.

'Has your brother ever thought about diversification?' she asked.

Cooper laughed. 'Yes, he's thought about it. He thinks about it the way a turkey thinks about Christmas. It's going to come, but that doesn't mean you have to like it.'

A piece of glass crunched under Fry's foot. She jumped, imagining the poisons that contaminated parts of Pity Wood. Battery acid and anti-freeze, iodine and drain cleaner. A toxic mix that had contaminated the farm beyond salvation.

'Ben, we shouldn't be here at all,' she said. 'It's much too dangerous.'

'There's just one thing, Diane.'

'What are you looking for?'

'I think I saw it around here somewhere.'

'You should be wearing gloves and a mask.'

'I'll be careful.'

'Famous last words,' she said, watching him anxiously, but trying not to sound like his mother.

Cooper was poking about in some of the rubbish that had been discarded when the skip had been searched. Finally, he dragged out a long pole, with a rusted metal plate attached to the top.

'What now?' asked Fry, as he scraped away at the metal. She could see the remains of some white enamel and black lettering, perhaps even a crude picture.

'The old Pity Wood Farm sign. I wondered where it had gone,' said Cooper.

Fry peered more closely. 'What's that animal? It has horns. Not more witchcraft?'

'It was never witchcraft, Diane. Only superstition.'

'What, then?'

'This is the last remnant of the Suttons' herd of pedigree Ayrshires, I believe. It must have been a very sad day when they took the sign down.'

'I don't know what you're talking about.'

Not for the first time that week, Fry sensed she was in unknown territory. What significance could there be in an old sign? It was a bit of advertising, that was all. And it had served its purpose, so it had been thrown away. End of story, surely?

But she could tell from Cooper's tone that there was some deeper meaning. She didn't ask him to explain it, and of course he didn't try. He'd given up hope on her, she supposed – and for a moment, she regretted that. There were times when she would have liked to be able to understand, to share the feelings suggested by the softness in his voice, by the way his fingers traced the rusty lettering, as if he was communicating with some other world that she just couldn't see.

Fry knew she would forever be on the outside at these times, always the uncomprehending stranger who didn't fit in. Her lack of understanding was deep and incurable, and it made her an unwelcome intruder into other people's lives.

The truth was, she could walk away from Pity Wood Farm now, step across the muddy track and disappear into those dank woods. No one would come looking for her, the way Mikulas Halak had come looking for his sister. She wouldn't be missed by the Ben Coopers of this world.

Fry drew her coat tighter round her shoulders and wiped the rain from her face. She didn't belong here, and she never would. End of story.